THE
American
ROOMMATE
EXPERIMENT

ALSO BY ELENA ARMAS

The Spanish Love Deception

THE
American
ROOMMATE
EXPERIMENT

a novel

ELENA ARMAS

ATRIA PAPERBACK

NEW YORK   LONDON   TORONTO   SYDNEY   NEW DELHI

ATRIA
PAPERBACK

An Imprint of Simon & Schuster, Inc.
1230 Avenue of the Americas
New York, NY 10020

First Atria Paperback edition September 2022

ATRIA PAPERBACK and colophon are trademarks of Simon & Schuster, Inc.

For information about special discounts for bulk purchases, please contact Simon & Schuster Special Sales at 1-866-506-1949 or business@simonandschuster.com.

The Simon & Schuster Speakers Bureau can bring authors to your live event. For more information or to book an event, contact the Simon & Schuster Speakers Bureau at 1-866-248-3049 or visit our website at www.simonspeakers.com.

Manufactured in the United States of America

1 3 5 7 9 10 8 6 4 2

Library of Congress Control Number: 2022937385

ISBN 978-1-6680-0277-3
ISBN 978-1-6680-0278-0 (ebook)

To those waiting on love,
be patient.
Love is a total drama queen.
It's just waiting to make an entrance.

THE
American
ROOMMATE
EXPERIMENT

CHAPTER ONE

Rosie

Someone was trying to break into my apartment.

Fine. Technically, it wasn't *my* apartment, but rather the apartment I was currently staying in. That didn't change the facts. Because if living in a couple of questionable neighborhoods in New York had taught me anything, it was that if someone didn't knock, they weren't interested in asking to be let in.

Evidence number one: the insistent rattling of the—thankfully locked—entrance door.

The sound stopped, allowing me to release all the air I had been holding in.

Gaze fixed on the lock, I waited.

All right. Maybe I was wrong. Maybe it was a neighbor mistaking this as their apartment. Or maybe whoever was out there would eventually knock and—

What sounded like someone banging a shoulder against the door startled me, making me jump backward.

Nope.

Not a knock. Probably not a neighbor, either.

My next breath was shallow, oxygen barely making it to its destination. But heck, I couldn't blame my lungs, really. I couldn't even blame my brain for not being able to accomplish basic functions like breathing after the day I'd had.

A couple of hours ago, what had been my cozy and beautifully well-kept apartment for the last five years had all but crumbled down on me. Literally. And we're not talking about a crack in the ceiling and some falling dust.

A section of my ceiling gave out and collapsed. *Collapsed*. Right before my eyes. Almost on top of me. Creating a hole large enough to gift me with a clear view of my upstairs neighbor Mr. Brown's private bits as he looked down at me. And allowing me to learn something I never needed or wanted to know: my middle-aged neighbor did not wear anything beneath his robe. Not a single thing.

A sight that had been as traumatizing as having a piece of cement nearly knock you down on your way to the couch.

And now this. The break-in. After I pulled myself together enough to gather my stuff—under Mr. Brown's careful scrutiny and still freely hanging . . . bits—and made it to the only place I could think of, given the circumstances, now someone was trying to force their way in.

What sounded like a curse in a foreign language came through, the noise against the lock resuming.

Oh, crap.

Out of the more than eight million people living in New York City, it had to be me being potentially robbed, hadn't it?

Turning on the tips of my toes, I stepped away from the door of the studio apartment I had fled to in search of shelter and let my gaze dart around the familiar place, studying my options.

Thanks to the open plan of the apartment, there were no decent hiding spots. The only room with a door, the bathroom, didn't even have a lock. There were no weaponizable objects, either, except for a crooked clay candleholder born from a lazy DIY Sunday and a flimsy boho standing lamp I wasn't sure about. Escaping through a window wasn't an option, either, considering this was a second floor and there was no fire escape.

The frustrated swearing came through more clearly now. The voice was deep, musical, and the words I did not recognize or understand were chased by a very loud huff.

Heart racing, I brought my hands to my temples in an attempt to subdue the growing panic.

This could be worse, I told myself. *Whoever is out there is clearly not very good at this. At break-ins. And they don't know I'm inside. For all they know, the apartment is empty. This gives me—*

My phone pinged with a notification, the loud and sharp sound breaking the silence.

And giving my presence away.

Crap.

Wincing, I lunged for the device that rested on the kitchen island. It couldn't have been more than three or four steps away. But my brain, which was still struggling with basic functions like, let's say, moving three or four steps forward, miscalculated the distance, and my hip collided with a stool.

"No, no, no," I heard the words coming out of my mouth in a whimper, one of my hands reaching out. Unsuccessfully. Because—

The stool crashed against the floor.

My eyelids fell shut. As if my brain was trying to at least spare me the sight of the mess I had made.

Silence followed the big bang, filling the room with what I knew was a false sense of calm.

I opened one eye, taking a peek in the direction of the door.

Maybe this was good. Maybe that had scared . . . him? Them? Away—

"Hello?" The deep voice on the other side of the door called. "Is anyone home?"

Dammit.

Squaring my shoulders, I turned around very slowly. There was still a chance that—

The jingle I had set for that stupid motivational app I'd downloaded earlier today blared through the apartment for a second time.

Jesus. Someone was out to get me today. Karma, kismet, fate, Lady Luck, or some all-powerful entity I had clearly pissed off. Maybe even Murphy and his stupid law.

I finally grabbed my phone to set the stupid thing to silent.

Involuntarily, my eyes scanned the supposedly inspirational quote on the screen: **IF OPPORTUNITY DOESN'T KNOCK, BUILD A DOOR.**

"Seriously?" I heard myself whisper.

"I could hear that, you know?" Intruder said. "The phone, then the bang, then the phone again." A pause. "Are you . . . okay?"

I frowned. How considerate for a possible burglar.

He pressed on: "I know there's someone in there. I can hear you breathing."

A gasp of outrage left me. I was *not* a heavy breather.

"Okay, listen," Intruder said with a chuckle. A *chuckle.* Was he laughing? At my expense? "I'm just—"

"No, you listen," I finally blurted out, hearing my voice crack and wobble. "Whatever it is that you're doing, I don't care. I've—I've—" I'd been standing there like a doofus, doing nothing. And that stopped now. "I'm calling the cops."

"The cops?"

"Exactly." I unlocked my phone with shaky fingers. I was done with this . . . this . . . situation. Heck, I was done with *today.* "You have a few minutes to leave before they get here. There's a police station right around the corner." There wasn't, and I hoped he didn't know that. "So I'd start running if I were you."

I took one miniscule, careful step in the direction of the door, then stopped to listen for a reaction. Hopefully, the sound of his steps fleeing.

But I heard nothing.

"Are you listening?" I called, then hardened my voice before speaking again. "I have friends in NYPD." I didn't. The closest thing I had to that was Uncle Al, who was a security guard for a company on Fifth Avenue. But that didn't seem to impress Intruder, because silence continued to follow my statement. "Okay, fine. I warned you. Now, I'm dialing, so it's up to you . . . *mother . . . clinking apartment-breaker!*"

"*What?*"

Ignoring my unfortunate and not at all threatening choice of words, I set the call on speaker and a few seconds later, the emergency dispatcher's voice filled the apartment. "Nine-one-one, what's your emergency?"

"Hi—" I cleared my throat. "Hello. There's . . . there's someone trying to break in the apartment I'm in."

"*Wait*, you're really calling?" Intruder yelped. But then, he said, "Oh, okay. I see." Following that with another chuckle. *Another. Chuckle.* Did he find any of this funny? "This is a joke."

Outrage filled my chest. "A *joke*?"

"Hello?" came from my phone's speaker. "Miss? If this isn't an emergency—"

"Oh, but it is," I said immediately. "As I was saying, I'm calling to report a break-in."

Intruder spoke before the dispatcher could, "I'm standing in the hallway. How have I broken in? I didn't even make it inside."

Now that he was saying more than a couple of words at a time, I could hear his accent more clearly. The way he enunciated certain words was familiar and set off a bell somewhere in my head. But I didn't have time or energy to spare for bells right this moment.

"Attempted break-in," I amended.

"Okay, miss," the dispatcher answered. "I'm going to need your name and the address to your apartment."

"I get it," Intruder said, loudly enough for me to take a step back. "This is one of those pranks. I've seen that show on TV back home. What was the name of that guy? The host. The one with the good hair." A pause. "Never mind." Another pause. "You got me! It was a really good one. See, I'm laughing," he added before breaking into a loud cackle and almost shocking the phone out my grip. "Now, can you please open this door and be done with it? It's past midnight and I'm exhausted." The humor had left his voice. "Tell her she's hilarious. We'll remember this as one of the best pranks in history."

Tell her?

Tell who?

Frowning, I lowered my voice and spoke right into the phone. "Did you hear that? I think he might be deranged."

"*Deranged?*" Intruder scoffed. "I'm not crazy, just . . . tired." Something dropped to the floor with a thud on the other side of the door and I prayed it wasn't him because I wasn't up for dealing with an unconscious man on top of everything.

"I heard," the dispatcher said. "And, miss, I'm—"

"Did I get the wrong door or something?" Intruder interrupted.

The wrong . . . door?

That caught my attention.

"*Miss,*" the emergency dispatcher hissed. "Your name and the address to your home, please."

"Rosie," I said quickly. "I'm Rosalyn Graham and . . . And, well, technically this is not my home. I'm at my best friend's place. She's away at the moment, and I needed . . . a place to stay. But I didn't break in, obviously. I had a key."

"And I have a key, too," Intruder offered.

A record scratched in my head.

"Impossible." I scowled at the door. "I have the only spare that exists."

"Miss Graham." The dispatcher's voice was laced with annoyance. "I want you to stop interacting with the individual outside your door and share your location. We'll send a unit to check on things."

My mouth opened but before any words came out, Intruder spoke again, "She really outdid herself."

She. That *she* again.

Neither of us said anything for a few seconds. Then, the silence was broken by a heavy thump. One that sounded a lot like he had just slumped against his side of the entrance door.

"*She?*" I finally asked, ignoring the "*Miss Graham?*" coming from my phone's speaker.

"Yeah," Intruder said simply. "My very funny and highly creative little cousin."

A breath got stuck somewhere between my rib cage and mouth.

Little cousin.

She.

The intruder's thick accent that is so terribly familiar.

The only possible explanation took shape in my head.

Had I—

No. I couldn't be that big of a dumbass.

"Miss Graham?" came from the line again. "If this is not an emergency—"

"Sorry, I—" I closed my eyes. "I'll call back if I . . . need to. Thank you."

Little cousin.

Oh God. Oh no. If this was one of Lina's cousins I'd messed up. Big time.

I terminated the call, pushed the phone into the back pocket of my jeans, and forced myself to take a deep breath in the hopes that oxygen would reach my clearly faulty brain cells. "Who exactly is your cousin?" I asked, even though I was pretty sure I knew the answer.

"Catalina."

It was official. I had messed up. Yep. And yet, because this was New York and I had dealt with my fair share of strange people and stranger situations, I still added, "I'm going to need more information than that. You could have checked the name on the mailbox."

A long and loud sigh was released on the other side of the wooden border that separated us, making the already souring sensation in my stomach swirl.

"I'm sorry," I blurted out, unable to stop the two words from coming out. Because I *was* sorry. "I'm just making sure that—"

"That I'm not a deranged person," Intruder answered before I could get through with the rest of my apology. "Catalina Martín, born the twenty-second of November. Brown hair, brown eyes, loud laugh." My eyes shut again, the swirling in my belly climbing up to my throat. "She's tiny but if she kicks you in the nuts, she'll knock the air right out of you all the same. I know that from first-hand experience." A short pause. "What else? Let's see . . . Oh, she hates snakes or anything that looks remotely like one. Even if that's a few socks sewn together and filled with toilet paper. Clever, huh? Well, that was what led to the nuts kicking. So the joke was really on me."

Yup.

I'd screwed up. Big time.

Big, big, big time.

And I felt horrible. Awful.

So much that I couldn't even bring myself to stop him when he went on, "She's away for the next few weeks. Enjoying her honeymoon in . . . Peru, was it?" He waited for my confirmation, but none came. I was speechless. Mortified. "Aaron's the lucky guy. A tall and intimidating-looking dude from the photos I've seen."

Hold on. That meant—

"I haven't met him in person. Not yet."

He hadn't met Aaron in person *yet*?

I—

No. No, no, no. This couldn't be happening.

But then, he said, "I didn't have the pleasure of attending the wedding."

Confirming that this could, indeed, be happening. And just like that, none of my earlier shock or embarrassment measured to what I started feeling right that moment.

Because this man was not a random intruder, or a deranged individual that had stumbled upon my best friend's apartment.

This man I'd called the cops on was Lina's relative.

And it didn't stop there. *No.* He had to be the *one* cousin that hadn't met Aaron.

The one person out of the long list of Lina's Spanish relatives that had missed the wedding.

He had to be *him*.

"I heard it was a great party," he said. And it felt like a physical blow to my chest. "Too bad I missed it."

Without really knowing how, I realized I was now clutching the handle of the entrance door. As if his words—the realization that it was *him*—had somehow brought me there and compelled the fingers of my free hand to wrap tightly around it.

It can't be him, a voice chanted in my head. *I can't be so unlucky*.

But it was. I knew it was. And kismet, destiny, luck, or whatever force in charge of deciding my fate, had packed its bags and left me to fend for myself.

Because this man was the one cousin I had secretly hoped would be at the wedding. The only one who had made my stomach flutter with anticipation at the simple thought of meeting him. Of getting those two mandatory cheek kisses from him. Of exchanging pleasantries. Of perhaps dancing with him. Of having him see me in my maid of honor gown. Of finally having him in front of me.

Of the possibilities.

My fingers moved and the door unlocked with a *click*.

Heart sprinting with the knowledge of this man *really* being him, I grabbed the handle. Anxiously, eagerly, hope clogging my throat. All the foolishness of whatever my head had fabricated in the months leading to the wedding tangled with new emotions from the mess I'd just made. Anticipation mixed with guilt. Embarrassment coiled around excitement.

Chest pounding, I threw the door open, and . . .

Something dropped at my feet.

I looked down, my eyes immediately finding the source of the thump.

He was lying on his back. As if he'd been resting his weight on the door and fell backward when I'd opened it.

Air seemed to barely get in my lungs as I took in a head toppled with wavy chestnut locks. It didn't match the image neatly kept in my memory. Memory, or the screenshot I secretly kept in my phone. I'd only seen him with a buzz cut.

"It's really you," I heard myself mumble as I stared at him. "You're really here. And your hair is different. Longer and—"

I clasped my mouth shut, feeling an intense blush covering my cheeks.

The handsome face I had looked at through the screen of my

phone more times than I'd ever be ready to admit twisted with a puzzled look. But just as quickly, chocolate-brown eyes twinkled with a smile. "Have we . . . met before?"

"No," I rushed out. "Obviously. I meant you look different from what I expected. You know, from your voice. That's all." I shook my head. "And I'm—*God*. I'm sorry. For all of this. I just—"

You just what, Rosie?

The blush spread to the tips of my ears, and I thought that if the ground under my feet were to open and swallow me right this moment—something I knew now was not that unlikely—I'd go willingly.

"I'm just so sorry," I breathed out. "Can I help you up? Please."

But *he*—the man who didn't even know I existed, but whose features I was able to summon in my mind if I closed my eyes—didn't give any indication of being in a rush to stand up. Instead, his gaze inspected my face, taking his time, as if I were the one that had just popped out of nowhere and dropped at his feet.

And just when I thought I'd collected myself enough to say something else—hopefully marginally smart—his lips stretched. That puzzled look dissolved completely, giving way to a smile, and whatever words had climbed to my mouth crumbled.

Because he was smiling. And it was big and bright and, quite frankly, beautiful in this blatant way you don't really know what to do with.

Possibly more than the smile he wore on *the one* screenshot I had allowed myself to keep and might still look at occasionally.

"In that case," he said through his sunny and upside-down grin. "If we don't really know each other then, hi. I'm Lucas Martín. Lina's cousin."

Yes.

I knew that. I knew exactly who he was. He wouldn't believe just how well I did.

CHAPTER TWO

Rosie

Lucas looked up from his position on the floor, probably wondering what the hell was wrong with me.

"I . . ." *Ugh.* This was *not* how I'd pictured meeting Lucas. This wasn't even in the same galaxy of how I'd constructed this moment in my head. And I'd had time—over a year of it—to come up with dozens of different scenarios.

"Hello, Lucas," I said. "It's . . . It's nice to finally meet you."

Finally?

Yep. I'd said finally.

Lucas's brows drew together, and I felt the tips of my ears grow even warmer. My face was probably flashing red, too.

"You're definitely not a burglar!" I blurted out to veer the conversation away from that stupid, stupid *finally*. "And I'm also so, so very sorry I assumed you were. I'm sure this was not how you imagined arriving in New York. Or Lina's apartment for that matter. Anyway, can I please help you up?"

But Lucas remained on his back, brandishing that grin that had taken shape minutes ago. As if all of this was okay. *Normal.* Which wasn't. It really wasn't. Because Lucas Martín was here. On my doorstep—or, well, Lina's doorstep. And I was making the worst first impression ever.

"Yeah, I didn't exactly see this coming," he said as he stretched his arm up, letting his hand hover above him, right at the height of my stomach. "But either way, it's really nice to meet you, Rosalyn Graham."

I stared at that hand, taking in the long fingers attached to it. Then, my eyes jumped to the tan skin of his wrist, which was swathed by a worn leather cord bracelet.

A small part of me wondered how his skin would feel against my fingers, but both my arms remained glued to my sides.

"How do you . . . know my name?" I asked.

Because Lucas had said my full name.

His hand remained in the air, waiting. Just like his smile.

"I heard it earlier," he answered casually. "You know, when you told the emergency dispatcher. Right after you called me deranged."

I winced. "Oh God, I guess I did that, didn't I?" I blew a breath out of my nose. "I'm so sorry about that, too." I blinked some more. My eyes now fixated on the section of skin on his forearm that had been gradually revealed as the sleeve of his sweatshirt slid down. But I still didn't reach for his hand and he let it drop down to his side. "I swear I had no idea you were arriving tonight. Lina never said anything. Otherwise, I wouldn't have called the cops. Heck, I wouldn't even be here if I had known you were coming."

Lucas tilted his head with what I assumed was curiosity. Probably wanting to ask why. *Why the hell are you here, then?*

"But you can call me Rosie," I continued. "Everyone does. You can, too. If you want, of course. But Rosalyn is also fine."

A soft chuckle escaped through his permanent grin, followed by a simple, "Rosie."

As if he was testing the name on his tongue.

And God, the way he pronounced it, coated in that strong Spanish accent that rolled his *R*s as if his whole body was pitching the sound and not just his tongue and vocal chords. It was so . . .

different from every other way my name had been pronounced. Interesting. Distracting.

"Rosie," he repeated after a couple of seconds. *"Qué dulce,"* he added in what I knew was his mother tongue, Spanish, but wasn't sure what it meant. "I like it. It suits you."

"Thanks," I muttered, my whole body feeling increasingly warm. I shifted in my feet. "You have a good name, too, Lucas. It's very . . . groovy."

Groovy.

Oh God. Oh Lord.

Did I just say that his name is *groovy*? Like a . . . a . . . disco ball? Or a seventies themed party?

"Thanks, I guess." Lucas let out a chuckle. "All right, as comfortable as I am on the floor, I'm tired of looking at your face upside down, Rosie."

And before I could process his words, Lucas got up on his feet in a quick maneuver I wasn't expecting. Distracted by the motion, the size of him, that alluring roll of the *R* that was still echoing in my head, and ultimately, the effect of having Lucas Martín—in the flesh—in front of me, I almost missed it when he winced and doubled over.

"Watch out!" I said as I lunged myself forward and grasped his forearms a couple of seconds too late. His head was down, and I couldn't see his face. "Are you okay?"

"Estoy bien," he breathed out, as if the words in his mother tongue had unconsciously slipped out. He shook his head. "I'm okay. All under control."

Slowly, he glanced at me from under his lashes, meeting my gaze and making all the blood in my body return to my face. Just before returning his eyes down, as if something had caught his attention.

I mirrored the motion.

My hands. They were around his upper arms in a death grip. Around what I now realized were very firm upper arms. Lined with muscles. Hard ones. Flexed ones.

We looked up at the same time, my now wide eyes meeting his brown ones.

Amusement entered his expression. "Good catch, Rosie."

I let go of him immediately, as if those three words had blasted me backward.

"Of course," I rushed out, clasping my hands in front of me and averting my eyes from his face. They set up camp on a point below his chin. "You sure you're okay?"

"Yeah, nothing to worry about." He waved a hand in the air. "I should have probably stretched my legs a couple times instead of sleeping through most of the flight."

"Right." I nodded my head. "You just got off a transatlantic flight." Because this was Lucas Martín and he had just crossed half the world to get here. From Spain, where he was from. And what had I done? Locked him out, called the cops, and then left him lying on the floor for a stupidly large amount of time.

"Oh no," he said. "I flew in from Phoenix."

Oh.

Oh?

"Was that a layover or were you already in—" I stopped myself, realizing it really wasn't my business whether Lucas had been in the country or not. "Either way, here I am anyway, keeping you at the door. Please, come in." I stepped to one side to let him into his cousin's apartment feeling all kinds of . . . out of place.

Lucas lifted a heavy-looking backpack off the floor and walked in, allowing me a clear view of his backside. Now that his eyes weren't on me, I finally let myself take him in. Take him really in, eyes traveling up and down the length of his body a couple of times.

And oh boy. He had long, lean-looking legs. Lucas was taller than I thought he would be based on what I'd seen of him during my online lurking. Even his shoulders were wider than I'd imagined. And the wrinkled gray sweatshirt he was wearing did nothing to hide them—or the muscles I'd noticed when I'd felt him up a few minutes ago. Or the way you could tell only by looking at his back that he was a professional athlete. That he surfed, competitively.

And we were talking championships and tournaments and beautiful but scary-looking waves that reached incredible heights. Lucas had probably spent most of his life on the water and his body could endure—

The sound of his backpack falling snatched my attention. He had come to a stop next to the island that separated the kitchen and living areas in the cozy studio apartment.

"So, Rosie," he said as he leaned down to pick up the stool I'd knocked to the floor earlier. He placed it upright next to its twin. "If you didn't know I was coming . . ." He turned around, facing me with an easy grin. "And you wouldn't have been here if you had known I was coming, then I guess you're not my welcome committee, huh?" His voice was deep, his tone kind but playful. It made something in my belly take notice, something I pushed down immediately. "Pity, I was starting to think I should really thank my cousin."

That something fluttered, making me stumble for an answer and immersing us in a strange silence.

Lucas's smile fell.

"It was a joke," he explained. "A really bad one, it seems. I'm sorry, I'm usually smoother than this."

I blinked.

Think, Rosie. Think. Just say something. Anything.

"Ashton Kutcher," was what my brain decided to go with. Lucas's brows drew together. "The host of *Punk'd*, the prank show. The one you couldn't remember." I threw my hands in the air and lowered my tone. "You've been *punked*!"

He tilted his head, and I wished I could take back the last ten seconds of my life. Rewind, and say something else. Something smart. Flirty. Because was that too much to ask? I wasn't even asking for the last ten minutes of my life. Or the last ten hours.

But then, he let out a laugh. It was a deep and happy sound. And for some strange reason, I knew it was genuine and not at my expense.

"Yes," he said, shaking himself off his laughter. "That was the show I was talking about. And that's him, the guy with the good hair."

I stared at him—at his face, his upward lips, his beautiful eyes, his hair, which was far, far better than Ashton Kutcher's ever was—and I felt myself smiling. I couldn't help it.

Lucas's gaze dipped to my mouth, though, and that kind of wiped the smile off my face.

"Okay," I said, squaring my shoulders and averting my eyes. "This was fun." It really hadn't been. "But I think it's time for me to go and leave you to . . . to it."

Without wasting any time or considering the knot that had formed in his forehead, I moved in the direction of my belongings and kneeled in front of my two suitcases—one of which was open, and half unpacked—a filled-to-the-brim blue Ikea bag, and the box containing all my perishable groceries.

I heard a few steps to my right. Then, a pair of white sneakers came into view.

"You're leaving," Lucas said, just as I grabbed a stray shoe I couldn't recall pulling out. "With all of . . . that."

It hadn't been a question, I knew that. But I answered anyway.

"Of course." I snagged the stack of sweaters I'd also apparently taken out. "I was just dropping by Lina's place to . . . to . . ." To occupy her clearly not vacant apartment while she was on her honeymoon because my apartment was uninhabitable at the moment. "To water her plants. Check on the mailbox. You know, that kind of stuff."

A beat of silence.

"That doesn't look like just dropping by, Rosie."

"Oh." I waved a hand, pushing the sweaters into the open suitcase with my other one. *God, why in the world had I unpacked so much stuff?* "This? This is all nothing."

Just me, trying to not inconvenience a guy I might have had a teeny-tiny little online crush on.

He sat down on the floor in front of me. As if we were just hanging out.

My mouth opened and closed a couple of times until I came up with something. "What are you doing?"

Smart, Rosie.

Lucas chuckled, the sound light and unconcerned and not at all how I was feeling. "I was going to ask you what you're really doing here, in my cousin's apartment. I would have asked sooner but we were . . . busy." A shrug of his shoulders. "I don't think I'm owed an explanation. All of this"—he spun a finger in the air—"is clearly Lina's fault. You didn't have any idea I was coming."

"I really didn't."

"Does she know that you're here, then?"

I let out a sigh. "No . . ." I trailed off, even though I did think Lucas was owed an explanation. "But not for lack of trying. I called her—and Aaron—to check if I could use my spare key and stay the night." Or more like a few nights, plural. "But neither of them picked up. Their phones must be out of reception."

His eyes roamed around my face, as if he was trying to piece something together. Then, he moved his hand, pulling a small object out from his pocket. "Speaking of keys," he said, holding it between his fingers. "I wasn't lying. I do have one."

My lips parted with another apology, but Lucas stopped me with a shake of his head. "Lina left it at the pizzeria down the street. Alessandro's? She left instructions for me to pick it up from there."

That made . . . sense. Although it didn't change the fact that she'd never mentioned to me that Lucas was visiting.

"Good man, this Sandro," Lucas pointed out with a nod. "I must have looked seriously beat, because he even offered me food." Lucas's face brightened impossibly, reminding me of an Instagram post where he's staring at a steak as if that piece of juicy meat had just hung the moon and stars for him. "Probably the best pizza I've had in a long while."

"Sounds like Sandro," I told him, thinking of the dark-haired, middle-aged man. "And I'm not surprised. We've been ordering pizza from Alessandro's at least once a week ever since Lina moved here a few years ago."

Probably the reason my best friend had felt safe enough to leave a set of keys with him.

"I was told as much," Lucas said, a twinkle in his eye, making me wonder what Sandro had said about us. Hopefully not that we always ordered enough to feed a small army.

We stared at each other for a long moment. And although it wasn't as awkward as a few minutes ago, it wasn't exactly a comfortable silence, either. Not when my secret infatuation with this man that sat on the floor in front of me seemed to be swelling like a balloon, taking all the space between us. And certainly not when all these facts and details I had collected over more than a year and kept hidden in a sealed cabinet in my mind started pouring out.

Like how I knew Lucas *actually* loved pineapple on pizza just because it was still food—something I'd never understand. Or how I also knew that he had gotten that tiny scar on his chin by tripping over the leash of Taco—his beautiful Belgian shepherd—and falling on his face. Or how I had learned that he prefers sunrises over sunsets.

Dear God. The amount of information one could learn from someone's socials when one looked long and frequently enough was terrifying.

"Rosie," he said so sweetly that I felt a ball of shame climb up my throat.

What had I been thinking, stalking someone like that? "Yeah?" I croaked.

"What are you really doing here?"

I debated answering that question genuinely. Not because I didn't want Lucas to know the truth, but because this encounter had been filled with enough dramatics, and adding my ill-fated day to it was too much.

"There was a little problem in my building." I swallowed, settling for a half-truth. "Nothing important, but I thought it would be better to leave for the night."

His brows arched. "And what was this little problem?"

"Plumbing issue." I shrugged. "Nothing that can't be fixed. I'll be back in no time."

A hum left him. "Is that why you packed all your stuff?" His head bobbed down, pointing at the bags and scattered items between us. "And all your . . . food, too? Just for a night?"

"I snack." I looked everywhere but at him. "I'm a big night snacker. I could easily go through all of this in one night."

"Okay," he said, but it sounded like he didn't believe me.

Fair, because I was lying.

I glanced at him, and I never knew what it was about his expression but I heard myself saying, "Okay. It wasn't a *little* problem. There's a crack in my ceiling. Big enough for me to pack everything, hail a cab, and come spend the night here."

Here, because Dad had moved to Philly and my brother, Olly, wasn't answering my calls. Here, because on top of that, I'd been lying to them for months—six, exactly—and going to spend the night with either of them would reveal the truth and expose my lies.

"Sorry, this is nothing you should worry about. It's all good, really." I looked around, taking in my best friend's cramped studio. "This is a one-room apartment and there's only one bed, so I guess . . . I *know* we can't both stay here." Frankly, I could and would take the couch but putting Lucas in that position wasn't something he deserved after tonight. And I was embarrassed enough. "I'll book a hotel for the night."

I looked at him in time to see his lips twitching. It wasn't a smile. It was some sort of grimace. "You're okay, though?" he asked.

I frowned, taken a little aback by the question. "What?"

"The crack on your ceiling," he said. "It sounds serious. Are you okay?"

"Oh." I swallowed. "I'm . . . fine, yes."

But Lucas didn't look like he believed me. Again.

"Seriously. I'm a New Yorker. I'm tough as nails." I let out a laugh I hoped sounded genuine and shuffled some more of the scattered items closer. "Just let me get everything and I'll call an Uber."

I inspected my disorganized mess. Then, I started to chuck everything inside the bags as fast as I could.

That was probably why I didn't notice that Lucas was on the move until he was on his feet and striding away. He stopped when he reached his backpack, picked it up, and flung it over a shoulder.

"What—" I started going up on my two feet. "Where are you going?"

Lucas rearranged the weight at his back. His smile was back in place, lopsided and . . . yeah, still distracting. "Somewhere else. I'm not staying here."

"What?" I gaped at him. "Why?"

He took a step in the direction of the door. "Because it's past midnight and you look like you're about to pass out."

I blinked. Then, I noticed my hand shooting to my hair. Did I look—

I let my hand drop. How I looked wasn't important. One, because there wasn't anything to do about that now. And two, because . . . there really wasn't anything to do about it. "Do you have a place to stay?" I finally asked him. "Any place other than Lina's?"

"Of course." He shrugged, his lips not bulging. "This is New York City—the options are endless."

"No." I shook my head, taking a step sideways and blocking his way to the door. "I can't let you do that. I'll be the one leaving. This is your cousin's apartment. You even have a key. You . . . can't go spend the night at a hotel."

His smile turned warmer. "That's sweet, Rosie. But unnecessary." He walked around me, making me turn around on my heels to keep track of him. "Plus, it's easier this way. I only have a backpack with me, and you have . . ." His gaze jumped to my big, messy pile. "You have a lot more than that."

"But—"

He met my gaze again, and the way his brows bent into a sort of frown was so at odds with his easy grin that I lost my train of thought.

"Listen," he said very calmly. "I'm a blunt man so I'm just going to say it, yeah?"

I swallowed.

"I'm under the impression that me being here is making you very uncomfortable." A pause. "I'm actually sure that's the case. And it's okay, we've just met."

What? Oh my gosh, and that was why he was leaving? He— "I'm not uncomfortable," I countered in the most not comfortable way. "It's not for the reason you think." He tilted his head and my mouth opened again to give him something else, anything else. But nothing came out. Only a stammered, "It's— It's not—"

"I'll make you a deal," he said, cutting me off, and for some reason, I had the feeling he'd done that to save me from myself. "You stay here for the night, get some rest, and tomorrow I'll be back. We'll start over. Forget tonight happened. Then, we'll figure out what to do in terms of accommodation." A careful pause. "What do you think?"

We'll start over. Forget tonight happened.

What I'd give for that to be something we could do. "But there's nothing to figure out, Lucas. Lina promised you the apartment. You should be the one taking it."

"Okay," he said simply. "But not tonight."

This wasn't right. This was *so* not okay. Everything about it had gone wrong and I . . . I only realized I was blowing air out of my mouth when I heard my mouth releasing it.

Lucas's chuckle was deep, masculine. "I'll be back tomorrow, I promise."

My lips parted, ready to fight him some more, to tackle him to the floor and make him stay if I had to.

But then he said, "It will be fine, Rosie." And his expression turned serious. Earnest. "Everything will be okay."

And all my determination to fight him back loosened up, letting the exhaustion in. The toll from years and years of trying to keep everything together, contained, always on my own, washed right over me. Head to toes, like a wave. And for once, just for this one time that I was being told those four words, *Everything will be okay*, instead of being the one using them to comfort someone else, I felt the need to let go.

"Okay. Thank you for doing this," I murmured, and I meant it more than Lucas would probably ever know.

He nodded slightly, then took another step away. "See you tomorrow, then. I'll knock this time, I promise."

I tried to think of something clever and funny to say, but what was the point anyway? I'd already ruined this. First impressions were like words penned with permanent ink. Once etched on paper, there was little one could do to change them. So, I simply stared at him as he turned the knob and threw the door open.

"Hey, Rosie?" he called before crossing the threshold. "It's been great finally meeting Lina's best friend."

Finally.

He'd said *finally*.

Just like I had a while ago. But probably for a completely different reason.

"Likewise, Lucas. This was all . . . *great*." A great freaking disaster.

A small smile turned his lips up. "Do me a favor and lock up after I'm gone, yes?" He turned around, giving me his back and striding away. "You never know who might try to break in."

And just like that, I watched Lucas Martín disappear down the stairs as swiftly as he had landed right on my doorstep—or Lina's doorstep.

As if this had been nothing more than a dream, all of it a product of my imagination.

A silly and bizarre dream about a man I had spied on through the screen of my phone for months and months, all thanks to the magic of social media.

A man I had somehow harbored the biggest, stupidest crush on, even when I hadn't even meet him in person and even when I'd thought I probably never would.

CHAPTER THREE

Rosie

*W*hen I woke up the following morning—at exactly 6:00 a.m., just like I had done every weekday for the last five years but didn't need to anymore—I did so with a certain brown-eyed, smile-wearing man in mind.

And for a split second, I was sure I'd dreamed it all.

Lucas Martín at the door. The disaster that followed.

But as seconds ticked by and awareness returned, I realized none of that had been a product of my subconscious. It had really happened. Lucas had really been here. I had really mistaken him for a burglar. And I had managed to make the worst first impression in the history of first impressions.

We'll start over. Forget tonight happened.

If only I could be so lucky.

Covering my face with one arm, I groaned loudly.

To make things worse, my much less dumbfounded brain realized now that I'd let him leave—venture into a city he had just arrived in—with barely any resistance on my side. I'd taken the apartment and left him on his own.

God, I was the worst.

23

I rolled on my side, refusing to get up and leave the comforting safety of my best friend's bed. My gaze fell on a framed picture of Lina and her grandmother that rested on a shelf, reminding me of how close she's always been to her family.

But then, why hadn't Lina said anything about Lucas's visit? Lina was an oversharer, especially with me. This was something she would have said at least in passing.

In Lina's defense, ever since Aaron proposed in September last year, she had been swarmed with the wedding preparations. Planning a wedding in Spain from the other side of the world wasn't exactly easy. And after tying the knot two months ago in a beautiful summer wedding by the sea, she had been overwhelmed by everything that followed, even if they hadn't left for their honeymoon until now, in October. So, I guessed . . . I guessed it must have slipped her mind.

Closing my eyes, I decided that either way, it didn't matter. Now Lucas was in New York, and Aaron and Lina were away, in Peru, enjoying their deserved honeymoon. I had no business feeling hurt.

Especially when I myself wasn't being truthful to those around me. Lina had no idea about my secret crush on her cousin. And that was nothing in comparison to consistently lying to Dad and Olly about my job situation for months. *Months.*

A surge of courage filled my chest.

All of that ended today. No more lying.

I'd give Lina a heads-up about what had gone down yesterday, and I'd go to Philly to see Dad. Maybe Olly could meet us there. If he stopped dodging our calls, that was.

Rearranging myself so my back rested against the headboard, I reached for my phone, clicked on Lina's name in the messages app, and started typing.

Hey, I hope Peru is treating you two lovebirds well 🖤 Listen, last night—

My thumbs hovered over the screen, hesitating.

Last night . . . I almost had your cousin Lucas arrested.
Surprise!

No. That was a definite no.
I deleted it and started again.

Last night . . . my ceiling cracked open, so I used your spare
key to let myself into your place (couldn't reach you but I
knew you wouldn't mind!). Anyway, everything was fine until
Lucas showed up and I somehow mistook him for a burglar.
Remember Lucas? Your cousin. The one whose Instagram
profile you showed me what feels like an eternity ago? Well,
I've been . . . checking it out. A few times. More than just a
few times. Something like every day? It's hard to explain but
think . . . Joe Goldberg. Minus the murders.

Yeah, also a no. That was too long for a text.
The word *murders* was probably a red flag, too.
With a long and noisy sigh, I deleted the text and let the phone
drop into my lap.
The truth was that I had kind of stalked Lucas online. In a totally
harmless way.
Ever since Lina showed me one of his social posts, I'd been
curious. And I hadn't started checking his profile regularly until
Aaron had proposed a year ago and I'd . . . hoped I'd meet Lucas at
the wedding. And just like that, what started as nothing more than
curiosity turned into something else.
Every photo he posted, whether he was in it or not, brought
butterflies to my stomach. Every short but always funny and honest
caption brought me a little closer to him. Every clip he uploaded
allowed me to get an insight into his and Taco's lives. Into the attractive and handsome man he was.
Sure, it hadn't hurt that as a pro surfer, he'd been shirtless in
most of his posts.
Some people had celebrities like Chris Evans or Chris Hemsworth

or any of the other Chrises, to inject that shot of serotonin before bed. A little daydreaming and a lot of wishful thinking. And I supposed . . . I supposed I'd had Lucas Martín.

It had been nothing more than a silly, innocent infatuation with someone I didn't really know. Plus, it had been put to rest the moment he'd mysteriously vanished and stopped updating—weeks before Lina and Aaron's wedding—and turned out to be a no-show at the ceremony. I had buried all of that nonsense and told myself enough was enough.

My phone rang in my lap, and all of that was immediately forgotten when I caught my little brother's face flashing on the screen.

"Olly?" I answered, heart dropping to my stomach. "Where the heck have you been? Why haven't you returned any of my calls? Is everything okay? Are you okay?"

A long sigh came through the line.

"Nothing's wrong, Rosie." My brother's voice was deep, that baritone texture reminding me he wasn't a kid anymore. Oh no, he was a nineteen-year-old adult that had been letting all my calls go to voicemail for weeks. "And I'm sorry. I've been . . . busy. But I'm calling you back now."

"Busy with what?" I asked before I could stop myself.

When Dad announced about a year ago that he was leaving Queens, where he had spent most of his life and where Olly and I had been brought up, to move to Philly, Olly had announced he wasn't leaving. He also informed us that, unlike me, he wouldn't be taking the college route. And we'd supported him, encouraged him to search for what it was that made him happy. I'd even helped him out with rent and living expenses until recently. But he struggled to find his calling. He struggled to keep a job for more than a few weeks, too.

The line was silent for so long that I feared he'd hung up.

"Olly?"

Another sigh came.

"Listen," I said, every single emotion brewing inside of me coating that one word. "I'm not attacking you. I love you, okay? You know I do, more than anything. But you've ignored me for weeks, only sending me short quick texts so I wouldn't lose my mind and report you as a missing person." And I would have. I *so* would have if it had come to that. "So, don't tell me you've been *busy* and expect me to take that as an explanation, please. Don't—"

"I've been busy with work, Rosie."

Hope inflated my chest for a second there, but it was quickly stifled by a hundred dozen new questions.

"That's great," I told him, pushing my concern down. "What kind of job is it?"

"It's . . . at a club. A nightclub."

"A nightclub," I repeated, forcing myself to remain objective. "As a waiter? You tried that and . . ." Quit about three weeks in. "You tried that, and it didn't work. At a café, remember?"

"I'm not serving drinks," he explained. "I'm doing something else. It's . . . hard to explain. But I'm making a good living out of it, Rosie."

"I don't care how much you make, Olly. I care about you being happy. About—"

"I am, okay? I'm not a kid anymore and you don't need to worry about me."

I was close to scoffing at his *you don't need to worry about me*, but I held the sound in. Olly was an adult, and I understood his need for boundaries. His wish not to be babysat. But I was still his big sister, and he was still the kid I used to feed Froot Loops to for dinner when our fridge was empty, and Dad was working night shifts. "Okay, okay, fine. I'll drop it." Then added, "For today."

He muttered a half-hearted, "Thank you."

"So, listen." I veered the conversation onto a safer ground. "I was thinking of grabbing a few sausage rolls and heading to Philly today. Surprise Dad with brunch. What about joining me? You could be back by evening. How about I meet you at the train station and we go together?"

A beat of silence, then he asked, "Aren't you supposed to go to the office today? It's Monday."

I winced, silently cursing myself for my careless slip. *Oh, crap.* "I . . . yes. You're right." And he was, technically. What Olly—or Dad—didn't know was that for the past six months, I hadn't been calling InTech's Manhattan headquarters *the office.* "But I have taken the day off. Just today. My boss is . . . more flexible with my time off now that I'm, you know, a team leader."

"Ah, yeah. My big sis is a boss-lady now. That's right." He chuckled and I wished I heard that sound more often. I wished I wasn't lying to him and he wasn't keeping things from me, either. "So that promotion you got last year is working out for you, huh? Planning on climbing even further up the ladder, big sis?"

"Oh, I have no plan to do that, believe me." Not when I had, in fact, climbed down and off the ladder. Stretching my legs, I set both feet on the floor and got out of bed. "So, are you coming, then? To Dad's?"

"I . . ." He trailed off, which was indication enough that I was about to be let down.

"Please, Olly. I have something I want to tell you. Both of you. And Dad misses you. I've been covering for you for weeks and I'm running out of excuses. Please, come."

He sighed. "Okay, I'll see what I can do."

Ah, progress, I hoped. "I'll text you the train timetable, yeah? We can meet at the station."

"Yeah," he answered, the earlier hope flaring up in my chest. "I . . . love you, Bean."

Bean. It had been ages since he'd called me that. "I love you, too, Olly."

And with those parting words I set to get ready and go confess the truth to the man who had worked multiple jobs to give my brother and me a good life after he'd been left on his own with us. The man who had raised us, alone, after our mother had taken off and left us behind. The man who had put me through college with the sweat of his brow and a determination of steel. The man to whom I owed the financial security my engineering degree had given me until recently. Until that day six months ago when I took a leap of faith to change my life. My career.

Oh boy.

How did one tell such a man that I had decided to quit the stable, well-paid position he—and I—had worked so hard for, only to chase dreams that were nothing more than ink on paper?

How did one tell a man who had sacrificed so much that I had exchanged an established career with amazing prospects for one that wasn't guaranteed?

I didn't have the slightest idea. And that was exactly why I'd let that secret sit on my shoulders for months.

But that ended today.

I kept repeating that mantra as I went through the motions of getting ready. I threw on the first thing I could pull out of my suitcase: a pair of light blue jeans and an oversized burgundy sweater. And like pretty much every morning, I unsuccessfully tried to tame the mess of dark curls on my head and settled for tying them loosely on top of my head.

Once I made my way out, I settled on a plan of action.

First, I'd get Dad's favorite sausage rolls from O'Brien's, a bakery here in Brooklyn, only a few minutes away from Lina's place. I'd wait for him to bite into the savory fried goodness and, *boom*, I'd drop the bomb.

It was a good plan.

At least, I was trying to convince myself of that as I entered the bakery, placed my order, and made my way out with Dad's bribe. That was probably why, when I stepped onto the sidewalk, I almost tripped when my gaze fell into the window of the diner across the street.

I did a double take. Then, a third. I probably stared for about a good full minute.

But how could I not, when Lucas was sitting there, in the window of the diner, hair an unruly mess, and lean and strong arms crossed over his chest. That mouth I'd seen mostly grinning, hung open as his head rested on the back of the seat and I could tell he had on the same clothes he had been wearing last night.

But I had to be wrong. That couldn't be Lucas.

He couldn't be sleeping in that diner, in front of a mug and an empty plate. He was supposed to be in a hotel. Unless . . .

That thought was left unfinished as my two feet carried me across the street and into the diner, this big, pressing question bouncing off the walls of my head. *Had he spent the night here? And if so, why? Why hadn't he gone to a hotel?*

I crossed the threshold and walked up to him, the warm bag of pastries still dangling from my fingers.

I took him in up close, the bags under his eyes and the impossibly wrinkled clothes. The start of what looked like . . . drool falling out of the corner of his mouth.

"Lucas," I whispered.

He didn't move. Didn't even hear me.

I cleared my throat and leaned down a little. "Lucas," I repeated.

Guilt tangled with worry in my stomach, making me want to shake him awake so I could demand answers and apologize a few hundred times. All at once. Because someone didn't just sleep at a diner unless necessary and I shouldn't have let him leave so easily last night.

Tentatively, I reached out, my free hand landing softly on his shoulder. "Hey." I shook him lightly, trying not to focus on how warm and solid he felt through his sweatshirt. "Lucas, wake up."

And . . . Still nothing. God, he slept like the dead.

I was left with no other option but . . .

"WAKE UP!"

His mouth snapped shut and one of his eyes popped open.

A brown eyeball took me in. Then his expression was relaxing back until a sleepy version of his smile took shape before me.

"Rosie," he half said, half slurred in a husky voice. "This really you or I did I wake up in heaven?"

CHAPTER FOUR

Lucas

J was an idiot. A big sleepy idiot.

That really you or did I wake up in heaven?

Really, Lucas? *Por Dios.*

I didn't need to be wide awake to know I'd regret saying that. But the corny, unoriginal, and unnecessary line left my lips before I even knew what was hitting me. I opened my eyes—or eye—and there she was. Rosie. Lina's best friend. The girl who had charmed the entirety of the Martín family. Heart-shaped face, soft features, plush lips, and bewitching green eyes. Like she was some kind of mirage, my sleep-deprived brain was trying to determine whether she was real. And look at the shit that came out of my mouth when my head wasn't paying attention.

"Wh— What?" Rosie mumbled when I didn't follow my spectacular opening line with anything else. Her eyebrows curled. "Are you okay?"

Question of the year.

Willing my other eye open, I shook my head and hoped my expression was casual when I said, "The sun was shining behind you." I pointed at the window with a hand. "It was framing your face. Like a halo."

Rosie blinked—twice—before answering with an "Oh. Thanks?"

Muffling a chuckle at her reaction, I stretched my arms above my head. All the muscles in my back complained, stiff from spending more hours than I should have in a sitting position. I shouldn't have stayed here for so long. I probably needed to stand up, get my legs moving and my joints working but . . .

Now, Rosie was here. Looking at me with a funny face. Her brows meeting with a small frown. Concerned and a little pissed.

"Are you mad at—" I started.

But at the same time, she said, "Can I ask you—"

I met her gaze, smiling to myself, and told her, "You can ask me anything."

"I know it's none of my business," she said, "but . . . What are you doing here, Lucas? You look like . . . Did you—" She cleared her throat, as if she was trying to soften her tone. "Did you spend the night here?"

I didn't want to lie to her. I'd never been very good at that. So I asked, "What do I look like?"

"Well, you look great—" She let out a strange noise before continuing, "You look fine, but you also look like . . . like someone who has slept in a diner."

"Attractive in an effortless and casual way?"

"You were drooling."

"Ouch."

"I'm serious," Rosie pressed.

"Oh, I believe you. And I bet I was a sight to behold."

"You . . . kind of were, I guess," she admitted with a shrug. "If you're into sleepy, drooling men." A pause. "Which I'm not."

I tilted my head to the side, pretending I was considering something. "So what's your type, then, Rosalyn Graham?"

Her eyes widened a little. "My type is—" she started, but she stopped herself. "You're deflecting." A pause in which her lips twisted with a pout. "You said that you would look for a hotel. You should have stayed at Lina's if you didn't have anywhere else to go. You should have told me instead of letting me kick you out."

I frowned. "You didn't kick me out," I told her seriously. Honestly. "I left on my own." Because I'd felt how uncomfortable she'd been in my presence last night. How thrown off she'd been by my arrival. And I wasn't a man who felt comfortable with invading a girl's privacy and personal space without so much as a conversation. "These are comfier than they look. Give them a try." I held out a hand, pointing at the maroon bank across from me. "Have a seat and see for yourself. I'll get us something to drink."

I turned around and called for the waiter with a smile. He shot me a nod, signaling that he'd be with us in a minute.

When I faced Rosie again, she hadn't sat down.

She hadn't even moved.

She was too busy scowling at me.

But that scowl . . . it made my lips twitch. Again. Because she was pissed at me, a grown-ass man who was mostly a stranger, for sleeping at a diner. And that was sweet.

"You said you'd be fine," Rosie reminded me in a wonky voice.

"And I'm fine." I pointed at myself with both my hands, working extra hard to keep my tone light and hide the exhaustion from my voice. "I've never been *finer*."

I met her gaze and winked.

Her cheeks turned pink and her scowl deepened. "The bags under your eyes tell me otherwise."

I patted my chest. "Harsh, Rosie. You have to stop throwing punches at me or my ego won't ever recover."

But she didn't budge—or smile at my attempt to joke—she only crossed her arms in front of her chest, making me notice a brown bag hanging from one of them.

After what turned into a ten-second stare down, I exhaled. Then, pointed at the seat in front of me again. "Do you have anywhere to be? Can you stay for a bit? Have that coffee with me and I'll explain."

She hesitated at first but then moved one tiny step forward. "I have some time. I could stay for a bit."

The waiter appeared with two clean mugs and a pitcher of fresh coffee just as Rosie folded her body into the booth.

"I didn't lie. Last night, I searched for a hotel," I admitted, watching the dark brew filling our mugs. "Thank you," I told the man with a nod before he left. "But I ran into some issues with my credit card while trying to check in and I was kindly invited to leave."

"What kind of issues?"

I added some sugar to my coffee, stirred it, and took a sip. The deeply bitter flavor biting into my taste buds for all the wrong reasons. "My card wasn't in my wallet. And apparently, I'm the idiot who travels with no backup so . . . " I shrugged a shoulder. "I have no idea where I might have dropped or left it, but all I had with me was my ID and some cash."

Fifty dollars to be exact.

Rosie's eyes widened, the pout returning to her mouth. "Why didn't you come back to the apartment? I was there."

"It was too late, Rosie," I answered simply. "I got into the first place I found open to make some calls and I kind of dozed off. Remember the sexy drool?"

I waited for her to laugh but it never came.

Tough crowd.

I continued, "Before falling asleep, though, I contacted my bank, reported the lost card, and asked them to send a new one. But it might take some time to get here from Spain."

"Oh, Lucas," Rosie finally said, looking down at her mug, her shoulders falling. "That really, really sucks. And I feel—"

"There's no reason for you to feel responsible about this, Rosie."

She seemed to disagree but didn't say anything. Instead, she limited herself to taking a sip of coffee. I watched her wince, jerking the mug off her lips.

Leaning forward, I lowered my voice and said, "Thank God you don't like it, either. I was beginning to think that this was the stuff you guys have over here."

"It's really not," she whispered back. "This coffee is terrible. God. How many of these have you had?"

"This is my fifth since last night."

What I was pretty sure was guilt returned to her expression. "I'm so sorry—"

"No more of that," I cut her off. Held my finger in front of us. "No more apologies or we'll never be able to be friends, Rosalyn Graham."

"Friends?"

I nodded, deciding not to delve into the way she'd said that word. As if becoming friends was something unfathomable. "So, what brings you here? I assume it's not the décor, the beverages, or the views, if drooling men are not your thing."

A snort left her mouth. It was a quick, sharp sound. But cute. I felt my lips bend as she shook her head. "I was leaving O'Brien's when I saw you from across the street." Her arm disappeared under the table and reappeared with the bag covered in greasy spots. "They have the best sausage rolls in the city. Well, they're probably one of the few bakeries that sells them in New York. Either way, they are a Graham breakfast favorite."

Enthralled by the scent coming off the bag, I couldn't help but gawk at her fingers when she pulled out a shiny and crispy-looking pastry.

An intense whiff of fried dough hit my senses.

"You hungry?" I heard her ask as she held it between us.

"Nah," I answered, even though I really was. "I'm good."

Rosie hummed, then shocked me by stretching her arm in my direction.

I followed the motion with my gaze, then looked up at her.

"Take it," she said, humor now dancing in her eyes. "You need it more than I do."

"I really shouldn't. It's your breakfast."

Deliberately slow, she shrugged a shoulder and inched the pastry closer to her mouth. I gawked at her parted lips, at the shiny and alluring roll, too. She halted right before closing that last inch, holding it midair. I looked up, meeting her gaze again.

My stomach growled.

"Oh," she said. "I think I just heard your stomach trying to tell me something."

If I hadn't been so focused on pretending I wasn't lusting after the sausage roll, her comment wouldn't have caught me by surprise. But it did, and it pulled a bark of laughter right out of me.

Rosie's mouth stretched, and she joined me with a chuckle of her own. A real one, I could tell. *Finally.* I liked it. "Eat it," she ordered through her smile. "I insist, Lucas. It will make me happy if you do."

I'll never know what exactly tipped the balance, but I stretched an arm and took the pastry off her fingers. "Thanks, Rosie."

Under her attentive gaze, I brought it to my lips, took a bite, and—

"*Dios mío.*" I moaned. "This is one of the best"—I took another bite—"things to ever bless"—and another one—"my taste buds."

Her laughter came again.

I glanced at her, finding her eyes on me. On my lips.

"Like it?" she asked.

"*Like it?*" I repeated, shaking my head. "This roll deserves more than 'like.'" I licked my index finger. "It deserves *love.*" I repeated the motion with my thumb. "It deserves to be seduced and worshipped."

Now her cheeks were flushed, probably from secondhand embarrassment for my shameless display. But I was a passionate man when it came to food. Especially pastries.

She recovered, only the tips of her ears remaining pink. "You Martíns really have a thing for food, don't you?"

I flashed her a grin, not caring to wipe the grease and runaway crumbs off my mouth. "Can't speak for all of us, but if you bring me one of these every day, I might fall to my knees and swear eternal loyalty to you, Rosalyn Graham. It'd take me about a week. Probably less."

That seemed to stun her into silence.

I tilted my head, wondering if she was that shy or just guarded around strangers. Either way, it really didn't matter, because I wasn't exactly deterred by any of those things. Especially after she'd fed me breakfast.

To my surprise, Rosie pulled another pastry out of the bag. "Here. Have this one, too."

"You really are an angel straight out of heaven," I told her, surprising myself when I realized I wasn't lying all that much. "But I don't deserve any more of your kindness."

"You do," she countered, pinning me with a serious look.

I waved a hand in front of me. "Can't and won't."

"Take it, or . . . we won't ever be friends. And you said . . . you said you wanted to, so . . ."

So, not *that* shy.

Grinning like she was giving me the world instead of a piece of deliciously greasy dough, I leaned on my elbows, getting closer to her face. I made sure to meet her gaze. "Only if we share." I snatched the upper half of the roll. "As much as I enjoyed putting up a show for you, I'd rather not eat alone."

Rosie seemed to consider my offer, but she eventually took the pastry to her lips. And when we were done, she pulled a third one, split it in two, and handed me a half, which I accepted with an even wider smile.

"So, Rosie . . ." I took a sip of my now lukewarm coffee, letting my gaze travel down her neck and taking in the off shoulder sweater covering her upper body. I wondered if she had been headed to the office. "You work at the same firm as Lina, right? What was the name . . . *Tech* something?"

"InTech," Rosie answered with some sort of grimace. "And I . . . did. Not anymore. I . . . It's a long story."

I waited for her to elaborate but even though her lips opened and closed a couple of times, she never did.

I hummed, tapping my fingers against the table. "I'll make you a deal."

She frowned. "A deal?"

My lips twitched. "A game. A 'get to know each other' game, you know. Because if we're going to be friends, we should break the ice somehow." I was trying my luck here, I knew that. She had no reason to share a single thing with me, but I knew stalling when I saw it. And Rosie could have been on her way already. But she was here. Sitting with me.

Rosie's head tilted, a lock of dark hair coming out of her bun. "So, we both get to ask questions?"

I nodded. "An answer in exchange for another answer. We take turns until we make it to five. And it doesn't matter how long the answer is. How does that sound?"

We stared at each other for a long moment, and I could see the battle in her face. She was hesitant. She also was curious.

Finally, she said, "Five questions. I can work with that."

I nodded slowly, pushing my growing eagerness down. "Because you just fed me, and I'm a man in debt, I'll let you start."

Her gaze roamed around my face, one of her eyebrows dipping in thought, as if she was readying herself to uproot my deepest secrets right out me.

It was adorable. And a little scary.

She laced her fingers together and rested her hands on the table. "Where were you? Before coming to New York? You said you flew in from Phoenix."

My shoulders relaxed. "I've been traveling across the States for the past six weeks." I didn't miss how that piece of information seemed to surprise her. "I started up north, in Portland, Oregon. Then headed south, rented a car, and drove from New Orleans to Phoenix."

Rosie nodded her head, processing my words. Then she went with a simple, "Okay. Your turn."

"Easy. Who were you going to share the rolls with? There were three of them, so unless you have a huge appetite . . ."

Averting her eyes to where the empty bag lay in a ball, she sighed. "My dad, hopefully my brother, too, but it's a long—"

I tsked. "No breaking the rules. Long or short, I want the answer."

She breathed out a laugh. "I am heading to Philly—Philadelphia—where Dad lives now. And I am hoping my little brother—who has been dodging all my calls for weeks because of what I suspect is something that's either going to make me upset or mad or both—will show up. There's something important I want to tell them. Hence, breakfast." A soft sigh left her. "These really are Dad's favorite. He goes crazy over them."

I remained in silence until her gaze lifted from the table and returned to me. There was something she was leaving out. I could guess as much from her expression.

I pretended to think about something, then said, "Should I be worried your dad is going to hunt me down for tricking her daughter into feeding me his all-time favorite?"

That pulled a laugh out of her. One more time, it was short-lived, but . . . enough to appease me. For now. She sobered up and pinned me with a look. "Is that your second question?"

"Not the biggest fan of angry dads, so yes. That's question number two."

"Do you have a habit of going around pissing dads off?"

Without breaking eye contact, I leaned on my elbows. "Is that your second question?"

Her eyes narrowed, but she nodded.

"Not anymore. In the past, though? I might have angered one or two." I winked, and I didn't miss the way her cheeks turned pink this time around. "You owe me an answer."

I watched her throat bob. "No, Dad won't hunt you down. He didn't even know I was dropping by. It was a surprise, and the rolls were my emotional leverage."

That last part sparked my interest, but Rosie beat me to the next round.

"My turn," she announced. "How long will you stay here? In New York."

"Six weeks. Without applying for a visa, I can stay in the country for just three months, so I decided to make my New York stop the longest because Lina offered her place. She said she couldn't break her lease until December and the apartment would be empty after she moved in with Aaron anyway, so . . ."

Rosie's lips were pursed but I couldn't tell why exactly, and I wouldn't spend a question on that when there was a more important one I wanted to ask.

I rested my chin on my fist. "Why do you need emotional leverage? With your dad."

Her chest deflated. She was quiet for so long that I thought she wasn't going to answer, that perhaps she was done playing this game with some man who had barged into her life less than twenty-four hours ago.

But then she said, "I quit my job." And her following words seemed to topple right out of her. "My well-paid, indefinite position as a team leader in an engineering firm. That's why I said that I no longer worked at InTech. Because I resigned. Six months ago." I opened my mouth to speak but more hurried words left hers. "My dad doesn't know. Neither does my brother. Only Lina does. And Aaron, of course. Not because he's her husband but because he was my boss and I had to hand my resignation letter to him. And everyone at the office, obviously, because I'm no longer there. So, I guess, some people know. What they don't know is what prompted it." She bothered her lip. "Anyway, that's why I needed leverage with Dad. Because I've been . . . keeping this huge thing from him. And I've never lied to him, not ever. We're very close. We've always been a team, Dad and I."

"Will he be mad?" Something unexpected stirred in my gut. *Protectiveness*. I shook it off, attributing it to Rosie being my little cousin's best friend. And to how much I hate bullies. "About you quitting? Is that why you haven't told him?"

"Oh no. He'd never be angry at me for following my dream. Even if it's a relatively new one." That somehow appeased me, but it also made me all the more curious. *A relatively new dream?* "But I don't think he'll be happy about it, either. He's always been so proud of me. Of his daughter being an engineer. Working in Manhattan. We didn't have much growing up." She paused. "When I graduated, it was the first time I ever saw him cry. Big, fat tears that wouldn't stop falling. I think he cried for hours. And when I got a promotion last year, back when he was still living in Queens, he told everyone in the block. 'My Bean leads a team now. She's a leader!' He threw me a party and invited the neighbors as if . . . I don't know, as if his daughter had just won a Nobel Prize or something." She shook her head with a sad smile. "He will be terrified that I'm throwing everything away for something he probably doesn't fully grasp. That's why I haven't worked up the courage to tell him. I'm scared he won't . . . understand and support me. And that would break my heart."

"So, what is it?" I couldn't stop myself from asking, craving more. "This new dream you are chasing."

I watched Rosie all but fold into herself, her shoulders falling and her eyes leaving mine. And I knew she was pulling away. "You'll think it's silly."

"There's no such thing as silly when it comes to dreams. No matter how new or old they are."

Those emerald-green eyes shifted to me with a new weight.

"Lay it on me, Rosalyn Graham," I continued. "You don't know this about me, but I don't judge. Ever."

Her chest rose with a deep breath. "I wrote and published a book," she finally said. "A romance book. Over a year ago. Around the time I got the promotion."

As if she was saying something completely ridiculous.

I frowned. "That's amazing, Rosie. That's more than amazing. It's incredible, and not at all silly."

"There's . . . more to it."

Nodding my head, I encouraged her to keep going.

"I self-published it, under a pen name, not my real name. And I didn't tell anyone at first, except for Lina, because I . . . Well, I was scared my colleagues wouldn't take me seriously if they knew I was writing what they'd consider steamy novels for bored housewives." She sighed. "How stupid is that, huh? Instead of being proud of myself." A shake of her head. "But I was scared someone would think less of my work as an engineer, or belittle my book just because it's in a genre that's so unfairly judged, or belittle me, because of something I love. Okay, not someone, but them, the guys at the office. Mostly men. Maybe even my dad, too. Society in general? I don't know."

Rosie seemed lost in thought for a second, then continued, her expression brightening a little. "Anyway. The book started getting some attention. Nothing huge, but more than I ever anticipated. It slowly but steadily escalated from there, until I was offered a book deal. And it was then that something in me snapped. I signed the contract with the publisher and quit my job, which is something very out of character for me. Taking leaps is not my thing. Making decisions without minimizing risks, without having the assurance that it will all work out is not something I've ever done. But dammit, it felt good. Terrifying but liberating. As if I had been waiting my whole life to be . . . free." Her smile fell. "And then, it all went to sh—"

She stopped herself.

"It all went where?" I asked, realizing only now that I had inched forward in her direction. Over the table.

Rosie squared back her shoulders. "You've already met your question quota."

"*What?*" I grunted.

"You've asked your five questions," she explained. "So, no more for you."

I had forgotten we were still playing this game.

"Me, on the other hand," she pointed out with what I was pretty sure was satisfaction, "I've got two more questions."

I leaned back on my seat. "I feel like I've been cheated here."

Rosie's lips tipped up the slightest bit. "I always play by the rules." Her chin lifted. "So . . . what are your plans, Lucas?"

While that was a simple enough question, it somehow felt like a punch to the gut. Because it only reminded me of the truth: I didn't have a plan. I was no longer a man who thought in terms of plans. I was *No Plan Lucas*. "Nothing special. Just . . . tourist stuff."

Silence settled between us as she weighed my curt answer.

I cleared my throat. "You're down to one question."

It only took her a few more seconds of scrutiny, and then she said, "Why weren't you at Lina and Aaron's wedding?"

My eyes widened. Her question had caught me completely off

guard. Memories of the weeks preceding the wedding poured in, stealing the breath right out of me.

Rosie, who must have seen everything playing in my face, hesitated.

"Lucas—"

"It's fine," I cut her off. I could play by my own rules. One question, one answer. No matter how long or difficult it was. "I couldn't attend," I forced out, feeling like it was hard to breathe. "I was not able to make it in time. I . . ." I blew out a shaky breath. "I was—"

I shook my head.

Long, short, easy, or hard, I didn't seem to have an answer for her. Because how did one finish a statement that represented everything they were running away from? Hell if I knew.

Something warm brushed the back of my hand, pulling me out of my head.

Looking down, my gaze stumbled upon five long and delicate fingers loosely wrapped around my hand.

"Hey," I heard her say, my eyes glued to our hands. "You couldn't go. That's a valid answer, Lucas. You played by the rules."

Torn between shaking her off and turning my hand to lace my fingers through hers for no other reason except because I needed the physical contact, I needed the closeness of another human being, I settled on neither.

I went for what I did best.

I pulled myself together and gave her a grin I hoped did the trick.

"Our five questions are up," I told her. "What time are you leaving for Philly?"

Her lips parted, but before she could give me an answer, her phone rang. She fished it out of her bag and looked at the screen with a frown. "Sorry, I better get this." Picking up the call, she brought it to her ear. "Hey, Dad, is Olly—"

She was silenced by whatever was being said on the line.

Her eyes widened, panic etching in her otherwise soft features. "You *what*?" She breathed out. "An ambulance?"

Something dropped in my stomach the moment that last word registered. And it tumbled further down when she ended the call a few seconds later and stood with a jolt, barely looking at me.

"I need to go." She scrambled for her things. "I'm sorry. It's my dad." Her hand shot for her purse, snatching it a little too briskly and dropping it to the floor. "Dammit."

"Rosie," I said, kneeling with her to pick up the things that had tumbled out of her bag. My joints complained fiercely but I ignored the pain as I picked up her keys and something that looked like a lipstick bar. "Hey, Rosie?" I searched her gaze, placing the items in her hands, and when she didn't look at me, I slid my fingers to her wrists. Her skin was warm, soft. I squeezed gently but firmly. Just enough to get her attention.

Her gaze finally met mine.

"Take a breath," I instructed.

She obeyed, filling her lungs with air while we remained crouching on the floor, facing each other.

"Do you need me to come with you?" I said very slowly. "You are a little shaken."

"*What?*" Her features softened. "That's . . . No. It's okay." She took in another breath. "I'm being silly. Dad's probably fine. It's his hip. An old injury, but he slipped, and a neighbor called an ambulance. He didn't even need me. He was calling because Mrs. Hull threatened to. Anyway, I was going to go to Philly today either way. So it's okay."

Words of reassurance rose to the tip of my tongue, but she distracted me by standing up.

I followed suit, taking extra care not to lean my weight on my right side so we wouldn't have a repeat of last night.

Rosie pulled out her wallet, extracted a few twenties, and placed them on top of the table. "Here." She smiled before pinning me with a serious look. "I think this will cover our tab."

Our tab?

I shook my head. "Rosie, no. You don't have to."

"Take it," she insisted. "Please, Lucas."

"Rosie . . ." I trailed off. But what did I expect after telling her I'd lost my card and that I only had a few bucks with me. God. I was a *zopenco*, like Abuela loved to call me when I pulled off something this stupid.

She smiled. "I better go, now." She took a step away from the booth. "I'll be back to the apartment to pick up all my things in the evening. Okay?"

"Good luck." I nodded my head. "And . . . thank you, Rosie. I'm returning this, I promise. I wasn't joking when I said I'm in your debt."

A new emotion crossed her face. "See you later, Lucas."

I watched her as she approached the exit of the diner, and just before she walked out, I called, "Oh, and please, don't tell your dad about me eating his sausage rolls! I'd like to make a good first impression."

She didn't turn around, but just as the glass door closed behind her, I heard her laugh.

It was a sweet sound. Soft and guarded, just like her.

"Ah shit," I said under my breath, looking down at my empty mug and the borrowed bills. *"Lina me va a cortar las pelotas."*

CHAPTER FIVE

Rosie

*O*lly didn't show up at the station.

A part of me wasn't even surprised. I guess I had expected him to blow me off. But that hadn't softened the blow when he dodged my call—again—and shot me a text that read: Can't make it, big sis. Sorry.

Luckily, once I arrived in Philly, I discovered that Dad was fine, just a little sore from his fall. Not that he'd admit it. Oh no. At home, he'd refused to lie down, take painkillers, or let me prepare tea or food for him. Repeatedly. But that was Joe Graham for you. "I'm fine, Bean," he'd said about a thousand times. Following that up with "I relied enough on you when your mother left all these years ago, Bean. You shouldn't worry, Bean. Why did you take a day off work to come fuss over your old man, Bean? You are a team leader now, Bean. People depend on you. Have you heard from Olly, by the way? He's okay, isn't he, Bean?"

So, by the time I was taking the train back to Manhattan, my lie tally was the same, if not higher after covering for my little brother— again—and I was so emotionally drained from dealing with a stubborn Dad that I no longer had the energy to guilt-trip Olly.

And then there was Lucas.

Something took flight in my stomach, making me feel giddy and nervous and all kinds of flustered at the thought of him.

Here I was, a mostly reasonable and independent woman, feeling like a sixteen-year-old fussing over the idea of seeing her crush.

Only Lucas Martín wasn't my crush. Nope. He was a man I didn't really know, whose online presence on social media I had . . . *appreciated* a perfectly normal amount.

He was also a man I had spilled a good portion of my guts to only this morning. And it had felt good. Not just fine, but *good*.

And now here we were. Him, on the other side of Lina's door, probably wondering if I was going to show up at all, given the time, and who knows, maybe considering throwing my ginormous, messy pile of belongings out the window if I didn't. *No, because he would never do that*, a voice countered. And me, standing in the hallway, staring at that door for a wildly inappropriate amount of time wishing I had X-ray vision so I could . . . *So I could what?*

Shaking myself, I let myself in.

The moment I turned the knob, though, I second-guessed not knocking. Because what in the holy hell was I doing barging in like this? What if Lucas—

Whoa.

I stopped cold in my tracks with the door fully open, the most amazing, out-of-this-world-delicious scent hitting me like a wave.

"Rosie." My name—off Lucas's lips, with that roll of the *R*—made it through the haze. "You're finally back."

Blinking a couple of times, I zeroed in on him. He was standing in the kitchen of the studio, in front of the stove, with his back to me. He wore a fresh T-shirt, and his brown hair fell in a disheveled mess of wet locks. He must have showered recently, I assumed, as I could see tiny droplets of water on the back of his neck. A strong neck. And the visible skin was tanned and smooth-looking, and . . . and I was staring. Ogling, really.

I cleared my throat. "Hi," I croaked. "I'm back, yes. And you're here, like we agreed. Which is great and nothing I should be surprised about." Cursing myself for not being able to turn off my awkwardness in front of this man who had done nothing to deserve it, I closed the door behind me and strode in. "It smells incredible in here, Lucas."

Finally. Something *normal* to leave my lips.

"I'm glad you think so." He chuckled. "I hope it tastes that way, too."

Taking in everything already laid out on the surface of the narrow kitchen island that also served as breakfast bar, dinner table, and desk, it was hard to believe otherwise.

Like a bee drawn to a flower, my legs carried me closer, my gaze gobbling everything in awe. A plate of fragrant rice sautéed with colorful veggies sat in the middle. Something that looked like charred Feta cheese drizzled with what had to be honey was to its right. And to the left, a tray filled with slices of roasted bread spread with peppers and onions.

Another chuckle reached my ears, making me realize Lucas was no longer at the stove but on the other side of the island. Looking at me, his expression one of pure amusement. "Come on," he said. "Have a seat before it gets cold."

My eyes widened. "Have a . . . seat?"

"Where else would you eat?"

"You're inviting me to have dinner?" I swallowed, a mix of surprise and more of that nervous giddiness making my tummy drop. "With you?"

He tilted his head to one side, studying me. "Only if you're hungry."

"I . . ." Didn't know what to say. Which I realized happened way too often around Lucas.

Did I want to sit down and take this chance to spend more time—before we went our separate ways—with Lucas, or did I want to politely decline, pack my things, leave, and figure out a plan of action for tonight?

Before I could make up my mind, my stomach growled, providing Lucas with an answer.

I winced in horror.

"Ah." Lucas pointed out with humor. "How the tables have turned. I think your stomach is trying to communicate with me this time around, Rosalyn Graham. And I'm taking it as a compliment."

His smile was big and easy as he grabbed two plates from the counter and set them on the table. Then, he walked right where I was standing, stretched an arm, and pulled out the stool closer to me. He met my gaze and patted the plush surface. "You're hungry, so it's settled. Sit. Tell me how your dad is."

My mouth opened, then closed.

His offer, his words, were sweet. Considerate. And in a not-so-shocking turn of events—given my long online lurking history—this was something I had fantasized about a couple dozen times. Having dinner with Lucas Martín. Dinner he had cooked. Dinner we would eat together.

But I hesitated. Standing there, not moving, except for my eyeballs, which were busy tracking Lucas's movements as he set everything up.

"Rosie, a seat?" he repeated. "I can't promise I won't bite, but I will try not to."

And my next breath got stuck in my throat for a second there.

My cheeks flushed hot while I told myself to react. To laugh it off. The man was flirty, fun, easy to be around. He was just being nice.

I opened my mouth and a boisterous, loud cackle came out.

Lucas's eyebrows shot to the roof of his forehead.

Too much, Rosie. "That was funny." I patted my chest, my screech still echoing in my ears. "A funny, funny joke, of course. Because you're not going to bite me. Obviously."

Lucas shook his head. "I'm starting to believe I've lost my touch," he murmured. But when I finally let myself fall onto the stool, the frown disappeared from his face. His expression eased and turned somewhat serious. "Thank you, Rosie."

"Why are you thanking me?" I answered, my voice thankfully getting back to normal.

He shrugged. "It's been a while since I've shared a meal with someone. Traveling alone has its perks but it can also get a little lonely. I think I was beginning to feel that way. Until this morning." He met my gaze. "And now."

I stared into that pair of brown eyes for a few seconds, feeling something inside of me softening, melting: my hesitation, my awkwardness, and most likely, something else, too. "Thank you for inviting me to have dinner with you, Lucas. It's really my pleasure." *And you wouldn't believe how much*, I wanted to add.

He smiled, and once more it was big and happy and . . . *trouble*. So much trouble, I seemed to realize as I stared at those lips of his. I was in sticky, up-to-my-knees trouble if he really planned to flash that smile like it was nothing.

"So, how's your dad?" he asked again, offering the platter of sautéed rice.

Taking it from him, I served myself a big spoonful. "He's okay. He has a bad hip. He tripped on one of the creepy yard gnomes he loves so much." I let out a soft snort. "But luckily, he's fine. Just a little sore. It could have been so much worse. The gnome was the only casualty."

"I'm happy to hear that, Rosie."

I was, too. And for some reason, I doubted Lucas had said it just to be polite.

"Thank you, Lucas." Looking to occupy myself with something that wasn't his face, I reached for a slice of bread and brought it straight to my mouth. "Oh my gosh." I pretty much moaned the moment I tasted the first bite. "What did you do to these peppers? They taste—*Whoa*. They're amazing."

"I caramelized them with red onions and a few spices I found in Lina's cupboard." He winked, biting into his slice, too. "The rest of the groceries I bought with my change and some of what you gave me." His expression turned hesitant. "Rosie, I feel like I owe you—"

"Don't worry about it, okay?" I told him before he could even try to explain himself. "I'm more than okay lending you a few bucks until you get your replacement. You don't know anyone in the city and it's really the least I can do. Plus, you've invited me to eat." I gestured at the absolutely moan-worthy feast he had served. "So, I hardly see how this isn't a good deal for me." I spooned some of that gooey and shiny Feta cheese onto my plate. "I'd do outrageous things for cheese like this."

"I'll make sure to remember that. For next time."

Next time. Did that mean—

No. It was just something people said.

He continued, "Cooking—followed by eating what I cook—is one of the very few pleasures capable of taking my mind off things when I'm having an off day."

I readjusted the napkin on my lap and returned all my focus to my food. "I can really see why, Lucas," I told him, keeping myself from asking about the off day and assuming he was talking about last night's mess.

"So, Rosie," Lucas said after a couple of minutes. "I've heard all about how you and Lina met and I'm going to be honest, I've been dying to hear your version of the events."

Frowning, I sneaked a quick glance at him. That big, distracting smile was there again. *Dammit.* I returned my gaze to my plate. "My version of the events? We met during Intro Week at InTech."

"Oh, that's so not what Lina has been telling around." He chuckled, and it was low and deep and . . . knowing. "You're kind of a legend back home."

"A *legend*?"

"Yeah, it's not every day that a kind soul pulls my cousin out of the way of an escaped horse and saves her life."

"A *what*?"

And just like that, the events he was referring to flashed through my mind and the only logical response to them was triggered.

A genuine deep belly laugh burst out of me.

"That's what Lina told everyone?" I asked, and Lucas nodded. "*Unbelievable.* Well, actually, I should have expected that from Lina."

"You're telling me my very low-key, absolutely not-dramatic cousin embellished a little?" He laughed. "You know, she even describes in terrifying detail how her life flashed before her eyes." He tilted his head. "All of it before opening them and finding her green-eyed guardian angel standing before her."

I scoffed. "I guess that explains why your grandmother cried when we met."

Without taking his gaze off me, Lucas pushed the cheese platter in my direction. "Are you really telling me, then, that there was no horse dramatically rearing?" When I didn't serve myself, he reached out and spooned a piece onto my plate. "No you swooping in and saving her life?"

"Well," I said, watching him retrieve his hands with a satisfied look. "Are you familiar with the horse carriages in Central Park?"

Lucas nodded, reaching for one of the last slices of roasted bread.

"They are mostly for tourists, or the occasional grand gesture date, which is a little . . . unoriginal, if you ask me. I have nothing against gestures, of course. But romance—big, grand gestures— should be about something personal. Well thought out, like—"

Our gazes met again, bringing my words to a stop when I spotted the amusement in his eyes.

"Anyway." I shrugged a shoulder. "Don't ask me how, but one of the horses was loose and marching across Central Park at the slowest pace known to . . . well, horses. Enter Lina, headphones on, clearly lost, looking at Google Maps app on her phone." Only later, I had learned my best friend had no sense of direction. "That same morning, I had seen her spill a pot of coffee on someone's pants, so I knew her basic reflexes weren't exactly super sharp."

Lucas snickered. "Oh, definitely not her forte."

"Right?" I chuckled. "Anyway, I yelled for her to watch out, and when she didn't move, I just went and pulled her out of the way."

Lucas tsked. "That's definitely *not* the version I've been hearing about every single Christmas since she met you."

Every single Christmas?

Lucas had been hearing about it—about me—every single Christmas?

"Sorry to disappoint you." I picked my fork back up, loading it with rice. "I'm no guardian angel. Or heroine. Just your run-of-the-mill engineer turned romance writer." I tilted my head. "Oh. That's the first time I said that out loud."

His smile turned warmer. "And how did it feel?"

I thought about my answer. "Good. It was good to say it. To hear it."

I just wished I *felt* confident in these new shoes I had slipped on. But I didn't, not right now. Mostly because . . . could someone who had written one single book be considered a writer? How could someone who had hardly made it past the first chapter of her second one *feel* like a writer?

My stomach dropped at the thought.

I didn't know if Lucas missed that or not, but he said, "Can I ask you something else? It's a little personal."

"Of course," I answered with a sigh, remnants of self-doubt still stirring in my gut.

"You never told me how you felt about giving up your engineering job. You told me how those around you might feel about you writing, and how you expected your dad to feel about you quitting. But you never said how *you* felt."

And that was . . . a question I hadn't expected him to ask. A question no one—from the people who knew—had thought to ask.

How did I feel, though? I knew why I had resigned. But had that been the right thing to do? Did a part of me regret it? Was the fact that I hadn't been able to write a single freaking word since then a sign of how big a mistake I had made?

"It's none of my business, I know," he said after a long silence on my part. His smile was lopsided, almost self-conscious. "It's okay."

"I . . ." I trailed off.

He watched me for a few seconds, and when I still gave him nothing, he resumed eating, acting like it wasn't a big deal. Probably because he really thought it wasn't.

"I wasn't unhappy," I finally managed to say, and he glanced up at me very slowly, as if a sudden movement would somehow scare me away. "I think I would still be happy working for InTech if I hadn't found something that I . . . finally *loved*. Something that made me understand what really loving what you do is. Something that completed me in a way engineering never did, even if I didn't yet know and was never unhappy." I released all the air in my lungs, feeling like a pricked balloon, deflating. "That's probably why it's so hard for me to talk about it. Because this new thing, this new dream, seems so fragile. Like, I'm holding it in my hands, but the feel of it is so . . . new, so unfamiliar, that I'm terrified I might drop and shatter it, so I just . . . stand there and look at it in silence."

And because every day that I inched closer to that deadline—now eight weeks away—every day that passed without me writing a single word or being able to access whatever had been inside of me not so long ago, I felt like it was falling. Like I was failing.

"Hey." Lucas's voice registered, making me realize I had been staring into empty space. "You're ballsy, Rosie." The right side of his mouth tipped up. "That's something you should never forget. And something you should be proud of."

Ballsy. I'd never been called that. Not even once. Cautious, responsible, driven, but never ballsy.

"Thank you," I said, so quietly I wasn't even sure he'd heard it. "But enough about me." I straightened on my stool. "What, aside from food, makes you feel better when you're feeling off?"

Lucas thought about my question for just an instant. Then, he leaned on his elbows. Slowly. His voice dropped down, as if he was letting me into a secret and I felt myself lean forward, too. "It's something almost as fun as eating, but it involves far less clothing."

My breath stuck in my throat, not caring that I had been in the process of swallowing. Consequently, a runaway rice grain went down the wrong pipe, making me break into a fit of coughing.

"*Por Dios*," I heard him say between my shallow puffs of air. "Rosie, are you okay?"

Nope. I wasn't. Clearly. Because the mental image of Lucas—in *far less clothing* than he was now, doing *fun* things—had sent my most basic body function into shock.

When I didn't answer and only kept coughing, a curse in what must have been Spanish left him. He stood up and shot in my direction.

Before he'd think of wrapping his arms around me and Heimliching me, I took matters into my own hands and reached across the table for a glass of water.

"Hold on, Rosie," Lucas warned just as I tipped the glass up. "Not so fast! That's—Oh. Okay."

I downed the contents of it and placed it back on the table. "Wine," I said a little breathlessly. "That was white wine." Which I hadn't even noticed on the table. Because, well. Because I'd been busy noticing Lucas.

"Yeah," he admitted, and I could hear the amusement dancing in his words. "Well, it did the trick."

"Yep." I cleared my throat and straightened in my stool, refusing to look up at him. *God, this really needs to stop.* "Can I . . . Can I get a refill, please?"

His answer didn't come for a long moment. "You sure? You just downed a full glass of it."

Feeling Lucas's eyes on the side of my head, I finally dared to meet his gaze. He was studying me. "I rarely ever drink." I sighed. "But today might be a two glasses of wine kind of day. Or week, maybe. Plus, we're mostly done with the food, so I might need something new to take my mind off things." He looked a little surprised by my admission and I felt the need to add, "Something that doesn't involve less clothing."

Slowly, and almost reluctantly, Lucas poured more of the golden liquid. "Your brother," he pointed out simply. "You mentioned he'd been dodging your calls. Is that why it's a two glasses kind of day?"

"You have good memory," I murmured.

"I'm a good listener." He returned to his seat across the island, making sure to meet my gaze. "He wasn't there today, was he? At your dad's."

I narrowed my eyes to thin slits. "Who are you? Dr. Phil?"

"Doctor . . . who?"

"He's a psychologist and talk show host." I reached for my glass. "People go on his show, Dr. Phil has a little look inside their souls and *boom*, uproots and fixes all their deepest concerns."

Lucas smirked. "Is he handsome? Is that why I remind you of him?"

A laugh climbed up my throat, leaving me before I could stop it. "Oh God, no."

Lucas's lopsided smile fell off. "Oh."

"I mean, you're handsome," I felt the need to clarify. Then, immediately regretted it. "*Objectively*. To the people out there. Not subjectively, as in, to me. You're objectively handsome, I . . . guess."

"You . . . guess?" Lucas's lips pursed. "I feel like there's a compliment somewhere, but I'm having a hard time finding it."

If you only knew, I thought. But instead, I said, "It's the fact that I seem to be using you as my therapeutic crutch a lot. We've known each other for a total of what? A day? And you know more about me than most people that have been in my life for years." I shrugged a shoulder. "That's why I was comparing you to him."

His smile returned. "Being used by beautiful women is something I don't mind in the slightest."

Beautiful women.

My heart did the silliest, stupidest cartwheel.

I returned the glass to my lips just to buy some time, trying to focus on *women*, plural, and not *woman*, as in me, Rosie. Although what did it matter, really? This was Lucas Martín, and after tonight, there was nothing tying us together. Not when Lina wasn't in New York to supply an excuse for us to meet again, and definitely not when in about a month and a half he'd be jumping on a plane and leaving the country. The continent. So it didn't matter if he was referring to me or not.

"So, my brother," I said, taking the conversation back onto a safer ground, "didn't even show up. He blew me off. Again."

Lucas nodded. "Did he say why?"

"He didn't. He never tells me anything anymore." I reached for my napkin, just to occupy my hands with something. "And that's the whole problem. I just . . . don't know what's up with him. It's as if I no longer know him, like he doesn't want me in his life anymore." I shook my head, squeezing the cloth between my fingers. "And that makes me incredibly sad."

I looked up at Lucas, finding his attentive gaze on me as he chewed on the last of his food. "And your dad?"

"He's probably blaming himself. He probably feels like he could have done something if he'd stayed in the city." I dropped the napkin next to my plate and reached for the wine again. "That's why I always cover for him. Tell Dad that he's busy. That he has a new job. That he's living his life. That he's an adult and we need to give him some room to grow on his own. But I'm not sure I believe that myself anymore." I downed the contents of my glass. "I think there's something he's not telling us. Something he's keeping from me."

Lucas nodded, momentarily averting his gaze. "What do you think that could be?"

Closing my eyes, I shook my head. "I don't know, Lucas." I zeroed back on him and forced a smile. "See? A two glasses kind of night."

Lucas remained silent for a few seconds, seemingly lost in thought. Then he said, "Sometimes we keep things from those we love for reasons we don't even understand ourselves."

And for some reason I couldn't really explain, his words felt like a confession.

He continued, "Give him some time. He'll realize on his own how isolating secrets can be."

A little lost in the shadows crossing his expression, it took me some time to answer. "I hope you're right, Dr. Phil."

Shifting in my seat I remembered that I wasn't the only one in the room that had had a strange day. "I should probably go. You must be exhausted after the weirdest twenty-four hours of your life."

He chuckled, returning to his lighthearted self. "I wouldn't say weird," he admitted.

I wouldn't, either, I thought. But I didn't say anything and rose to my feet instead, the couple glasses of wine I'd ingested in the span of a few minutes racing straight to my head and making me wobble for the tiniest second.

Lucas's brows wrinkled.

"Whoops, I stood up too fast." I played it down with a light laugh. "Well, dinner was great, Lucas. Seriously. The best I've had in a while. Thanks again for inviting me."

His mouth twitched, making me hope for one last sunny grin before leaving but it never really happened. Instead, he stood up and walked to the living room area of the studio. Leaving me there, staring at the way his wide and lean back shifted with every step. He plopped himself down on the large couch I knew my best friend had splurged on about a year ago.

He reached for the remote and turned the TV on. He tapped on the smart TV options, displaying the subscription apps. "She really has every single streaming service I can think of."

"Uhm," I muttered, wondering if I was getting a goodbye from him. "Yeah. We spend a lot of nights in." More like all of them. "Or used to, before Aaron and the wedding."

And it hit me right then, that maybe Lucas wasn't the only one that had been feeling a little lonely lately. Maybe I was, too.

He turned, looking at me over his shoulder. "Are you coming?"

I blinked.

Lucas's smirk returned. "Don't look at me like that. I'll let you pick."

I hesitated. "I . . . I should probably start gathering my things. I have a lot of stuff and I unpacked more than necessary. I also didn't get around to booking something for the night and I should do that." And that was evidence of how scattered my thoughts had been today. Because I was "Always Ready Rosie," and any other day that would have been at the top of my list. Done and ready.

"Or," Lucas pointed out, "you can relax while we watch something, and then I'll help you get your stuff." He looked down at his watch. "It's only 8:30 p.m. And I don't give remote rights to just anybody."

"I guess . . ." I took one small step forward, feeling my head sway.

This is why I don't usually drink. "I guess relaxing for a bit won't hurt." Another step. "I guess . . . I could stay."

"Then, what are you waiting for, Rosie?"

Yep. I didn't just guess. I wanted to stay badly enough to close the rest of the distance, snag the remote out of his grip, and join him on the couch. Or at least the wine did.

A couple of episodes of my favorite show later, I had not only re-laxed but succumbed to the mental exhaustion of the last hours—and days and weeks.

Shifting my lax body on the couch, I turned and let my head fall on the pillow. My drowsy eyes took in Lucas's profile.

Defined nose, strong jaw, high cheekbones, full lips . . . and that hair. Those locks that were on the longer side and that still managed to make my stomach dip with surprise and something else. Some-thing . . . warmer that I didn't want to think too much about. Not when I could just look at him.

Yeah. This new look suited him. Far more than the buzz cut one he sported on Instagram.

Before I knew what I was doing, I heard myself whisper, "Lucas?"

I saw the corner of his lips turn up before he whispered back, "Rosie?"

I chuckled. "I might still be a little tipsy. And I'm so tired, too. I might doze off if I don't stand up right now."

It was his turn to laugh. "You might," he said, but then, his mouth fell and his neck somehow tensed. He rolled his head toward me and made sure to meet my gaze. "Does that worry you?"

I frowned, a little slow to follow.

His brows bunched up. "It shouldn't. You know you're safe with me, right?"

Oh.

Something in my stomach took a deep dive at the seriousness in his tone. "I know," I told him. And I meant it. I did know I was safe with him.

His expression and shoulders relaxed, causing me a deep sense of satisfaction I didn't understand.

"You know why I know?" I asked.

He waited for my answer.

"Because I know you noticed I was tipsy, and that's why you insisted I stayed. You were making sure I was okay before I left."

Nodding his head, he seemed to think about something. To my surprise, he turned back to the screen, and only when he was facing away, he lowered his voice and said, "Now quiet. I'm trying to watch my show."

Which brought the stupidest smile to my face. Because it wasn't his show. It was *mine*. My supernatural teen show filled with vampires and werewolves and magic rings and enchanted lockets and mystic cures and more than a fair share of over-the-top drama.

"Lucas?" I repeated after a few moments.

The corner of his mouth twitched again. "Yeah, Rosie?"

"Thank you." *For listening. And for tonight. And for making me feel . . . less alone. A little less burdened, even if only for a little while.* "I think I really needed to talk to someone, and I want to make sure you know."

He looked over at me again, and he must have seen the gravity of my words in my face because he asked, "What's wrong?"

The wine had probably obliterated the last of my filters, and his expression was so kind, so gentle, that it was impossible not to answer.

"Remember my new dream?" I asked with a big, long sigh, bringing my hands between my cheek and the pillow underneath. "I have a deadline, for my second book, and I'm running out of time." I lowered my voice to barely a whisper. "This is my chance to prove to myself that I didn't make a mistake, Lucas. And I might not make it."

A part of me realized I wasn't telling him much. In fact, I was really telling him nothing about the real problem: me, feeling like someone was cutting off the oxygen supply every time I opened that manuscript; me, drowning in pressure, in paralyzing fear; me blocked. Stuck.

But Lucas just rolled his body, angling himself in my direction, and rested the side of his head on the cushion behind him, mirroring my posture.

His lips pressed in a stern line. "You'll figure it out, Rosie." His gaze burned with a confidence that I hadn't yet earned. "You've gotten this far. I don't need to know much about you to know that you'll keep pushing. That's what ballsy people do."

Ballsy. I liked how it felt to be called ballsy. By him.

But I still wanted to tell him that he couldn't know for sure. That I could be a fraud or a failure. I could have made a mistake rushing into this. But it was hard for me to be negative around Lucas when he managed to shine a bright light. "I hope you're right."

His voice lowered, turning solemn. "Want to bet on it?"

I chuckled. "I'd rather not."

"Good, because it would be my easiest win."

He smiled, and I think I did, too.

Time ticked by as we stared at each other, the show playing in the background. And at some point, seconds or minutes later, I felt my eyelids grow heavy and consciousness slowly slip away from me as an unexpected and vague thought took shape in my head.

What would have happened if Lucas had attended Lina and Aaron's wedding? If we'd met that day? Would it have been this . . . easy, this effortless, to talk to him?

But before I could conjure an answer, sleep won the battle, taking me over with it.

CHAPTER SIX

Lucas

*M*y eyes snapped open; a breath stuck in my throat.

One of my hands landed on my chest and I . . . couldn't breathe.

I . . . *Joder*.

Slowly, I managed to force my fingers to rub circles over my rib cage, attempting to relieve the pressure gripping my lungs.

I'm not in the water, I reminded myself. *I am breathing.*

And I was sleeping.

Disoriented, I let my gaze roam, taking my surroundings in what had to be the morning light. A colorful painting hung on the wall above me. Two wineglasses rested on top of a kitchen island a few feet away. My shabby backpack lay at the feet of the couch I was lying on.

The couch.

Had I fallen asleep at Abuela's again? No, this wasn't her beat two-seater that had seen better times. It wasn't her living room, either. Every piece of furniture and the décor was trendy and vibrant. It reminded me of—

It all came to me, then.

This wasn't Spain, or my grandmother's house. I was in New York. In Lina's apartment. And I'd spent the night on her couch.

Passing both hands up and down my face, I rubbed my eyes, all the while repeating the mantra I had used innumerable times in the last months.

It was just a dream. I'm okay.

Although that last part might be a lie. I was as okay as I'd ever be. Because this was my new life. Not New York, but *this*. Waking up covered in cold sweat with muscles that had once been in prime condition now sore and tight and unreliable.

Soft snoring from a few feet to my left caught my attention. With a wince, I threw both my legs off the couch and looked for the source of the sound. It didn't take me long to zero in on the figure lying in the middle of the master bed. Dark curls splayed on the pillow.

Rosie. Rosalyn Graham.

I wasn't surprised that she'd fallen asleep last night. In fact, I was shocked it hadn't happened until the fourth or fifth episode of that vampire show she knew by heart. As much as we both had fought to stay awake—her because she had every intention of leaving, and me, because, damn, that show was laced with crack—we'd dozed off. And it hadn't been until later, after what I assumed was a couple of hours, that I'd woken up to a cramp traveling down my right leg and found her snoring next to me. So, without giving it much thought, I'd turned off the TV, picked Rosie up as best as I could, and carried her to the bed.

Our conversation from the night before came back to me—we weren't that different, she and I, both afraid of the future. Only, Rosie had the world at her feet, and in my case, mine had opened up under me. I ripped my gaze from Rosie's sleeping shape and headed for the bathroom. My skin felt clammy and my body tight, so I closed the door behind me and jumped into the shower.

After an indecently long time under the scalding hot water, I made myself turn off the shower, wrapped a towel around my hips, grabbed my discarded clothes, and walked out of the bathroom.

Feeling a lot more like myself, I shook my head as I stood there, inspecting again the nice albeit small apartment in Brooklyn, New

York. What had Lina called it? Her . . . studio? Loft? I couldn't re-member. But considering it was an open space with no rooms but the bathroom, I guessed it had one of those fancy sounding descrip-tors to make it sound chicer. Like in those American remodeling shows Abuela loved so much, that got dubbed into Spanish back home.

"Lucas?" Rosie's voice dragged me back to the present.

Turning, I found her sitting in the middle of the bed with the comforter curled around her legs. She looked like she had just woken up, but her eyes were wide, the green in them impossibly light.

My lips stretched into a smile. *"Buenos días."*

Her gaze dipped down, then back up again. "Oh my . . . Hi, yeah. Hello," she stuttered, her cheeks turning pink. "G-Good morning."

I frowned. "You okay?"

Her eyes trailed down my chest again. Slowly at first, then a little frantically. As if she couldn't decide where to look.

"You showered," she pointed out. "And now, you're in a towel."

Following the direction of her gaze, I looked down, too, check-ing for wardrobe—or towel—malfunctions, making sure the scars on my knee and thigh weren't visible. Everything was in order and the towel covered the now mostly healed marks. My eyes returned to her face.

"Is something wrong?"

She shook her head, her eyes diving one more time.

Oh. Nothing was wrong. Rosie was just checking me out. Bla-tantly. Probably a little unknowingly, too.

Her eyes settled on the tattoo I had on the left side of my torso, covering a big part of my rib cage. She studied it for a long moment.

Incapable of helping myself, I asked in the most serious tone, "Enjoying the view?"

Her eyes jerked to my face. "Sorry, what?"

"Are you enjoying the view?" I repeated, barely holding my laughter.

"Oh . . . *Oh.* I wasn't ogling you. I . . . happen to love tattoos," she rushed out. "I'm a *huge* fan of them, actually. That's all I was check-ing. Is it a wave? It's beautiful. Stunning line work. Did it hurt? I bet it did." She took a deep breath. "I . . . yeah, I love tattoos on men. Or people in general."

Instinctively, my palm went to my side and framed the design. I rubbed my fingers over it, driving her gaze back there.

"I'm glad you approve." A chuckle finally left me. "For a second there I thought I'd crossed a line walking around like this. But I guess you were just a little distracted." I paused. "Because of the tattoo."

"Oh yes." Rosie nodded her head vigorously. "Totally. You could stroll around completely naked and I wouldn't even bat an eyelid."

"Good," I answered, letting her think I believed her. I didn't. She'd be affected. If I dropped my towel right this moment, she'd probably blush so hard she'd pass out. And I found myself enjoying that knowledge a little too much. "I'll make sure to remember that. Nakedness, okay."

"Awesome," she croaked. "Really great."

Hiding my smile, I turned away from her. "Did I wake you? It's a little early for long showers."

"You didn't," she said as I walked where my backpack was and threw it open. "I'm always up at dawn. I'm not much of a sleeper."

"That makes the two of us." I snagged a change of clothes and glanced at her. "Do you need the bathroom before I go change?" I asked, crossing my arms in front of my chest and flexing my bi-ceps the tiniest bit because my ego was a little too pleased with her attention. Her eyes tipped down quickly and widened. "Or I could change right here. With you being okay with naked—"

"No!" she rushed out. "Go ahead, *please*. I'll get the coffee started."

With a satisfied nod, I disappeared into the bathroom again. When I returned Rosie was placing two mugs on the counter. She had changed out of last night's sweater and into a black sleeveless top. Her hair was wrapped in some kind of colorful tie at the top of her head. Inadvertently, my gaze trailed down her neck, following the line of her throat and shoulders, all the way down her arms and back, taking in the soft curves of her body and hopelessly reaching her backside. It was a good, rounded—

I shook myself.

No. I couldn't check her out like this. Not when I was about to suggest the plan I'd come up with in the shower.

Rosie turned to face me, an apology shining in her eyes. "I swear, I meant to leave last night. I'm sorry I dozed off."

"Nothing to be sorry about." I waved a hand in front of me, meaning every word. "You were exhausted, and I was, too. We both fell asleep."

She seemed to consider something. "You put me to bed, though, didn't you? You really didn't need to do that." She grabbed the coffeepot and placed it on the island. "I could have stayed on the couch."

"It wasn't a problem." I shrugged.

She pulled out a stool and sat down in front of me. "It was very sweet of you to do that." She averted her eyes and busied herself with the coffeepot. "You know," she said, filling both mugs, "Lina mentioned how much of a *brute* you are, and I keep wondering why she ever said that."

"Oh." I let out a laugh. "Trust me, she has more than a couple of reasons to say something like that. I was a bit of a nightmare when we were kids. As a teenager, too." I snickered. "And, well, I still am on occasion."

"You seem to be on your best behavior now."

I met her gaze as I dragged my coffee toward me. "I'm actually glad you think that way."

"You're glad?" A small frown tugged at her brows. "Why would you be?"

Readying myself, I waited until she took a sip of her coffee, then I said, "Because I think you should stay."

Rosie lowered her mug very slowly. "Like, now? For breakfast?"

"No, I mean for as long as you want or need to." I let that sink in, then added, "Stay here, in Lina's apartment with me."

She arched an eyebrow. "What? I can't."

"Why not?" I sipped my coffee.

The conviction in my voice must have worked in my favor because she stuttered over her words. "Because you're . . . you're . . . Lucas. And I don't . . . live here?"

"You can't stay in your apartment," I pointed out, holding my mug between my hands. "And it doesn't seem like you can stay at your dad's, either. Otherwise, you would be there right now. But correct me if I'm wrong."

Rosie's shoulders sunk. "No. You're not wrong."

She hadn't explicitly said so last night, but I'd guessed. And I got it. I *understood* that. Far more than I was comfortable admitting. "So, stay here, give yourself some time to work things out."

"But it's a studio apartment with one bed, and Lina promised you the place, Lucas."

"We can share it if you're okay with that."

Rosie's ears turned pink.

I tilted my head. "The apartment, not the bed."

She let out a humorless laugh. "Of course." A pause. "But if *I* am the one okay with sharing?"

"You said we couldn't both stay here the night I arrived, so I thought I'd check."

"I did say that," she murmured. Then, her voice dropped with something that sounded a lot like regret. "But I didn't mean it that way. I don't mind sharing the apartment with you. You're . . . surprisingly wonderful. Actually, I shouldn't even be surprised."

I frowned, wondering what she meant by that.

Lost in thought, Rosie's hand went to the top of her head, absentmindedly fixing locks of hair. "My plan was looking for a cheap hotel, or an Airbnb or something. I started checking yesterday on my way back, but it's just . . ."

"Expensive," I finished for her. "Exhausting, too. I know. I searched before Lina offered her place." I straightened on my stool, making sure to meet her gaze. "Stay here, Rosie." I offered her for what would be the last time. I wasn't going to push this on her. "For as long as you want or need to. But just . . . don't throw away the money on an overpriced room rushing out of here just because you think you'll inconvenience me. I'm the one offering."

Something new crystallized in her gaze. Something I was pretty sure meant she was considering it.

She hesitated, then asked, "Won't I crowd you?"

"Do I look crowded to you?"

She shook her head.

"We stayed the night and it worked, didn't it?" I said, and she shrugged. "And you're forgetting I'm a tourist. The apartment will be empty most of the day anyway. Plenty of quiet for you to concentrate. To work and make your deadline."

She perked up, but just as quickly she sighed. "But I can't let you sleep on a couch."

I checked the piece of furniture, not seeing the problem. "I've slept in far worse places than a couch in a trendy apartment in Brooklyn."

"What places?"

"On Abuela's thirty-year-old sofa, on an air mattress, a towel on the sand, or the floor of my van whenever the mattress got drenched by the rain, which was often." I shrugged a shoulder. "I can go on. I've lived on the road for long periods of time. So trust me, that plush and fancy couch is a dream."

Rosie took her time to process that. "On the road because of the competitions?"

A wave of cold and heavy reality washed over me.

"Lina bragged about you every time you qualified for a tournament," Rosie explained. "She'd show me pictures. Of you."

That settled like a stone deep in my stomach because neither Lina nor the rest of the Martín family was aware of how much that had changed.

Rosie brought the mug to her lips, and then shocked me by asking, "Is that why your English is so insanely good?"

Thankful for the slight veer in the direction of the conversation, I chuckled. "Yeah. Over the last five years I've spent more time around international people, away from home, than in Spain. So, at some point I guess I had no option but to . . . learn. I picked up lots of common expressions."

Something seemed to flicker in Rosie's eyes, spreading out across her face. "I'll stay," she said. "Until I find out how long before I can go back to my place. I should hear from my landlord this week."

I nodded, ignoring the deep sense of relief invading me. "As long as you need."

"Oh. And I'll take care of all the groceries while I'm here." She pointed at me with her finger. "Even after your credit card arrives. It's the least I can do."

I opened my mouth to complain but she stopped me, waving her index in front of my face. "Not negotiable."

"All right." I accepted with a sigh. "But only if I cook for both of us."

"Okay." She let that threatening finger fall. "But I'll do the dishes."

"Deal."

"Oh." She straightened on her stool. "And you take the bed. I'll sleep on the couch."

Not a chance in hell, but it was adorable that she believed I'd ever accept. "Rosie—"

My ringtone blared through the apartment, interrupting us.

"Might be important," she said. "You should take it."

With a nod, I sprinted to the phone. My sister's name flashed on the screen, notifying me of an incoming video call.

I held my phone in front of me. *"Hermanita."*

"Lucas!" she screeched, her flaming red hair bouncing with her enthusiasm. *"¿Cómo está mi persona favorita en todo el mundo mundial?"*

Her favorite person in the world? My sister never said stuff like that unless . . .

"What did you do, Charo?" I asked her in Spanish.

She gasped, pretending to be outraged. "Excuse you. I'm a saint, you know that."

I snorted. And because she really wasn't one, I asked, "Is Taco okay?"

My sister rolled her eyes just as a bark sounded in the background. "You are an overbearing pup dad. Do you know that? Taco is perfectly fine under my care."

There was movement on her side, the image blurring for a couple seconds. Then, a familiar snout appeared on the screen.

"*¡Hola, chico!*" I told my best bud, barely keeping the emotion off my voice. "*¿Estás siendo un buen chico?*"

Taco tilted his head at the sound of my voice, then a whimper came from the phone.

"I miss you, too, buddy." That earned me an excited woof. "Is Charo taking good care of you?"

Taco turned and licked my sister's face, then faced the camera and did the same with her phone.

"*¡Taco, no!*" Charo's voice was muffled by my dog's tongue, presumably on the microphone. After a couple seconds of wrestling, both of them were back in the frame. "Your dog will lick or eat just about anything, is that normal?"

I chuckled. "Yeah. Like daddy, like son. Right, Taco?" He barked in confirmation. "A few months ago, he sneaked into *Mamá*'s pantry and slaughtered the *jamón*. The good one. She was furious." And therefore, wouldn't dogsit him while I was away for three months. "But he's a good boy, aren't you, Taco? You're just a little hungry all the time."

Charo shook her head while Taco sat proudly at her side.

"Hey, buddy, I want you to meet someone." I turned around, looking for Rosie. I found her right where I had left her, sitting on a stool, only now her eyes were wide.

She pointed at herself. "Me?"

"Yeah, you." I walked up to her, placed myself behind, and stretched my arm in front of us. "Who else would I be talking about?"

Lowering myself, I scooted closer to Rosie's back to make sure Charo and Taco could see us both. With the change of position, I brushed the back of her shoulder with my chest, and it was hard to miss how she stiffened.

"Taco," I said, wondering if I had crossed some line invading her personal space. "This is Rosie, my new friend. And, Rosie." I glanced at her profile, taking in her flushed cheeks and neck, noticing the freckles under the pink covering her skin. "This is my best and closest friend, Taco. And my sister, Charo."

Rosie's lips parted with a breath just as she turned her head to look at me, and the moment our gazes met I realized that this had nothing to do with Rosie being uncomfortable with me standing so close. She was affected, just like she'd been earlier today. When she was checking me out.

I couldn't stop my lips from twitching.

She shook her head lightly and returned her attention to my phone, the quick motion leaving me with a taste of a sweet and fruity scent. Like—

A happy woof snagged back my attention.

"Hi, Taco," Rosie finally said. I could see her smile in the little square on the screen. "It's so good to finally meet you."

Finally, huh?

Rosie continued, "And, Charo, how are you? It's good to see you. I had no idea Lucas and you were siblings. Nobody said anything. Not that it matters, of course. Just surprised because you two are so . . ."

"Different," Charo offered. "I know, *cariño*. It's the hair, isn't it? You know, everyone thought Lucas was going to be a redhead, too. It was either that, or early balding. Both things run in the family, you see? Everyone just assumed he was cutting his hair so short to hide a receding hairline. And you know what? No one would have blamed him."

I sighed. "Charo, you know it was for—"

"Competition, yes," she finished for me. And I felt the pang of pain that accompanied the reminder. "Because it's easier and more comfortable with the salt water and the sunlight and all that jazz. But now that you're on vacation," she added, and it was hard to keep my face neutral. Not to give her any indication that even if my stay in the US wasn't permanent, my vacation was. "Now you proved them all wrong, didn't you, *ricitos de oro*?"

I huffed.

Rosie asked, "*Ricitos de oro*?" And while her pronunciation was nowhere close to being right, it sounded so . . . *sweet* that the heaviness in my gut receded for a second there.

"Goldilocks," I translated for her. She snorted and I nudged her softly with my shoulder. "I'm not even blond. And my hair is not that long or curly, either. So—"

"Whatever you say, *ricitos*," Charo said before turning all her focus to my new and temporary roommate. "Anyway, Rosie. I haven't heard about you since Lina's wedding. How are you, *cariño*?" She paused but before Rosie could even open her mouth, my sister was shooting more questions. "Is Lina around, by the way? Wasn't she supposed to be leaving for her honeymoon? Did she introduce you guys before that?"

Unaffected by Charo's antics after a life of dealing with them, I rolled my eyes. "What was it that you wanted?"

She ignored me, her eyes narrowing for only a moment. "I'm just saying because this is an odd time to be hanging out. Isn't it, like, super early in New York now? What time is it there?"

Rosie seemed to be holding her breath for some reason.

And I was not about to entertain whatever my big sister thought she was doing. "Breakfast time. And you know how seriously I take the most important meal of the day. So if you don't mind . . ."

Charo clapped her hand against her chest. "How fun! A breakfast party!"

Overlooking the irony lacing her words, I looked over at Rosie. "I was thinking French toast. What do you think, Rosie?"

Her head jerked in my direction, the tips of our noses almost banging together.

"Oh dammit," she breathed. "Sorry."

I held my ground, unbothered. "Why are you sorry?" I asked, getting a more intense whiff of . . . *peaches* now that I was so close. She smelled like peaches. "Unless you don't like French toast. We could also make churros. I put a spin on the original recipe that will have you licking your fingers."

Her green eyes twinkled with interest.

"Churros it is, then." I winked.

Rosie mumbled something under her breath.

Something I could have heard if not for my sister's squeal. *"Ay! Ay, Lucas. ¿Sabe Lina que estás—"*

"Charo," I interrupted her. There was no reason to bother Lina because there was nothing to tell Lina, regardless of what Charo was implying. This was just us, sharing her apartment for a few days. And us, having breakfast. "If there's nothing else—"

She gasped theatrically. "Are you getting rid of me already? We've barely chatted!"

I narrowed my eyes.

"Speaking of chatting . . ." My sister shifted her attention to the woman beside me. "Rosie and I have a lot to catch up on, I'm sure. We haven't talked since the wedding. And we had such a fun talk that day." Rosie let out a strange sound that Charo decided to ignore. "Remember? About how surprised I was that you attended alone. And you told me that you had been single for a while and—"

"Oh my God, Lucas," Rosie interrupted, putting a hand to her ear. "Did you hear that? I think it's the fire alarm of the building."

It took me a second to understand what she was doing.

I brought a hand to my ear, too. "Holy shit, I think Rosie's right. Hold on." I paused. "Is that a fire truck right outside?"

Charo's eyes turned to thin slits, her gaze flashing with well-founded suspicion.

"I think you're right, Lucas. That means we should really go," Rosie added quickly. "One is never too fast to evacuate. Before the fire spreads."

"Hold on," Charo complained. "I can't hear—"

"Sorry, Charo," Rosie cut her off again. "We'll catch up another day, maybe?"

"That is if we survive," I added.

Rosie glanced at me. I dipped my head, holding her gaze, fully aware that the grin I had been fighting during our charade was now parting and bending my lips upward.

Rosie's smile was there, too. A much smaller one. And I wondered if she did this often enough. Smile.

Charo scoffed, bringing my attention back to the phone. I managed not to give her an in to speak. "*Adiós, hermana!* And, Taco, I will miss you, *chico.* Be a good boy, okay?"

To that he whined, breaking my heart in two.

"Bye, guys!" Rosie said quickly. "It was great meeting you, Taco. And talking to you, too, Charo."

Then, I *finally* terminated the call and lowered my phone until it rested on the kitchen island.

"The fire alarm," I said, releasing a slow breath and not caring to move right away. "A classic," I added while I simply stood there, with my head roughly at the same height as Rosie's, and my body only a few short inches behind hers.

Rosie's chuckle was sweet and soft, her posture not as stiff as when I'd first come so close. "I'm so sorry I lied to her. I feel so bad."

"I'm glad you did," I admitted. I was also surprised she had. Gladly. "I love my sister, but I needed some saving—and you were quicker than me."

"I needed as much saving as you did, Lucas."

I was going to ask why and if it had to do with my sister's comment about her attending the wedding on her own, but before I did, Rosie's back relaxed, coming into contact with my chest.

The sudden warmth of her body against mine took me by surprise, and the change in my breathing was enough to fill my lungs with her scent. *Peaches.*

Rosie's breath hitched at the contact, and the motion somehow brought us even closer. On instinct, my arms went around her sides, my hands gripping the edge of the island. Peaches surrounded me, the soft heat coming off her body as my arms caged her, reminding me of how long it had been since I'd let anyone this close. Or close at all. Reminding me of how natural physical contact and touch had always come to me. And how I had isolated myself after what happened.

A warning flashed behind my eyes. *Step away, off-limits. You're in no place or shape for any of this.*

So just as quickly as I'd moved forward, I pushed back.

Rosie was safe with me. I hadn't made that statement lightly. I might be labeled a brute by my cousin for my lack of . . . refinement or manners, but I wasn't a caveman. I had every intention of respecting Rosie. Especially now that we were going to share this apartment. Even if only temporarily.

"All right." I turned around with a clap. I opened a few cabinets, looking for the flour. "I promised you churros. So, you're getting churros for breakfast, *roomie*."

CHAPTER SEVEN

Rosie

*W*e were roommates.

Temporary roommates, as I'd been sure to make very clear.

Because I wouldn't take advantage of Lucas's kindness.

It was one thing to stay in Lina's empty place while she was on her honeymoon, like I'd intended when I'd shown up two nights ago. But it was Lucas who had been promised the apartment. I'd only accepted his help because I . . . I was a little desperate.

And I didn't mind the company.

And fine, okay. I was tempted by the idea of spending more time with him, too; temptation encouraged by my—totally under control—crush. But most of all, I was running out of time. I had eight more weeks until my deadline and I couldn't afford wasting them searching for an alternative, affordable accommodation if I was being honest. *Realistic.* I needed every minute and penny I had, because worse come to worst, if I didn't hit my deadline and cash in part of my advance, my savings account would suffer.

So I'd stay with Lucas. For a few days. Until the repairs at my apartment were done. Which I was hopeful would be soon.

Returning my gaze to my laptop as it sat in front of me, I reminded myself that my focus should be on my manuscript, and not on everything else going sideways in my life. Particularly, not on Lucas.

I checked my word count for the day.

One hundred out of my daily goal of two thousand words.

A sad hundred words in three long hours. Half of which were notes for me. Setting the nonexistent scene.

I returned my gaze to the mostly blank page in front of me. My fingers hovered over the keys and I . . . I closed my eyes, tried to summon something, anything, and nothing solidified. Fear sprouted. Spread. Settled right in the middle of my chest. Like a stone, heavy and solid. And just like it always happened, that familiar urge to scream rose.

And once more, I suppressed it.

Because I was Rosie. Keeping it together was my thing. I planned, rationalized, took a deep breath, and adjusted without losing my shit. I was the reliable friend and daughter.

When I'd written my first—and only other—book, everything had just . . . come to me. It had been like opening a valve and releasing something that had been locked inside, waiting to be let out. The yearning to be loved, fiercely. The wonder of becoming someone else's world. The joy of finding that person—that one person—that . . . fits. Someone who isn't necessarily perfect, because nobody really is, but someone who is perfect for *you*.

The time-traveling spin had been just for fun, because I'd always had a soft spot for a lost, fish-out-of-water hero. So I created a man from the past, an officer stuck in the present day, battling his demons and trying to come to terms with a love he thinks he doesn't deserve. Because he might have been lost, but that never meant he couldn't be found by someone. *His* person. Even when all odds are against him and even after being flung forward in time a century or two.

So why couldn't I—

A loud screech caught my attention.

Lucas?

It couldn't be. He'd left to explore the city a few hours ago and wasn't supposed to return until late afternoon.

I walked to the door and looked through the peephole.

An old woman dressed in red dungarees stood in front of her door across the hall, her hands on her hips. A loveseat seemed only halfway inside her apartment.

I stepped into the hallway and ventured a "Hi there! Do you need help with that?"

No reaction or acknowledgment. The woman was busy pulling at one of the arms of the mustard-colored leather loveseat, which was lodged into the doorframe.

"Hello?" I said a little louder, taking a step forward. "Can I help you moving that?"

Still oblivious to my presence, the woman—who must have been somewhere in her seventies from the mane of gray hair and crooked posture—shoved the piece of furniture forcefully. And when it didn't move, she took a couple of staggering steps back.

Closing the distance between us quickly, I gripped one of the arms of the loveseat.

Her gaze finally zeroed in on me, her brows shooting up her wrinkled forehead. She screeched, "Oh, for the love of all that is holy!" A hand patted her chest. "You scared the bejesus out of me, girl!"

I gave her my friendliest smile. "I'm so sorry, I tried to get your attention a couple of times, but you must have somehow missed me."

Her eyes narrowed.

My smile fell. "I'm Rosie." I waited for her to introduce herself, but she didn't. "It looks like you're struggling with this, and I wouldn't want you to hurt yourself."

The woman's eyes swiped up and down my body very slowly. "I don't know."

"You don't know if I can help you?" I frowned. Her gaze settled on my arms. "I'm stronger than I look?"

For whatever reason, I formulated that as a question.

The woman tilted her head. "Maybe." Still unconvinced, she continued her perusal. "You don't live here."

"You're right." I pointed behind me with my thumb. "But I'm friends with Catalina, your neighbor. I'm staying at her place for a couple of days."

"I don't know any Catalina."

My expression fell. "Catalina Martín. Short? Brunette? Around my age? You don't know her?" The lady blinked. "She . . . She . . ." Why couldn't I think of anything that would describe my best friend? "Oh God, I swear I know her—"

She waved a hand in the air, stopping me. "I was testing you." A low chuckle left her. "Always says hi, no partying, no stinky animals, and a very tall boyfriend. I like her. And I like him, too."

"That's the one, yes."

"Did she have anything to do with the hassle going on in the hallway two nights ago?"

I flinched. "Oh, that was actually me and my . . ." I trailed off, not knowing how to finish that. My roommate? My best friend's cousin I mistook for a burglar? "Lucas. Not *my* Lucas, but just Lucas. I'm sorry for the trouble." I paused, growing uncomfortable. I looked at the loveseat once again. "So . . . Do you think we can move this? Together?"

Lina's neighbor gave me one more once-over. "Fine, I guess you'll do. I'm Adele, by the way."

"Thanks, Adele," I said, gripping the side of the seat with both hands. Rolling my shoulders back, I readied myself to give Adele some instructions. "I think we should push it back inside, so we can maneuver it. So, at the count of three we are going to do that, okay?"

She nodded, murmuring something that sounded a lot like *smart-ass*.

"Okay." I sighed, deciding to ignore that. "Three . . . Two . . . One . . . Push!"

And . . . the thing didn't budge an inch.

Mostly because Adele had pulled.

"It's all right," I said, keeping my frustration off my voice. "We can give it another try. Make sure to *push*, yeah? Push it back inside."

Adele shot me a dirty look. "Don't use that tone with me, missy. I know what I'm doing."

Oh dear God. I really didn't have time for this.

I gave her a big, toothy smile. "Just trying to help, Adele."

"Trying with those spaghetti arms," she muttered under her breath.

I winced, looking down at my arms.

Something occurred to me. "Adele, are we moving this in or—"

"Let's give it another try." She ignored me. "Now."

Battling whether I should question her further, I braced both hands on the edge.

I looked over at her, waiting for instructions, but Adele's expression had changed. The blood had drained from her face, her skin paling and her eyes going glassy.

I placed my hand on her shoulder. "Adele? Are you okay? Do you need to sit down?"

The woman stared into space for what seemed like a full minute, not responding to any of my attempts at moving her or making her return to herself.

Alarm pounded through me.

I couldn't get her back into her apartment because the entrance was blocked by the loveseat. Calling for help felt like a waste when she wasn't hurt. She was just . . . not here. As if her mind had left her.

Small beads of sweat formed in the back of my neck.

I called her name one last time with no response.

Right as I was pulling my phone out to dial for help, though, Adele's eyes zeroed back in on me, confusion knitting her brows. Her eyes jumped to the stuck loveseat. Then down, right where my hand gripped her shoulder. What couldn't be anything but alarm flickered in her expression.

"Adele?" I tried again, taking my hand back slowly. "Are you okay?"

But the lady in front of me had nothing to do with the snappy Adele from a few minutes ago. This woman was disoriented, looking as lost as someone who had just woken up from a dream.

Crap. Now I was feeling pretty panicky myself. "I—"

"Rosie?" A deep and musical voice filled the hallway.

Lucas.

He was here.

The relief at hearing his voice was so sudden and unexpected that it almost felt like too much. Like I had to close my eyes and take a breath.

I heard his steps approaching us. "What's going on here?" A pause. "What's that sofa doing there?"

I turned in his direction, finding him standing only a few feet away from us. "We're trying to move it out." Our gazes met, and that bright grin he seemed to brandish so easily fell the moment he took a good look at me. "Or in. I . . . don't really know, if I'm being honest."

Lucas frowned, processing my words, his eyes scanning my face.

"Mateo?" Adele said, disbelief and joy loud in that one single word.

I blinked, my gaze jumping between the woman, who had her hands clasped under her chin, and Lucas, whose expression remained as calm as a millpond.

Mateo?

"Adele, this is Lucas," I told her as sweetly as I managed. "The Lucas I was telling you about earlier? My Lucas, remem—" I stopped myself, paling the moment I realized what had come out of my mouth. I made sure to look only at the woman. "He's Catalina's cousin."

Adele glanced at me with a small frown. "But this can't be your Lucas. He's my Mateo."

I smiled tightly, not knowing how the heck we had gotten here or how to veer the conversation far, far away.

After what seemed an eternity, Lucas said, "How about I get that thing out of the way, and get you back inside, Adele? I'm all about feminism, but I'm willing to take this one for the team."

I finally dared to glance at him, just in time to meet his gaze briefly before he started in our direction.

He set a palm on Adele's back and ushered her out of the way, then he returned to my side. Slowly, he leaned down and said only so I could hear, "*Your Lucas* to the rescue."

Your Lucas.

A strange sound left my mouth.

Thankfully, Lucas got to work and a few minutes later, the love-seat was unstuck and back inside Adele's apartment and my temporary roommate was guiding the frail woman back inside.

"Are you hungry?" Adele asked as they stepped inside the apartment, leaving me behind. "I think I have lasagna leftovers, and you look a little skinny."

"You think I'm skinny?" Lucas replied so casually and naturally it seemed they'd known each other for a long time. "I'd say I'm in pretty good shape." He lifted his free arm and flexed his biceps. "Have you not seen how big these are?"

Adele giggled and smacked his arm down. "Oh, you rascal."

And I stood there, so enraptured by the odd and bittersweet scene—and enthralled by the way Lucas radiated this soothing and commanding kind of energy—that it caught me off guard when he looked back over his shoulder and met my eyes.

You coming? he mouthed.

And I'd never know what he saw in my expression as our gazes remained locked for the next seconds, but when I didn't move, he said more gravely, in this firm yet sweet tone, "Come, Rosie." And my two feet pushed forward and I followed them in.

After preparing some tea and chatting for a while, Adele assured us her daughter was coming over later in the evening. And when she eventually drifted off, we returned to Lina's place. *To our place. For now.* A part of me seemed to note.

Just as the front door closed behind us, we let our backs fall against the wooden surface.

"That was . . . intense," I whispered. "And a little heartbreaking."

"Yeah," he admitted, his voice lacking his usual liveliness. I glanced at him over my shoulder, finding him with his eyes closed. He continued, "But that's life for you. Intense and heartbreaking."

The shadow I had seen cross his face a few times returned.

Before I knew what I was doing, the words were leaving my

mouth, "Was your heart broken, Lucas? Is that why you're here, away from Spain?"

Lucas's eyes opened and fell heavily on me.

"Yes and no," he admitted in a low voice. "Only no one broke my heart, Rosie. I don't think anyone ever got the chance to."

Gazes locked, I pondered what his answer meant. Had he never been in love, then? Was he or was he not escaping a broken heart? And if he was, and no one was responsible for it, then *what* had caused it?

Lucas broke the silence. "Abuelo had Alzheimer's. He used to confuse me with his little brother. At some point I stopped correcting him and pretended there was nothing wrong with his assumption. So even if I didn't know if Adele could have been experiencing the same, I . . ."

"Did that with her, too," I finished for him. "I'm sorry, Lucas. Going through something like that can't have been easy." And I wasn't sure if it was because of this or his earlier admission, but his words left a spot so tender, so exposed in my chest that I found myself reaching out and setting my hand on his arm. "I think you made Adele happy today. Even if just for a little while."

Lucas looked down at where my fingers rested against his forearm, and I focused on how warm he felt beneath the sleeve of his sweater. He seemed to consider something, and then, without any kind of warning, he moved and wrapped his arms around me, pulling me into a hug.

"I really fucking hope this is okay," he murmured somewhere close to my temple, warmth surrounding me as an odd sense of comfort mixed with the shock. "Is it, Graham?"

"I . . . huh, yes?" I mumbled. Then closed my eyes. "*Yes*. It's more than okay."

"Good." And one hard and fast squeeze later, I was released and left there, watching Lucas turn and stalk in the direction of the kitchen as if nothing had happened.

He opened a drawer and pulled a pan out. "I'm thinking frittata, roomie. Then, I have a couple of ideas for a white chocolate cheesecake I've been dying to try."

With head and chest scrambling for composure after his hug attack, it took me a couple of seconds to make my vocal cords work. "Sounds okay."

"Rosalyn Graham," Lucas said, throwing the fridge open. "Your lack of enthusiasm is appalling." He pulled out a cardboard of eggs and a few veggies before turning and pinning me with a hard look. "You're doubting my frittata, and what's worse, my white chocolate cheesecake." He pointed a whisk in my direction. "And I accept the challenge. You just wait and see. You'll love everything."

Oh, I didn't need to wait and see a single thing.

I was starting to understand that where Lucas Martín was concerned, chances were, I'd never find anything I didn't like.

And what was much, much worse, nothing I wouldn't love.

We had been about to start the third consecutive episode of *our* show—as Lucas had called it—when Netflix decided to shut down our improvised binge party.

ARE YOU STILL WATCHING? My temporary roommate scoffed, reading the message on the screen in front of us. "Of course we're still watching. They just killed one of the main characters and without that *goddamn* magical cure they just lost because of some stupid mind game, she's not coming back to life anytime soon!"

I chuckled, amused by his frustration. "I warned you," I said from my side of the couch, still finding it hard to believe that he was this invested in the paranormal teen drama. "I told you not to get attached to any of the characters . . ." I trailed off, needing to muffle a yawn. "Especially not her."

I glanced over at him and found his eyes on me. "You tired?"

I wanted to say no, but unable to stop it this time, my mouth opened widely of its own accord.

Lucas laughed. "Okay, *Bella Durmiente.*"

Bella Durmiente.

The words sounded like a spell conjured just for my ears, alluring and distracting, and I knew I probably felt that way about them only because they had come from Lucas. "What does that mean?"

"Sleeping Beauty," he translated, and before I could even process that, Lucas was stretching in my direction.

One second, he'd been right there, in his corner, sitting at a safe, conservative distance of three feet, and the next, he had closed the distance and his chest was pressed against my side.

The first thing I noticed was how warm he felt. The next thing that hit me was his scent. Salty, soapy, fresh. Undeniably Lucas in a way I couldn't explain or understand how I'd missed earlier, when he'd squeezed me against him like he hadn't been able to help himself. But now, it was all I could think of. All I could smell.

"Ehm, Lucas?" I stuttered, trying to hold my breath so I wouldn't dig my grave a little deeper, because dammit, how could he smell so, so freaking *good*. "What are you doing?"

He stretched over me, as if he was looking for something somewhere on the other side.

"Lucas?" I repeated, my voice barely there.

He shifted so he could look me in the face, bringing our noses inches apart. "Did you hide it?"

"Hide what?" I thought I asked, but in all honesty, I couldn't think straight with Lucas's face so close to mine. Oh God, were those little, tiny freckles on his nose?

I sensed his hand moving around the pillow I was sitting on. "The remote. You're about to pass out, so I'm putting you to bed, *Bella Durmiente*."

His tone was teasing, friendly. And I could *see* how unintentional and harmless his actions were. Heck, apparently he was just looking for the remote and I happened to be in the way. But all I could think about was him, right there, smelling amazing and so close that if I moved an inch to my left his chin would graze mine and I'd feel the stubble covering his jaw. All I could focus on was him, calling me things in Spanish. Or him being so sweet, that he wanted to put me to bed.

Ugh. I probably was better off finding the remote for him, smacking myself with it, and putting an end to this.

"Ah, here!" I watched him extract the black device from the pillow tucked against my side, holding it in the air as if he had just found the Holy Grail. "Got it."

"Thank God," I croaked.

Lucas laughed, and before moving away, he tapped the tip of my nose with his finger. "Next time, hide it better."

"Trust me, I won't hide anything around you ever again." Regaining a decent amount of space between us, I took a deep breath and ordered myself to get a grip. I couldn't act like this every time Lucas got within a foot radius if we were going to share this apartment.

"Sounds good to me, roomie," Lucas said, standing up and stretching his arms upward. "You know, I don't think they'll find the cure in time. I think they'll . . ." His shirt rode up, revealing a strip of tan skin and distracting me from whatever he was saying. And just like that, the two- or three-inch section of flat and hard-looking stomach I'd seen in all its glory that morning sent all my plans to get a grip down the drain.

Cursing myself silently, I closed my eyes.

"Rosie?"

"Yeah?" I answered, eyes still shut.

He waited a few seconds. "Did you . . . fall asleep while I was talking?"

"Nope." I shook my head. "Just resting my eyes for a second. It's like a night routine. I always do it for a few seconds every day." I waited one, two, three beats and then added as I sprung off the couch, "Okay, done!"

And because this was me, and I *had* to fail at acting normal around this man, I miscalculated the distance to the coffee table and banged my knee against it.

"*Por Dios,*" Lucas muttered, rushing to my side. He leaned down as if he had every intention to check the bump on my knee. "Let me see—"

I stepped back before his hand ever made contact. "I'm fine," I reassured him. "It was nothing."

Lucas straightened, coming to his full height. He looked down at me as if he was trying to piece something together. Then, he leaned his head to one side slowly, and to my utter surprise, he chuckled. "Yeah, not *Bella Durmiente*. You're a tougher princess."

And that unexpected observation, for whatever reason, made my heart do a cartwheel in my chest.

Perhaps I wanted to be tough. Or maybe, I simply wanted to be called a princess by someone. Or not just someone, but Lucas. And that— That was something I shouldn't have been thinking of in that moment. Or any moment. So, I answered with the cheeriest "Thanks!" Then I grabbed my sleeping clothes and sprinted to the bathroom.

When I reemerged, all those dangerous, dangerous thoughts parked aside, I found Lucas leaning against a kitchen cabinet as he typed something on his phone.

"You can go in now," I told him. "I'll pull out some blankets and a pillow for the couch. I know where Lina keeps everything."

Lucas looked up from the device, zeroing in on my face. He nodded, and his mouth opened with words that never left him. His gaze descended, as if compelled by something, making its way down my body while I stood there in nothing but a sleeping tee, shorts, and all the glory of my messy hair. One pass, that was all he did. One single, leisurely pass of his eyes as they traveled from my head to my toes and then back up again.

His gaze met mine again, and he said in a voice that sent a tiny shiver down my arms, "Thank you, Graham."

Graham. I couldn't remember if he'd ever called me just by my last name. Maybe earlier today? After the hug attack.

Distracted by that thought, I watched him as he pulled some clothes from his bag and headed to the bathroom. When the door closed behind him, I thought about that quick peek he'd taken. At me. At my legs. But I threw a sheet over the couch and told myself that I wouldn't dwell on it. They were nice, female legs. And Lucas . . . was into that. Women. Legs, apparently. So what?

If he were to stroll out of that bathroom showing off his calves, I'd do the same. Heck, I'd done it this morning, when he'd been wearing nothing but a—

"You really didn't need to prepare the couch for me, Rosie."

Lucas's voice came from somewhere behind me. I was ready to tell him he had another thing coming if he thought he'd be sleeping on the couch again, that I was preparing it for myself, but the words died on the tip of my tongue when I turned and encountered the sight before me.

It wasn't naked calves.

It was far, far better than that.

It was Lucas. In sweatpants—*gray* sweatpants—and a thin cotton tee.

But the *sweatpants*.

They hung low on his hips, and the fabric clung to his legs. His oh-so-not-naked calves. And his two strong-looking thighs. And those much, much more interesting parts that hung right in between.

And I— *Jesus*, what the hell was I doing?

There were about a hundred rules in the *Roommate Handbook for Civil and Not Creepy Cohabitation* that I might have broken by looking at his crotch. Even through the fabric of his sweats. Which wasn't leaving much to my—

"Rosie?"

Feeling my cheeks flaming hot, I dragged my gaze back to his face.

Lucas was smiling. Grinning, really. As big as I'd ever seen.

"Sorry," I breathed out, the blush I knew was covering my face spreading throughout my whole body. "Did you . . . hum . . . Did you say something?"

He crossed his arms over his chest and the cotton of his shirt stretched. Goddammit. "I said many things, if I'm being honest."

"Oh, okay." I swallowed. "Anything . . . important that we should discuss?"

He pointed behind me. "Yeah, that you're not sleeping there. But that's not open for discussion."

"Why not?" I frowned. "It was part of the deal."

Lucas drifted in my direction. Leisurely, as if he had all the time in the world to stroll across the small studio. He stopped only when he was right in front of me.

"Rosie," he said in a low, warning voice that made my stomach flop for some reason. "Take the bed." He smiled, but it wasn't light-hearted and fun. "Don't make me fight you over this. Because I will."

How? That part of me that had my stomach flip-flopping wanted to ask him. *How would you fight me exactly?*

But instead, I murmured, "Fine." I decamped to the bed on the other side of the studio. I huffed as I threw the covers back and slipped in. "We'll see who takes it tomorrow night."

"We'll see," he added right before turning the lights off. "Roomie."

I heard Lucas ruffle with his blankets, and I forced my eyelids shut so I wouldn't search for his shape in the dark. So I wouldn't make a big deal out of this. Lucas Martín, sleeping a few feet away from me. In his outrageous gray sweatpants.

"Rosie?" he called, in what couldn't have been more than a minute later. "Are you still awake?"

My eyelids lifted. "Yeah."

"Me, too."

I laughed lightly. "It's only been about . . . sixty-five seconds since we turned the lights off, so I'd be surprised if you were sound asleep."

"I could be narcoleptic for all you know, smarty-pants."

"Are you?"

"Nah," he answered, and I had no choice but to smile at the ceiling. "Hey, Rosie?"

Turning onto my side, I stared in the direction of the couch. I could barely make him in the dark, but I still looked. "Yes, Lucas?"

"How many pages away from your dream are you?"

I thought about all the words I hadn't written today. About how

I'll need to recalculate my daily goal again. Just like I had to do every day.

"Writers count in words and not pages."

I heard a deep *hmmm*, before he countered, "So how many words away from your dream, then?"

Many. "Still a few."

Only meeting a word count wasn't the problem, wasn't it? It was about so much more than just that. It was about writing. Inspiration. Or the lack of both things.

Neither of us said anything for a long time and then, when I was no longer sure whether he was asleep or not, I heard him say, "*Buenas noches*, Rosie."

CHAPTER EIGHT

Lucas

*N*ew York. The Big Apple. The City That Never Sleeps.

Anywhere I looked, there were either people rushing through the day, vehicles dashing through the streets, or buildings bustling with activity and . . .

Noise. So much noise.

It was different from every other American city I'd visited during the first half of my trip and a far cry from home.

Home. Spain.

But that had been the whole point, hadn't it? A change of scenery.

I had willingly exchanged waking up to the waves crashing against the shore for skyscrapers and hot dog vendors. I had willingly left behind the freedom of taking the coastal road and driving whenever and wherever I pleased and committed to an itinerary of sorts. I had traded Taco and my people for crowds of faceless strangers.

And the only reason I had done any of that was because that peace, that freedom, that scenery I knew like the back of my hand, and the people who loved me—or the version of Lucas I had been—

were no longer comforting. They loved someone who now felt like a stranger.

New York City was my last chance to escape. To postpone the inevitable. Of everyone finding out the real reason why I'd taken this trip. Of them wanting to fix it. To fix *me*. Because that was how the Martín family operated.

Just like Abuela said: *"Ay, Lucas, no vas a arreglar nada tumbado ahí como un monigote."*

You won't fix a single thing lying there like a stick man.

But there was nothing to fix. I sure as hell didn't need fixing, either. That would mean that the possibility to restore what I'd lost existed. And it didn't. I couldn't get on a board anymore. I couldn't do the one thing I knew how to do. Surf. The one thing I loved and was lucky enough to make a living doing. The one thing I had *thrived* doing. The water, the waves, feeling the roughness of the wax under my feet, the sand sticking to my skin. It had been my life. The adrenaline, the constant traveling. I had just reached peak performance, and even in my early thirties, I'd had a few more good years in me. Releasing a rough breath as I stood on the Manhattan side of the Brooklyn Bridge, I noticed I'd been staring into the swirling water of the East River for what had to be an unacceptably long time.

I checked the time on my phone. It was early enough to cross one more city sight off my list: either walking around City Hall Park or checking out the Charging Bull on Wall Street. Both attractions were free, which was a requirement since I was still waiting for my replacement card. Rosie had lent me more money—money she'd slipped in my jacket when I hadn't been looking and which I planned to return with interest—but that was reserved for public transportation.

"Como un monigote," I muttered to myself, repeating Abuela's words.

She might be right. I was one. Purposeless. Just like a plastic container in the river. Floating around with no course. Just being dragged around and . . . existing.

I was tired. Exhausted, really. And now the simple thought of going sightseeing, drifting in the current of strangers didn't seem like something I could do.

Rosie's face popped up in my head. Unexpected. I'd promised her that I'd be out of her hair during the day so she could work, and I'd had every intention of keeping that promise. Today was an exception. Today, I was feeling extra sore. So much so that I'd be shocked if I didn't end the day with that goddamn limp that had taken me weeks to lose.

Today, I felt extra lonely, too.

And Rosie was good company. Sweet, smart, and . . . Lina's best friend.

Something I should make sure to remember. Not because I had intentions of being anything else than roommates with Rosie, of perhaps becoming friends, good friends, but because . . . Because what, Lucas?

With a shake of my head, I opened the maps app in my phone, checked for the best route back to Lina's place, and started for the closest subway station. Forty minutes later, and with the start of that goddamn limp already affecting my pace, I finally spotted Lina's building.

Pulling my keys out as I stood on the narrow steps before the entrance, I could almost taste the wave of relief from sitting my ass down when a blur of dark curls slammed into me.

"Holy crap!" A female voice muffled against my sweater.

Still plastered against my chest, the mass of curls shifted, and a wave of sweet peaches I immediately recognized hit me right in the nose.

I breathed out a laugh. "I've missed you, too, roomie."

Rosie, whose face was still inserted somewhere between my right pec and collarbone, cursed.

Without thinking about it, I threw my arms around her shoulders and shifted us both off of the steps and onto the sidewalk.

"Oh," she let out a little breathlessly. "Oh, okay, thanks."

Ignoring how soft she felt against me, I released her. "If I'd known you'd be welcoming me home like this, I would have come back earlier."

Her laugh was self-conscious, and her cheeks a deep shade of pink. "Oh, funny. I didn't see you there, obviously. Otherwise, I wouldn't have plowed into you."

"I don't mind being plowed into, Rosie," I told her with a smile, noticing how easily her blush spread to her ears and neck. "Where are you headed? Looks like you are in a rush."

"Oh, right!" Rosie's eyes widened, as if she was just realizing that she had been racing down the stairs. "My landlord called. We're meeting in my apartment with the contractor in less than an hour. The crack, remember?"

I nodded my head. "The little incident that wasn't so little. I remember. That's good news, though. It means things are moving forward?"

"Yep." She averted her eyes, looking at my feet. "So, anyway. Sorry for the plowing. I should really go now. My landlord is a little . . . moody."

I frowned. "Moody?"

"Well, he's not really pleasant to be around." She smiled. But it was toothy and tight, and I could already tell it wasn't her real one. "Nothing I can't handle, though."

"I'm done for the day," I fibbed. "Can I come?"

"You want to come?" She repeated, blinking a couple of times.

"I'm curious by nature. Have you not met my sister, Charo? It's genetic."

"It won't be an exciting or fun meeting," she warned, but I didn't miss the quick flash of relief crossing her face. "Lots of standing around while the contractor evaluates the damages."

My right knee throbbed. "Perfect. Lots of snooping around your place," I countered, taking a few steps backward and keeping the grimace off my face. "You know, as the newly established town gossip and all."

As anticipated, Rosie's landlord—a man that had introduced himself as Mr. Allen—wasn't only moody. He was also a verified asshole.

One that apparently owned the entire building, as he made a point of sharing immediately.

Not a moment too soon, a dark-haired man around my age arrived, dressed in dark cargo pants and a hoodie with Castillo & Sons printed across his chest.

"Sorry I'm late," he said, encountering us in the hallway. "My previous visit ran a little over. I got here as soon as I could."

"*A little,*" Mr. Allen scoffed, his words dripping sarcasm. "You're ten minutes late. I specifically asked you to meet us at 6:45."

Asshole remark, when Mr. Allen himself had just gotten here.

The contractor was quick to ignore that, though, and moved straight in Rosie's direction.

"Hi," he said. "I'm Aiden Castillo."

"Rosalyn Graham," Rosie answered with a small smile before unlocking and opening the door for us. "Thank you for coming, Mr. Castillo."

"Oh, no need to thank me." Aiden's gaze remained on Rosie's face as he stood beside her, not walking inside immediately.

Before I knew what I was doing, I was shifting closer to Rosie and shoving my hand in his direction. "Lucas Martín." I paused, making sure I met his gaze. "A good friend."

Aiden took my hand in his without missing a beat, pinning me with an understanding glance that automatically made me feel like a jerk for whatever the hell I had just tried to pull off.

¿Pero qué coño haces, Lucas?

Scolding myself internally, I shook his hand and a few moments later, we were inside and Aiden was on the move, pulling out a pad and pen.

Mr. Allen, who started pacing behind us, released a long sigh. "We're meeting the tenant upstairs, too, so make it quick, yeah?"

The contractor ignored that, too.

Rosie, on the other hand, worried her lip as she glanced back at a restless Mr. Allen.

"Hey," I said, shifting closer to her and getting in her field of vision. "Nice place you have here, Rosie."

I wasn't lying, it was a nice apartment. Also in Brooklyn, but a different area. Roomier than Lina's, which wasn't hard, but also *homier*. Rosie's place screamed comfort and calmness, everything about it—from the plush-looking chaise longue to the soft buttery glow of the lamp and the little trinkets and books she had lying around—as if designed to provide solace. A home.

And it . . . suited her. It fit her perfectly.

Parking that thought aside, I pointed my head to the left. "Especially that one picture hanging over there."

It was a framed picture of her and Lina—shockingly large in size—where they were dressed up as Minions. They even had their faces painted in yellow and had two toilet paper rolls glued over their eyes. The costumes were ridiculous, but the fact that this was two adult women proudly staring into the camera was . . . captivating. Goofy.

"And cute," I said under my breath before turning to look at her face. "Do you think we should take it back to Lina's? Maybe you miss having it around. I would if I were you."

"Hilarious." She pouted. "It was a gift from Lina, okay?" Of course, it was. "And I think I'll survive without it."

I snickered, feeling a strange satisfaction at the lightness in her tone and the way she'd seemed to forget about the other two men in the room.

"Miss Graham," Aiden called from the other section of the living room, breaking off the moment. Rosie and I looked over at him, finding him with his head tilted back, inspecting the ceiling. "Is this all the damage? No more sections of the ceiling collapsed?"

Collapsed?

Hadn't Rosie talked about a *crack*? With all my focus on keeping an eye on her, I'd forgotten to check that myself. I glanced up, searching the ceiling and I—

"*Pero qué cojones.*" The Spanish curse slipped right out.

Mr. Allen scoffed at me, and Rosie shuffled to Aiden's side. "Yes, that's all."

"That's *all*?" I blurted out, disbelief coating my words. "Rosie, that could have knocked someone down. You said it was a *crack*."

"Yes," Aiden confirmed. "This could have gotten ugly real quick if someone had been standing right beneath this section of the ceiling when it went down."

"*Jesus,*" I muttered as I stared at Rosie's profile.

"But no one was," Rosie said softly. "It just fell at my feet."

A strangled sound climbed up my throat.

"Miss Graham," Aiden said before I could speak. "Is there any other damage elsewhere in the apartment? Bedroom, bathroom, kitchen?"

Rosie shook her head. "Just this. Or at least, this is all I could see."

The contractor slipped the notepad he had been scribbling on under an arm. "All right. If you don't mind, I'd like to have a look in all rooms. Would that be okay?"

"Yes, of course." Rosie let out a sigh. "Please, take your time. And sorry for the mess. I left in a rush when everything . . . went down. No pun intended."

With a nod, Aiden turned around and left the room.

Rosie's lips fell, pressing in a tight line.

Getting a hold of my shock and, quite frankly, frustration at her downplaying the risk when she could have been hurt, I regained the distance she'd put between us and nudged her shoulder with mine. "Hey."

She glanced at me, her expression neutral, seemingly passive, but her eyes telling a whole other story.

"I'm sorry I just got a little mad," I told her.

She shrugged a shoulder. "You shouldn't apologize." Her lips turned down. "Or get mad over nothing."

I ignored that, the need to make her smile sprouting deep in my gut. "I can't believe I missed it when I came in," I started, and she looked over at me. "Who knew that I had a thing for women in yellow paint," I added as casually as I could. "And by women, I really don't mean my cousin."

She blinked, then let out a half laugh, half snort. "Feeling funny today, huh?"

"I thought I was always funny." I winked, and that seemed to distract her enough for her to give me another one of those half-assed laughs. "Now seriously, are you okay?"

A shrug. "Yeah."

"It's okay if you aren't." I paused. "This is a lot, Rosie."

She held my gaze, as if she wanted to say something, but she seemed to change her mind. "This." She threw her head back and looked at the hole—and definitely not just a crack—above us. "This is nothing, really. No big deal. Just a little inconvenience. It'll be fixed in no time."

It wasn't little. It really wasn't.

Mr. Allen, who had been surprisingly quiet, scoffed, reminded us of his presence. "There's nothing little about this, Miss Graham."

Upper lip curled upward, he appeared in front of us, his fingers tightening the knot of what looked like an expensive tie. He reminded me of the crazy guy from that black comedy horror movie from the early 2000s. The one with the psychopath.

And while I agreed with him on this one, I still took a small step forward at his tone.

Mr. Allen's gaze bounced from Rosie to me before returning to Rosie. "I suppose you don't own property, Miss Graham."

"No, I don't. But I was just trying to make light of the situation—"

"Exactly," Psycho Landlord interrupted her, making my spine straighten at the change in his voice. "And that's only because you aren't aware of the cost that patching this *no big deal* is going to entail. But of course"—he paused, his lip now impossibly high on his face—"this is my time, Miss Graham. My money, too. Do you know how much I lose by standing here, dealing with this?"

Rosie's answer was quick. "I completely understand that. I'm not here by choice, either. I'm not the one that caused—"

"Oh, I think you don't understand," he cut her off for the second time, and my body moved closer to Rosie's. Our shoulders brushed. Psycho Landlord continued, his smile turning knowing. "You really don't if you think this will be fixed in"—a pause—"*no time*. In fact, I think it will be the opposite of that."

I sensed Rosie's body freeze in place at Mr. Allen's last words. So

I looked over at her, finding her staring back at him with a hard jaw and a serious frown. At first glance, one would have thought she was unbothered, handling the news like a pro, but then a shaky breath escaped her mouth, and her eyes blinked a couple of times. This was her brave face, I realized. She was putting up a façade, for whose benefit, I didn't know. But I happened not to care, because my hand left my side and reached out in her direction, landing softly in the middle of her back. Right between her shoulder blades.

She didn't move or give me any indication that my touch was doing anything to her as she laser-stared into space, but I kept my palm where it was. Drawing slow circles and letting her know I was here if she needed me, that I had her back.

"Nothing concerning in the rest of the rooms," Aiden announced, returning to the living room. "Except for a couple spots I noticed in the bathroom's drywall that I'd like to check with one of my guys." He looked over at Rosie, his expression turning cautious. "I'll need to check the upstairs floor to be sure of the extent of the damages, though." He pointed upward with his pen.

Rosie's voice was rocky when she answered, "Thank you, Mr. Castillo."

Aiden slipped the pen in the side pocket of his pants and turned toward Psycho Landlord. "After that, I'll get my crew in."

Mr. Allen clicked his tongue. "What about the quote? You won't get any crew in without me getting a quote first, Aiden."

"A quote," Aiden said very slowly. "You haven't asked me for one in ye—"

"I want it for this," Psycho Landlord interjected. Something crystallized in his gaze, something I didn't like one single bit. "Take as long as you need but no crew will get in without one."

"Mr. Allen," Rosie interjected with a squeaky voice. "I have a request of sorts, I—"

"Let me guess, you'd like me to prioritize your apartment over Mr. Brown's? Or to get this expedited, Miss Graham?" he spat out with such disdain that I felt myself drifting forward until positioning myself partly in front of Rosie. Not that Psycho Landlord was deterred, because his tone rose and he added, "If you're not happy with how I handle repairs in *my* property, feel free to break the lease. I'll have a new tenant in . . ." He trailed off. "How did you phrase it? *In no time.* As you might already know, apartments like this one go on and off the market in a flash."

Rosie sucked in a breath, but she recovered quickly enough to say, "There's no reason to be unreasonable and—"

"'Unreasonable'?" he bristled, his face morphing, as if he was getting a kick out of this. As if this man was enjoying playing power games with Rosie. I felt my blood rise to my head, the temper that so rarely manifested in me, boiling to the surface. "Miss Graham," he said in a tone that had me straightening, "don't be a—"

"Don't," I cut him off, getting in his face so he had no choice but to look at me. "I suggest you don't finish that sentence."

The man held my gaze, but there was no mistaking how his throat bobbed.

"In fact," I pressed, noticing my voice dropped down, "I suggest you stop talking altogether."

The man limited himself to gawking back at me, not responding. Slowly, ever so slowly, even daring to smile. Just like the Psycho Landlord he was, he *fucking* smiled.

I felt my body move forward, eating away the last inches of space between us, to do what exactly, I'd never know, because something stopped me before I could find out.

Delicate fingers wrapped around my forearm, pulling at me. When I didn't back down, they pulled again, and that second time it was hard to ignore what they meant. *Stop. You're crossing a line. Back down.* But I didn't want to. I've never liked bullies.

But Rosie pulled at me again, so softly I barely felt it, and I had no choice but to return to her side.

"How uncivilized. Some friends you have, Miss Graham," the openly relieved man in front of us muttered.

I expected Rosie to side with him, as I probably would have after what I'd just done, but instead, her fingers shifted, gripping my wrist. The pad of her thumb slipped inside my sleeve, falling against my skin and grazing it softly. As if she was trying to tell me that it was okay and that she wasn't mad.

And because I clearly had no respect for boundaries, I turned my hand and clasped hers in mine.

"There's nothing uncivilized about him," I thought I heard Rosie murmur.

A part of me wanted to take notice of that, to look at her, but Psycho Landlord said, "Aiden, let's go. Mr. Brown is waiting."

And with that, he turned around and headed for the door.

Only after he disappeared, Aiden said, "He's an asshole." He sighed. "I'll try to get that quote as soon as possible." And with a nod of his head, he disappeared after Psycho Landlord.

Rosie stepped away, severing the contact between our hands. When I finally glanced at her, she was looking up at the ceiling.

"Well, that sucked," she said under her breath, her hands coming to rest on her waist. "I wonder . . . How much space will the crew and whatever equipment or tools they bring in take."

I frowned at that.

"If you think about it," she continued. "Kitchen, bathroom, and bedroom are . . . free."

Free? I didn't like where this was headed.

And I liked it even less when Rosie's brows met in her forehead as she inspected her ceiling, thinking really hard about something. And—

A sound must have come out of my mouth because Rosie's attention was back on me. "Are you okay?"

Was I? "Please tell me you're not thinking of staying here."

She worried her lip but didn't answer.

"You can't stay here, Rosie." I tried to bend my mouth into a smile but failed, judging by her reaction. In fact, I was probably scowling.

She crossed her arms over her chest, her expression one of shock. "You don't need to worry about me. Or babysit me."

"Rosie." I breathed out a bitter laugh. "I'm not babysitting you."

"I'm just your cousin's best friend." She thought about something. "You've done enough already. You've let me stay with you. You've listened to my . . . nonsense. And you've even stepped up for me with Mr. Allen, when that's something you really didn't need to do."

It was my turn to look perplexed. "But we're friends."

"Are we?"

Before I could say anything else, a voice came from . . . above us. "What's all this shouting about?"

My head jerked, my gaze going up and finding a man dressed in a checkered robe peeking down. My brows shot up my forehead, almost fusing with my hairline.

He continued, "We're trying to have a conversation up here."

Unable to believe what I was seeing, I took a step forward. I narrowed my eyes, inspecting the man and—

"*Por el amor de Dios,*" I scoffed, shivering at the sight. "There's nothing under his robe." I glanced back at Rosie. "Rosie. His balls are hanging free like—"

"Hi, Mr. Brown!" Rosie interjected before giving me a shrug. "I hope everything's going okay!"

"*Rosie.*" I groaned. "Why . . ." I started, too bewildered to continue. "Jesus Christ."

"It's fine." She rolled her eyes. "Not the first time I've seen that."

My mouth opened, then snapped close. I didn't even know what to say. The only thing I knew was that my flight switch had been flipped, and it begged me to grab Rosie by the waist, throw her on my shoulder, and get her out of there as soon as possible.

"Rosie," I said slowly. Carefully. "Let's go home."

A tremor rocked her, and she said, "But all my things are here."

"I'll cook something for dinner and we'll call it a day," I told her, watching her closely. "Tomorrow you'll be fresh as a rose, ready to get all the words in."

"Sure." She huffed with frustration, her expression turning defeated. Worn out. "Because that's something I can do."

That got my attention. "What do you mean?"

She shook her head.

"Why did you say that?" I gentled my voice, guessing—knowing—there was something that she wasn't telling me. "You can trust me, Rosie."

More of that jerky head shaking followed, her arms going around her waist.

"Rosie?" I stepped a little closer, growing concerned. "What's wrong?"

She didn't answer; she wasn't even looking at me.

I tilted my head. "Hey, Ro—"

"Nothing!" she blurted out loudly, startling the shit out of me. "Nothing's wrong!" Her voice came out high-pitched, a tremor rocking her lip and making her jaw clatter. "Everything's fine and dandy!"

"Rosie," I whispered, closing the distance between us faster. "Hey, *cariño*, what's going on?"

A shaky breath was plucked out of her, her shoulders now falling and her eyes getting watery by the second. "Nothing's wrong," she repeated, right before the dam broke. "There's a freaking hole in the ceiling of my apartment. These stupid repairs are going to take a much longer time than I thought. I'm inconveniencing you because I've been lying to my dad for months and can't stay with him. I'm pretty sure my brother is in some kind of weird business. And I have less than eight weeks left until I have to hand in a manuscript that's nowhere near where it should because I'm stuck. I can't write, Lucas! And here you are, witnessing the complete and utter mess that is my life. Oh, and to make everything even better, I've been craving Cronuts ever since I got my period this morning and when we leave here it will be too late to get them because Holy Cronut will be closed!"

Rooted to the place, I could only watch her as she came up for air.

"So fine! Okay!" she continued, startling me again. "There might be more than a couple things that are wrong. But I'm *Rosie*. I'm supposed to keep my shit together." A hiccup broke free. "Because that's what I do best. Keeping it together. And now I just . . . I just . . ."

It was the lonely tear falling out of the corner of her eye that propelled my legs to close the rest of the distance between us.

In two seconds flat, my arms were around her shoulders and I was bringing her into my chest. "It's okay," I said, moving one of my hands to the back of her head, so I could secure her against me.

"I'm not losing it," she muffled against my sweatshirt. "I'm Rosie and I can't *lose it*."

Squeezing her a little tighter as her body shook under my arms, I let my chin rest on top of Rosie's head. "You *can* lose your shit, Graham," I told her, as I swayed us left to right. "You're entitled to that every once in a while."

"But I hate it when I do. I don't want anyone seeing me like this. Especially not you." She hiccupped again. "I'm such an ugly crier."

"Ugly? Impossible."

A strangled sound left her, warming the skin beneath the fabric of my sweatshirt. "Stop being so nice to me."

"I'm just being honest," I told her, and I meant it. And I hadn't missed the *especially not you*, but it wasn't the time to inspect that. "It's healthy to let it all out." I trailed my hand up and down her back. Massaging along her spine. "Especially when you are under so much pressure."

"Maybe," she said, still buried in my chest. "But I still don't like it."

Something occurred to me, something that might make those tears stop. "You met Abuela, right? At the wedding?"

Rosie nodded.

"The last time I did something like this, something like pretending nothing was wrong, that it was all . . . *good and dandy*"—I used her words—"Abuela flung a wooden spoon at me. Hit me square in the face."

I'd expected Rosie to gasp, or laugh, but instead, she went with a thoughtful, "I love Abuela."

"It's hard not to love her. And let's face it, I probably deserved it."

She let out something that was close to a laugh. Kind of.

Good, as long as she stopped crying I could embarrass myself a little more. "The spoon had been covered in the Bolognese she'd been cooking, and I looked like I'd gotten into a brawl with a can of tomato sauce." In Abuela's defense, I'd deserved it. "Oh, and after hitting me, she proceeded to yell, *Tontos son los que hacen tonterías.* Stupid people are those that do stupid stuff." I let my fingers reach Rosie's hair, absentmindedly stroking the soft curls. When she didn't flinch, I let my hand rest there. "Abuela was right, though. It's not smart to pretend everything's okay when it isn't. When you bottle something up so tightly, the lid will blow up. Sooner rather than later."

Rosie didn't speak, and my last statement left me with a bitter taste in my mouth, so we stayed in silence after that, swaying left and right without caring to release each other.

When Rosie finally spoke again, her voice no longer quivered. "Lucas?"

Fully aware that there was no reason to have my arms around her at this point but not caring to move, I answered with a Hmm.

"What had you been bottling up? When she threw that spoon at you."

It really shouldn't have after my almost-confession, but her question caught me off guard. "I . . ." I trailed off, not following my own advice and shoving everything I'd been keeping locked in even deeper. "I'll tell you if you stop fighting my help. And if you come back to the apartment with me. You can't stay here."

"Can't you tell me now?"

"Show me that you trust me."

Rosie extricated herself from my embrace, looking up at me.

I met her gaze. "That's how this works, Graham. It's a two-way road."

She considered something for a long time, then said almost reluctantly, "Okay." She followed that up with a loud sigh. "If that's your way of asking me if we can be friends, then fine. I guess we can be friends."

Something raced across my chest, one moment there and gone the next.

"Friends," I said, finally letting my arms drop to my sides, because friends comforted each other but knew where to draw the line. "Let's go, then. I don't want to risk Mr. Brown flashing us his balls again."

"Okay," she repeated, now with more conviction. "Let's go home, roomie."

CHAPTER NINE

Rosie

I closed my laptop, unable to look at my manuscript for one more second.

Zero out of 2,500 words.

"God, this sucks," I said into the silent and empty studio apartment.

Because I'd written zero and I'd had to recalculate my daily word goal. Again.

I thought back once again to yesterday's epic meltdown. To how I'd dumped a crap-load of emotional baloney on Lucas. To how I'd then proceeded to slobber all over his sweatshirt for an indecently large amount of time. And most of all, I thought of Lucas's calm and careful comfort. Of how he'd stepped in without me asking him to. Without me expecting him to.

And I thought of that hug. A full-body hug. Soothing, healing, *intentional*—because Lucas hugged like he meant it, like all his focus was on that embrace and that embrace only. A life-altering hug, if something as simple as a hug was ever meant to do that.

All my life, I've been the person others relied on. I shared the burden with Dad when my mother walked out on us and left us with a ten-month-old Olly and a ten-year-old me who had to learn how to grow up fast. I carried the weight alone at times when Dad wasn't there. I've been the rock in the middle of the pond for my friends, that person they could count on for a good cry or honest advice. I've taken any role I've been needed for, always making sure to be there, to keep a tight grip on any situation or any crisis. Always calm, always in control. That was probably why my job as an engineering consultant had been so . . . fitting, so natural. I'd been paid to plan projects, to provide my expertise, and to advise in the case of a crisis. And that was probably also why quitting that to do what I really loved—something that could be ruled by emotions—had been so . . . liberating.

Even if it had led me to this. To the meltdown. To Lucas's immediate reaction, him lending me his strength. Taking over.

I sighed.

Blinding smile, wide shoulders, mad cooking skills, the superpower to give the best full-body hugs in the world, *and* a big heart.

Life really was unfair sometimes.

"And here I am," I muttered under my breath. "Thinking about a man instead of writing."

Not that it would have changed anything; I still couldn't write.

Pushing the stool back, I strolled to the window and threw it open, welcoming the chilly October breeze. I leaned on the sill, wondering if I should try to call Lina again. Maybe—

My phone buzzed from the other side of the apartment.

"Freaky," I murmured.

I stalked back to the kitchen island, picked up my phone, and smiled at the name lighting up the screen.

"BESTIIIIIIIIE!" a voice I knew well screeched. "Why do I have a million missed calls from you? Do you miss me this badly or did you finally spot Sebastian Stan and I totally missed it? Did you two hit it off? Is he as cute in person? If he's a jerk, don't tell me. Don't ruin Seb for me."

"Lina." I let out a half sigh, half laugh. "I was just thinking of you. And it wasn't a million calls, it was just two."

"Hmm, I'll take that as no. Poor Seb. It's really his loss."

"Ugh, I've missed you." Walking over to the couch, I let myself plop down on it, turned the speaker volume to the max, and placed the phone on the coffee table. "How is everything, *Mrs. Martín-Blackford*? How is Peru? Is the honeymoon going as planned?"

"Ah, Rosie, I could get used to this. Do you think they'll miss us at work if we stay a little longer?" She lowered her voice. "Or forever?"

"Well, considering your husband is the division head of an engineering firm in thriving New York City and you are leader of a team in said division, I'd say . . . probably?"

"Ugh. I should have stayed a consultant," she said, even though I knew she didn't mean it. Lina loved her job. "Or, you know, I should have married someone without responsibilities."

I opened my mouth to tell her how ridiculous that was, considering those two were hardly able to keep their hands off each other, but before I could get a word out, Aaron's deep voice was distinguishable in the background.

Then, I heard Lina tell him, "Don't get your panties in a bunch, *amor*! I was only joking. I'd marry you one hundred times over."

Some more muffled words were said in the back and a giggle left my best friend. Based on experience, it was the kind of giggle that usually preceded a kiss, a touch, or a hooded-eyed Lina and Aaron.

A pang of jealousy surged through me. The good kind. The kind of longing that made me wonder if I'd ever find what they had. Ironically, this had been the kind of longing that had pushed me to flirt with the idea of writing all that time ago. To bring to life the kind of love that never seemed to happen for me.

Look at me now, though, one book and a half-assed try at a second one later, and not only did the well of inspiration seem empty but I hadn't managed to find love, either.

"Rosie?" Lina's voice brought me back. "I was telling you about my *honeymoon sexletics*, now that my husband left to get empanadas peruanas, but you totally spaced out on me."

"Sorry, sweetie."

The line was quiet for a few moments.

"Is everything all right?" Lina finally asked, and gone was her teasing and lighthearted tone. "I was joking about the calls, you know? You can always call me. As many times as you need."

"I know," I told her, because I did know that. "But—"

"You won't burst my bubble," she finished for me, reminding me why she was such an essential and important person in my life. She knew me inside out. And that was why she knew what to say next to appease me. "I'm as happy as I've ever been in my entire life and talking about whatever is going on with you won't change that."

I let that sink in, and I didn't feel jealousy this time, even if healthy, but pure unfiltered joy for her. For them. Aaron and Lina deserved nothing but happiness.

"Actually," she continued. "It's you thinking that you can't count on me that's breaking my poor, fragile heart. I—"

"Okay, okay." I breathed out. "You can stop the emotional blackmail. It's not like I don't want to talk about it with you. I just . . ."

"Don't want to bother me while I'm on my honeymoon with my swoon-worthy husband, I know. But we've established that you're not doing that. So, start talking, bestie."

Start talking.

There was so much I needed to tell her. To confess, really. Starting with the fact that my apartment was out of commission for the time being. And that I was sharing her studio with her cousin. And that I'd harbored an online crush on said cousin and spending time with him wasn't making it any better.

And yet, what came out of my mouth was, "I think I might have made a terrible mistake."

"Okay." Her tone was careful. "Was that an 'I added salt to the batter instead of sugar' mistake, or a 'honey, remember the zinc phosphide we got for the rat infestation problem, well I'd stop chewing if I were you' mistake?"

I closed my eyes. "The second one?" I thought about it a little better. "Maybe not exactly the second one but something close to it.

Minus the accidental poisoning of my family. Let's say I was the only one poisoned. And I kind of did it to myself. Let's say—"

"Rosie?" She stopped me.

"Yeah?"

"I think we took the metaphor too far, and now I don't know what we're talking about."

I released a deep breath. "Quitting my job at InTech. That was the mistake, Lina."

"*What?*" She gasped with what I knew was honest shock. "Why would you think that? You're living your best writer's life now, no distractions and a book deal in the bag."

"Yes, only I'm not living my best writer's life." I looked up at the ceiling, bringing my fingers to my temples. "I haven't been writing. I'm less than eight weeks away from my deadline and I'm . . . I'm nowhere. I've been stuck for a long time, and now, I don't think I'll make it. I've got nothing, Lina. Not *a single thing.*"

There was silence, and then my best friend said, "Oh, Rosie."

A tremor rocked my lower lip, the lock on the gates that had busted open less than twenty-four hours ago rattling again. "So there's that," I blurted in a strange-sounding voice. "I'm a failure. I haven't even had my dream yet and I'm already a failure. Do you . . . Do you think that Aaron will take me back if I ask for my old job?"

"No."

"Okay, well. I get it. I guess someone else—"

"No," she repeated. "You're not asking Aaron for your job."

"Lina—"

"Shut up and listen. And listen carefully." My mouth snapped closed, my eyes growing more watery by the moment even though my best friend's tone was harsh. "You, Rosalyn Graham, are a *boss-lady.*"

I let out a sound I refused to acknowledge as a hiccup.

"You have an engineering degree. You were promoted to team leader in a top-tier tech company in goddamn New York City." She paused, letting all that sink in. "You wrote a book—in your free time. A good freaking book, Rosie. A beautiful and epic love story about a war veteran that travels through time and fights to find a place, his place, beside the woman he so helplessly loves in the present day. Do you know that Charo is still calling him 'My Officer'? The woman has claimed that fictional man as hers and she genuinely gets pissed at people if they so much as mention him." I knew that. Lina had sent me screenshots from more than a few aggressively enthusiastic messages. "The day she finds out that you are *the* Rosalyn Sage, she's going to flip and pester you for the rest of your life." A pause. "And that's only because you smashed it. You knocked it out of the park."

"I didn't really smash it, Lina. I—"

"That publishing house didn't offer a deal because of your pretty face."

"Okay," I reluctantly agreed. "I guess my first book was *okay*."

Lina huffed. "It wasn't just okay, Rosie. It was laced with crack, I told you. The small albeit enthusiastic part of my family that speaks English *adored* it." I heard some ruffling noise in the back, as if she'd just opened a chocolate bar or a snack bag. Both possible options with her. "And on top of all that, you had the balls to quit a job that no longer fulfilled you and pursue a career that did. In writing. Because you're good at it, Rosie."

The balls.

That reminded me of Lucas when he'd called me ballsy. Ballsy. *Me.*

My heart resumed the funny flip-flop business it performed every time I thought of him.

"Am I ballsy, though?" I heard myself ask out loud.

"Yes!" Lina confirmed right away. "This whole thing about you being stuck is your fear talking. You're terrified to fail, Rosie. I know you. But you need to get out of your head, stop whining about not being able to fix the problem, and start believing that you can."

"Ouch," I muttered.

"I'm saying it because I love you." I could picture her waving a finger at me. "Don't let the pressure you're putting on yourself paralyze you. You are the only person limiting yourself, Rosie."

Her words cut a little deeper than they should have. Not the whining part, but the one about *me* being the problem. Because I was starting to believe that I was.

"Writer's block is common," Lina added. "So, we'll unblock you."

"Unblock me?"

"We'll pop you right open."

My hands dropped to my sides, my palms resting on the soft fabric of the cushions. "I don't know, Lina. I don't . . . even know what's wrong with me. I'm just . . ."

There was a beat of silence. "You're what?"

"I'm . . ." I trailed off. "It's as if there were a hundred million things stopping me from writing and I just flatline when I try." I shook my head. "I've tried everything, even acupuncture, because I read on some blog that it helped releasing endorphins that aided inspiration. It didn't work."

The line was silent, then a tentative, "There might be something you could try."

"And that is . . . ?"

Lina didn't answer right away, which told me enough about whatever was coming. "Your second book is in the same universe, isn't it? You told me you wanted to give his best friend his happily ever after."

"Yes."

"You mentioned that this time around the story would be a little more . . . lighthearted. That it would be about him battling modern life and adjusting to how things have changed in the wilderness that is dating nowadays."

"Yes, I suppose I said that."

"So," Lina said very slowly, so much that the two-letter word dragged for a few seconds. "You could do the same. You could get back out there."

I frowned. "Out *where*?"

"Dating," she answered with confidence. "You've been holed up for . . . how long?" she asked, but I wasn't given the chance to answer. "Too long. Maybe that's the problem. You're a romance writer. Trying to write about a man from the 1900s dating in present day.

Maybe you should just . . . do that. If you think about it, you two are not so different. You haven't dated anyone for at least two years." A chuckle left her. "You and your hero are two beautiful and old-fashioned fish dumped in the twenty-first-century dating pond."

A strange sound left my throat. I opened my mouth to tell her all the many and different ways her idea could go sideways, but I stopped myself. Because maybe, just maybe . . .

"It could work," Lina said as if she'd just read my mind. "Listen, my first idea had been sex. Orgasms. I was going to suggest you get a new vibrator when you mentioned the endorphins, but I think you need the real thing this time around."

I blinked, trying to process everything.

"You know I'm not good with hookups and one-night stands," I replied.

"Exactly," she answered quickly. "You need to be romanced before getting to the hanky-panky."

"The *hanky-panky*?"

She ignored my question. "That's why I think you should re-download Tinder. Or Bumble. Or whatever app the Zuckerberg of dating software has come up with this week."

"A dating app." I could hear the thick skepticism coating my voice. "What about the old-fashioned fish? I think I liked that better. Can we get back to that? Nothing good has ever come out of a dating app. Not for me."

"Listen." Lina cleared her throat. "I know you've sworn off apps—and men—for a reason, a good one at that. The last man you dated in particular, Assface Number Five, was . . . well, let's just say he was lucky I didn't borrow Aaron's car and accidentally run him over."

"Lina!" I gasped. "We've talked about you saying stuff like that."

"Just a soft brush of the bumper against his ass. That's all I'm saying."

I shook my head. "You want to run over every man I've ever dated."

Lina laughed but it sounded dark and . . . bloodthirsty. "Maybe because they've all been assfaces." I closed my eyes, feeling . . . helpless and tired. Mostly because she was right. "My point is," Lina continued, "that the long line of idiots you've dated is what somehow led you to write that phenomenal debut. And you can't count on going down to Central Park, dropping a scarf, and hoping the man of your dreams finds it and proceeds to search the city—"

"Yeah," I cut her off. "I don't have the time, I get it."

"You don't," she agreed gently. "So maybe, just maybe, down-loading a dating app and getting back out there might change something. It might find you some inspiration. Jump-start the whole thing. Or clear your head and have some fun. That can't be so bad, either."

I hugged my middle with my arms, not wanting to accept that what she was saying made sense.

"Maybe you could even treat this as . . ." She trailed off, then continued more enthusiastically, "As research. Field work. As if you were running an experiment. Pick a man and do whatever you need to get those creative juices running. You don't even need to tell him."

An experiment.

I didn't like the last part, though. I didn't think I had the guts to trick someone into . . . whatever Lina was implying. Being dishonest had never been my thing.

Although I had lied to Dad for months, I reminded myself. And now I was lying—by omission—to Lina by not telling her that I was living in her apartment while she was away. *With her cousin.*

"It's worth the shot," she encouraged.

"It probably is," I admitted quietly. "At this point, I'll try anything if it means I have the chance to get out of this stupid funk." Pressure returned to the back of my eyes, and I even surprised myself when the next words left my lips. "Who knows, maybe I'll even manage to find love for once?" The sliver of hope dawning in my chest at the thought faded quickly. "Or if it's just not in the cards for me, I guess I'm fine daydreaming of the real thing for the rest of my days if I can manage to write about it."

"Don't say that, Rosie," Lina said so softly that I felt my throat close up with . . . *emotions*. Lots of messy, intense emotions. *God, I am being such a baby lately.* "Of course it's in the cards for you. Who knows, this could become one of those Hallmark movies you love so much." She lowered her voice and announced, "*Romance writer dates in search of inspiration and falls in love. Spoiler alert, it was a bestseller.*" She chuckled. "And if you don't and the guy's a jerk, then we'll borrow Aaron's car, and we will make sure that man never crosses on red ever again."

God, I loved my best friend. I loved her even if her good-intentioned but violent nature was going to get us in jail any day now.

Once more, my stomach tangled in knots at the reminder of everything I was keeping from her. But just as I opened my mouth, a creaking sound from the entryway caught my attention.

I jolted around, my gaze stumbling upon a large form that I'd have to be blind not to recognize immediately.

Lucas. My roommate. Lina's cousin.

He was back, and he was standing by the threshold of the door with his shoulders drawn up, and his eyes wider than usual. In fact, he was the image of someone that had been caught doing something bad. Something they shouldn't have been doing. Something—

Oh God. *Oh no.*

Just like that, I knew. I *knew* with a certainty I had trouble processing what he'd been busted doing.

Snooping. Listening.

"Rosie?" my best friend called, her voice coming out the speaker that I'd set to the maximum possible volume when I'd picked up. "You still there?"

"Sorry," I croaked, my eyes laser focused on his profile. "I'm here but I . . . I need to go now."

Because I couldn't rip my eyes off Lucas, I watched him move as my mind was flooded with chants of *Why, Lord, why?* Why did he have to overhear this one particular conversation?

Lucas walked in my direction, and my gaze—which was still doing its own thing—decided it was a good time to check him out. To marvel at the way his emerald-green hoodie hugged a chest I *knew* felt solid against my cheek. To get a little lost in the way a lock of chocolate hair fell over his forehead.

Sexy and disheveled snooper, he could at least have the decency not to look so . . . distracting.

"Fine, okay," I heard Lina say, just as Lucas reached me. He sat down on the coffee table, right in front of me, and placed a blue and pink box I hadn't noticed, right beside my phone. I swallowed, noting how his knees were half an inch away from brushing mine. Lina continued, "I'll tell Abuela to light a candle and ask for a decent guy that can at least give you one or two orgasms because—"

"Thank you, Lina," I quickly interrupted, jerking forward and grabbing my phone. I deactivated the speaker and brought it to my ear. "I'll call you later, okay? I really need to go."

"All right," my best friend relented. "I'll let you off the hook, but just because I love you and only if you promise me to remember that you can do anything."

I could feel Lucas's eyes burning holes on the side of my face, but I kept my gaze down. "Love you, too, Lina. Give Aaron a hug and enjoy the rest of the honeymoon, okay?"

Heart in my throat, I ended the call, trying my best not to look like I was scrambling to come up with a plan of action while my mind threw questions right and left. *Lucas has heard about the orgasms. But what about the rest? God, how long has he been standing there?*

"Hey," I heard him say so softly that the word set off about a hundred alarms in my head. Yesterday, he'd had to hold me while I lost my ever-loving shit, and today this. "You're not gonna say hi to me, Rosie?"

"Hi," I answered, keeping my eyes down. Because if I looked up at him and found the barest trace of pity in his face, I'd be so . . . sad. Devastated, really. "So, that was Lina on the phone."

"I noticed."

My lips pursed. "I didn't get the chance to tell her that we're both staying here. Together. Until . . . you know, I can go back to my place." I swallowed, keeping my eyes trained on the corner of the coffee table that he wasn't occupying. If I wanted nothing to seem wrong, I had to act like it. "Anyway, how was your day? Did you go to the free exhibit in the New York Public Library I told you about? Did you like it? Was it as cool as it seemed on their website?"

"Yes," he said, as if that one word answered all four of my questions. Then added, "I brought you something."

He moved the blue and pink box toward me, and I did a double take when I noticed the logo on the lid. Something in my chest expanded just like a balloon being pumped with air, and it grew bigger the longer I gawked at that pink and blue cardboard container I recognized.

"You remembered," I mumbled in a wobbly voice. "Cronuts. From Holy Cronut. Just like I mentioned yesterday."

I hadn't just mentioned it. I'd screamed it, right after I'd informed him that I was on my period, and right before I'd covered his sweatshirt in snot.

"I did," he admitted, the balloon taking all the space in my rib cage. "I got my replacement credit card in the mailbox this morning, so I thought we could celebrate." He pushed the box in my direction. "If you'll share because, as I said, these are for you."

"If I'll share?" I asked. Because was this man real? Was he actually, really, truly real? I slid my gaze from the blue letters that read *Holy Cronut* to his knees. "Of course, I'll share." A pause. "You got the big box."

"It was the biggest they sold."

One of his hands came to rest against his left thigh, and I thought about the piece of tan skin I could see through the rips in his jeans. The urge to reach out and see how that felt under my fingers swarmed me.

"What do you say?" Strong-looking fingers tapped against his leg. As if he'd known I was focused on that exact spot and wanted to get my attention. "Should we have them now, or save them for later? Maybe after dinner?"

Something that sounded a lot like a complaining grunt left me.

"Now it is." Lucas laughed, and that, his laughter, turned out to be reason enough to make me finally look up. At his face.

"My breakdown must have been of epic proportions," I murmured, studying the way the corners of his eyes wrinkled with a smile. "Or maybe you're terrified of me now and you're just appeasing the ugly crying monster."

"There's nothing ugly about you."

My lips parted, his words echoing in my ears.

As if he hadn't just said something meant to stay with me forever, he threw the lid open, unveiling the six pastries inside. "Plus, I love being cried on every once in a while." The box was pushed in my direction again. "It's good for my skin."

I shook my head lightly and fished out one sugary and cinnamony crispy piece of heaven. "Thank you, Lucas. You really didn't have to do this."

He grabbed one, too, and then cheered his Cronut against mine, as if there was something worth celebrating. "Friends don't do stuff for friends expecting a thank-you, Rosie."

Friends.

"Right." I willed my lips upward and ended up giving him what I knew was the smallest smile in the history of smiles. He frowned, so I felt the need to distract him. "I guess we'll have to find something to say instead of *thank you* then."

His eyes danced with something I liked knowing I had put there. Even after that reminder of us being *friends.* "Like a code?" he asked. "Just for us?"

"Sure," I said, loving the idea way more than he did. Far more than I should have. "Something like that."

Lucas thought about it for a few moments, then waved his pastry-holding hand. "*Cronut you.* How about that?"

His smile was big, bright, all megawatt power on display.

And I looked at him as he sat there like this was nothing, like he wasn't wonderful and he wasn't making it very hard for me not to like him more and more, so much that I had to physically restrain myself from telling him that I believed he was the sweetest man I'd ever met. Sweeter than any pastry he could get me. "*Cronut you,* Lucas."

And without another word, we dug in, equally delighted moans leaving our mouths. The contents of the box disappeared in record time. And by the time we'd both finished licking the tips of our fingers, I had successfully managed to forget about almost everything.

"So, Rosie," Lucas said, pinning me with a look that should have warned me of what was to come. "Will you finally tell me about your writer's block and this long line of assfaces you've dated?"

CHAPTER TEN

Rosie

"So you heard all of that, huh?"

I knew he had, and I glanced in embarrassment at the hair-thin space that separated our knees.

"I think the whole neighborhood did; you were having a very loud conversation with the window wide open."

I covered my face with my hands. *"Great."*

I felt what had to be his fingers gently wrap around my right wrist. A breath got stuck in my throat at the unexpected contact. He pulled softly, tingles spreading down my arm, and I . . . well, I couldn't do anything but let him retrieve that one hand off my face.

I gave him a one-eyed appraisal.

"I'm going to be honest, Rosie." He went for my other wrist, and when I resisted a little, the small smile that had been playing on his face widened, dazzling me enough to let him take that other hand down. *Ugh, stupid, stupid beautiful smile.* "I might have accidentally listened to a fair chunk of it from the street. But when I sprinted upstairs and stood outside the door to listen to the rest, I did so completely intentionally."

"Okay," I answered slowly, bringing my hands to my lap. "Thanks for your honesty."

Because what was I supposed to say? For some reason, I wasn't even mad about it. I was . . . many things. But mad wasn't one of them.

"I like you, Rosie," Lucas said, and my heart tripped at the words. "I think it's pretty obvious." He gave me an unapologetic shrug, the drumming in my chest resuming at an increasing pace. "But you believing that you're a failure? Just because you have writer's block? I didn't like that. Not one bit. And as your friend, I'm going to tell you, just like my cousin did."

As your friend.

Because he liked me as a *friend*. Of course, I knew that. That wasn't new information.

He continued, "And as your friend, I also want to help. My cousin is not here, so I could take over for her. Be your *bestie*?"

My bestie. That sounded equal parts wonderful and stomach-turning. I sighed. "Okay?"

Lucas inched forward the tiniest bit. "Lina said you've sworn off men. And dating apps." His expression turned serious. "Why?"

I shook my head, feeling the tips of my ears burn. "I don't think I want to take a walk down Memory Lane: Depressing Dating Edition with you, Lucas," I muttered.

"I'm trying to understand. I'm at a clear disadvantage here. I'm missing all these pieces of Rosie that Lina has." He shifted to the very edge of the coffee table, the inside of his knees now touching the outside of mine. I swallowed. "And I'm a man who has dated. Plenty. I don't scare easily."

That *plenty* he'd dropped so casually sparked my curiosity. Fine, it did more than that. It also did a teeny-tiny bit of jealousy. "So . . . you're like a dating expert or something?"

He tilted his head, thinking of his answer. "I wouldn't say an expert, but no woman has ever complained."

Was he a serial dater, then? His words from a few days ago came back to me. Together with a new flare of jealousy. "I thought you didn't date anymore."

Lucas had also said that no one had ever broken his heart, but I kept that remark for myself.

"You have good memory, Rosalyn Graham," he admitted. "And no, I don't date. I'm not in the market for that. I can't be."

I wanted to dig deeper. Ask him why. "So, you're a dating expert that doesn't date."

"If that's what you want to hear, then I am."

No, it wasn't what I wanted to hear. But what did that matter?

Sighing, I pulled both my legs up, folding them under me and severing the light contact of Lucas's knees. "I don't even know where to start with my history."

Lucas dragged one of his feet up, too, resting it on the side of the couch, right beside my thigh and somehow coming closer. "Assface Number Five," he offered with a serious expression. "You can start telling me about him. Full name? Address? Date of birth? Just for reference."

"*Ha.*" I shot him a look. "Ted, no last name, location and date of birth unknown." I ignored Lucas's frown and asked, "What else do you want to know? What went wrong?"

He nodded.

"If you are into that kind of boring stuff . . ." I joked, but he didn't even smile. "Okay, so Ted and I dated for . . . a few weeks give or take." Six, to be exact. "I'd always been very clear about us being exclusive, not seeing other people because I just . . ." I shook my head. "It's how I am. He agreed, told me he didn't want to share me, either. Then, one day, by pure chance, I saw him attached to someone else's lips. When I confronted him, he pretended he didn't know me." And that had stung like a bee. "The complete tool made such a scene that I even doubted myself for a second, thinking I had the wrong guy. But nope, it was Ted. And he'd been dating that girl longer than me."

Lucas stared at me, remaining oddly quiet.

I filled in the silence. "So, yeah, that was Ted. Assface Number Five." I leaned back on the couch, making myself more comfortable while I waited for him to say something, anything. He didn't. "It's okay. It only took me a couple days to get over him. He wasn't even the worst."

Eyebrows up, Lucas said very slowly, "There's worse than him."

I realized it hadn't been a question, but I answered anyway. "Nathan. Your cousin calls him the King of Assfaces." I shifted, bringing my knees up and hugging them to my chest. And because I seemed to have no brain-to-mouth filter, I told him about him, too. "He was a screenplay writer. Funny, witty, charming. Our first date was probably the best first date I ever had, and that should have been a red flag considering he showed up drunk."

Lucas flinched, his lips pressing into a tight line.

I continued, "He excused himself saying he'd had the worst day at work and downed a couple beers before our date. Told me that he hadn't wanted to cancel on me because he liked me *so much*." And if anything, Nathan had been convincing. "Anyway, all the dates that followed that one were . . . just like dating multiple men at the same time. He'd be his charming, perfect self and then a switch would be flipped, and he'd turn into someone completely different. I wouldn't know if I'd get someone weird, moody, or just . . . crazy."

A muscle in Lucas's jaw jumped. "Did he ever—"

"No," I stopped him. "It was never like that. He never laid a hand on me. It was more about things he'd say or the way he'd act during a date." Stuff straight out of comedy sketches. Bizarre. "But he'd always apologize after, tell me it was nerves making him act strange because he was crazy about me." And silly naïve me believed him every single time. "Anyway." I laughed to make light of the sucky experience. "To sum it up, it turned out he had been testing stuff on me. Scenes. For the screenplay he'd been working on."

Lucas sat so still I could barely see his chest moving. I didn't even think he'd blinked for a minute or two.

I averted my eyes, letting them rest on my toes. "I told you it was depressing stuff, Lucas."

"This Nathan," he said, ignoring my last comment. "How long until you left him?"

Wiggling my toes inside my socks, I made sure to keep my eyes there. "Oh. I guess I didn't . . . exactly leave him?" I swallowed my embarrassment with as much dignity as I could. Because I should have, I really should have terminated that relationship on date one. "He was the one that broke things off. The reveal was his big *plot twist.*"

Lucas didn't speak. Not a word. And I . . . God, what in the world was I doing? Why was I telling him all of this? We could be friends without me revealing stuff that didn't exactly reflect well on me.

"And that's enough of a rundown for today, *friend.*" I finally met his gaze, finding him with an expression that I decided to ignore. "That's why I swore off men and dating apps." That much was true. After that trail of failed pseudo-relationships, I decided to take a break from . . . real-life love and focus on the fictional kind. "Lina might be right, though. Maybe all I need is to go out and experiment with dating again. And by going out, I guess I mean re-downloading Tinder."

His forehead furrowed in a strange way.

I felt the need to fill in the silence again. "It's far from ideal but I can't afford or think of anything else." I started fidgeting with my fingers, so I decided to sit on them. "I could prepare a checklist with all the things I need to take home from this . . . research, like Lina said. An experiment. So, I'll pick a man and go through the motions. The phases of dating. The natural arc of getting to know someone emotionally, from fun or basic things like getting flowers or experiencing the butterflies of going on a first date, to the more . . . advanced stuff. Like that first brush of his hand against mine. Or when he leans forward and I know he's—" I stopped myself, noticing that I was rambling. "Anyways."

I eyed the man in front of me again, waited until a few more seconds passed.

"Ehm . . ." I trailed off, wondering if I should maybe nudge him with my finger, check if he was okay. "I think we had one or five Cronuts too many. Can you feel the tips of your fingers tingling? Cold sweats? Maybe I should get you a glass of water."

I'd shifted by about half an inch when Lucas's hand shot in my direction. His palm fell on my knee, and I looked down just as he said, "No."

My brows rose. "No to water?" I gawked at that warm and heavy palm as it heated the skin through my jeans, feeling the tiniest bit breathless. "Would you like a glass of milk?"

"No, Rosie," he repeated with a determination that made me look up as his fingers squeezed my thigh softly. "I'll do it."

Blinking, processing, I mentally recapped, searching for whatever he could possibly be offering to do. "You'll . . . get me flowers?" I asked as I felt his hand lift off my leg. I sagged back, a little relieved that now I could think more clearly. "I don't think I've ever gotten flowers from any man I dated, but—"

He shook his head and something that wasn't really a laugh left him. "No, I'll be your experiment partner."

My breath caught in my throat. My stupid crush—the one I tried so hard to pretend wasn't real—started banging against the bars of the cage I had shoved it in.

Silence, I commanded the loud screaming in my head. *He has said we are friends.* Numerous times.

I tried to summon a smile and failed. "You'll be my experiment partner?"

He nodded, returning to his easygoing self. "It's perfect if you think about it." *Perfect?* In all honesty, I was having a hard time hearing my own thoughts through the thrumming in my temples. "You won't have to download Tinder or whatever app those"—a tiny grimace curled his lips—"*men* came from."

I opened my mouth, but nothing came out.

Lucas continued, "It simplifies everything."

The following two words left my lips in a breath. "What does?"

"Me, you, us doing this," he answered with a confidence that had me wondering if he really was riding a sugar high. Or maybe I was. Because was Lucas Martín really suggesting we date—experimentally—in hopes I could find my writing muse? "You said you'd pick a man and go through the motions," he pointed out. "Were you planning to tell the little guy about the experiment? The phases? The natural arc of connecting with someone?"

"You . . ." I swallowed. "You were listening."

He smiled and I couldn't miss how smug he looked in this moment. "You're not the only one with good memory, Rosalyn Graham." Something seemed to occur to him. "You never told me your pen name, by the way."

"Rosalyn Sage," I answered without thinking.

Lucas's eyes narrowed as mine grew in size with realization. "Hold on," he muttered.

Oh crap.

"You are *the* Rosalyn Sage?" His mouth formed an *O*, and even though it was the worst possible moment, I couldn't help but think how much I liked his lips. They were full. Masculine. "You're the Rosalyn Sage whose book I've been hearing my sister yell about nonstop for months? The book that is a permanent fixture on Charo's coffee table? You—" He stopped himself.

"Yep." I sighed. "That's me."

A grin split his face slowly, his lips stretching in this grand and magnificent way, as if Moses himself was parting the Red Sea.

With all the might I could summon, I ripped my gaze off his face. "Anyway, I hadn't worked out the details yet, so I didn't really know if I was going to be outright honest or just, I don't know, go with the flow and hope for the best." I frowned at how impractical all of this sounded. How . . . dishonest. "I wouldn't want anyone to get hurt if they found out I was using them, though."

"Enter Lucas," he quipped.

I looked up, finding his Moses grin staring right back at me. That smile was so . . . confident. Reassuring. Comforting. Like a safety net, just there, just in case you fell. "Lucas . . ." I trailed off, questioning my own sanity for actually considering his offer. "You don't date. You're not in the market for that. You said so yourself."

"This is not dating; it's experimental dating."

"This is . . ." This was madness.

It isn't, a greedy and reckless voice countered in my head. *It's a chance to get closer to him without needing an excuse. Before he leaves for good.*

No.

I needed to be reasonable. "You'll be in New York only for a few weeks," I pointed out. Six to be exact. "I wouldn't want you to spend your time doing this instead of whatever you had planned."

Lucas looked down at his hands for a few seconds, then back at me. "That won't be an issue, Rosie."

I tilted my head, watching him closely and catching one of those shadows crossing his expression. "Don't you want to continue exploring the city?"

"No." A shake of his head. "I'm going to be honest with you, Rosie," and the way his voice dropped had me holding my breath so I wouldn't miss a word. "I've been traveling alone for six weeks. By choice, because it was something I thought I needed. But it has . . . backfired in a way I wasn't expecting. I wasn't lying when I told you I was feeling lonely." He shrugged a shoulder as if it was no big deal, as if it didn't make me want to reach out and hold his hand. "So, you can say I have more time on my hands than I know what to do with, alone, and I'd welcome the company. And I know you've noticed, but"—he patted his right thigh—"I'm not exactly in the best shape for all this walking around."

My gaze shot to his hand as it rested on his leg. It hadn't exactly been obvious, but I'd noticed he favored his left side. I remembered that first night, too, when he nearly fell over.

What happened to you, Lucas? I wanted to ask.

But I didn't, because something told me that him opening up and admitting this out loud was already . . . big enough. Out of the ordinary. And I wanted to treasure it, but above all, I wanted to show him we could do this at his own pace, on his own terms, and I wouldn't pry him open just because I was curious. "So, you're saying that I would be doing something for you, too? If we were to be . . . experiment partners?"

"You would, Rosie." He met my gaze. "More than you know."

I liked that. So much that I felt a tingly, fuzzy sensation filling up my chest.

"These experimental dates need to feel real, though. I'm not talking about . . . kissing or canoodling or holding hands. But about everything else. About being . . . romanced. Connecting. Sharing things you would in real dates."

His chuckle was deep. "What's *canoodling*?"

"You know, getting . . . close, physically." Some of the amusement left his eyes, but I ignored that. "That could mess up things between us. Our *friendship*."

Lucas didn't hesitate when he said, "Then we'll be honest with each other if that ever happens."

Honest with each other.

Honest like one of the parties confessing to having harbored a crush on the other?

Strike one for Rosie.

Lucas leaned forward, a whiff of his soapy, clean scent hitting me straight in the gut. "I'll tell you what," he said, and I swallowed. Mostly because he was now much, much closer. Right on the edge of the coffee table, his long legs caging me in. "I promise you that I won't let this interfere with our friendship." He moved another inch forward. "You'll tell me all about those dating phases you need to experience, we'll go on the dates, be the best experiment partners we can be, and at the end of the day, when we come back home, we'll be Rosie and Lucas. Roommates. Friends. Soon enough, best friends."

"Best friends?" I croaked.

"Yeah." He nodded, then repeated, that deep, musical voice of his enunciating the words, "Best friends."

Clearly dazzled by his scent, his words, the way his brown eyes seemed to twinkle up close, I didn't say anything.

That was probably why Lucas felt the need to add, "And if you're still on the fence, I can promise you something." A pause. "I promise I will not fall in love with you and make things awkward, *Rosalyn Sage*."

I swallowed, giving myself time, because I had no reason whatsoever to feel this . . . heartbroken over that vow.

In fact, I had no reason whatsoever to feel anything but excited. Lucas was offering to help me. And whether I did this with him or not, at the end of the next five weeks, he was leaving. Either way. To a different continent. And two weeks after that, I needed to hand over my manuscript.

So, what did I have to lose?

"All right," I said. "Let's do it."

He flashed me one of those smiles I didn't know what to do with.

"Four dates—*experimental* dates," I corrected myself and stuck my hand in front of me to be extra safe. "Five would be . . . too many if you're staying here for only five more weeks. And three wouldn't be enough. So, four."

"Four dates it is," he agreed, unfolding his long body and coming to a standing position in front of me. "So, I guess we're research partners now. Experiment buddies. Field . . . workers? You're the mastermind."

I laughed, and it came out choppy and helpless. Exactly how I felt. "All I do lately is strike bizarre deals with you."

"*Bizarre?*" He huffed dramatically as he offered a hand I didn't take. "You wound me, Rosie. All I have are amazing ideas."

"We'll have to draw lines. Terms," I said more for myself than for him. "Like what I've mentioned earlier. No matter what, nothing changes. No awkwardness." *You heard that, crazy silly crush? Don't make it awkward.* "And you don't go around spending unnecessary money on me. I'm cheap and low maintenance. We always split the bill."

"I can get on board with some of those rules." That hand still dangled in the air, fingers I knew were warm and strong wiggling in front of me. "But you'll have to trust me on the rest."

Oh, Lucas I trusted fully.

Me? Not so much. "Okay but—"

Lucas snatched me by the wrist and pulled me up. And straight into his chest for what I knew would be a Lucas Martín full-body hug.

"We'll shake on it with a hug, Graham," he said, wrapping his arms around my shoulders and squeezing me against him, and boy, I wished someone would come up with a way to bottle these up. I'd buy them all. Stack my cabinets with them and save them for a bad day. Or any day. "Do you like capers?"

Caught off guard, I let out a laugh against the fabric of his sweat-shirt and asked, "Capers?"

He released me from his arms and took a step backward, once more leaving me to deal with the effects of one of his hug attacks. "All this plotting made me really hungry."

Before I could tell him how ridiculous that was after he'd just ate half a box of Cronuts, he shot in the direction of the kitchen. He started pulling things out of the fridge. Then went for the pantry. The pan drawer.

He looked at me over his shoulder. "Help me with dinner."

I walked over to the island and plopped down on a stool. "If by helping, you mean watching?"

He hummed in appreciation. "Oh, I love having an audience."

"So, what are *we* cooking?" My gaze fastened to the muscles on his back as he pulled out a chopping board.

"Aubergine lasagna." He turned, flashing me a grin over his shoulder. "And I want to prep the dough for a rustic ciabatta. For tomorrow."

Oh Lord. Lucas kneading dough?

He pressed, distracting me from my thoughts: "So what do you say about those capers, then?"

"Love them."

His eyes lit up. "That's my girl."

That's my girl.

Ah, crap.

CHAPTER ELEVEN

Rosie

One week.

It had been seven days since we agreed to be partners in this dating experiment and besides my stomach flopping every time I thought about it, nothing had happened. As in, no experimental dates had taken place, no muse had been rediscovered, and no word count had increased. Granted, I had needed a couple days to come up with the dating phases I told Lucas I'd provide him with. Together with a couple of pages of notes that contained anything else I could think of that might help.

When I'd finally handed him everything, Lucas had smiled his megawatt grin, shoved my notes inside his bag, and told me he would *study* the material.

God, the whole thing was so clinical I often found myself battling between wanting to laugh hysterically and scream warning after warning at myself. Because what in the world was I doing? The man I had secretly daydreamed about for over a year was about to take me on "experimental' dates I'd sort of designed. And then, he'd pack his bags and leave the continent.

My heart had had enough of getting through the day now that we were living together. It had had enough of not toppling out my mouth every single time Lucas strolled out of the bathroom in nothing but a towel and an army of droplets dangling off his skin. It had had enough of not thrumming straight out of my chest at the sight of him turning around—still in that goddamn towel—and making the muscles that lined his neck, shoulders, and back dance when he lifted his backpack. My weak, silly heart had had enough of fighting the urge to fall at my feet when every evening he was back with a bag of groceries and a dashing smile and he asked me "How many words today, Rosie?" as he unpacked everything and got started with dinner.

And that last part in particular? Took a lot to survive.

Because Lucas cooking? *Lucas at the stove?* It was like having a first-row ticket to a show designed to fulfill sexual fantasies I didn't know I had. Like the Magic Mike of Doughs and Pans. Lucas could be kneading bread and my sad and neglected lady parts would riot at the sight of his fingers pressing and stroking the smooth surface, working the mix with a diligence and iron hand that had me sweating and shifting on the stool. He could be flipping an omelet and I'd sigh in longing at the way his biceps flexed.

Ugh. And to make things worse—harder for my weak, silly heart and lady parts—the result, Lucas's food, was brilliant, incredible, amazing, showstopping, and all the rest of Lady Gaga's superlatives.

So my heart and I had had enough.

My phone pinged with a text, shaking me off my Lucas-induced thoughts. I reached across the island, where I set camp every day to work, and unlocked it.

Unknown: Date night, today. 6pm?

Ignoring the flutter at the words *date night*, I reread the message a couple of times.

It had to be Lucas. There was no one else who would send me a text about a date. But then again, it wouldn't be the first time I got an accidental message, either.

Rosie: Who's this?

Unknown: Lucas.

Unknown: Are you waiting for somebody else to take you out?

Unknown: I thought I was your only one 🙁

"If only you knew," I muttered under my breath, saving his number while trying to come up with a reply that wouldn't expose me.

Rosie: fine, we'll be experimentally exclusive 🙂

Lucas: we weren't?

Shaking my head, I decided to cut to the chase and answer his initial question.

Rosie: 6pm sounds good. Thanks!

I was going to ask how he'd gotten my number—honestly, it was a little strange he hadn't had it, considering we'd been living together for over a week—but the explanation landed in my inbox in a trail of texts from my best friend before I even hit Send.

Lina: Hey bestie! Just arrived in Trujillo. How is NYC?

Lina: Sorry for the radio silence, we were hiking and out of reception.

Lina: BTW I forgot to mention that my cousin would be visiting for the next few weeks. He's staying at my place.

Lina: Okay, fine. I didn't forget, I messed up the dates and thought he was arriving today. I suck. I still have wedding brain.

Lina: Anyways, I gave him your number. ONLY for emergencies, 'kay? Don't feel obligated to waste your time on him. He's a grown man.

Lina: if he texts you with unimportant shit, tell him to google it.

Guilt lodged itself deep in my stomach. Lina didn't know about the rooming arrangement Lucas and I had. In *her* apartment. Nor did she know about our newly established experiment.

God, I really needed to stop lying by omission to every single person in my life.

Another text notification popped up.

Lucas: check this out.

Tapping on his conversation, an image opened on my screen.

A selfie of Lucas wearing an *I* ♥ *NYC* blue cap. His smile was lopsided, smug, and I could see the Empire State Building nearby in the background.

My rib cage squeezed, feeling a little too tight all of a sudden.

Rosie: living the full tourist experience.

Rosie: I love the cap!

I didn't just love it. I loved it so much that before I knew what I was doing, the photo was saved to my gallery.

Rosie: Lina just texted me. She said she confused the dates and thought you were getting here today.

Rosie: she also mentioned she gave you my number.

Rosie: For emergencies.

I was working out a way to tell Lucas that we should probably tell her about the current situation, but his incoming text disrupted my train of thought, derailing whatever intention I had to confess. It was another selfie, this one from an angle that showed that wide and strong upper body I had ogled more than once or twice, and he was looking down at the camera. His crooked smile had been promoted to a full-fledged grin and the earlier flutter in my stomach had no choice but to revel, pulling out the big guns and turning into a riot.

Lucas: looking this good and not having anyone around to share it with was an emergency, Graham.

He wasn't wrong. He did look good. Emergency-good, good.
And he's a shameless flirt, too, I reminded myself. *Remember his words: No woman has ever complained?*
I rolled my eyes at myself because I really had no business feeling bitter or jealous.

Rosie: Hi Lucas's ego. Nice to finally meet you.

Lucas: He says hi back.

The three dots jumped on the screen for a few seconds, making me bite my lip in anticipation. Then, one last message came.

Lucas: I'll let you get back to work. Be ready at six. See you later, roomie.

Roomie.
I'd tell Lina about this. I would. The moment she and Aaron landed on US soil, I'd tell her everything.

Later in the afternoon, at exactly 5:45 p.m., I had just slipped into my favorite pair of jeans when I heard a knock.

"One sec!" I called, zipping them up as I sprinted through the apartment barefoot. "I'll be right there!"

Throwing the door open, I was not expecting to find Lucas casually leaning against the frame.

"Lucas," I said a little too breathlessly, before stepping back. "Did you forget your keys this morning?"

He straightened. And boy, I don't know what was about him in that moment, but he seemed larger than usual. Bulkier, taller. But before I could process that, he took the smallest step forward and let his gaze trail down my body, slowly, in a way I had trouble processing.

Whoa, what . . . was that?

A slow smile bent his mouth. "Nope," he said. *Nope.* Nope to what? What the hell had been my question? "You look very nice, Rosie. Beautiful."

Very nice. Beautiful.

I thought my lips bobbed, opening and closing in some strange fish-like manner. "Thanks," I finally mumbled. And then I felt the need to point out, "These are my favorite jeans."

We looked down at the same time.

And when Lucas's gaze returned to my face a beat later, that grin had somehow stretched. "I think they might be my favorite, too."

More of that fish bobbing took place, but this time I recovered faster. "Good."

I'd recovered faster, but clearly, not better.

"So . . ." Lucas began, his expression turning serious. "Are you going to invite me in, Rosie?"

I cocked a brow. "You live here."

Amusement entered his gaze but he repeated, in that commanding yet gentle tone he'd only used once around me, "Invite me in, Rosie."

Something tugged at my stomach. "Would you . . . like to come in, Lucas?"

"I would love to," he said quickly, firmly. And then, only then, did he step inside the apartment.

I walked up to the bed, sat on the edge, and busied myself with the shoes I'd set apart for tonight. They were high heels. Blue velvet. Another treasured item in my closet—or, well, suitcase.

I strapped them on quickly and stood up, coming to a stop when I found Lucas's eyes trained down on my feet.

"Do you think these are okay?" I asked because he was studying them with such rapt attention. "You never said what we were doing and I didn't ask so . . ."

He didn't hesitate when he answered, "They're perfect."

"Okay, good. That's good," I murmured.

But was it? With this intense way Lucas had been looking at me, I couldn't tell, I couldn't decide whether this was good or bad. Inspiring or distracting. Exhilarating or overwhelming. Real or . . . experimental.

My head swarmed with thoughts, questions, and speculations, while the flopping sensation, the up and down and up and down, in my chest continued. And I . . . "Lucas?"

He might have sensed something in my voice, because all that intensity coming off him softened. "Yeah?"

"I think I'm messing this up," I confessed. "I'm making this awkward. I said I didn't want any awkwardness between us and I'm already—"

His palm fell on my shoulder, the touch bringing my words to a stop. His strong fingers felt warm against the thin fabric of my blouse. Comforting and thrilling. "Do you trust me?" I nodded, and he smiled. "Then, relax. You're not making anything awkward. This is just Rosie and Lucas, Date Night. Phase one of the experiment. Just like we agreed."

I swallowed. "Do you think we can take a break for a second? Be . . . just us? Rosie and Lucas, every other day, just for a few minutes before we leave?"

"We can be anything you need," he said, his hand remaining exactly where it was. His thumb now moving back and forth. And my thoughts scattered. Because of his words. His touch. *Dammit.* He tilted his head. "You know, I thought it would be a good idea to slip into it right away," he admitted, that thumb now trailing along my collarbone and leaving a path of tingles behind. "Knock on the door, have you invite me in, but maybe I'm rustier than I thought. So, I hope you don't fire me just yet, Ro."

Ro.

That was new.

I liked it. Loved it. A lot.

Which was bad. Real bad. I shook my head, trying to focus, ready to tell him just how not rusty he was based on how he'd affected me, but his hand left my shoulder, and the absence of his touch distracted me.

He slipped his hand into the pocket of his bomber jacket. "I guess this is a good time to give you something I got you. It's nothing special but . . ." He pulled out that *nothing special* and placed it on my head. "You said you loved it."

His palm returned to my shoulder, and he turned me around until we were both facing the large mirror against the wall behind me.

I took in our matching blue and pink *I ♥ NYC* caps in our reflection, thinking how very wrong he was to think this wasn't something special, and I realized that I'd made a big, big mistake.

"Look at that," he said as he stood right behind me. "Someone call 9-1-1, because double the good, double the emergency."

My heart flipped in my chest. No, it might have pirouetted straight out of it. When my lips parted, and instead of words, only laughter came out. An eruption of giggles. Happy, chaotic giggles that released whatever tension or awkwardness I had been feeling minutes ago and replaced it with pure, unfiltered giddiness.

And that right there had been my mistake: a miscalculation of what I could or couldn't take; an overestimation of my control, of what would be experimental or real to me. The answer to my own question, what did I have to lose by doing this? Turned out, more than I thought. And we hadn't even gone on our first date yet.

"Cronut you," I told him, using the code for *thank you* we'd agreed on. Because *friends don't do stuff for friends expecting a thank-you*, like he'd said. And I needed the reminder. *We are friends. Lucas doesn't date. This is all research.*

His smile faltered for an instant, too quick for me to guess why or how. And then he was taking off both his and my cap and tossing them on the bed.

"Hey!" I complained.

"Break's over," he said, spinning on his heels and throwing open the entrance door. "Do you think we're ready now, Rosie?"

Rosie, not Ro.

I swallowed, my earlier anticipation and nerves returning, but different. Bigger, scarier, but more . . . manageable, if that was even possible. So, I grabbed my leather jacket, threw my arms in, and said, "As ready as we'll ever be."

After walking a few blocks, Lucas broke the mostly comfortable silence. "Phase one," he said. "The meet-cute, a spark of interest, the sweet anticipation that leads to that first date. First dates are like first impressions: you only have one chance to make it count."

My cheeks flamed at hearing my own words on his lips.

I wasn't exactly proud of myself for looking at romance through the lens of an engineer or a project manager, as I'd been in my job at InTech. As if I was optimizing a process. Setting these four pivotal points in a relationship that I needed to check in the hope of jump-starting my inspiration. But I guessed habits die hard, and this *was* an experiment anyway. We needed structure. Efficiency. A plan.

And Lucas had definitely studied the material, as he'd promised.

"I think we have the meet-cute in the bag," he continued. "Remember the whole you thinking I was trying to break in and calling the cops?" How could I forget. "So, I've focused on the rest of phase one."

"The first date."

"In my experience." He returned his gaze forward, checked a

street sign, and made us take a turn. "The best first dates are goofy. Lighthearted. A little silly. They're about clicking, seeing if you laugh at the same jokes, if there's a spark there when you do, one that urges you to make the other person smile again. One that could lead to . . . more."

"I have never experienced that on a first date," I heard myself saying.

Lucas's voice dropped when he spoke. "And I'm going to fix that."

I looked down at my feet. "Maybe it should be you writing a romance novel." I tried to joke. "We could look for a nice pen name for you, too."

His chuckle rang in my ears, and I smiled in response. "I've never been good with my words, Rosie." He came to a stop, his hand brushing my elbow. And only when I turned and met his gaze, he added, "But I make up for it with my hands."

I thought my jaw fell open, all kinds of images—involving Lucas's hands—invading my mind. And none of them had anything to do with him kneading dough. Or doing origami.

Before I could say anything, Lucas was spreading his arms and gesturing at the store behind him. "We're here."

My eyes jumped to the sign hanging above the door, and there was no point in denying my voice came out a little rocky when I said, "A record store."

He opened the front door for me with a flourish. "Beauty before age."

Ignoring how that comment didn't make things exactly easier for me, I walked in, the characteristic scent of vinyl and cardboard triggering a succession of memories.

Before Olly was born and our mother left, Dad would take me to shops like this one. A different one every Saturday morning. We'd browse records for hours, each of us picking our favorite cover, the one we'd thought was the weirdest or even the one we deemed the ugliest. We'd never buy anything, though, but even that way, it had always been something I looked forward to.

Making my way inside with my head stuck in the past, I wasn't aware of Lucas trailing close behind me until he placed both hands on my shoulders. *For the second time today*, I mentally noted.

He pushed me forward gently, leisurely, moving us farther in. I felt his breath on my temple before I heard his words. "You okay?"

"I wasn't expecting this," I answered honestly.

"In a good or a bad way?"

I looked at him over my shoulder. "A good way, definitely a good way."

That earned me one of his slow smiles. "Good," he said before walking around me. "Because we're here on a mission."

Letting my hand move above a stack of records, I couldn't ignore the rush of anticipation at his words. "A mission?"

Lucas pinned me with an all-business look. "You"—he pointed a finger at me—"are going to pick a record. Any record you want. And I'll buy it for you."

I frowned, but he waved that pointer finger, stopping me.

"My date, my rules," he said, and I rolled my eyes. "You'll pick a record, but pick wisely, because whatever you choose will be our soundtrack."

My throat seemed to go instantly dry. "Our soundtrack?"

He nodded. "Lucas and Rosie's Soundtrack."

Oh boy. Oh man.

A cheer, loud and chaotic, erupted between my temples.

Lucas and Rosie's soundtrack.

"That's . . ." I trailed off, busying myself pulling a random vinyl from a box, just so I could take a deep breath and not look as elated as I felt at the idea. "That's . . . kind of cheesy." And I loved it. I really, seriously, thoroughly loved it.

"*Cheesy?*" he rasped.

I moved on to the next crate, my fingers grazing the edge of a record, and I'd never know what the heck came over me, but the need to tease him over it overwhelmed me. "Yeah, it's a little cheesy. But cute, I think. I guess that after that one line about me falling out of heaven or something, I shouldn't be surprised." I glanced at him over my shoulder. "Maybe you're just a little *cheesy*."

Lucas narrowed his eyes at me, his expression morphing. "You remember that line. Of course you do," he muttered under his breath.

"Hard to forget something like that," I said.

His expression morphed and before I knew what was happening, he was moving.

Somehow, in what seemed the ninja version of one of his hug attacks, his arm wrapped around my shoulders and he tucked me to his side. The first thing I felt was his minty breath on my cheek, then the line of our bodies pressing together. Him, solid and warm. Me, nothing but butter at the contact, molding myself to him. And then, he tickled me.

Lucas Martín was tickling me.

Pinching my side.

Pulling a yelp right out of me.

"You making fun of me, Rosie?" His voice was low, a grumble, and so close to my ear I shivered.

He tickled me again, and I broke into a fit of giggles, the skin under my sweater tingling for many different reasons.

The tickle attack itself lasted only a few more seconds. But when he seemed to be done, Lucas didn't release me from his hold. Instead, he kept me right where I was, gently lodged into his chest, my side against his front. And as my laughter died, his chin came to rest on my shoulder, bringing our faces so close that I felt, rather than heard, his chuckle on my cheek.

"I'm sorry," I thought I said, but it came out so breathy I wasn't even sure he'd heard it.

"No, you're not," he said, still in that low grumble. His chin moved the tenth of an inch closer, my heart picking up. "You liked teasing me," he added, and he wasn't wrong. "And I loved that you did."

"Oh," I let out, together with all the air in my lungs. "Glad that we're on the same page."

At that, his hold loosened the slightest bit, and I took the chance to jump out of his reach, out of pure self-preservation.

His smile was nowhere to be found for a few seconds, then, the side of his mouth tipped up. "Get to work, Rosie. Find us a soundtrack."

And he sounded so bossy that I had no choice but to do exactly that.

After a while, I pulled out what was probably the hundredth vinyl and inspected it in my hands. I glanced over at Lucas. "This is harder than I thought."

"You're overthinking it," he pointed out, leaning forward so he could see the record I was holding. "What's wrong with that one? Talk me through your thinking process."

"It's Coldplay, so technically, there's nothing wrong with it."

He hummed. "I feel a 'but' coming."

"*But*, I had my first kiss to a Coldplay song," I told him, unable to keep the grimace off my face.

"What the hell did he do?"

I pretended I wasn't surprised by his assumption. "How do you know I wasn't the one who messed it up?"

"I just do," he said with so much confidence my gaze returned to his face. He smirked. "So? What happened?"

"In Jake Jagielski's defense, he hadn't known someone had spiked the punch."

"Oh no."

I sighed, because *oh no* indeed. "Prom night. Jake had been trying to kiss me the whole night, and I'd been dying for him to finally do it." I chuckled at the memory of us dancing with almost three feet of space between our bodies. "He'd been so nervous, though. He'd forgotten my corsage, his tie was all crooked, and his palms were sweaty on my shoulders."

"I feel that. Poor little guy."

"You get sweaty hands, too?"

Lucas made sure he was meeting my gaze when he said, "I would if I was trying to work up the courage to kiss a girl like you."

I stared at him, my head spinning with the possibility. The thought of Lucas's lips on mine. Of his mouth moving against mine. Would he really be nervous? Was his admission . . . true?

This is experimental flirting, I reminded myself.

I cleared my throat. "So, anyway. We were dancing, spinning in slow circles, song after song after song. 'Speed of Sound' comes to an end, Jake leans forward very slowly, and I start thinking, *Oh my God, he's going to do it. Here comes my first kiss.* I close my eyes and wait for that brush of his lips against mine and then, boom, they are there. Pressing tightly against my mouth. Just a peck. But I was so shocked that I opened my eyes just in time to see . . ." I trailed off, shivering at the recollection of what happened next. "Jake rearing back and hurling all over my dress."

Lucas's eyes grew wide, just as his mouth formed a big *O*. He whispered, *"No."*

"Oh *yes.*"

He plucked the Coldplay album from my hands and put it back into the crate. "Okay, let's stay away from Coldplay. I don't want you thinking about that."

He pulled a new vinyl out and held it in the air. "What about the Smiths?"

"Too sad. Reminds me of *(500) Days of Summer.*"

He frowned. "Isn't that supposed to be a good thing? That's a rom-com, isn't it?"

I gasped, a little outraged. "The first line of the movie is literally a warning that it's *not* a love story."

Lucas chuckled and picked another one. "Elton John?"

I sighed and patted my chest. "Uh, I couldn't."

"Another sad soundtrack?"

My brows rose. "Can you think of Elton John without thinking of 'Your Song'? Of *Moulin Rouge*?"

Lucas frowned. "Wasn't that a—"

I turned my head very slowly. Pinned him with a look. "The most beautiful yet heartbreaking movie ever made? Yes, it was."

He dropped the Elton John record back on its box with a snicker and something in Spanish I didn't catch.

I decided to ignore that as we continued browsing, something occurring to me. "I've told you about my first kiss. I think it's only fair you tell me about yours."

One corner of his lips tugged up. "My first kiss wasn't memorable in any way. Good or bad."

"What about any other firsts? I feel like I'm owed an embarrassing moment from you."

He tilted his head. "I might have one. But it's not nearly as good as yours."

"I still want to hear about it."

Lucas thought about it for so long that I thought he wasn't going to tell me. But then, he said, "It's the story of the night I didn't lose my virginity."

My hand came to a halt just as I was lifting a record off a crate.

My jaw might have dropped to the floor.

I stuttered over my words. Words that were not even leaving my mouth.

Did that mean . . . ? No.

Impossible.

It couldn't be. There was no way.

Lucas threw his head back and let out a laugh. "Oh, you should see your face right now. I'm tempted to take a picture, actually."

Out of the corner of my eye I saw him pulling out his phone, and that snapped me out of it. I patted at his arm. "What face? I have no face whatsoever."

"Oh, you do." He shook his head, pushing the phone back in his pocket. "It's the face you made while you wondered whether I'm still a virgin."

I looked around, checking for other customers close by, concerned on Lucas's behalf. But Lucas didn't seem to care.

And when he leaned forward, and lowered his voice to say, "I'm not, Rosie. I lost it a long time ago. I'm very, very far from being a virgin," I somehow knew it wasn't so people wouldn't overhear.

And boy, was it hot in here? Or was he doing that thing, the one where he turned up the intensity and I felt breathless and warm?

I went with the first thing that crossed my mind and fist-bumped his shoulder. "Good for you!"

Amusement entered his gaze, but he didn't smile or laugh.

I refocused on my task and moved along the row of crates. "Okay, so what's the story? I'm intrigued."

"Lorena Navarro," Lucas said, following close behind me. "She was my on-and-off girl all through high school. First and only relationship I've had." My ears perked up at that piece of information, pocketing it for later inspection. He continued, "My parents were visiting some family we have in Portugal for the weekend, and Charo, being five years older than me, was doing her own thing. So, I had the house to myself."

I tried to convince myself that I wasn't the tiniest bit jealous of this Lorena, even if she belonged in Lucas's past. "You got her a beautiful bouquet? Lit up the whole place with candles? Put on some body oil?"

Lucas did a double take. "Body oil?"

"Some guys are into it." I shrugged. "Assface Number Three being one. I—"

"Don't." Lucas grunted. "I don't want to hear more about those idiots." Yep. The memory was putting me off, too. He scratched the stubble on his chin. "I wasn't exactly refined as a teenager. My version of a romantic night was convincing Abuela to bake me something and getting the girl her favorite gummy bears."

"Lucky Lorena Navarro," I muttered under my breath, meaning every word.

Lucas continued, "I rented a movie, laid the cake and the gummies on the coffee table, and sat really, really close to her. By the time the credits were rolling, a few pieces of clothing were on the floor, and I was doing my thing." He chuckled. "Or what I thought was my thing back when I was seventeen."

Holding my breath, I waited for a mental image I knew would stick.

Lucas's grin was big, unashamed. "I was kneeling on the floor, between Lorena's legs, trying my best to . . . you know. Make sure she was enjoying herself, feeling good." He tipped his head down. And I knew exactly where he was pointing. "And the next thing I know I'm being dragged out of the house by the ear. No recollection of how, except for the fact that Mamá and Abuela were somehow there. And they were pissed."

My hands flew to my mouth, and God, I tried to hold it in, but laughter escaped through my fingers.

"You laugh, but Abuela refused to bake anything ever again for me." He shook his head. "The following day, she threw an apron at my face, sat down on a chair, and bossed me around the kitchen until I baked my first cake."

Finally sobering up, I said, "Well, at least some cherry was popped that week."

Lucas looked lost in thought for a second, then a burst of deep-belly, boisterous laughter left him.

Feeling elated at being the one that had caused that rowdy, happy sound, it didn't even come out bitter when I added, "And I'm sure Lorena was happy when she got her Lucas cake."

He waved a hand in the air. "Oh, I don't think I ever baked anything for her."

"Why not? Did she not take you back after that?"

"She took me back. Eventually," he said, stepping closer to my side, leaning forward until the side of his face lined with mine. "But I don't go around putting on an apron for just anybody."

I turned my head and peered into those two chocolate-brown eyes, warmth spreading across my chest, filling every nook and cranny of my rib cage until there was no spot left.

"You don't?" I asked, feeling my breath coming out choppy and shallow. *But you do, for me*, I wanted to add.

Lucas's answer never came. He just said, "Now, stop distracting me and get back to it, Rosie. We're two embarrassing stories down and no soundtrack yet."

CHAPTER TWELVE

Lucas

"*I*sn't that another movie soundtrack?" I asked on our way home from the store.

Rosie huffed, staring down at the record in her hands. "Sort of, but this one is different."

"Different." Snatching it out of her grip, I inspected it closely. "'Dancing Queen' by ABBA, the single." I turned the album around. "Isn't this a little too . . . 'girls night out' for a date?"

"Experimental date," she murmured. "And it was either this or 'Ice Ice Baby' by Vanilla Ice, a hip-hop classic."

The owner had been rushing us out of the store at closing time. And I wasn't going to lie, I was a little relieved that she hadn't gone with Vanilla Ice. Nothing against him—or ABBA, for that matter—but hip-hop wasn't what I'd pictured when I asked her to pick our soundtrack.

She continued, sliding me a skeptical look, "Have you not watched *Mamma Mia*? This song is Meryl Streep's revelation moment. It holds the whole movie together. I once read an article about how it's actually a sad track, and it made some very good points, but . . . I don't know . . . it has always made me happy. It's more than a song you dance to."

Her admission was enough to satisfy me. In fact, knowing she had picked a song that meant something to her did a little more than just satisfy me. "So, you're one of those people, huh?"

She narrowed her eyes, and it was hard not to smile. "What people?"

"One of those *Mamma Mia*–obsessed people."

Rosie seemed outraged by my question. "It's a musical *and* a romantic masterpiece." She snatched the record back from me. "What's not to love about having multiple love stories, all rolled up into *the* perfect musical? Nothing. Because it's literally impossible to not love that."

"Okay, okay." I held my hands in the air. "It's not exactly ideal for what's coming next, but we'll just have to roll with it."

She shot me a quick glance, and I could see the question taking shape in her eyes.

"Ask me, Rosie." I smiled to myself and returned my gaze to the sidewalk, happy that I was starting to get familiar with all her cues. "Always speak your mind around me."

She lifted the record in the air with both her hands. "What's coming next and why isn't this"—she held it in front of her face—"amazing, outstanding, ahead-of-its-time musical masterpiece ideal for it?"

Laughter rolled straight out of me in a loud rumble for the second or third time today.

Rosie lowered the album, revealing a small frown. "What's so funny?"

Nothing was funny about how much I loved that she made me laugh like this and how clueless she was. "You have no idea," I told her simply, spotting Lina's building in the distance. "And you'll find out what we're doing soon enough."

I quickened my step and when I noticed she wasn't keeping up, I peered back over my shoulder.

Rosie was standing in the walkway, looking in my direction with a cocked brow, all long legs in those shoes I was having a little trouble not paying any attention to, and greener-than-ever eyes in that leather jacket that made them stand out.

"I don't know how I feel about surprises," she said, her expression telling a different story. She was curious. Excited. I could tell. "Can't you tell me now?"

"Nope." I flashed her a grin and pivoted away. "My date, my rules."

"Cheesy *and* bossy," she muttered. "I didn't think that was possible."

Another laugh erupted out of me, this one chased by something else. Something that demanded my attention. But I shook my head and said, "I heard that!"

Back at Lina's building, I stopped Rosie and headed to Adele's side of the hall. I knocked on Lina's neighbor's door, and before I could catch Rosie's questioning look, the old lady's head was peeking out.

"Ah, you're back." Adele gave me a crooked smile before moving over to let me into her home. "I was wondering when you'd pick it up. It's right where you left it."

"Thank you, *hermosa*," I told Adele as I slipped in and grabbed the box I'd dropped a few hours earlier. Now that I had learned that this Mateo she sometimes confused me with had been Hispanic, I made sure to say a few things in Spanish when I saw her or came over to check on her. *"Eres la mejor."* She really was the best. "Have fun with your daughter later, okay?"

Adele's face lit up when she said, "I will." She eyed Rosie and added, "Have fun, too, you little rascal."

Snickering, I returned to a dumbfounded Rosie, finding her blinking at the scene. "Could you please take care of the door?"

Rosie gaped at me for a long moment as I held the heavy cardboard box in my arms, before snapping into action. "Yes! Of course, yes. The door."

I followed her into the apartment, throwing the door shut with my left foot. Something I realized a little too late was a bad idea when my right knee buckled.

"Lucas!" Rosie called, running to my side. "Oh my God!"

Wincing but regaining my step quickly, I tried to play it off as nothing, but Rosie was already holding the other side of the box.

There was no point in denying anything, so I repeated my words from that first night, "Good catch, Rosie." I pointed to the left with my head, and added, "Let's place it there, beside the TV stand. I think there's a free plug."

As instructed, we moved, together, and set it down on the floor.

Rosie took a step back but didn't go too far.

Throwing the box open under her rapt interest, I extracted the object I had made sure to leave with Adele so Rosie wouldn't catch on.

"Oh," I heard Rosie say softly. "*Oh.*"

I looked up at her, taking notice of how her lips were forming a little *O.*

"It looks a little beat," I admitted after a moment. "But the lady that sold it to me swore that it works."

"You bought this?" she asked. "For m— For the experiment?"

"Of course." Plugging the old record player into the outlet, I straightened and took a step back to admire my acquisition. "It was fate, really. I was walking around and found this woman selling a bunch of stuff from her basement, right there on the doorstep. I got it for only a few bucks and a favor."

"What kind of favor?"

I snatched the ABBA record from the coffee table, where Rosie must have left it to help me carry the box. "She needed help moving a dresser." One that the woman had forgotten to mention weighed like a motherfucker.

Rosie let out a strange noise. "You went into a stranger's house? Just because she asked you for a favor?"

Shrugging a shoulder, I kneeled in front of the player. "It was actually her basement."

She audibly gasped. "Lucas. You can't . . . You can't do that kind of stuff."

I placed the vinyl on the plate. "Why not? She asked me to help her. And I was getting a record player in exchange."

"What if . . . What if she was just luring you inside? To axe murder you. Or sell your organs. This is New York, Lucas. The ratio of crazy people per square foot is too high to do that. Especially if the word *basement* is thrown around."

"Cute," I said, and she just blinked.

But it *was* cute that she'd get worked up over the possibility of me being murdered.

"All right, Rosalyn Graham." I stepped closer to her, and she tilted her head back. "Shoes off."

"What?" she mumbled. *"Why?"*

"Because we can't dance with you in those sexy heels without bothering the downstairs neighbors."

Her eyes widened, as if I'd said something crazy. "Dance—We're dancing?"

I pulled off my shoes. "Of course." I kneeled back down and toggled with the few settings the player had. "I told you you'd be picking up our soundtrack. And that's what a soundtrack is for. Dancing."

Rosie looked at me like I was asking her to sprout wings and fly.

I tilted my head to the side. "Should I help you with those shoes?" I offered. "I can do that if you really, really need me to." And I'd do it gladly, in all honesty. Those shoes had been driving me a little crazy ever since she'd put them on.

Her mouth bobbed a couple of times, not emitting any sound.

Only when I took a step in her direction did she seem to snap out of it. In a few seconds, the pair of blue heels was behind her, and her toes were peeking out from under the hem of her jeans. And what a pair of jeans. I hadn't been lying when I told her they were my favorite, too. They definitely were when they hugged her—

Lucas, I told myself. *Focus.*

I pressed Play on the record player. The opening notes of "Dancing Queen" filled the apartment.

I cracked my neck left and right. Then I made sure to meet her gaze as I started moving left to right.

This song might not have been exactly my jam—definitely not what I had pictured us dancing to—but at least I knew how to keep a beat. Abuela had made sure of it when I was a kid, for when the occasion needed it. And so, I gradually added my arms to my motions, then my hips, and then, just so I'd get a reaction, any reaction, out of her, I spun in a perfect circle.

Rosie's eyes turned to plates.

"You look so shocked, Rosie," I teased, not stopping my solo performance. "Is it so surprising to see me dancing?"

Fine, I didn't *just* know how to keep a beat. I *knew* how to dance.

The pink coloring her cheeks deepened, but the corner of her lips twitched.

Biting back my own smile, I did the only thing I could. I strode very slowly in her direction, matching every step to the beat of the song and making sure to keep my eyes on hers.

"Come on, Rosie," I told her, then added a little louder, "You can dance." I moved my hips left to right. "And you can also jive."

By the time I closed the distance between us and I was only a short two feet away from her, I was fully singing to ABBA, swinging my arms and shoulders around her.

The smallest snort left her.

Almost there, I thought. And my leg wasn't even bothering me all that much.

I moved forward. "Am I not a good enough dancing queen?" I asked her, stepping much, much closer. "I'm not seventeen but I'm young and sweet, anyway, don't you think?"

A small smile tugged at her lips now. And naturally, that only fueled my need to take more from her. To make her give me more.

"Okay, that's enough. Come here," I said right as I snatched her hand and spun her in a circle.

Rosie yelped, loud and pitchy, and a second later she broke out laughing.

There it is.

Because there it was, that laughter I had been craving.

I spun her one more time, her body now slowly beginning to move to the rhythm of the song. And when she was facing me again, it was with a full-fledged grin parting her face that I had no choice but to return.

The chorus started just as if we'd choreographed it, and we screamed the lyrics at the top of our lungs.

And just like that, Rosie's limbs loosened, her eyes shut, and her body got lost to the seventies hit. I held one of her hands and watched her sing like it was nobody's business, so loudly that I could hear her voice over the music. And boy, she wasn't a good singer. Not by a long shot.

Not that it stopped me from taking her other hand and spinning her in another circle. We whirled and whirled, singing and laughing, perhaps one too many times, because with that last twirl, Rosie lost her footing and spun right into my chest.

Our bodies clashed, my arm going around her waist. Our gazes locked, chests heaving in breathless sync as we stared at each other. The sweetest wave of peaches wrapped around me, making my nostrils flare.

My throat worked as I started noticing the way her breasts pressed against my chest, moving up and down with every heaving breath. One of my legs was thrust between hers, and somehow, in a basic reflex I hadn't been able to control, I pulled her closer. Tighter against me. Our hips coming into contact as our legs tangled further.

Her breath caught, and when her mouth released the air, shakily, rockily, it hit me on the jaw. Something inside of me stiffened, hardened.

My fingers splayed on her waist. And I—

The record scratched, bringing everything to an abrupt stop.

"*Lucas,*" Rosie breathed.

My arm kept her secured right where she was, against me, giving myself a few more seconds to . . . think. I needed to think. "Yeah?"

"The music," she added quietly, breathlessly. "It stopped."

"Yeah."

"Was that—"

A strange noise cut off her words.

Rosie's head peeked over my shoulder, in the direction of the sound. "Lucas?" she whispered loudly.

I opened my mouth, but the sound grew louder, stopping my words.

"What is that?" she asked over the *scratch scratch scratch*. "What the heck is that?"

That was a damn good question.

I spun us around, now holding her for more than one reason.

The scratch continued, increasing in intensity, and I took a tentative step forward. *"Pero qué cojones . . ."* The Spanish curse slipped out of me as I stretched my neck.

"Oh no," Rosie loud-whispered. "Lina says that a lot when something's about to go wrong."

I moved us forward.

"Lucas, I don't like this. What are you—"

"Shush," I told her softly. "I think there's something behind the record player."

A pitchy screech left the vicinity of the box, so I peeked down in time of . . . *Ah, mierda.*

"Okay." I softened my voice. "I want you to remain calm, Ro." Because if that was what I was pretty sure it was, and Rosie happened to be scared of—

A scream pierced my ears.

Okay. So, she was.

"Lucas!" Rosie bellowed, jumping and managing to climb up my body as if I had been nothing more than a pole. "A rat! Is that a rat!?" A hand landed on my face, another one on my shoulder. One of her knees reached my armpit. "No, no, no, no. Please, tell me that's not a rat!"

Throwing my arms around her waist, I adjusted her around me so her legs would close around my hips. "I'm not going to tell you any of that."

"Why the hell not?!"

Chuckling, I placed my hands on the back of her thighs and turned us around so she'd face the opposite way. "Because there's a huge rat in the apartment and I'm not going to lie to you, Ro. Not ever."

Another scream.

Pivoting, I tried my best to carry her to the other side of the studio while she squirmed in my arms and left me with no choice but to place one of my palms on a perky and rounded ass I promised myself I wouldn't think about. "Hey, Ro?" I told her, holding back a groan when she wiggled right against my crotch. "I'm going to put you to safety, okay? But it's going to be easier if you stop moving. *Please.*"

That seemed to put a stop to all her squirming because she froze in my arms. "Oh my God, I'm so sorry, Lucas." She tried to hop off from my embrace, but I didn't let her. "Am I too heavy? I'm such a jerk. Let me—"

"Stay right where you are," I told her as I carried her the rest of the way with only a light limp and placed her on the counter very gently. "It's all right."

"No, it's not." Her expression was remorseful, pained. "I shouldn't have jumped on you like that."

And yet, I hadn't even cared about her doing so. I hadn't cared about the tightness gripping the now weak muscles under her weight. Or the soreness I'll suffer in a few hours after our dancing session. To be honest, I was sick and tired of paying attention to any of that. I was sick of not being able to do whatever I pleased because of this goddamn injury.

Swallowing, I answered the only way I could: "Don't worry about it. I don't."

She nodded her head, and one more time, she shocked me by not pressing. Pushing me to talk about it. Instead, she lowered her voice. "I'm terrified of rodents." She lifted both legs and placed her bare feet on the counter. "And now I can't stop thinking about that . . . "—she shivered—"that creature eating away at my toes."

Her expression was of pure disgust, and it made me smile. "It won't eat your toes."

"It could," she hissed.

"I mean, sure, it could. But you're high up now. It won't reach you here."

Rosie groaned. "You're not making it better. I'm going to have nightmares now, Lucas. We'll have to sleep with the lights on and I might have to wake you up to bring me water to my bedside table because I'll be scared of something biting my feet if I step on the floor. You're digging your own grave here, really."

I sighed, but it was more for show. "I'll do that if you need me to. That's who I am. A good roommate and an even better friend."

Rosie's lips fell and she muttered something under her breath.

"Now stay put, okay?" I told her before she lost it again. Then, I moved back to the record player, located the rodent, and not without effort, managed to corner it and shove it back into the empty box with a magazine that had been lying around.

Once ready, I held the box—with the rat—and started making my way back to Rosie.

She stopped me with a hand. "Do not move one more step with that thing in there, buddy."

"*Buddy*? Really?" I feigned outrage. "How about 'Oh, Lucas, my sexy and skilled knight in shining armor'? Now that's a nickname that suits me and I can get on board with."

She shot a threatening glance in my direction.

Before I could say anything, a knock on the door came.

"Oh my God," Rosie whispered. "What if that's another one of them?"

"Well," I said, heading for the entrance. "Then, I hope they brought snacks."

Leaving a fuming Rosie on the counter behind me, I opened the door with the box under my arm and I was welcomed by a face with features I recognized from a much older woman.

"Hi," a brown-haired woman with one of those edgy haircuts I'd seen around said. "I'm Adele's daughter, Alexia. I hope I'm not . . ." She trailed off, her gaze falling behind me. "I hope I'm not interrupting something."

"Oh no. Don't worry," I told Alexia with an easy smile. "She just likes it up there. Right, Ro?"

Rosie's answer didn't come for a few seconds. "Yeah," she called. "Right. I love climbing on furniture. It's really a pastime of mine."

I chuckled before returning to Alexia. "It's very nice to meet you." I offered my free hand. "I'm Lucas. And the pretty lady on the counter is Rosie."

"Nice to meet you . . . both," Alexia said, shaking my hand. "I wanted to come by to introduce myself and thank you for looking after my mom. Either my wife or I come by every evening, and God knows how hard we've been looking for full-time care for her, but it's proving . . . " She seemed a little overwhelmed for a moment, leaving that statement unfinished. "Anyway, you're really good to her, and you absolutely didn't need to check on her, so I appreciate it. More than you know."

I shook my head. "It's nothing." And I meant it. It really was nothing.

"It's not nothing." Alexia reached out and patted me on the arm. "The last time she talked about Dad this way was right after he passed."

Dad.

So, Mateo had been Adele's husband, like I'd suspected.

Alexia stared at me for a long time, a heavy emotion filling her eyes. Grief. Clear as the day. "God, you look so much like his old photos. He was Argentinian, *mi papá.*"

There wasn't anything I could say that would make it better, so I didn't.

"All right." Alexia cleared her throat. "I won't keep you from"—a knowing smile replaced the sadness that had been there—"whatever you two were doing that definitely looks like fun."

I nodded, relieved that she hadn't asked about the box under my arm. "I'll see you around, Alexia."

"Yeah. I guess I'll see you around, too, Lucas." She peeked behind me. "Bye, Rosie!"

"Bye!" she hollered. "It was nice meeting you, too!"

Only when Alexia was gone, I looked over my shoulder. Rosie

was exactly where I'd left her, though her expression was now different. "You've been visiting Adele? Every day?"

"Yes."

"You . . ." she started, her gaze roaming around my face, her eyes filling up with something. "Ah crap."

I frowned but our little boxed friend moved, bringing our attention back to where it should have been. "I'm guessing that picking up stuff from the street is a no-go around here."

The left corner of Rosie's lips twitched. "I'd probably stay away from basements, too."

"Fair enough." I sighed. "All right, I'll take our little friend out to the street or . . . to a park?" I frowned. "You know what, I'll google what to do with it. Just, come down from there when I close this door, okay? You're safe."

Because invader rodent or not, I had promised Rosie that much.

And I wasn't going to forget that.

CHAPTER THIRTEEN

Rosie

Olly was blowing us off. Again.

After he'd promised he'd be here, that he would come to prime the walls of Dad's studio after he had asked for our help.

The worst part, though, was the realization that Dad didn't need any help. The fact that I was standing behind him holding the bottle of multisurface soap while he did all the work was proof enough. He'd asked for help just so he would get us here. Just so he'd have an excuse to see his children. See Olly.

God, I wanted to shake my little brother. What the hell was wrong with him?

"Are you sure you should be doing this?" I asked him, closing some of the distance so I could see his face. "Your hip okay, Dad? We could take a break and have something to eat."

"I'm fine, Bean," he said quickly.

Ugh, not the *I'm fine* routine.

Snatching the sponge out of his hand, I stood by his side until he looked at me. And when he finally did, reluctantly, his expression confirmed that he wasn't, in fact, fine. "Liar, liar, pants on fire."

Dad chuckled, and I kissed his forehead just so I wouldn't shake him, too.

"Just a little worried, is all," he finally admitted with a sigh. "Have you heard from your brother? He's coming, isn't he?"

"I . . . Yes." I busied myself with the sponge so he wouldn't see my face. "Let me see if I have any missed calls from him. He's probably just running late."

Dad snatched the sponge back. "I'll finish this off while you do. We're only missing a few spots."

"*We*?" I muttered as I turned to fish my phone out of my bag.

Not a text, not a call, nothing.

I texted him again.

Where are you, Olly? I'm at Dad's and it's already 6PM. You said you would come.

Then, I invented an excuse for him with Dad, the man who had fought tooth and nail to keep us afloat while making us feel loved every single day, even when he couldn't spend much time at home. "Olly might be on the train, maybe without reception?" I explained, hoping Dad bought the lie. "I'll try again in a bit."

Dad sighed. It was a quiet sound that most people would have overlooked, but I knew it well. It was the Olly sigh. Because Dad blamed himself for whatever was going on with my brother.

Almost as much as I did.

I was about to attempt to reassure him when a female voice entered the room. "How's my favorite neighbor doing?"

I turned to find a woman with graying hair high in a bun, her eyes twinkling with warmth and humor.

"Ah, Nora. You're here," Dad answered, his whole face brightening. "I hope we didn't bother you by moving the furniture around. Is your book club meeting over? Did you bring some of your delicious red velvet cake?"

Her book club meeting? Her delicious red velvet cake?

Dad lowered his voice. "I've been thinking about it all day."

I blinked. Oh Lord, what was happening here?

Nora lifted a bag she'd been keeping behind her back. "I'm glad to hear that." She smiled before turning to look at me. "I didn't know you had company, Joseph. Is this your daughter?"

"I told you to call me Joe," he corrected her with a wink. A wink that had me doing a double take. "And yes, this is her. Rosie is an engineer. Works at a fancy company in Manhattan, remember I was telling you about that yesterday?"

Guilt sliced through my chest at my dad's words. "That's me." I swallowed. "Hi, Nora, it's nice to meet you."

She smiled at me over the bag. "Your dad is very proud of you, honey. He told me all about that well-deserved promotion."

I felt my blood drain from my face, but I gave her a nod.

Nora's gaze slid to my dad. "She has those beautiful green eyes of yours, Joseph." She chuckled. "I sure hope she's not as stubborn as you are, though. Because those are some genes you don't want to pass on."

"Joe," Dad corrected her. And without turning to me, he added, "Did you hear that, Rosie? Beautiful eyes."

I searched Dad's face, then Nora's. They were both grinning. Dad at her, and Nora at the bag that contained that *delicious red velvet cake he had been thinking about all day.*

My phone buzzed in my hands, snatching my attention from the flirtation-fest happening right in front of me.

Lucas: How's the home project? Your dad's hip okay?

I bit my lip just so I wouldn't smile at the screen. At his name. At his words.

And just like that, memories of our first and only experimental date toppled down my mind, making me feel all kinds of breathless.

It had been goofy, fun, sweet, and cheesy in the best possible way. As much as I teased Lucas, the truth was that I *loved* cheesy, and he had surpassed any expectations I'd had for our experiment.

Every single thing about it—about him—had been a romance writer's dream come true. *A woman's dream come true.* Even thinking of that rodent running around the apartment didn't make my skin crawl anymore. Instead, I thought of my legs around Lucas's hips as he carried me to safety. Of his solid and warm body under mine. Of the intensity burning in his brown eyes as he'd looked at me when we danced.

It all had been in the name of research. Experimental flirting. Experimental dancing. Experimental . . . wowing.

But this wasn't. The care he took in checking up on me and Dad—as Lucas, my roommate and friend, not Lucas from Date Night—wasn't experimental. It was real. And that . . . was hard to ignore.

Rosie: He's okay. He's busy flirting with his neighbor. In front of me.

Lucas: 😄 Go Mr. Graham!

Rosie: Don't encourage this kind of behavior.

Lucas: Why not? Flirting is healthy for the soul.

Rosie: He's my dad 😬 And they are watching each other with googly eyes right here.

Lucas: He still deserves to eat, you know.

Rosie: EW LUCAS. NO.

Lucas: Fine 😖 but you're a romance writer. You should encourage this. Maybe even give him tips.

Lucas: How far do you think the flirting has gone? Do you think they'd had a little pow-pow fun?

Pow-pow *what*? Jesus Christ.

Rosie: okay gossip girl, let me stop you right here.

Rosie: you're supposed to side with me.

Lucas: I'll always be on your side.

Those words sat there alone for several seconds as I stared at them, not really knowing what was about them that made them stand out.

The three typing dots appeared again.

Lucas: I'll let you go, just wanted to check on him. And you.

Lucas: #TeamRosie

Lucas: xoxo, you know you love me.

Lucas: and before you ask . . . I have a big sister, Ro. I know Gossip Girl.

Ah dammit. God freaking dammit.

Why did he have to go around being so . . . good and funny and . . . and . . . so Lucas?

Rosie: that's sweet of you, Lucas. You really didn't have to check on us.

A few seconds passed, and just when I thought I wouldn't receive any more messages from him, a new bubble appeared on my screen.

Lucas: One last thing, will you be eating at your Dad's or should I leave dinner in the oven for you?

That expanding sensation in my chest I so often experienced when Lucas was around came back with a vengeance. Heightened, intensified. As if it was there to stay. He was so unbelievably sweet, and he probably had no idea.

This truly was a curse and a blessing. Because—

"Rosie?"

Looking up from my phone, I caught my dad's interested gaze. "Sorry, were you saying something?"

"Who's that you're texting?"

His question brought me back in time, when I was sixteen and he'd asked me if there was any boy I liked. *Remember to pick the boy that will plant a garden for you instead of just getting you the flowers, Bean.*

"Oh," I said as casually as I could. "Just a friend."

"There was a lot of grinning going on there for 'just a friend.'"

"I was laughing at something he said." I locked my phone and slipped it in my bag. "He's funny like that."

"Oh yeah?" Dad's smile was knowing. "What was the joke?"

Out of the corner of my eye I watched Nora slip out of the room with a nod in our direction. I used her disappearance to my advantage. "One not as *funny* as seeing you with Nora." I pointed a finger at him. "Someone's been busy."

He laughed, like outright deep belly laugh, and I loved hearing that sound. I loved it less when it died off too quickly the moment Dad checked his watch.

"I guess your brother's not coming then," he admitted with a sigh.

I thought about making up a new excuse for him, but we had reached the point where there was not much else I could say. "I guess not, Dad."

"Right." He nodded. "Let's get this done so you can catch an early train back, Bean."

Hours later, I was finally getting off the train and making my way out of Penn Station. Feeling surprisingly drained of all energy and it being dark and a little late, I opted for spending the extra bucks on an Uber instead of taking the subway back home.

I had been waiting for my driver to arrive, when the outline of a man pacing the intersection across from where I stood caught my attention.

His head hung low as he walked back and forth, fidgeting with his hands in a way that immediately struck me as familiar.

I stared for a little longer, then felt my feet carrying me forward. *Olly?*

It took me at least ten feet to confirm that the man was my little brother. God, had he changed so much in the time I hadn't seen him? His shoulders seemed wider, and he even looked taller, but it was *him*. Man or boy, that was my little brother. And . . . What was he doing here? Was something wrong?

I rushed the last feet between us.

"Olly?" I called, watching his head immediately bounce up at my voice. "What are you—"

The last stride that brought me face-to-face with him stopped whatever I was about to say.

Something wasn't just wrong. Everything was. Because my brother stood in front of me with a black eye and a busted lip.

"Jesus Christ, Olly." I watched my hands reach for his face. My fingers brushed his cheeks. He winced. "What happened? Who did this to you?"

His eyes closed, and I knew, I just knew that the nineteen-year-old man in front of me needed comfort. He might have been at least five inches taller, and no longer the boy that stared at me like I had hung the moon when I sneaked him an ounce of chocolate, but I still wanted to wrap him in my arms and protect him from the world. From whoever had done this.

"I'm fine," he grunted.

I felt something snap inside of me. Something dark and hostile. "I swear to God," I growled, my voice shaking with frustration, "if you Graham men don't stop this *I'm fine* crap, I'm going to lose my shit."

Olly's exhale was close to a gasp and I knew it was because I had cursed, but it managed to appease my anger. Just the tiniest, littlest bit. "I think you might have lost it already, Bean."

I sighed, studying his black eye. "How, Olly? How did this happen?"

"It's a black eye. It just happens."

Taking my time to fill my lungs with a deep breath, I willed my voice to remain steady. "Is this why you're here, outside the station? Why you didn't come to Philly?"

A nod. "You texted me you were on your way back. I wanted to apologize for not showing up."

My thumb grazed the cut on his lower lip. "Does it hurt?"

He shrugged and I sensed the words rising to my mouth. Words he wouldn't want to hear. "Olly, what the hell is going on?"

"I'm young, it'll heal quickly," he had the nerve to say. Deflect.

"*Because* you're young, you shouldn't be getting into situations that leave you with a busted lip. Nobody should, young or old."

I saw my fingers start shaking, bewildered by the whole situation. Overwhelmed. Helpless, too. Because I didn't know what to do to make him listen. To trust me. "You should be enjoying life. Having fun. Doing whatever nineteen-year-olds do now." I shook my head, something occurring to me. "Does this have anything to do with the mysterious job at the nightclub?"

He recoiled, stepping out of my hold. "Just trust me for once, okay? I make good money. I'm fine. This was just a little brawl over a misunderstanding."

I reached out for him again, but he stepped farther back. It was only then that I took notice of what he was wearing. Nice clothes, expensive ones. Brands I could hardly afford myself.

He looked down, too, and he shook his head.

I wanted to scream, but I didn't. If I did, I probably wouldn't stop. "Is it drugs?" I demanded.

Olly's head snapped up. His eyes widened.

"*What?*" He gasped, as if I'd just asked him if he was pooping golden pellets.

"Are you dealing drugs, Olly? Is that what this is?"

"Jesus, Rosie." That shock turned into disgust, frustration. "I'm not dealing anything. It's not that, okay? You just don't understand. I'm . . ."

He shook his head, his raven hair falling over his forehead.

"You're just *what*?"

"I'm . . . dancing?" he finally said, but it came out as a question. Which only made me more confused.

More skeptical. More suspicious.

"At the nightclub," I said slowly. "Making enough money to afford clothes worth my rent."

Olly shrugged.

Jesus, was my brother . . . dancing for money? Was Olly *stripping*? My heart thundered in my chest while I remained very still.

Not long ago, I was thinking of Lucas's cooking as the Magic Mike of Doughs and Pans, and now it turned out my little brother was actually reenacting the whole thing. In real life.

Didn't he trust me enough to tell me?

Overwhelming sadness slipped in, making me feel dizzy. I opened my mouth to say something, anything, but the blinding lights from a vehicle stopped me.

Olly threw an arm over his eyes and cursed under his breath. A car pulled up beside us, and the window rolled down.

"Okay, pretty boy. Get in," a man that wasn't much older than Olly demanded from the driver's seat.

"Olly," I tried. "Don't go."

But my brother moved toward the car.

"There's so much we need to talk about—"

"Rosie," my brother cut me off. "It's fine, I called him. And I'm okay. I swear."

The man in the car smirked, his expression setting off about ten different alarms in my head.

"Let's go," he told Olly. "Shift starts in thirty. We'll have to use a crap ton of makeup to cover that number you have, but Lexie will manage." *Lexie?* "You'd better hope she was worth the trouble."

My head whirled in Olly's direction. His jaw was hard.

The black eye. It was about a girl. But—

"Bye, Rosie," he said. And in a swift motion, he was kissing my cheek and throwing the back door open.

In a blur, I was left alone, dumbfounded and standing on the sidewalk while I watched the car's taillights turn into two red spots in the distance.

Ironically, it was exactly then that my Uber arrived.

A while later, when I finally stepped inside the apartment, the encounter with Olly weighed so much on me that not even the sight of Lucas asleep with his mouth hanging open and our vampire show playing made me smile. After pulling a blanket over him, I tiptoed to the kitchen to grab a glass of water, where I found a note he'd left on the counter. *Dinner's in the oven in case you're hungry.* And not even that made me smile. I didn't even answer his text, and he still went through the trouble of cooking for two. Because he hadn't written *leftovers*, he'd written the word *dinner*. And he'd made sure that the note was somewhere I'd see it. Waiting for me. In case I was hungry.

It should have made me smile. Grin like a fool, overwhelmed with giddiness, just like earlier. But it all had the opposite effect.

The situation with my writing, Lucas, my brother, even my dad. The complete mess that was my life. How big of a hypocrite I was for demanding the truth when all I did was keep secrets. Everything was . . . too much.

I was standing there, with the note in my hand, when I heard my name.

Lucas stood in the middle of the studio, about ten feet away from me. He held the blanket in one hand, and his hair pointed in all directions.

Summoning the best smile I could manage, I said, "I'm sorry I woke you up."

"I was only resting my eyes." He blinked a few times, as if he was willing himself back to life. His eyes roamed around my face. "What's wrong? Your dad—"

"No. Dad's fine." I shrugged, doing what we Grahams did best. Hide whatever was wrong. Swallow it up. "Nothing's wrong, Lucas."

He was silent for a long moment, looking at me. I knew what he was doing. He was worrying, wondering how he could make it better for me. Probably wondering if I was going to burst into tears again.

And the fact that he was doing all those things made me mad. Lucas was doing so much. And I was giving him nothing. Just the company of someone who moped around a lot.

I vowed in that moment that I'd do something for Lucas Martín. Something to make him happy.

"Hey, Rosie?"

I sighed. "Yeah?"

He looked at me with something that was a lot like that intensity from our experimental date, but different. Fiercer. Softer. "Do you want a hug?" he offered.

He was such a good man. But I wouldn't have another breakdown in front of him after he'd done so much.

"No. It's okay. I'm fine," I whispered.

He was quiet for a few seconds. Then he said, "Do you think you can give me one, though? Maybe I'm the one who needs it."

I swallowed, the urge to step forward and lunge myself at him invading me. But I didn't, because I knew what he was doing. This was for my sake, not his.

Lucas caught on, because he went with something I wouldn't be able to resist: "I really miss Taco today. So that hug would really help." His voice was so deep and gentle, so soft. "Can I get one hug, Rosie?"

And as much as I knew that this hug was for my sake—because I must have looked like I was about to come apart at the seams—he still managed to make it look like I'd be giving him something precious if I said yes. Like I'd break his heart if I denied this one thing to him.

"Okay," I heard myself say. Knowing with alarming certainty in that precise instant that I'd never be able to look into Lucas's face and not give him whatever he asked from me. "Only if you need it that badly."

It didn't take him any time to cross the few feet between us and throw his arms around me.

Once more, I buried my face in his chest. But this time, I let myself lean into him. Completely. I gave myself the green light to give up. I inhaled his scent and relished how warm and big and solid he felt around me. I took as much strength from him as he was willing to give me. And I imagined this, his hug, his body, *him*, being my safe haven. My normal. My bad days, my good days. My *every* day.

"Thank you, Rosie." I felt—more than heard—his chest rumble with the words. "I feel much, much better, now."

My arms tightened around his torso, feeling every muscle, every bone underneath, every inch of warm skin under his shirt. Even the beat of his heart.

CHAPTER FOURTEEN

Rosie

"Alessandro's?" I asked when Lucas came to a stop in front of the pizzeria right around the corner from Lina's building.

Just like he had done with our first experimental date, Lucas had sprung this one on me, too. He'd texted me earlier today to be ready by 9:00 p.m. "Spanish dinnertime," as he had called it. Expecting him to take me out to a restaurant, I'd dressed up. I was wearing a midi pencil skirt, a light sweater tucked at the front, and my black leather boots.

But we were here. At Alessandro's.

Lucas had ushered me across the street and now we were standing in front of the one place in New York City whose menu I could recite by heart.

And it was . . . closed. Even the metallic blinds were down.

I frowned. "Are you sure this is where we're going?"

Lucas peered at me over his shoulder. "Yep."

Okay.

"But before we go in," he said, pulling a key out of the pocket of his bomber jacket, "I want to make sure I got everything right."

I knew he didn't need to do that because he'd gotten it just right. He seemed to get everything right.

"Phase two," he said, reciting the plan I'd come up with. "The second date. While usually underrated, the second date is where curiosity turns into interest. You explore the spark you've felt on the first date."

The spark.

I averted my gaze as heat climbed up my neck. I had some nerve talking about curiosity, interest, or sparks when I was starting to feel far more than just that. If Lucas and I—our experiment—was a romance book, I'd be pages beyond this phase. And that had slowly started showing in my writing sessions. My head hadn't been as empty and my chest hadn't felt as stiff, suffocated by all the pressure that had been pushing everything down, and instead of worrying about my running out of time and possibly becoming a failure, I'd found myself daydreaming about Lucas, transforming those thoughts into words on the page. The truth was, however, that time was still ticking, Lucas would leave in three weeks, I had five until my deadline, and I still was a long way from having something— anything—I could send to my editor.

Lucas's fingers came to my chin, and he tipped my face to the side and up. He met my gaze.

"No take-backs, Rosie." His expression was one of no nonsense. "Do you still want to do this?"

There wasn't much to think of, not when he was looking at me like that. All sharp determination in his gaze. "Yes."

That slow grin broke free, making me a little weak in the knees. Inevitably, I matched him with one of my own. "There it is," he said, his fingers still on my chin and his eyes dipping down to my lips. *"Deslumbrante. Como el mismo sol."*

And my heart started strumming like it was playing a goddamn set of kettledrums.

It didn't matter that I didn't understand the words he'd said in Spanish.

It didn't matter that until him, I had never had a thing for accents.

It was Lucas, and that seemed to be enough. "What does that mean?"

"It means that I hope you're hungry."

I frowned, doubting the accuracy of the translation. But before I could complain, he was stepping away and taking care of the security gate, and poof, the sight of his backside—his ass, in particular—as he kneeled and stretched, dissipated whatever I was going to say.

Life was really unfair. On top of that smile, he also had to have a great ass. One that I'd bet my complete Jane Austen special edition collection was as firm as—

"Rosie?"

My gaze snapped up to his face, finding him looking at me over his shoulder. The biggest smirk known to man tilted the corner of his mouth. "Whenever you're done checking me out."

"*What?*" I screeched, my voice coming out high-pitched and squeaky and obvious. So obvious. I cleared my throat. "I was not checking you out."

Lucas snickered and stood, throwing the glass entry door open and gesturing for me to go in first. "It's okay with me, you know? I love the attention." He paused. "And it's good to know that you're an ass woman."

I was an ass woman. I *really* was.

With a defeated sigh, I stepped forward and focused on doing damage control on what I knew were flaming red cheeks once I gave him my back. "I wasn't checking your ass, Lucas. I was just making sure that you . . ."

The words died the moment I set foot inside the pizzeria and saw what was waiting for me.

Dozens of tea lights formed a trail that parted the pizzeria and led to what I knew was the kitchen.

"I . . ." I trailed off, my jaw starting to chatter for a reason I couldn't explain. My whole body trembled. And I didn't know why. "Lucas," I somehow managed. "I don't even know what to say."

I felt him come closer. "No better way to explore the spark and prove to the other person that you're worth the effort." A pause, in which I heard a few more steps. "That you're worth lighting dozens of tea lights."

I thought I heard him chuckle, but I couldn't be sure. I had been sucked into a vacuum. A Lucas vacuum. "How?" I thought I whispered.

"Sandro closed early today. Family celebration. So, I thought we could have the place to ourselves."

I hadn't been asking about *that*, but my head still swiveled in his direction, "You thought we could—" I stopped myself, processing the information. "How the heck did you convince Sandro to give you the keys? This pizzeria is like—"

"Like a third daughter to him, yes." Lucas chuckled, that easiness about him taking over. "He told me about his whole family tree. Also explained in detail how he considers this place his legacy. His home outside home. Built with the sweat of his back and—"

"The calluses on his hands." Lina and I had sat through that explanation on many occasions.

"Yes." He shrugged a shoulder. "I guess I made a good first impression."

"So, he simply agreed?"

Sandro was a great man but not one you could win over easily.

"A few promises I'm not sure I can keep might have been thrown around, but it's all under control." He winked, like this was normal. Like him going through the trouble was nothing. "Let's keep the fire hazard to ourselves, though. It can be our first ever secret."

The fire hazard.

The beautiful candles he had lit.

Our secret.

Just like my secret crush. Or the many other secrets I kept.

I swallowed, nodding my head and soaking up the sight of the pizzeria. The feeling. The fact that Lucas had gone above and beyond and out of his way for me.

For the experiment.

"If you'll follow the path, please?" Lucas whispered in my ear, bringing me back with a delicious shiver that curled down my spine. "I'll show you our main activity."

"Oh," I murmured, moving forward. "This wasn't the main activity? We're not eating surrounded by tea lights?"

"Not yet." Lucas walked close behind me, setting one of his hands between my shoulder blades and bringing me to a stop in the kitchen. "We're eating. But for that, we need to take care of the food first."

I stood there, wishing my skirt had pockets so I could slip my hands in and not fidget. God, why didn't all skirts have pockets?

I glanced over at Lucas, finding him toggling with the temp controls of the large oven. "You love Alessandro's, right?"

"I'm a New Yorker. It's genetically impossible for me not to love pizza. But Sandro's in particular? I adore, yes."

"Well," Lucas said, pulling out a large and squared plastic container and placing it on the counter. "I'm not Sandro. I'm not even Italian, but I think you love watching me cook."

"I might," I teased. I loved watching Lucas cook more than I loved that first sip of coffee in the morning. Or biting into a lava cake. Or that feeling you get when you know you're reading a new favorite book. Or waking up on Christmas morning. I loved watching him cook more than I loved most things in life.

Lucas moved to the fridge and pulled a few things out of it. Tomato sauce, a few greens, a huge wedge of what looked like Parmesan cheese. "Sandro gave me a few tips, told me where everything is, and made me promise to do it justice."

Lucas had *really* won Sandro over.

"So, you're going to cook?" I asked him as he placed a package of flour on the counter. Without any kind of warning, the image of Lucas covered in flour, smiling down at me, ambushed me and I almost stumbled over my next words. "You'll cook for us? And you'll let me watch?"

"Nope." He walked to where I was, and only when he reached me, I noticed what he was holding. An apron. "We'll cook. Together. Because I deserve a little watching, too. Don't you think?"

Before I could react to that, he moved behind me, his arms going around my sides.

"The spark," he said, referencing phase two of the experiment, "can be explored in many different ways." I could feel the warmth of his body radiating into mine, my breath catching in my throat. "It can be about more than lighting candles." He moved closer, his chest almost brushing my back. "It can be about sharing something that's important to you."

His chin came impossibly close to my shoulder. So close that I was pretty sure we'd share our next breath if I tilted my head to the side.

"It can and should be about seeing if those glimpses you've offered of yourself are appealing to the other person. Seeing if they reciprocate and reveal something of their own," he said softly, his words falling very close to my ear. "Let's suit you up."

I nodded my head, my heart thrumming with a steadily increased pace.

Lucas placed the apron against my front and wrapped the ends around my waist. They were too long, so they furled around me twice, keeping him on the task for a little longer.

His head peered over my shoulder to get a clear view of his own hands, and the side of his jaw brushed my cheek.

One soft and quick flick of his stubble against my skin. That simple of a touch, and it sent my pulse all over the place.

Before I could stop myself, before I could restrain the need to lean into the contact, my body was moving back. My shoulder blades came to rest against his chest, and the back of my head against his throat. Warmth draped around me, turning me supple and alive in his arms. All at once.

He held his ground, welcoming my weight, reminding me of yesterday, of our hug, only different. This time, it wasn't about comfort and support. This time, every nerve ending in my body crackled with electricity.

"I'm making sure the knot holds," he said in a low, gravel-like voice.

I nodded my head, remaining very still while I watched his fingers work. Once done, his palms came to rest against my belly. As if incapable of letting go.

My eyelids fluttered closed at the contact, at how his hands were now pulling me to him ever so lightly.

Then, I heard him rasp at my ear, "You're ready now."

Opening back my eyes, I swallowed the need to tangle my fingers with his and pull him even closer. All around me. "Thanks," I breathed out. Then, looked down. "It looks like you did a very thorough job."

Lucas's jaw brushed against my cheek again and all the air from my lungs caught somewhere in my throat.

"I'm a thorough man," he answered. "I don't do things halfway."

And without another word, he stepped away, my whole body turning cold at the loss of his body heat.

I heard Lucas clear his throat before he moved back to the counter.

"Aren't you going to wear an apron, too?"

"I don't think I'll need one." The corners of his lips tugged up when he faced me, as if nothing had just happened. *Although, what just happened?* "Now, come here, Rosie. You won't be able to cook all the way over there."

"Okay." I obeyed, making a move in his direction. "But don't think I've missed the way you're implying I'm messy."

He barked out a laugh and muttered something I didn't catch in Spanish.

I leaned on the counter and frowned. "What did you just say? It's a little unfair that I can't understand those little things you mutter under your breath."

"I said, *Dios, dame paciencia,*" he admitted. "Which means, 'God, give me patience.'"

My eyes narrowed. "What do you need patience for? I'm not that bad of a cook."

Lucas ignored my teeny-tiny lie and dragged the plastic container toward me. "Step one, we stretch the dough."

He took the lid off, revealing two smooth balls. His index finger delicately pressed into one of them. "These have been proofed already; see how the dough bounces back?"

Imitating him, I patted one of them, too. "Yes. I see that. And I can also tell you, mine never looks like this when I attempt it at home."

A low chuckle came from my left. "I can show you how it's done some other day. Now, let's dust the counter so it doesn't stick to it."

He turned away and dragged the flour closer to me.

"So, an experimental date *and* a master class. I'm a lucky girl." I took some flour with my fingers and sprinkled the counter. "Did Sandro leave these for us? He must really, really like you."

"Oh, I wasn't joking when I said I totally won him over," he said, adding some more flour himself. "He even wants to introduce me to one of his daughters."

I stiffened.

Lucas continued, "But I prepared these myself. I came by early today and left everything ready for us. Minus the candles. Those I brought only when the boss wasn't around."

Whatever jealousy I was feeling was wiped clean. *He spent the day at the pizzeria? While I was home working and thinking he was out and about exploring the city?*

"Before you complain." Lucas snatched one of the dough balls and placed it in front of me. "I was very curious about the hydration rate he used. And the only way he was going to talk about that was by infiltrating his kitchen." He extracted the other piece of dough from the container and put it down on his side of the counter. "He was reluctant at first, but when I told him . . ." He trailed off, and he shook his head. "But he shared it with me."

"When you told him what?" I asked, so eagerly that I felt the need to cover for myself. "That you would marry his daughter or something?"

He shot me a quick glance, amusement entering his expression. "You know what? He did offer his blessing."

"Fab," I said, returning to the dough.

He nudged me with his hip. "I told him I wasn't in the market for it."

Somehow that didn't make me feel any better.

Another bump of his hip against my side. "As cute as you get when you're jealous, I don't want to see you frowning, Rosie."

"I'm not frowning," I muttered. "And I'm not jealous, either."

He laughed. "All right, index and middle finger out, press softly into the middle of the ball. Just like I'm doing."

With maximum care, I followed his lead. Switching to my knuckles when he told me to and trying really hard not to get caught up in the meticulous and confident motion of his hands, which became a hardship really quickly, because the sight of Lucas's hands working was turning me . . . unproductive.

"So, Rosie," Lucas said, lifting the dough with a slow spin. "How many words did you get in since our first date? Any luck with that inspiration?"

Imitating him, I held my dough in the air but it just . . . stretched down languidly. "I think I'm doing something wrong."

His hands came over mine, sending a sharp flare of electricity up my arms.

"Thanks," I told him quietly, letting him take over control of my motions. "Some words," I answered just so I wouldn't think of his warm palms pressed against the back of my much smaller hands. "Not many with Olly and everything. But some. Definitely some. I'm . . ."

His strong fingers intertwined with mine for a moment, distracting me.

"You're what?" He pressed.

Our fingers worked the dough in circular motions, and I had to clear my throat. "Starting to feel the inspiration."

Lucas moved our hands to the counter, resting them on both sides of the stretched dough.

"Just so you know, I'm dying to hear all the details about Officer Burns's best friend."

Officer Burns? Hold on. Did that mean that Lucas had—

"Have you read my first book?" I blurted out.

"I'm a thorough man," he said, repeating his earlier words, not answering my question. "And I won't ask about the second until you're done. I don't want to jinx what we're doing here."

I wrinkled my nose, not thinking about Lucas reading the steamy scenes of the book but focusing instead on how happy it made me to hear he was that invested in this. In me. In my writing. My books. I'd been so busy trying to protect myself from what anyone could say, writing in secret, hiding behind a pen name, that I hadn't shared this with anybody but Lina. And I . . . God, I loved how it felt hearing that this man cared. "Jinx it, huh? You're superstitious?"

"I'd love to say no, but I'd rather bite my arm off than walk under a ladder."

A laugh burst out of me.

He froze, as if the sound had caught him off guard. Then, I felt more than heard him exhale through his nose before finally stepping away, leaving me a little unbalanced without the safety of his hands on mine.

"So . . ." I trailed off, recovering as best as I could. "What toppings are we using?"

"We have a little bit of everything. But I want you to be creative."

"Creativity hasn't been my strong suit lately."

"Rosie," he said in a way that made me look over at him, "I believe in you. I'm Team Rosie, remember?"

I smiled to myself, reveling in how good, how confident, hearing that made me feel. Then, I reached for a few slices of some cured sausage and worked in silence for a while.

"I know this is not exactly date—*experimental* date—night talk, but I've been meaning to tell you that Mr. Allen called this morning."

"The Psycho Landlord?" Lucas grunted.

His reaction made something in my belly tumble. "He said the contractor might take some additional time to finish."

Lucas didn't say anything, not right away. Then he sighed. "You're right, this is not date night talk."

Nodding my head, I took a few more slices of the sausage. "I know, but I just wanted to say how grateful I am for you letting me stay in Lina's place with you and that if this is turning into too much, I could still look for someplace else. Just say the word."

He seemed to think about his answer. "You're comfortable staying with me."

My hand halted in the air. "Of course, I am."

"And if there's something that bothers you, you will tell me." He held up a piece of juicy mozzarella. "This will complement the *finocchiona* you've picked." He shredded it with his fingers roughly. "Even if it's me snoring."

"You don't snore."

"Or me being a little chaotic in the kitchen. Or the music I play when I'm cooking. You'd tell me, right?"

He was ridiculous. "Lucas, it's you, the one sleeping on a couch when you were promised a complete studio apartment. Bed included." I shook my head, observing my work. "Meanwhile, I have a handsome man cooking delicious, five-star meals for me every night of the week. Why would I ever be uncomfortable?"

"Hmm, okay," Lucas said, seemingly appeased. "And I'm also happy to hear you think I'm all that handsome and irresistible."

Oh, dammit. That had totally slipped.

I rolled my eyes. "I didn't say anything about being irresistible."

"Ahem."

"And it's not like you didn't know you're handsome." Or irresistible.

I glanced to my left to find him leaning on his side, his arms crossed in front of his chest casually, his gaze on me. In fact, he looked like he'd been done with his pizza for a long time.

Without thinking too much about it, I said, "You've dated plenty." I used his own words. "All those girls must have told you you're handsome."

He shrugged. "You've been my first date in a long time so maybe I needed the reminder."

Experimental date, I felt the need to correct him. Even if only for myself.

I searched his face. "You never said why you're not dating anymore."

"It's not something I can focus on right now."

"Because of your career as a pro?"

Lucas hesitated, and I watched a shadow cross his features. "Something like that."

I didn't want to reveal myself, my feelings, but I had to ask. "Are you excited to return? After you recover from . . . whatever happened?" His eyes narrowed slightly and I felt the need to say, "Lina said you were smashing competition after competition. You had sponsors, and social presence . . . You were killing it. Before the break." Lina had never told me all that much about Lucas. I'd gathered most info from his social media. From how much he had shared online before he'd vanished completely weeks before the wedding. "So, I just wondered."

Lucas swallowed. And he stayed quiet so long that I thought he wasn't going to say anything. I started turning away from him, just to hide the disappointment of him not confiding in me, but just as I moved, his hand wrapped around my elbow.

"I can't do any of it anymore, Rosie," he said, and I could feel the weight behind his words, as if these were rocks he was hardly able to lift. "I . . . won't be able to surf ever again. Not at the level I did. Not even close." His gaze tipped down to the leg I knew bothered him more than he wanted to show. "So, that career as a pro? It's not exactly stopping me from anything. Especially not dating. What will I be offering anyone anyway, huh?"

And *oh*.

Oh my God. This wasn't just a vacation. He wasn't taking time off to recover from anything.

And I . . . Lord, I wanted to wrap my arms around him. To smack myself for asking those questions because it must have been so incredibly hard for him to answer them.

I also wanted him to tell me everything. How he felt and how it had happened. I was on the quest to know all there was to know about Lucas Martín and it wasn't because I was curious, but because I cared.

But Lucas looked at me like he'd just been cut open, exposed, and had nothing left in him to deal with that conversation. So I didn't ask. This was big enough already. He'd given me a meaningful, crucial part of who he was today. Now. Not the social media persona he once had been that I had happened to spy on.

"You're not defined by a career, Lucas." I let my hand fall on top of his, very briefly, just so I didn't lace my fingers with his like I was desperate to do. "You're way more than just that. You have more to offer, too."

He blinked, a muscle in his jaw jumping, his gaze clouding with something that looked a lot like wonder. Awe. Also, surprise.

And just as quickly, he was walking off, severing the contact, and reappearing with a large wooden spatula.

He leaned down on the counter, assessing my work like we hadn't had that conversation. "Good job, Rosie. I think you might have a knack for this."

He slid my pizza onto the spatula and left to put it in the oven. I took the opportunity to check his toppings choice. "Whoa. Is that honey that you drizzled on yours?"

"Yes," he said when he came back and repeated the process with his pizza. "Pear, walnuts, some prosciutto because I couldn't find any *jamón* that was worth our time, and a little of blue cheese, too."

He walked back to the oven, and my gaze followed him this time, getting caught up in the way his back shifted as he slid the spatula in and out. Muscles moved and rolled, making me think of him in the water. Him, a board underneath his body. And him, not able to jump on one anymore.

". . . Or in other words," Lucas was saying, "any Italian's nightmare."

He strolled back to where I was at the counter, and I nodded my head, fully aware that I had spaced out. "Yes, total nightmare."

"You didn't listen to a word I said, huh?"

"What? Of course, I did."

He snickered knowingly. "Rosalyn Graham, and you dare deny I'm irresistible."

I was ready to deny it again, but now that he was standing closer, not more than a foot away, I could see that the tip of his nose was covered in flour so I told him, "Your ego is so big that I should probably let you walk around the rest of the night like this but . . .

you have something on your face." I brought my index finger to my nose, pointing him in the right direction. "Right here."

He dragged the back of his hand across his nose and cheek, but only made it worse. He asked, "Now?"

"Yep," I lied through my smile. "Much better."

He narrowed his eyes, inspecting my face. "It's not gone, is it?"

I shook my head and finally let out a laugh.

Lucas's palm returned to his face, but he must have covered his hands in flour when he slid the pizzas onto the spatula, because he somehow managed to paint his chin white, too. "How about now?"

I laughed harder. Smiled bigger.

"Come here and take pity on me, woman." He held both hands in the air, looking at his palms. "Fix me up, before I end up completely covered in it."

"But you look *soooo* cute."

He sent me a dark look that made me immediately move, closing the small distance between us and stopping right in front of him. I held my hand up in the air, reaching for his face but not making contact. And I swore, I'd never—ever—understand what got into me to say what I said next.

"Maybe I like you covered in flour."

Lucas's eyes sparkled with surprise. Something warm and sultry, too.

My smile died slowly. My left hand reached for the remnants of flour that had been covering the counter and I covered my fingers in it.

"Rosie," Lucas rasped. "Don't."

But that only encouraged me.

I made sure to meet his gaze when I smudged the flour all over his left cheek.

Lucas's expression morphed, that intensity I'd gotten glimpses of in our first date swirling in. And just as I was about to retrieve my hand, his fingers closed around my wrist. He asked in a gravel-like tone, "You want me messy or cute, Rosie?"

My belly took a deep dive at the quality of his voice, of his gaze, of his words. I swallowed. "Both."

Without breaking eye contact, Lucas leaned forward, towering over me with his flour-covered face and making me tilt my head back. "You can't have both. Choose. What will inspire you tonight, Rosie?"

"Messy," I breathed out.

Out of the corner of my eye, I watched him stick his thumb in the tomato sauce container. Then, he was moving, shifting us so my back was against the counter, my wrist still in his hold.

Before I could fully process any of that, his thumb was sweeping over my nose, leaving a sticky trail behind. "Then I'll make a mess of you, too." I felt his breath on my mouth. His body coming closer. "Ever since I tied that apron around you, I've been stopping myself from doing exactly that, anyway."

An uproar took place at the pit of my stomach at his confession, but just as I was about to answer, to ask him to please shred the apron to pieces if he had to, his thumb reached the corner of my mouth. It swept right and left.

"Have you ever felt this on a date before, Rosie?" His voice was low, barely a grumble, but it reached deep inside of me.

I shook my head. My pulse raced through my body, reaching areas that had been neglected and were now wide awake.

"Is this a strong enough spark for you?" His gaze dipped down to my lips, where I was smeared with tomato sauce. I watched his throat bob. "Because I can try harder. For you, I will."

A shiver curled down my spine when his hand moved and cupped the back of my neck. Lucas leaned forward, pushing me softly against the counter at my back, his body heat now blanketing all around my front. My lips parted at the contact and his gaze moved to my mouth again.

The brown in his eyes flared like chocolate fire.

His brow furrowed.

His brow furrowed?

And then the smell hit us.

"*¡Joder!*" He released me and sprung backward with a trail of curses in Spanish.

I had to catch myself on the counter.

What the hell had just happened?

Regrouping, I tried to make sense of the pounding in my chest, the tomato sauce trickling down my face, the scent of smoke flooding Alessandro's.

The scent of . . . smoke.

"Oh crap!" I snapped into action, joining Lucas at the oven and peeking at the charred remains of what had once been two pizzas.

CHAPTER FIFTEEN

Lucas

Sandro was going to have my head. Knock me out with one of his spatulas and fling my unconscious body into the East River, just like he'd threatened.

Maybe Rosie would help him. Because talk about ruining a date. I seemed to have a knack for that.

Something else I had a knack for? Getting distracted. Parking common sense at the curb and losing perspective of the lines that were drawn around me. The ones that had seemed to blur tonight. Or had they? Because that had been the whole point of the experiment. Jump-start her inspiration. Helping her forget about everything weighing on her and make her feel something else. That was all I wanted.

No, not all I wanted. The image of Rosie in my arms, all supple against me, ready to let me lick that goddamn tomato sauce off her lips, flashed behind my eyes.

Until today, I had been somewhat able to ignore the pull she'd had on me, to hide it beneath the fact that I genuinely enjoyed her company as a friend. That I truly, honestly, wanted to become even better friends than we were. But now? After tonight? After the lines had blurred long enough for me to lose myself to that all-consuming *spark*?

Long enough for me to burn something? Not something, but food.

Por Dios. Now, pretending she didn't have any effect on me didn't look like something I'd be able to do.

"I think we did a pretty good job cleaning," Rosie announced beside me as we made our way back to the apartment. "Sandro might not even notice anything."

I looked both ways at the intersection, as I placed my hand on the small of her back before crossing. "Hopefully," I answered, still a little lost in my head.

We had spent a good hour scrubbing that oven—after waiting for it to cool down so we wouldn't burn ourselves. I *hoped* we'd removed every last black speck of charred dough from the oven. "Either way, I don't think it's about our cleaning skills. I think we just make a great team, Ro."

Rosie's mouth twitched, returning my smile. "I guess we do."

"So." I checked the time on my watch and threw the door of the building open for her. "It's past midnight and I haven't fed you yet. How hungry are you?"

"I'm okay," she said climbing the stairs before me. "But I wouldn't mind ordering something if you're not too tired to wait for delivery."

My eyes, which had been glued to the back of her head, traveled down her spine, reaching her backside. Her hips and ass swayed as she made her way up, and I found myself a little mesmerized by the motion. By her beautiful curves.

I felt my pace pick up, as if I was in a rush to get closer to her. Shaking my head, I made myself chill. Told myself that I couldn't pant after her like a horny teenager. I was her friend. Her roommate.

Just look somewhere else, Lucas.

Rosie stopped in front of the apartment door, giving me a strange look. "So, what do you say?"

What do I say? "To . . . what?"

She frowned. "Should we get something delivered? I don't think

I want pizza after scraping burnt dough." She paused. "How about Japanese?"

"Ah . . . I don't know." I pulled out my keys and turned the lock.

"Let me surprise you," she insisted as I let her in first. "You're always cooking for me. And I can't really return the favor, so let me. It's my turn to feed you."

I liked that. I liked hearing that from her.

She walked to the coffee table, slipped off her boots, grabbed her laptop, and plopped herself onto the sofa. "You'll love it, I promise."

I joined her on the sofa, letting myself fall with a sigh. "I don't know . . ."

She glanced at me over her laptop. "You don't trust me?"

"What?" I said, but it came out as a grunt. I crossed my arms over my chest. "It's not that."

"Then what is it?"

I exhaled through my nose, confident I was pouting, too.

Her socked foot nudged my thigh. "What is it? Tell me."

"I'm hungry, okay?" I grumbled. "I'm starving and I was very excited about those pizzas. But now, I'm not in the mood for pizza, either. I can't get that smell out of my nostrils."

"And?" She nudged me again with her foot, and because I couldn't help myself, I grabbed it, wrapping my fingers around it and securing it in my hold.

I swept my thumb over her instep. "And you want Japanese, but sushi always leaves me . . . unsatisfied." Hungry. Soon enough, *hangry*.

Rosie was taking her time answering, so I looked at her. She was staring at my hand, right as it massaged her foot.

Lines, Lucas. Lines. My fingers stopped but I didn't release her.

"We'll get something that's not sushi. And you'll love it, you'll see." She returned her gaze to her laptop. "I'm a little offended that you won't trust my taste, though. So, if you want to make it up to me, you should continue with that foot massage."

Keeping the sweet, delightful surprise to myself, I obeyed. Happy to be gifted with yet another green light tonight.

That, until she muttered under her breath, "Cheesy, bossy, and grumpy. Who would have thought?" And I stopped massaging her foot to tickle her instead.

That night we only lasted two episodes of our show before calling it a day and heading to sleep.

"Lucas?" Rosie whispered loudly from the master bed.

I smiled up at the ceiling from the couch. "Rosie?"

"Did you like the Chicken Karaage?"

"It was okay." It hadn't been *just* okay.

My head was already pondering how to reproduce the way they'd breaded the chicken and maybe even give it a twist. I could add crumbled crackers or even very finely chopped nuts marinated in soy sauce. I could—

"Liar," Rosie called. "I saw you licking the container lids when you took everything to the kitchen."

Busted.

I threw an arm up and rested my hand under the back of my head. "Fine, it was fucking fantastic. You were right, and I'd lick those containers again if there was anything left on them."

She laughed and the sound made the corners of my lips inch even higher. It was a beautiful sound and it didn't come out nearly often enough.

"Why are you trying to play the tough guy card and saying it was just okay?"

I went with the truth. "Because the plan had been to feed you those pizzas. And burning them bruised my ego."

We fell into silence for a couple of minutes, my head going straight back into my gutter. Thinking of her, of tonight. Of her parted mouth and how I'd wanted to dip my head and lick her bottom lip—

I cursed myself when my sweats got a little tighter at the crotch.

"Lucas?" Rosie called.

When I answered my voice was thicker. "Yeah?"

"Tonight was amazing. Regardless of the pizzas."

"I'm happy it helped, Rosie."

"It wasn't just that," she replied. "Sure, it helped. More than you know, but I . . . loved it. It was the best second date I've ever been on. I don't deserve you going out of your way so much for me—for this," she corrected herself. "For the experiment."

Something in my rib cage shifted. "Your bar is so low, Rosie. It drives me insane."

A beat of silence.

"Why do you say that?" she finally asked. "I think my standards are normal."

The fact that she believed that made it all even worse. "You shouldn't be content with a date that ends up with you scraping an oven clean," I told her, and I could hear the frustration in my voice. "Or standing on top of a counter, terrified." I closed my eyes for a couple of seconds, needing the time to stifle the urge to say more than I should. "You deserve so much better than any of that. Whether it's an experiment or not, you deserve more."

No answer came from her. And I hated that I had snapped like that and couldn't see her face in the dark.

Only when I'd given up and thought she'd fallen asleep, she spoke, "I wish you'd attended Lina and Aaron's wedding, Lucas. I . . ." She trailed off, what sounded like a shaky breath chasing her words. "I really wish I'd met you that day."

My chest constricted.

And I thought about that for the first time. That alternative reality where we—Rosie, the maid of honor, and Lucas, the bride's older cousin—would have met and perhaps had a glass of wine or two. Maybe a dance. Hopefully a little more than just that. God knows I would have tried.

But I wasn't that man anymore. I couldn't . . . hope for more with anybody when I didn't even have my own shit together. And we were friends, roommates. And I loved that. Spark or not, I loved having Rosie in my life.

For now, I reminded myself. Because in three weeks I was going to leave.

And that was something I shouldn't forget.

Whatever existed between us didn't change the facts.

And I'd been dead serious when I told her she deserved more.

My leg acted up during the night.

And that meant a longer than necessary shower.

After weeks of traveling and staying on my feet almost all day, a long day like yesterday had this kind of effect.

It was the price to pay for ignoring physical therapy and skipping more than a third of the sessions advised. But what point was there? I'd been told since I'd woken up in that hospital bed in France that there was no going back to hundred for me. So, I just . . . didn't bother trying. I let them do whatever they needed to and the moment I could walk without an obvious limp, I went home. *Home*.

Taco's image flashed in my mind.

But besides my best friend, and my family, what did I have left in Spain to call it home? The feeling of belonging had dulled since the accident. It was as if something was missing. It no longer called me back. And I had no family of my own. No one I called mine and longed to go back to. With all the traveling and demands of my career that had never . . . happened.

With a shake of my head, I turned off the water and wrapped a towel around my waist before stepping out of the bathroom. Feeling strangely weary, I came to the decision that I'd ask Rosie if she minded having me around today. Even she was planning to write, I could be quiet and keep to myself.

I threw the bathroom door open, and my gaze immediately zeroed in on my roommate as she stood there in her sleeping shorts and tee. *Dios*, those shorts were going to be the end of me one of these days. "Morning, Ro—"

"*Te voy a matar.*" The threat to my life cut my words right off. It came from somewhere to my side and it was delivered by a familiar voice that shouldn't be here. Unless—

"*Lucas, ¿qué está pasando aquí?*"

The query was sputtered, and it was only then that I noticed Rosie's face. The warning. The pained expression.

I turned very slowly. *"Hola, prima,"* I said, welcomed by Lina's contorted face. My eyes jumped to the man standing beside her. His eyes were on me and while they looked a little less murderous, they still managed to be threatening. "Nice to meet you, Aaron," I continued. "Congratulations on the marriage to this little treasure here."

Aaron didn't even give me a dude-nod; he just cocked a brow and greeted me with a curt, "Yes."

Yes, to what exactly, I had no idea. But by the looks of it, it probably meant that a double ass whooping was in the cards for me today.

A strange sound came from my cousin, returning my attention to her. "Why are you roaming around half *naked*?" That last word was a high-pitched squeak. I looked down, taking in my bare chest, the towel wrapped around my hips. My mouth opened, but Lina let out another strangled sound, stopping me. "Why is my best friend here, in her pajamas, so early in the morning, with you"—she paused—"*half naked*?"

"Lina," Rosie interjected, coming to my side quickly. "It's not what you think."

Lina's forehead vein, the one I had memorized from when we were kids, pulsed. "It's not what I think?" she asked before pointing a finger at me. "Is he wearing some kind of invisible sweater?"

I snorted, and I felt Rosie's elbow on my side. On reflex, without even thinking about what I was doing because I hadn't even had my goddamn breakfast and not thinking seemed to be my thing lately, I grabbed her arm and muttered, "Not nice, Rosie."

Which clearly was a mistake because my cousin stiffened, her face turning even redder.

"Before you start jumping to crazy conclusions—"

But Lina lunged forward, succumbing to all and every crazy conclusion she could possibly come up with.

Luckily, her husband intercepted her, snaking a strong arm around her waist. "Baby," he told her, securing her against him. "Don't."

At the same time, Rosie cried, "What the hell, Lina?"

But Lina was busy growling and pointing a tiny fist at me. "This is my best friend, you *nitwit.*" She waved that arm in the air. "My best friend in the whole world. Couldn't you keep your Lucas *juju* to yourself? Couldn't you keep your penis in your silly nitwit pants?"

I should have probably been offended by Lina acting like my *Lucas juju* had just ruined her best friend, but I wasn't. In that moment, I could only focus on how distressed Rosie looked, and how her lip was doing that thing it did when she was upset. Trembling. And I knew the reason. I knew Rosie well enough by now to guess that she was feeling responsible for this. That she felt guilt over not telling Lina that we had been sharing the studio.

That was why I lowered my head a little and whispered to her, "What the hell is a nitwit?"

Her head turned very slowly toward me, and when she looked up at me, it was with wonder in her eyes. Also, a little humor. Just like I'd wanted. "*Lucas*, be serious," she reprimanded me. But at least, her lip was not doing that thing anymore.

"Aaron, *amor mío*," Lina said, returning me to the matter at hand. "Can you please put me down so I can kick my cousin's nitwit nuts? Apparently, he thinks this is all a joke."

Aaron rolled his eyes slightly, but then, he pinned me with a serious look. Intimidating-looking dude, he was. All tall and scowly. Not that he was intimidating me, though. The only person in the room I was slightly scared of was 5'4" and had a vein that might pop out of her forehead.

"Okay." I sighed. "You need to calm down," I told my cousin. "We spent the night together, here, in your apartment. But it's not what you think, all right?"

Lina's eyes narrowed. Aaron's head tilted.

I could see my cousin's skepticism all over her face. "There's only one bed, Lucas. And should I repeat that you're practically naked?"

I knew Lina; I knew she wouldn't drop this until . . . the end of times. She was as stubborn as they came. So, I said it as clearly as I possibly could: "Rosie and I haven't fucked."

I heard my roommate's sharp intake of breath at my words, but

I ignored it. I had to. I was in a towel and trying to make a point, for Christ's sake.

Lina let out a strange sound.

After a few seconds, Rosie took a small step forward. "Remember those missed calls? Soon after you left?"

Lina nodded, her murderous eyes softening when they switched to Rosie.

"Well, that night there was a . . . a little incident in my apartment."

I huffed. "The ceiling in her living room caved in. Nothing *little* about it."

"Fine," Rosie relented. "Little or not, I couldn't stay there. In fact, my place is out of commission until the repairs are done. That's why I'm here. That's why I called you that night, to see if it was okay to spend a few nights in your apartment. But you guys were somewhere off the grid, so I just packed my stuff and used your spare key. That was the night Lucas arrived in New York."

There was a long silence in which Aaron resumed his frowning and Lina's vein eased off until becoming barely noticeable anymore, *gracias a Dios.*

My cousin finally said, "So you two"—she waved a hand in our direction—"have been living here? Together?"

I nodded and caught Rosie doing the same.

"Which means," Lina continued, "that you haven't hooked up and that we haven't walked into you two engaging in post-sex shenanigans?"

Rosie croaked, her cheeks turning red, *"Post-sex shenanigans?"*

I just crossed my arms over my naked chest and answered a simple, "No."

Lina seemed to process that, her expression falling when she said, "Why didn't you tell me?"

Rosie spoke before me, "I feel awful and—"

"It was me," I took over. "I convinced Rosie that we shouldn't bother you. That there was no point in telling you anyway."

Rosie's head turned, looking at me for a beat before returning to her best friend. "I'm so sorry, Lina. We should have told you. We really, really should have. But we didn't want to worry you over nothing. And I . . . well, with everything going on I forgot you were returning today so I couldn't even give you a heads-up."

Lina nodded slowly, assessing the information, looking more sad than pissed off.

I sensed Aaron's gaze on me. His eyes were narrowed, but not in a disapproving way.

"Lucas has been so great to me," Rosie murmured, taking a couple of steps forward. And when she spoke next, her voice seemed to pick up, turning steadier. "No. He's been the best. In fact, I don't know why you've been so hard on him. Because he's a kind man. Considerate, too. And he's done nothing but make me feel safe. So, no one's nuts should be kicked here. Especially not his."

Hearing Rosie say those things about me made me wish I wasn't standing in a towel in front of my inquisitive cousin and her husband. Because I wanted to wrap my arms around her and bring her to my chest. Squeeze her right into my body for what I knew would be a wildly inappropriate amount of time.

Because she'd stood up for me.

Not even I'd thought of doing that. I'd been ready to take the beating.

I swallowed, pushing down how that made me feel.

Lina's mouth parted, her body now lax in Aaron's arms. And Aaron was . . . smiling? If the barely there bent of his lips could be considered one.

It was Lina who broke the silence, and her voice was back to normal, her tone gentle and sweet. "So, you're sure you're not hooking up?"

Rosie huffed. "*Lina.* Would you just stop asking that question? We're not having sex."

"No flirting?" my cousin continued. "Intense staring? Sensual touching? Heavy petting? Kissing? French or not, both count in my book."

"*Déjalo ya*, Lina," I told her, even though she might have been onto something. I didn't have a single issue admitting to her that Rosie and I were going on experimental dates, for her book, but I'd never do that without checking in with Rosie first. Being research *partners* meant something. We were a team. "Rosie and I are friends."

And above all else, we were.

My cousin stared into her best friend's eyes for a long time, and when she finally looked at me, she said, *"Ella es mi mejor amiga. Como una hermana para mí."* She's my best friend. Like a sister to me. *"Es demasiado buena."* She's too good.

For me.

Lina hadn't said that, but I knew it followed that statement.

And I didn't disagree.

Rosie was out of my league. Women like her didn't go around with men that had lost so much, who had nothing left to offer. Men that wouldn't even stay in the country for more than a few weeks.

Lina locked eyes with me for a long moment, then pointed a finger at Rosie. "A moment." She waved it in the hallway's direction. "Alone, please."

Aaron finally released his wife, but not before kissing her temple, and murmuring, "Be good."

Rosie sent me a quick look, and I winked at her before watching her follow her best friend out, leaving Aaron and me behind.

"So . . ." I said with a sigh. "Do you think my nuts are out of the woods yet?"

His eyes jumped to the entrance door, as if he could see right through it, then back at me. "If you play your cards right."

I cocked a brow. "And by right you mean . . ."

The man crossed his arms over his chest and considered his answer. "Lina's more bark than bite." His gaze darted in the direction of his wife again, then back at me. "She loves you, Lucas. She was so excited to see you that we came here straight from the airport. Unannounced." That warmed a spot in my chest. I loved Lina, too. Of course, I did. "But I don't think I'll be able—or want—to hold her down if you hurt Rosie."

I could tell he wasn't bullshitting me. He'd probably help if I ever hurt Rosie. And I liked that, I liked knowing that people like Aaron and Lina had Rosie's back.

That was why I looked at him straight in the eye when I said, "I'd never hurt her. I could never do that."

Aaron's lips tipped up in a surprisingly bright smile. "I know."

CHAPTER SIXTEEN

Rosie

$\mathcal{L}$ina shook her head.

"What?" I whispered. "What's that exasperated look for?"

We were in our favorite café in Manhattan, hours after Lina had shown up at her apartment and learned of Lucas and my arrangement, and demanded we meet again in the evening to talk.

Not just talk. But *talk*. Away from the men.

"Don't *what* me," Lina answered, exhaling forcefully for what had to be the hundredth time. "You know what. I go on my honeymoon for a few weeks and when I come back, I find you all . . . cozy and homey with my cousin."

"You're right," I told her, because she was. "We should have told you about it from day one. I feel terrible, Lina. Awful for occupying your apartment like this without you knowing."

Lina groaned. "It's not that I'm upset about, Rosie."

The impulse to come in Lucas's defense resurfaced, but I told myself to push it down. I had officially known the man for close to three weeks, so it wasn't my place, I guessed. I'd said enough this morning. "What is it, then? What is it about Lucas and I being friends that bothers you so much?"

"I love him, okay?" She held both hands up. "Out of all my cousins, Lucas is the one I'm closest to. So, when I say I love him, I don't mean it in a 'I put up with him because he's blood' kind of way. He's like the big brother I never had. And that . . . I don't know. Maybe that's part of the issue. The idea of him getting between us and hurting you makes me want to cut his—"

"Okay." I stopped her there, before she started throwing threats around again. "First of all, no one's getting between you and me, okay? I'm serious."

She nodded.

"Now," I continued. "Why do you assume he's going to hurt me? Is that related to whatever *Lucas juju* you mentioned this morning?"

Lina shrugged. "Maybe."

"Can you explain it to me? Tell me why?"

Lina's hands draped around her coffee mug, bringing it to her lips. "Fine." She took a sip before continuing: "Lucas's superpower is making people love him, and as annoying as he was when we were kids, he *is* lovable. Sometimes. And trust me, I know he has a pantie-dropping smile, and that he's good-looking in this . . . easy way. And I also know he can be funny, too, okay?"

"Okay," I murmured. Because he was all those things. On top of the many, many other things that made me like him so much.

Lina tapped her nails on her mug. "He is all of that, and yet he's never brought a woman to a family gathering. He's never had a serious relationship. Not since . . . I don't know, high school?"

"Lorena Navarro," I was saying before I knew what I was doing. "How the heck—"

"We talk," I said quickly. "He mentioned her name."

I looked behind her, pretending I was inspecting the beautiful flowers adorning the window, because, God, I was getting so good at this "lying by omission" game I was playing. And the skill didn't feel good. I hated myself for it. But how could I tell Lina that her fear was in fact a disaster waiting to happen? That Lucas's *juju* worked, and that it worked so well, his magic was actually helping me with my book? That today, after Lina and Aaron had left I'd been *finally* writing? That a nozzle had been turned on and a stream of emotions and ideas and inspiration was starting to pour out?

Lina frowned but seemed to buy my explanation. "It's not like he's been in a place long enough for a relationship to stick. And with all those tournaments all around the world, he spends six months away and then he's back home for another six. Or just three. Or who knows. So, I guess it makes sense that he's never settled down?"

No one has ever broken his heart, he'd said.

And yet, no matter how much he traveled, it seemed like a wonder to me that no one had snatched him up so far.

"Him being here, on vacation, it's no different," Lina continued.

I thought back to last night, Lucas confiding in me about his injury. No one but me knew that his break was permanent.

I needed to be careful with my choice of words. "How is it not different?"

"Who's saying he won't use his *juju* on you? You'll giggle. He'll smirk. You two will do the nasty. He'll leave. And *boom*."

I swallowed, the thought of him leaving making me dizzy for all kinds of reasons. "And *boom*, I'll get hurt?"

"Yes, exactly. And I'll have no choice but to murder him." She blew air through her mouth. "And as I mentioned, he's kind of my favorite. And I . . . ugh, I really don't want to. Not when I'm actually worried about him."

I didn't say anything, waiting for her to continue.

Lina's mouth fell. "I think there's something wrong. Abuela told me she caught him having a panic attack. Before his trip."

My chest hurt at that. At the thought of such a solid, strong man undergoing such a thing. It made me wonder what had happened to him exactly.

Sadness coated my best friend's face when she continued. "Apparently it was Taco that went to fetch Abuela and brought her to Lucas. Thank God he had emotional support training."

"He does? I had no idea, Lucas never pos—" I stopped myself, catching my slip on time. "Lucas never said anything. Neither did you."

Lina nodded. "When Taco was a pup, he was placed with one of Abuela's neighbors, a retired policeman that suffered from PTSD. The man passed away soon after." She sighed. "Heart attack. The family was so devastated that they couldn't deal with a pup on top of everything, so Abuela offered to take care of him for a few weeks. In one of Lucas's visits, the two of them met and, well, they fell in love with each other. When weeks turned into months and the family wasn't showing any signs of wanting to take care of Taco . . . Lucas adopted him."

"So, it wasn't Lucas who named him?" I said, when in reality, this story was making me feel all kinds of new things for Lucas.

"Oh no." Lina chuckled. "That was the man's granddaughter." She shook her head. "Anyway, after the panic attack, Abuela suggested he take a trip. A change of scene to clear his head."

"And he came to the States," I concluded, and Lina nodded. I felt my throat work as I tried not to let everything I was feeling affect my voice. "I'm sure that whatever it is, Lucas will come around and tell you. He loves you guys, and maybe he just needs time to do it on his own terms." I paused. "Sometimes, when we're in pain, we need to come to the realization on our own that we need help. Before we can ever accept it."

Lina's hand reached out across the table and grabbed mine. "Ugh, you really are wise, best friend."

I wasn't. I really wasn't. But I gave her a smile and hoped she'd still love me when I told her everything that I was keeping from her about Lucas.

"Anyway." Lina waved her hand in the air. "Are you sure you don't want to come stay with Aaron and me? There's a spare room and more than enough space in his apartment. Our apartment, now."

"I'm sure," I told her confidently. The last thing I wanted was to disturb two newlyweds.

"All right. If you're sure." She shrugged, checking the time on her phone. "It's getting late, and I told Aaron I'd help him with dinner."

"Yep, let's go." I braced my hands on the table and pulled my chair back. "I should get back, too. Lucas has probably started with dinner already."

Lina tsked. "That's why you don't want to leave him for us."

I knew exactly what she was talking about, but I played dumb. "Huh?"

She cackled. "I don't blame you. Lucas is an amazing cook. He's somehow elevated Abuela's recipe book to a whole different galaxy. Tía Carmen is always trying to get him to audition for one of those cooking shows."

I smiled at the idea of Lucas on TV. God, he'd win the damn thing and everyone's hearts in a heartbeat.

"Oh." She caught my attention with a waving hand. "Before I forget. Do you have plans for Halloween?"

I grabbed my jacket from the back of my chair. "You know I don't."

Lina joined me at the side of the table, her lips twitching with a devious smile. "Well, you might now." She grabbed her own jacket and slipped her arms in. "Aaron was invited to a—brace yourself— Masquerade Ball. Next Saturday."

My eyebrows shot up my forehead. "Fancy."

"It's really a costume party, but you New Yorkers have a sexy name for everything. Anyway, it's one of the charity things he gets invited to every year, but never attends. You know Aaron."

"Yeah, I can imagine how dressing up is not his thing." Or socializing, in general. "But I'm guessing Aaron is going to RSVP yes to this one? For you?"

"And it barely took any convincing," Lina bragged, a glint in her eyes. "My husband is kind of the best."

Her face brightened. Just like it always did when she talked about him.

That sharp bite of longing returned. It was quick but threw me off balance all the same.

Unaware, Lina continued, "The organizing committee was so happy he was attending, that they sent him two extra invitations."

Oh. "I don't know, sweetie. I'm—"

"You're under a deadline, I know." Lina seemed to consider something. "Did you re-download Tinder? Like I suggested?"

The tips of my ears turned warm. "No, I didn't. I somehow found a different . . . method. It's a long story that I can tell you tomorrow because we're in . . . er . . . a rush now."

She looked skeptical. "Is it working?"

"Yes," I confirmed without thinking. Because it was. It *so* was.

"Then," Lina pointed out with a smile, "maybe you can afford to take this one night off? Have a little Halloween fun? Fun is good for the mind."

We started for the exit of the café, and I heard myself say, "You have two tickets, right?"

Lina sighed. "Does that mean you want to bring my cousin?"

I pinned her down with a hard look.

"Are you sure you two are not . . . *doing smoochies*? You know you can tell me if you are, right? Even after everything I told you, and even if he's my cousin and that would be a very gross conversation."

"We're not," I quipped. "And where are you learning all these expressions and euphemisms? They're either old-school or . . . weird."

"I have my ways." She shrugged. And before getting to the door, she gave me one last glance. "So, Lucas and you are not an item. Right?"

"No," I answered as casually as I could. "That's never been in the cards for us, Lina."

The first thing I noticed as I walked into the apartment were the two women fussing over Lucas at the stove.

"Hello . . . everyone?" I greeted the room, getting three head turns—Lucas, our neighbor Adele, and her daughter, Alexia. "This is a surprise. A good one."

"You're back," Lucas said. "Finally."

Ugh. That *finally* made me feel so . . . hopeful, that it almost distracted me from the confident way he strolled in my direction.

When he reached me, he leaned down slightly and said just for my ears, "We have company, as you see. I hope that's okay."

"Of course," I answered, taking notice of how close he was standing. How he towered over me. I swallowed. "Adele is always welcome, you know that."

His brows furrowed momentarily. "Did my cousin give you a hard time?"

I shook my head. "No, she's just . . ." Worried. About me, about you, too. "She means well but the whole thing caught her by surprise. I set her straight, and I didn't . . . I didn't really tell her about the experiment."

I couldn't bring myself to say dates. Lucas seemed to notice my hesitation, because a thoughtful expression dimmed the lightness in his eyes.

I watched his gaze trail down my body in almost an absent-minded way, as if he wasn't aware of what he was doing.

"All right," he said, grabbing the grocery bag I had forgotten I had in my hand. "You're just in time. I needed to throw these in the pan right now."

Oh.

That was why he was looking down. That was where the *finally* came from.

He'd texted me to get some parsley and fresh red chili peppers if I had the chance. He'd been waiting for the ingredients. Not for me.

And that was okay. I didn't have a reason to be disappointed. I—

Lucas brushed a quick kiss on my cheek, my thoughts coming to a halt at the contact. "Thanks for picking these up," he said. "Now, come on, dinner will be ready in a minute."

One moment his lips had been touching my skin, right there, barely an inch from my mouth, and the next, he was striding away leaving me . . . dumbfounded.

Because he had kissed me. On the cheek.

As friends, I reminded myself. Because in Spain, friends kissed friends on the cheek all the time. Roommates did, too, when friendly.

Trying really hard to ignore the way that tiny patch of skin still tingled, I followed him to the island to chat with the women. "Hi, guys, how are you doing?"

"Hi, Rosie," Alexia greeted me with eyes that were like her mother's. "We're doing okay. *Now*."

Adele ignored her daughter's sideways glance. "This young man here is cooking dinner for us." She looked over at Lucas, who was back at the stove. "He said he knows what he's doing and made me promise I'd sit down and stop nagging him about everything."

"Which you didn't," her daughter muttered, placing both hands on Adele's shoulders and ushering her to a stool. "So, how about you stop hovering around us like an opinionated fly and get off your feet, huh?"

Adele mumbled but took a seat, and a satisfied Alexia returned to Lucas's side, seemingly engrossed by my roommate's cooking.

The first time I'd met her, I hadn't been able to get a good look at her. Mostly because I'd been standing on the kitchen counter, terrified out of my mind by the rat. Also distracted by the fact I had just been dancing with Lucas—had been in his arms minutes before Alexia had knocked. But now, I noticed that she was in her early fifties, making Adele a little older than I'd initially thought.

Lucas looked at me over his shoulder and said, "Have a seat, Ro."

Ro.

That nickname, again. Doing silly, silly things to me.

"I'm okay," I replied, keeping the effect in check as best as I could.

"I'm sure you are. But it'll be good for your back. I've seen how tense those shoulders are from writing all day." He followed that with a quick wink, leaving me no choice but to obey before I fell on my ass.

I've seen how tense those shoulders are.

I took the only other stool left in the kitchen and sat next to Adele.

"Good," he muttered before returning to the pan at the stove. "Okay, ladies, a few more minutes and this will be ready."

A happy sigh left all of us at the same time.

I laughed and when I looked in Lucas's direction, I caught Alexia's eyes on me, holding back a smile. "You're a lucky girl, Rosie."

My puzzled expression must have given away my total confusion because she explained, "Men like Lucas are hard to find."

I started nodding but stopped myself quickly. "Oh no. We're just friends. We're not together. Just roommates. *Friends.*"

Alexia's brows rose, and her eyes bounced to Lucas, who said in a confident voice, "Best friends, soon enough."

"You keep saying that," I murmured. "But either way, us living here is all temporary. I'll return to my apartment and he'll . . ." I trailed off, having a little trouble finishing that, "go back home. To Spain."

Lucas's motions seemed to come to a stop for a moment before he resumed chopping parsley.

Alexia nodded. "Too bad, really. We could use a man like him around." She sighed. "The way he all but ran to Mom's rescue . . . He really is a true hero."

"What rescue?" I asked. "Did anything—"

"I was barely rattled, dear." The old woman pursed her lips. "No need to fuss."

"My mother here," Alexia remarked, "left a pressure cooker sitting on the stove and went to take a thirty-minute bubble bath."

Adele exhaled loudly. "The thing was malfunctioning. And the long baths are good for my bones."

"Lucas must have heard the explosion," Alexia explained, ignoring her mother. "Because when I got here to bring Mom her prescriptions, I found him scraping stew off the walls with Mom."

"It was a small explosion," Lucas finally said. "And it was no problem."

"See?" Alexia laughed. "He won't even take the credit. And believe me, that was a lot of cleaning. It was splattered all over the place." She shook her head. "Guys like him . . ."

"Are very rare to find," I finished for her.

Lucas's motions halted again, making me wish he wasn't facing away and I could see his face.

Something occurred to me. "So that's why you guys are over for dinner?" Not only had Lucas gone to Adele's rescue and helped with the cleaning but he'd offered to feed them afterward.

"Yes." Alexia beamed. "We both were a little rattled after that. My wife will pick us up in an hour, though," Alexia added. "Mom will come to stay with us for a few days, right, Mom?"

Adele sighed. "Not like I have a choice anyway."

"Anyway," Alexia said, angling her body in Lucas's direction. "I have to admit that I've been driving myself crazy trying to figure out what apartment all these rich and distinctive scents came from every evening I've visited Mom. Most people do takeout around here."

Lucas stepped back, turned off the stove, wrapped a cloth over the handle of a large cast-iron pan, and lifted it in the air.

"It was all Lucas, yes," I said, not wanting her to get any ideas about my cooking talents.

He walked to the island, where Adele and I were, and placed the pan between us. Seared steaks dressed with red chimichurri glistened under the kitchen light, making my stomach growl.

Alexia joined us at the table, and with only two stools available, I jumped off mine and offered it to her. "Please, sit. You're a guest."

"Oh, I wouldn't want to—"

"Rosie can sit with me," Lucas announced.

Frowning, I turned around and found him holding a folding stool in his hand. "Where—"

"Found it behind a cabinet," he said, unfolding its legs. "Just the one, so we'll share it."

"I don't know . . ." I eyed him as he flopped down.

I couldn't sit in his lap, could I? He had an injury I didn't know the extent of.

As if he had a way to peek into my head, he gave two firm pats to his left thigh. "This one's fine," he said. "Now come here, Ro. Let's eat, I'm starving."

It was the determination in his gaze that pushed me forward. The way he looked at me like I'd be doing something for him if I gave him this one thing. So, I walked all the way to where he was and I let myself fall on his lap. In a nanosecond, Lucas wrapped a strong arm around my waist and squeezed lightly. "Cronut you," he said, so low I almost missed it.

And that code for thank you that was just ours, did something to me, something powerful and not at all expected. Something that made me wish it was code for something other than thank you.

I tried to focus on the amazing food laid out in front of us instead of on the man whose lap I was currently sitting on. "This all looks incredible, Lucas."

I felt more than heard his sigh of relief, right there, very close to my ear. And my body immediately reacted to the contact of his breath against my skin. So much that he probably felt it because he told me, "Eat."

"Oh Lord, these sweet potatoes." Alexia moaned. "What's this sauce? Yogurt with . . ."

"Roasted garlic, lemon, and tahini," Lucas answered as he drizzled some of the sauce Alexia was praising over my potatoes.

Alexia stoked her mouth with a new bite. "You roasted the whole head with the potatoes. Then used it for the sauce?" Lucas nodded and she added, "Well played."

And just like that, Alexia took over the conversation, interrogating Lucas about each and every step he had followed with the searing of the meat, the red chimichurri, and what I'd discovered was our dessert: rhubarb and pear *milhojas*. Which happened to be an absolutely delicious twist on a Spanish dessert.

"Okay," Alexia said once all the food was gone and the dessert plates were wiped clean. "I suspected you knew what you were doing, but I had no idea you were this good."

Lucas answered with a grunt and a shift of his body that brought me further into his lap. I tried to shift away, but his arm secured me against his chest, every part of me that was in contact with every part of him coming alive.

"So, what's your deal, Lucas?" Alexia pressed, while I tried to catch my breath. "You work at a restaurant back in Spain? Attending cooking school by any chance?"

Lucas let out an incredulous laugh. "None of that. I never considered cooking school. Never had . . . the time, I guess."

"You could go, now. If that's what you wanted," I said, not able to help myself. "You're an amazing cook, Lucas."

His hand tightened on my waist, his body heat now impossible to ignore. His tone softened when he told me, "Thank you, Ro. But . . . I don't know. I'm a little old for school."

"You're not too old." Alexia's eyes narrowed. "Where did you learn to cook like this? The all-butter flaky pastry from the *milhojas* was divine and definitely not store bought. And that wasn't your first time prepping a sirloin. I've seen sirloins being *assassinated* by people who attended school."

Lucas's palm fell on my thigh, making me catch my breath. "I learned from my *abuela*, my mother . . . I don't know, everywhere. I'm self-taught, I guess. I like to experiment, try new things. There's a wild amount of information online. So, I just . . . you know, learned on the go. Nothing fancy or worth comparing to someone with an education. Or someone with any real talent. My call is—*was* something else."

I disagreed, Lucas wasn't defined by one single thing, but I remained quiet and let my hand fall on top of his. He twined his fingers with mine, and I swore all my nerve endings flared at that simple contact.

Which was why I almost missed Alexia's next words.

"I'm the executive chef of Zarato, so I know what I'm talking about. You *are* talented. Cooking school wouldn't be a walk in the park, because it never is. But it's not out of your reach."

"Oh, whoa," I breathed out. Turning to look at Lucas over my shoulder, I explained, "Zarato is *the* hotspot in the West Village. People wait months to get a reservation. I think it's in the top three restaurants in New York right now."

Alexia chuckled. "Top five, but the competition is savage in Manhattan, so you never know where you'll drop down to when the next year rolls."

She was being humble. If even I—someone who didn't know a thing about cuisine and only dined out on occasion—had heard of and longed to live *the Zarato experience*, that meant the buzz around the place was as strong as it could get.

"That's truly amazing," Lucas said, and I could hear in his voice that he meant every word. He turned to Adele. "You must be so proud of your daughter."

"I couldn't be any prouder," Adele answered, her eyes watering. "But you know that don't you, Mateo?"

A silence settled around us at Adele's words, who had remained quiet during dinner, the atmosphere immediately turning heavy with the reminder of Adele's looming illness.

"Yeah," Lucas finally said. "Of course, we are."

Alexia threw an arm around her mom, squeezed her shoulders, and mouthed a *thank you* at Lucas. Then, she said more firmly, "And Lucas, I'm serious. I know how to spot talent. That's how I met my wife. She started low in the kitchen, all raw potential, and now she's the sous chef at Zarato, so you never know." She tilted her head. "You know, I think you two should come. It'll be on the house, for everything you've done."

Oh, oh wow.

"You don't have to, Alexia," Lucas answered, voicing my thoughts. Although I could hear a spark of curiosity in his words. "It's really okay."

"I insist," she answered firmly. Then, she pulled out a card from her bag, placed it on the table, and added, "Rosie will love it." As if that fact changed something.

And Lucas's hand left mine and reached out for the card.

It was much, much later, well into the night, when a noise woke me. It was like a whimper, but deeper. Guttural.

At first, I thought I was dreaming, but then, the sound came again. That time louder. More urgent.

I sat up in bed, surveying the dimly lit space, stopping where I knew Lucas would be asleep on the couch. Only he wasn't. He couldn't be sleeping, shifting so restlessly.

Another whimper left him, now tangling with his rocky breathing, and it froze me on the spot. Because it sounded like . . . like he was struggling to get air into his lungs. Like he couldn't breathe.

Icy fear propelled me off the bed and forward. Until I was kneeling on the floor by the couch.

I whispered, "Lucas?" But Lucas thrashed from one side to the other as my hands reached out to his shoulders. I rose my voice to a gentle but firm tone. "Lucas, wake up."

He muttered something, but it must have been in Spanish, because it was something I didn't understand.

With all the gentleness I could muster, I trailed my hands up, all the way to his cheeks. "Lucas, please. You need to wake up. You're having a nightmare."

His jerky motions came to a sudden stop, and his eyes blinked wide open, revealing two brown wells of fear.

My chest constricted at the sight, finding it hard to put up a calm front for him, and even harder not to think about how much I cared for him and how much I hated seeing him in pain.

"You were having a bad dream," I told him, the nerves creeping into my voice. "But it's all right, now. You're awake."

His gaze started clearing very, very, slowly. But the fear, the despair, was still there. Etched into his expression.

My grip on his face grew a little desperate. "You're fine. It was a bad dream, but you're okay," I repeated.

Lucas's palm fell on top of my hand. His skin was cool, damp.

"Rosie," he breathed out. "You're here." No explanation, no smile, no attempt to brush it away with a joke.

"Scoot over," I told him, so I could climb on the couch with him.

Without a word Lucas moved as much as he could while remaining on his back. I lay down, facing him, tucking myself into his side. I locked one of my arms around him. His shirt stuck to his chest.

"I'm all sweaty, Rosie. I—"

"It's all right," I said, scooting even closer and letting my fingers draw soothing circles over his chest. "I like my men sweaty and sleepy," I told him. "So go back to sleep. I'm here now."

Lucas didn't say a word, didn't move a muscle. He didn't even try to squeeze me against his body, like he had done so many times before. And that was okay. Because right now, he was the one who needed me. So I stayed right where I was. My body hanging on the very edge of the couch as I warmed his body with mine. My touch and voice somehow soothing him back to sleep.

Only when his breath fell into a slow rhythm, did I relax. But I stayed awake for a long time. Thinking, keeping watch, I recalled my conversation with Lina. Lucas, always on his own, isolating himself now, not confiding in anyone. I thought about how he always gave away his smiles so selflessly. About how much he had given me in the short amount of time we'd known each other. And as I held him, I couldn't help but wonder if someone had ever done the same for him.

CHAPTER SEVENTEEN

Rosie

I was applying the last touch of powder when the doorbell rang.

Frowning at the mirror, I placed the brush on the surface of the vanity and had a quick look at my reflection.

My curls were falling in an orderly manner that had taken me a full hour—and five different YouTube tutorials—to accomplish. My lips were a pale shade of pink and I'd done my eyes in natural tones, achieving an almost no-makeup look. I looked good. I knew that. I wasn't a fashion or lifestyle influencer by any means, but I usually took care of what I wore, of how I looked. Except for my hair. That, I always neglected. Let it fall in a disarray of waves.

But not today. Not tonight. Because we were going to a party. The Masquerade Ball. And if the butterflies in my stomach were any indication, I was as excited about it as I was anxious.

Good nerves, bad nerves, I wasn't sure.

I didn't know what to expect, really. Because this felt a lot like a double date, only it wasn't one. When I'd told Lucas about the Masquerade Ball, he'd just said he was in and we'd started talking about costume ideas. Couple-costume ideas, although we were going as friends. Just friends, not even experiment partners, considering Aaron and Lina would be there.

Which reminded me that they would be picking us up soon and Lucas wasn't home yet. Two hours ago, when I'd pulled my costume out of the closet, he'd said he had to pick up a last-minute thing and vanished.

The bell rang again, getting me out of my head.

I raced across the apartment, the swoosh of the fabric of the Victorian-inspired ball gown I was wearing chasing every one of my steps.

In a rush, I threw the door open and— Whoa.

My eyes widened with a mix of emotions. Surprise, awe, and . . . lust.

Yes, most definitely, lust.

"*Lucas.*" My gaze leaped up and down, my head scrambling for something to say as a powerful rush of heat climbed up my body. I somehow managed to croak out, "*Wow.* You look so, so, so, so good."

He stood there in his Victorian velvety tailcoat jacket and burgundy vest, unbothered by my ogling and the *so, so, so, so good* I had just blurted. His hair was combed back and his sun-kissed face on full display, making his handsome features demand more attention than ever.

And *my* attention was definitely happy to comply.

He snickered. "You like?"

"Yes." *So, so, so, so much*, I thought. Because one single *so* would have not sufficed. "You look one hundred percent amazing. No, one hundred and twenty percent because you . . . you've broken the scale."

He laughed again, and I had to clamp my mouth down to keep myself from exposing myself anymore.

Granted, I was exhausted from working on my manuscript all day. Which was good, amazing, really. Today, inspiration had hit like it hadn't in . . . heck, I didn't even know. Probably ever.

I couldn't remember writing ever feeling this way, as I imagined riding a wave would feel. Wild, freeing, unpredictable. Just like I felt with Lucas.

"Your dress," Lucas said, all humor gone from his voice. "It's beautiful. It matches the color of your eyes."

He let his gaze roam up and down my body, just like mine had done a moment ago. Intentionally checking me out. And I . . . liked it. Loved it. Seeing that profound appreciation on his face was making me feel all kinds of things. Fluttering things. Warm and fizzy things. Things I should keep under check for my own good.

Collecting myself, I swooshed from left to right and repeated his words to him. "You like?"

His lips parted with a wide, wicked grin, revealing the pointy ends of prosthetic fangs, and it was hard not to smile back.

"Like it?" He shook his head. "You look incredible, Rosie." His smile dimmed, that intensity of his that I didn't know what to do with showing on his face. *"Estás preciosa."*

Preciosa.

I didn't need to know what that meant exactly, not when he was looking at me the way he did, making that flutter intensify. Multiply. So much that I'd never know how I stood there and took the compliment with a straight face when all I wanted was to swoon straight into his arms.

"You clean up pretty well as a Victorian vampire," I managed to say after a few seconds. "You're giving the protagonist of our show a run for his money." *And I'd take you over him any day of the week*, I wanted to add.

But Lucas didn't smile like before, he only hummed in response, all that intensity still there.

In an attempt to appear unaffected by that and by the way those chocolate eyes were staring right into mine, I averted my gaze to his chest. I spotted a button that had come undone in the visible section of his vest and reached out for it. I let my fingers make a work of it, the warmth of his chest seeping through the layers of fabric, making me clumsy and my breathing choppy. "Where did you find these clothes?" I asked in a quieter voice than I'd intended. "They look exactly like the ones from the show."

Because we were going as our favorite vampire couple, but the version of them from one of the flashback episodes in Victorian times.

Lucas's head tipped down, watching my hands as they remained latched onto that button. He stepped forward, bringing us closer. "I had a little help," he answered, and I could feel his breath on my skin. "And by little, I mean my feisty 5'4" cousin."

My fingers were fidgeting with the button that was now done, searching for an excuse to remain there, on his chest. "She's not that feisty. Or short," my loyalty pushed me to say. "She's cute."

"I think you're cute," Lucas said, making my fingers freeze. He expelled one slow pull of air. "No. You're not cute. You're beautiful."

I swallowed, wanting to beg him to take back the words as much as I needed him to repeat them again so I'd never forget them.

But what I said was, "You're ready now." And I brushed my fingertips over the fabric of his vest for what I'd promised myself would be one last touch.

Before I could sever the contact, though, Lucas took another step forward, bringing us even closer. Flushed. My hands adjusted to the new position, the new nearness, my palms now flat against his chest. "I don't know about that," he said, voice husky, deep, distracting. "There might be other buttons needing your attention. You've done such an amazing job with that one, I want to make sure."

I looked up, finally meeting his gaze and finding the version of Lucas that had smeared tomato sauce all over my bottom lip staring back at me. My heart leaped, my whole body taking notice of the way his chest moved and of the intensity in his eyes. Of how stern and determined his features turned when he looked at me like this. As if all the amusement and lightheartedness had left him.

He remained exactly where he was, waiting, but what was I supposed to do? Ask him to undo all his clothes so I had an excuse to secure them back around his solid and beautiful body?

Yes, a voice encouraged me. *That would be a good start.*

"I . . . I think I got them all," I said instead, because anything else would be crazy. Stupid. Reckless.

The tip of his tongue peeked out and swiped over his bottom lip before he said, "Okay."

"Okay," I repeated.

And all too soon, he was stepping back and opening the space between our bodies. "Before we go," he said walking backward, disappearing down the hallway for a moment and returning holding something behind his back. "This is for you."

He revealed what he was hiding and my jaw dropped to the floor, joined by my heart less than a millisecond later.

"For— For me," I stuttered, looking at the stunning corsage of pink magnolias in his hands. A corsage I'd never gotten from Jake during prom night. Like I'd told him. And he'd remembered. "Lucas you didn't have to. This isn't one of our—" I caught myself before I said dates. *One of our dates.* "Tonight isn't supposed to be part of our research."

"It doesn't matter," he said matter-of-factly, and I wanted to ask him, *How?* How could this not matter to him when it did to me? But he continued before I could: "I know I didn't plan this date, so it technically isn't one. But after how the last one ended, how I couldn't even properly feed you dinner, I thought I could take the chance to make it up to you. Consider it part of phase two. Exploring the spark."

So this was nothing more than research.

"That's why you were away?" I asked, taking the arrangement from him and bringing it to my chest. "You were out getting me a corsage?"

"Yes." He gave me a small bashful smile, and despite everything, it was really freaking hard for me not to fall a little bit more for this man. God, I was doing that, wasn't I? Falling for him. "I wanted to surprise you. And also, I knew you'd be changing and wanted to be sure not to catch you running around in your *undergarments*, Lady Rosalyn. There are lines that mustn't be crossed."

I nodded, disappointment flooding my stomach. "Yeah. I guess you wouldn't want that."

Lucas tilted his head. "What do you mean?"

I shook my head with a weak smile. "Nothing."

Before I could even register him moving, Lucas crowded me against the doorframe and tipped my chin up. I had no choice but to meet his gaze, and when I did, I wished I hadn't. Because there was something in his eyes I didn't understand.

His thumb grazed along my jaw very softly. "What did you mean, Rosie?"

I shook my head a little. "I just mean that as my friend and my roommate, that's something you don't want to see." Because that was all we were. Our experimental dates were research, and Lucas was just trying to help me. Until he went back to Spain.

He stared, his eyes looking straight into mine, while he seemed to work out something in his head. And when his lips finally parted, he could only say, "Tonight—" before he was interrupted.

"What's taking you two so long?" Lina's voice thundered in the empty hallway before she even made it upstairs. "I can hear you up there and we're double-parked."

"Later," Lucas said in a low voice. Just for my ears.

Reluctantly, he peeled himself off me, as if he was not looking forward to facing what was a few feet behind him.

Lina appeared in front of us.

"Hola, prima," he greeted his cousin with a sigh. "We were just coming down."

She eyed the situation in silence for a long moment. "You look amazing, Rosie. And are those magnolias? They are beautiful," she told me. "Where did you get them?"

Lucas said something in Spanish, too quick and complex for me to try to understand.

Lina's eyes narrowed when she replied.

And before I could ask or open my mouth to say anything about that exchange, Lucas was tugging at one of my perfect curls. He looked down at me with a grin that didn't reach his eyes. "Let's grab your fangs and go, Ro."

"Yes," I conceded, glancing down at the corsage.

Lucas went into the bathroom to fetch the prosthetic teeth for me as I fastened around my wrist the pink magnolias he had gotten me for no reason other than research.

Because he was set on helping me.

And I should have been happy and grateful for it.

It shouldn't have made me sad.

"Holy shit," Lucas said from my side.

"Holy shit indeed," I muttered, picking up my jaw from the floor.

Lina stood in front of us, partly blocking our view of the impressive hall where the Masquerade Ball was taking place. She wasn't exactly tall, not even in heels, but her blueish-tinged hair and matching body paint covering her face, neck, and arms was distracting enough.

Lina and Aaron were going as corpse bride and groom, a job she had taken to heart. The costumes were the closest I'd ever seen to the real thing. Even Aaron was wearing makeup, his eye sockets covered in smoky black shadow, making his blue eyes pop even more than usual. That, together with his height, the two-piece suit, and the undead bride hanging off his arm, was a powerful image.

They looked like the power couple of the underworld. Unlike Lucas and I, we were most definitely *not* a couple, despite the matching costumes. Not that it mattered. One glance at our reflection in the elevator's mirror had almost knocked me straight to the floor all the same. Especially after we'd put on the beautiful masks Lina had surprised us with. *For the flex*, she'd said with a wink, unaware that the addition made Lucas all the more . . . distracting for me.

"Don't you guys love everything?" Lina beamed before turning around to take in the venue. "I'm going to sound super uncool but do you think we will spot any celebrities?"

"It's possible," Aaron answered. "This is New York, and all kinds of personalities get invited."

Lina clapped her hands under her chin. "I'm still hoping for Sebastian Stan."

Aaron mumbled something unintelligible under his breath.

I chuckled. "Oh, I wouldn't mind that. Not at all."

Lucas shifted somewhere to my right, and when I looked at him, he was frowning. "Who is that? This . . . *Sebastian Spoon*?"

Lina waved a hand in front of her. "*Sebastian S-tan*. And he's only the funniest, cutest, most charming actor in Hollywood? Totally underrated."

Nodding my head, I added, "He's been spotted in New York enough for Lina to believe that one day we'll cross paths with him."

Lucas shrugged. "Well, I hope *Sebastian Stong* doesn't mind bumping into stalkers."

Aaron snorted, which earned him a glare from his wife.

"Stop butchering his name, Lucas," she said before patting Aaron's chest. "And you don't have any reason to be jealous, *amor*. I want to meet Seb, but just so Rosie can keep him."

Aaron threw an arm around her wife's shoulders, fusing her to his side.

I looked over at Lucas, finding his gaze on me. I thought he'd say something else about the topic, or butcher Sebastian's name again, but he only winked at me. Smug, as if he knew how good he looked, winking in that costume and that mask. And dammit, all thoughts of maybe spotting Seb or any other celebrity vanished from my mind with a puff.

I stepped forward to Lina and Aaron's side and Lina untangled herself from her husband with a kiss on his cheek, linking our arms and walking into the party, leaving the two men behind.

After crossing the more dimly lit dance floor, we made it to the opposite end of the venue and took a spot at the bar, where the guys rejoined us.

"I think we might be a little early," Lina said, looking around us and pointing at the few and scattered groups of people that had gathered. "What time did it say on the invitation, Aaron?"

His arm came around her waist, his palm settling on her stomach. "Eight. People will come. Don't worry. This is one of the most popular events of the year. Only the bachelor auction beats it."

"Oh, I definitely remember that one."

"I do, too." Aaron's head inched even lower and he pressed his lips to her shoulder, turning my best friend into a Lina-shaped puddle of blue goo.

My face must have been showcasing every single one of my emotions—happiness, longing, that pang of good-hearted but sharp jealousy—because one of my curls was tugged by the man that was learning to read me like an open book.

I turned, finding Lucas a little closer to my side than he was a minute ago. "I'd love to have a drink," he said, looking down at me. "What about you, Lady Rosalyn? Would you care for a beverage?" He flashed me his prosthetic fangs. "Perhaps some O-Negative?"

I could not help but laugh, so I did. "With pleasure, Good Sir. But make it blood-free." I wrinkled my nose. "Only the thought is making me dizzy."

Lucas's lips twitched and he nudged my shoulder with his, his expression brightening his eyes.

After that, we ordered those drinks and hung out in our little circle, chatting animatedly while the place filled with more and more people.

And with every minute that ticked away and every newcomer arriving to the party, my side inched closer and closer to Lucas. So much that without knowing how, I was leaning my shoulder on his. And it felt good. The easy chatter, the way his arm felt against mine, our inside jokes, the times I'd see his gaze dipping down to meet mine, or the way he'd ask me if I was having fun. It all felt so goddamn good.

It felt exactly as if we were on a double date with my best friend and her husband.

Comfortable. Exciting. *Real.*

CHAPTER EIGHTEEN

Lucas

*A*aron had been right, this *was* a popular event.

It was hard to take a step without bumping against someone. The place was bursting with people. People, I assumed, who moved in social circles I knew nothing about. People who attended masquerade balls in impressive halls of hotels I'd never consider booking a night in. Not because I couldn't but because it wasn't my choice.

I wasn't used to being in crowds like this one. Or *any* crowds, unless we counted the folks attending a tournament or a competition. But I had to admit that I wasn't as uncomfortable as I'd anticipated. And sure, it had to do with tonight being Halloween. But it also had a lot to do with the girl pressing her shoulder against my arm. I was here for her.

And if it was up to me, I'd have her tucked into my side, much like Aaron had Lina. Not because I wanted to—which, don't get me wrong, I did—but because the free space around us was starting to run out. And the crowd was starting to get tipsy, and therefore, careless.

I hadn't liked it when some zombie pushed us from behind, and I hadn't liked it any better when it was some superhero I didn't know. At this rate, our drinks were at risk of being knocked out of our hands, Rosie might get hurt, and I might have to punch some drunk idiot in a mask.

Checking on Rosie's glass to see if she was done with her drink, it was physically impossible to stop my eyes from wandering around. All the way up to her face. Down her neck again. Hopelessly dipping back to her neckline.

It wasn't the first time I'd done it tonight, and it probably wouldn't be the last. I seemed unable to help myself.

Not when the swells of her breasts were pressing against the neckline of her dress in a way that made my blood swirl and flow to certain areas of my body that were starting to feel a little tight against my clothing. I was only a man. And I could only take so much when that soft-looking skin on display was making me think thoughts not appropriate for the current venue. Or company.

"You okay?" Lina asked, forcing my eyes away from Rosie. Lina tilted her head. "You look . . . weird. Are you hungry or something?"

I schooled my face into the easiest smile I could summon. "I'm always hungry." Out of the corner of my eye, I saw Rosie snickering. "Other than that, I'm okay. *Gracias, prima.*"

As if on cue, someone bumped into me and Rosie from behind. Again. Probably someone else trying to place an order at the busy and slightly chaotic bar.

With a curse, I finally stepped to the side and parked myself behind Rosie. Then, I snaked an arm around her side and leaned my elbow on the bar top, creating a wall behind her.

Rosie moved her head, her hair swaying with her scent.

Damn, those peaches were starting to drive me a little crazy.

It made me want to dip my head and place my nose at her neck. Take a good, honest whiff, as if I were nothing more than an animal. Like the unsophisticated man I was.

Aaron met my gaze and nodded his head with approval. Wondering what he could be approving of exactly, I returned it.

"Thank you, Lucas," Rosie said, her voice drawing my attention back to her. Those green eyes of her were dancing with warmth, with the awareness I was feeling, too. "You don't really have to, you know, protect me or something. But I appreciate it."

I don't really have to?

Dios.

I had told her once how much I hated how low she set her standards, and I'd meant every word. It infuriated me that someone who brought to life romance heroes, love stories people longed for, wouldn't expect all those things from real life. Because she really seemed fine not expecting any man to live up to her heroes. She was fine with it.

"There's nothing you should thank me for," I told her, stepping a little closer to her body because I just couldn't keep myself in line. My gaze trailed down again in time to watch her swallow, and that slow motion of her throat, and the way her breasts followed with her next breath, was enough to make me twitch in my pants. Jesus. Some friend I was. "I'm happy to protect you, Lady Rosalyn."

Rosie didn't answer, and when I met her gaze again, her eyes were . . . different. Surprised, hooded. Probably mirroring my own.

"How about dancing?" Lina suggested with bubbly enthusiasm, breaking the spell. "I think we've hung out here long enough."

Aaron remained silent. Rosie hesitated. And I . . . shrugged. My leg was sore after standing for so long, but I'd follow them to the dance floor if that was the plan.

"Come on," Lina insisted.

But before any of us could answer, someone else pushed into me, forcing my front to come into full contact with Rosie's back. Without thinking, my arm snaked around her just as I felt her ass press against my crotch. A new shot of awareness sparked across my body, making my dick stand to attention.

"Yes!" Rosie yelped. "Let's dance!"

Without giving me or Aaron any choice, the women linked arms and walked into the moving crowd.

Aaron shot me a glance, and whatever he saw in my face made him chuckle.

"What's so funny?" I asked him, summoning a casual expression.

His eyes scanned the sea of people in front of us and zeroed in on a point I assumed was his wife. "You didn't have to say anything," he said, gaze forward. "You know, it doesn't get easier. But it does get better."

I forced out a laugh, pretending I knew whatever he was talking about.

But you know what he meant, a voice countered. *Although it won't ever get better. Because she's not yours. And you are leaving anyway.*

With a shake of my head and one of Aaron's nods, we ventured onto the dance floor.

The women were dancing, doing their thing while lost to the song, spinning in circles with their arms up. It reminded me of the Rosie I'd seen swirling to "Dancing Queen." A smile parted my face at the memory, at the sight. In fact, I was pretty sure I was eating up every one of her motions in blinding awe, as if the sun was rising in front of me for the first time.

A strange thought infiltrated my mind. Rosie, straddling my board, floating in the ocean. Her wet hair sticking to her skin, a smile on her face. I'd love to take her, teach her to paddle, catch her first wave, hear her laugh over the sound of the waves. All things I couldn't do.

Rosie's eyes found mine, and whatever was on my face made her lips fall, her expression turning serious. Concerned. She immediately strode in my direction, and while I didn't want to ruin her fun, I was glad to see her closing the distance. Coming to me.

When she stopped in front of me, she was standing close enough for me to catch another whiff of peaches. Of her.

She went on her tiptoes so I could hear her over the music. "You're not dancing. Is your leg bothering you?"

Lina and Aaron were several feet away now—bodies fused together—getting swallowed by the colorful crowd.

Maybe that was why I felt free to say the truth. "I was too distracted to do any of that. Watching you."

The green in Rosie's eyes deepened. "Watching me?"

I nodded my head slowly, everything in me screaming to lean down. To dip my head and get close to her ear. To place my lips against the delicate skin there and feel her squirm with awareness. "It's really hard not to stare, Rosie. You make it hard."

Her lips parted, but before she could say anything, she was pushed into my chest. Forcefully.

Rosie gasped as my arms draped around her, holding her to my chest, my hands immediately feeling the liquid running down her back.

"This really has to stop," I gritted under my breath. "*¿Qué cojones le pasa a esta gente?*"

Because seriously, what the hell was wrong with everyone at this goddamn party?

I looked up, finding some person dressed like a . . . Chewbacca? He turned around and took his hairy head off and tucked it under his arm. "I'm so sorry. I didn't see you there, sweetheart."

Ignoring the way he eyed Rosie and that *sweetheart* he'd let drop like there hadn't been a man—*me*—holding her, I looked down at Rosie. "You okay, Ro?"

"Yes." She nodded quickly, not moving out of my embrace. "But I'm completely covered in whatever he'd been drinking."

She was. And from the way the fabric of her dress felt between my fingers, I could tell just how much.

Chewbacca stepped closer to us. "Please, let me take care of the dry-cleaning bill." He shoved a business card in Rosie's face, then added, "My number is there. You can give me a call. Or let me get you a drink, I'll make it up to—"

"It's okay, really." Rosie cut him off, not accepting it. "No need for any of that."

Good, now scatter, an illogical and basic part of me wanted to say.

"You sure?" Chewbacca insisted. "Not even the drink?"

"I'm sure." She gave the man a polite smile, leaning more into me. "But thank you."

Chewbacca stared at her for a beat longer than necessary, as if he'd been waiting for her to change her mind.

I frowned, holding myself back from barking something at this guy because one, I had no right to. And two, Rosie had handled herself fine without me.

So instead, I threw an arm around her shoulders like I'd been dying to do the whole night. Too damn bad it had to be now that she was drenched, and I was a little pissed.

"Let's get you dry. The bathrooms must be somewhere close. I'll help you clean up."

Treading the swarm of dancing creatures, superheroes, and more than a fair share of pop culture references I didn't get, we finally found the restrooms.

Rosie untangled herself from me, leaving me behind.

Choosing to ignore etiquette, or society rules in general, I followed her in, and the moment she caught my reflection in the mirror, she came to a halt. "Lucas, what are you doing?"

"Helping you out." I gave her my best smile. "Like I said. And before you think of complaining. Yes, I have to. And yes, I want to."

"This is the ladies' room. You shouldn't be here."

I looked around to make sure there wasn't anyone else in here. "I've always been curious about it," I lied. I only wanted to be there because of her. I felt a little overprotective at the moment. "Wondered why women spend so long in here."

Ignoring me, Rosie grabbed a few expensive-looking paper towels.

Spotting an upholstered chaise longue by a corner, I smirked. "See? Now that would be one explanation. You get to lay down for a bit. Unwind. Do you get refreshments delivered here, too?"

Rosie stopped patting her shoulders with the towels and looked over. "You're ridiculous." But she laughed, which I always considered a win. "I thought you were here to help me?"

I perked up. "I am."

"Then come over here and help me."

"Oh." I patted my chest. "I love when you boss me around, Graham," I said as I made my way to her, crossing the unnecessarily spacious and large room. Her arm was stretched over her shoulder, trying to reach a spot in her back. "Hold on, let me get that."

"Thanks," she said quietly.

I grabbed a couple of paper towels and took over for her, gently wiping the moisture off the visible skin on her back. "What the hell was that Chewbacca carrying around? A bucket?"

Rosie laughed, gathered her hair in her fist, and placed it over her shoulder, revealing the back of her neck. It was long and delicate, and the sight had me wetting my lips with my tongue.

Animal, I reprimanded myself.

But I still wondered how the nape of her neck would feel under my fingers if the layer of paper disappeared. Wondered if she would shiver under my touch. Wondered what would happen if I leaned down and—

Christ. *Don't go there, Lucas.*

With a silent groan, I resumed the dabbing, my hand going around her shoulder on automatic and reaching her front. I paused, fingers hovering over that spot I'd been so concentrated on tonight.

My heart leaped, that craving returning with a vengeance. That was probably why when I spotted a runaway droplet trailing down her chest, crossing the curve of her collarbone and falling dangerously close to her neckline, I didn't even think about going for it.

I retraced the droplet's path with the towel, slowly, delicately, watching Rosie's pulse come alive under my touch. Taking notice of the catch in her breath.

Because I wanted—needed—to see her face, my gaze shot up and met her eyes in the mirror.

There was a question in them. Wonder. Hunger. Curiosity, too.

"Just trying to get all of it," I told her in a low murmur, keeping my eyes on hers. "I wouldn't want you to walk around like this and catch a cold."

"Oh. Okay," she breathed out. And now, I could feel her heartbeat on my fingertips, even through the thin towel. "That's good. Really good."

"I love being helpful," I said, even though my hand wasn't even moving at that moment.

Her throat bobbed. "You know, that's not even half of it," she said, her voice joining mine in the underground. "The drink somehow got inside. Through my dress. And I think my underwear might be . . . you know, wet."

I swallowed so hard I even heard the sound. "You . . . think? You don't know for sure?"

She shook her head.

My own imagination turned against me, flashing all kinds of images behind my eyes. Her gown sliding off her body. Rosie in her underwear. Droplets trailing down her back. Reaching the band of her panties. Falling even lower, down her thighs, and—

"I think I need to take it off," she said, bringing me back. Sort of. But not really, because—

"Take it off? The dress?" I rasped. Or growled. I wasn't sure. *"Now?"*

Rosie moved out of my reach, severing the contact, and making my hand drop to my side.

"Yes, now," she confirmed.

I squeezed the paper towel in my fist.

Her arm flew to her back, reaching for the zipper but not stretching far enough to make it. "I'll just—" She stretched further. "I'll take it off and dry it under the hand dryer." Her arm was bent at a strange angle now. "I think you can leave now, Lucas."

Yes. No. I . . . I shouldn't be here if she was going to take off her dress. Because I'd lose it. I'd pounce on her, seeing how my self-restraint was struggling tonight. I'd want to do things to her. Like—

Cold head, Lucas.

I swallowed. "Rosie?"

"Yeah?"

"How about we get you inside a stall, I unzip you, and you take it off there? Does that sound like a plan?"

She jerked to a halt. Her back returning to a natural position and her arms falling to her sides. "Okay. I think that sounds reasonable."

"See?" I sighed, relieved but not really. "I told you I was here to help."

She made a face at me.

When we moved to the closest stall, I threw the door open, held it in that position with my hip, and positioned Rosie so she was facing the inside.

And . . . all my momentary cool went out the window.

"Ready?" I asked, just in case. Just so I wouldn't startle her with my touch. Just so I'd have a couple of seconds to prepare myself.

"Born ready," she murmured.

"I'm going to start with the tiny button at the top. Then I'll pull the zipper down."

She exhaled slowly. "You don't have to narrate it, Lucas. Just do it."

My lips twitched at her impatience, but the moment my fingers unclasped that first button, that smile died.

My jaw clamped down tightly as I started making a work of the zipper, sliding it down deliberately gently, telling myself that it was because the fabric was thick and heavy when in reality, I was having a hard time making my fingers function. Taking a deep pull of air through my nose, I kept tugging at the zipper and more and more of that smooth, rosy skin was unveiled, sending my pulse thrumming all over my body.

I itched to move the dress out of the way and touch her. Her skin. To feel if it was cold or warm under my fingertips. To trace her spine with the back of my hand and see if she would shiver.

We fell into a charged silence, the only sound in the enclosed space the slow hiss of the metallic teeth as my right hand kept moving down, pulling at the slider, and reaching something I hadn't been prepared for.

The band of Rosie's underwear.

Lace. Black.

The sight sent my heart into a sprint. My blood swirled and gathered down, down, down. In places that would make this situation very uncomfortable to explain if someone walked in on us right now.

"Lucas?"

"Yeah?" I thought I said.

"I think . . ." She trailed off, her voice thick. "I can take over from here."

And before I could open my mouth to attempt an answer, she was disappearing inside the stall.

My forehead fell onto the closed door. Ah fuck.

I wasn't forgetting about the band of her lacy, black panties anytime soon.

Rosie groaned from inside. "Oh God. Oh no." A pause. "I'm so . . . wet."

Wet. She was wet.

A pained sound left me at her declaration.

"Can you pass me a few paper towels?" she asked after a beat. "Under the door?"

"Of course. Roomie." *Roomie, from roommates, remember, Lucas?* I reminded myself as I grabbed a handful of towels and followed her instructions. "Here you go."

"Thanks," she said, snagging them off my hand. Two seconds later, her dress was hanging off the top part of the stall door.

I closed my eyes at the sight, summoning all my willpower not to think about what that meant. Her, mostly naked. In her black lace underwear. *Wet.*

"Lucas?"

I cleared my throat. "Yeah?"

"Can you put the gown under the hand dryer? Just for a couple of minutes." A beat of silence. "While I clean up."

Grabbing the dress, I walked to the hand dryer and placed it underneath the hot air. The task served as a distraction from my wildly inappropriate thoughts.

"Is it working?" Rosie asked a few minutes later.

It wasn't. Not fast enough. The fabric was heavy, and only mildly less damp in my hands. "Still a little wet."

"I think I'm going to put it back on. We've been in here long enough, and I don't think it's going to get any better than this."

I walked back to her stall and held the dress in front of me. And, of course, that was the exact moment someone decided to enter the restroom. Yet one more superhero I didn't recognize. Were those . . . horns on her forehead?

"Hi," I greeted her with a nod. "Please, don't mind me. I'm—"

And, before I knew what was happening, I was being pulled backward into Rosie's stall and the door was being closed behind us. I shut my eyes.

"Why were you striking up a conversation with her?" she whispered.

"I was being polite, Ro," I said, facing the door and giving Rosie my back to be extra safe. "Abuela taught me that good manners and a smile can get you a long way. No need to be jealous."

"I'm not jealous," she scoffed. "Dress?"

Still with my back turned—because I hadn't forgotten about the fact that she was standing in barely any clothing right behind me—I held it up over my shoulder. "Right here. But I'm not gonna lie. I'm not sure you're going to want to put it on."

I heard her groan when she retrieved it. "Dammit."

My impulse was to turn around and tell her that everything would be okay, comfort her in some way, but I couldn't, shouldn't, when she was basically naked, and I was trying to keep it together. "You can wear my shirt, Rosie. And my jacket. I think they're long enough."

"Just . . . that?"

Do not visualize it, do not visualize it, I recited silently.

But the provocative image—Rosie, in my clothes, bare legs, wet—took shape in my head so fast and so clearly that my next word barely made it out of my mouth. "Yes." I cleared my throat. "Sure. I have no problem walking around shirtless, you know that. Plus, I'll still have the vest."

Silence.

"Wear them," I insisted. "I can get you out of here. Take you home."

She sighed. And she must have been standing very close to me because I felt her breath on my back. Then her forehead falling somewhere between my shoulder blades.

"Home." Another burst of air left her lips. "The night is over. Ruined, isn't it?"

The clear disappointment in her voice made something in my chest twist.

Without thinking about it—about every reason why I shouldn't—I turned around and wrapped her barely clothed body into my arms so I could bring her against my chest.

Her skin was warm and sticky with the dried spilled drink, and I couldn't not breathe her in when I closed my eyes even more tightly for good measure.

"I'm sorry, Ro," I told her, resting my chin on the top of her head. "I'll make you popcorn. The caramel and salt one that you like. And we'll watch a scary movie. The night isn't over."

Her arms had been somehow trapped between our chests, and I felt how her palms shifted, coming to rest against my pecs, making me want to grab her wrists and pull her arms around my neck.

A strangled sound came out of her, muffled by my clothes, so I started to release her. But she clamped the fabric of my vest, pulling at it and keeping me in place. "You are . . ." She exhaled shakily, making me frown and wish I was able to open my eyes so I could see her face. "You are incredible, Lucas. And I think you have no idea."

Eyes still closed, I let my right hand wander down—only a few safe inches—so it rested in the middle of her back. My thumb grazed her warm, sticky skin. "Why do you say that?"

"Because you are here, helping me, instead of out there having fun and . . . and . . . I don't know, living your best life without having to worry about me."

My brows knitted further.

Having to worry about her?

Did she think I felt like I needed to worry? Did she not see that this came naturally to me? That I couldn't control it, even if I wanted to?

Before I could voice any of those questions, I felt her head move out from under my chin. "You're so incredible that you even shut your eyes so you wouldn't get a glimpse of me in my underwear." Her voice sounded off, and concern zipped straight into my gut. "I didn't even ask you to do that."

"Because you don't have to ask me, Rosie."

I felt her shiver in my arms. Then, her body started shaking under my hands, against my chest. My brain flipped into autopilot and I tried to pull her back to me, to heat her skin in any way I could.

But she resisted.

"You're shaking, Rosie." I didn't even recognize my voice for a second. It had been a long time since I'd sounded so . . . desperate. Pleading. But I wasn't ashamed of any of those emotions, so I patted my chest with one fist. "Come here. Let me keep you warm."

But I didn't feel her move. Didn't even hear her speak for several moments.

Until she said, "Open your eyes, Lucas."

My head gave a curt shake. "No."

Hands still holding on to the front of my vest, she pulled at it, bringing me closer to her. Making my pulse thrum faster. Wilder.

"This is what I meant earlier today," she said. "When you told me you left the apartment so I'd change. That you didn't want to see me running around in my undergarments."

I remembered, of course I did.

"Would it be so bad? You looking at me?" Her voice had a quality that I didn't like, as if I'd hurt her. Something I couldn't stand but didn't know how to fix.

She pulled at me again, bringing me even closer to her. Ripping at my restraint.

Now I felt the outline of her body—the curve of her breasts, the dip of her stomach—against me, pushing me to my very limit.

And when she said, "I want you to open your eyes, Lucas. I need you to."

I need you to.

It was that *need* that killed me, knowing that she needed me, wanted me, to do something for her. My willpower good and done.

I was long past the point where I could play the noble friend any-more.

My restraint snapped.

And I opened my fucking eyes.

My gaze bathed in the sight before me. Of Rosie, in nothing but her underwear, all curls framing her beautiful face, all plush curves that called out to me. To touch her—not like I'd done at any point in the past—but to learn her. To let my hands roam leisurely along her skin until there wasn't an inch I didn't know by heart.

She was gorgeous. Stunning. Everything and anything a man could want. And she was looking at me as if bracing herself to see me bolt when I'd do anything to stay.

"Rosie," I said after I caught my goddamn breath. "If you think this is something I don't want to see, then you have me figured out all wrong."

Her lips parted with surprise.

Surprise.

I shook my head, and because my restraint was gone, I finally, openly, let my gaze take their fill. My eyes ran down her smooth neck, taking in the soft curve of her shoulder and reaching the swell of her breasts, hardly contained by a matching black lace bra.

Because my restraint had vanished, I also allowed myself to touch her—finally, fucking finally—to circle her waist with my hands, feeling her warm and supple under them, to wrap my palms around her sides so I could move her as I pleased.

Rosie's breath left her in a puff, and she took hold of my shoulders.

My hands traveled up, until my thumbs were brushing the un-derswell of her breasts. "Do you think I don't want to see these?" The tips of my fingers grazed her again, the contact through the lace already doing mad, crazy things to me. "Touch you like this?"

Rosie arched her back in answer, bringing herself closer, and my dick twitched in my pants at the sight, the nearness of her body.

"There's nothing about you I don't want to see." My hands flew to her wrists, my fingers wrapping around them. I brought one to my mouth and said into her skin, "You're a sight, Rosie. A fucking sight. Like a mirage. An illusion. What man in his right mind wouldn't want to see you?"

Rosie's mouth released a whimper that spoke to that primal part of me I'd tried to keep at bay tonight.

Without any sense of rational thought, I stepped toward her, and in a swift motion, I turned us around until I had her against the closed door.

I leaned down, making sure my mouth was close to her ear when I asked her, "Are you even real?"

"I'm real," Rosie said so breathlessly that they were barely words. "You can touch me, if you don't believe me."

"Touch you." I groaned at the idea of me really doing that, not the simple brush of my fingers against her skin but really touching her, everywhere. *Want that.* I pulled Rosie's arms up, pinning her hands above her head. "Don't say things you don't mean, Rosie. Don't offer things you'll take back."

She arched her back again, pushing her breasts into my chest. "I won't take it back."

My hands tightened against her wrists as I leaned down, and I pressed my lips on her skin when I said, "I want to do the noble thing, Rosie." I dipped my nose in her hair, taking that deep whiff of her scent like the animal I was. "But I'm finding it really hard when all I want to do is sinful things to you."

Her chest heaved against mine before she said, "You can be both. Do both."

No. "Remember me telling you I couldn't give you cute and messy?" I rasped, stepping into her, pressing her harder into the door. She nodded her head, and I hummed deep in my throat. "This is the same. If I'm noble, I step away. Wrap you in my jacket and take you home."

Rosie pulled against the hold I had around her wrists, and when I didn't give in, she met my gaze and said, "No."

It was the need in her eyes, the way she shuddered at the thought of me pulling away, that obliterated that last thread and snapped something inside of me, something bigger, wilder. What poked at the beast.

"Keep them here," I grunted, pressing on her wrists to stay above her head. I swallowed, unable to rein myself in. "You want sinful," I told her, moving my hands down, palms open and ready. "It'd be so easy, Rosie." My thumbs brushed the swells of her breasts, then played with the puckered peaks over the fabric of her lacy bra before descending again and reaching the edge of her panties. I toggled with the thin fabric, my pulse racing, flying at the thoughts rushing through my head. "I could slip these to the side, and make you feel good. Fuck you silly with my fingers."

She gasped in surprise—in *need*—and the sound, the image of Rosie's parted lips in a pleasure I hadn't even given her yet, made me so hard that I had no choice but to press myself against her. Pushed my hips right against hers, one hasty, hard thrust, pulling another abandoned moan from her.

"Ah, Rosie," I grunted again, clasping the fabric of her underwear now, holding on to that last sliver of sense. "What's an angel like you doing with someone like me?"

A strangled, harsh sound left her lips before she whispered my name, "Lucas—"

"Rosie?" A familiar voice sliced right through the moment. "Hello, Rosie? Are you here?"

I cursed under my breath, my body freezing around hers.

Rosie's eyelids fluttered shut, and I could see the loss on her face. Loss I fought tooth and nail as I tried to pull myself back together, to cool down whatever was going on in my head, my chest, my pants.

"Hello?" Lina's voice came again, the distress was obvious in my cousin's voice. "Jesus, I've looked everywhere."

Rosie's eyes opened, a grimace twisting her lips. "I am! I'm here! Hey."

She looked at me and I forced myself to give her the easiest smile I could manage. Then, I placed a kiss on top of her head.

"Finally!" Lina exclaimed, her voice coming closer to the stall. "What happened? You disappeared and I couldn't find you."

Rosie's mouth opened, but no words came out.

"Have you seen Lucas?" Lina continued. "We can't find him, either."

I could see Rosie struggling to answer. To potentially explain how she ended up with me in a bathroom stall. To explain why she was half naked and I had the face of a starved man and a bulge pressing against my zipper.

"Aaron is in the restrooms, too, looking for him," Lina added.

Rosie's lips kept bobbing, and it became clear to me what she was having trouble with. What I had to do.

Shaking my head, I mouthed, *I'm not here.*

A frown curled her brows.

"Rosie?" Lina called. "You okay in there?"

I gave her another shake.

"Yeah," Rosie answered, averting her eyes. "Some guy spilled a drink on me. I was cleaning up."

"Oh no, that sucks. Did you manage okay or do you need me to get in and help—"

"No!" Rosie yelled, still looking somewhere to my left. "It's all under control."

Her cheeks had turned a deep shade of pink at some point. Probably when I'd been groping at her like the desperate bastard I was.

"Is Lucas waiting outside, then?" Lina chuckled. "He's not hiding in there with you or something, right?"

Rosie seemed thrown off by the comment, and I understood. I really did. Lina had made it perfectly clear how she felt about the possibility of Rosie and me together.

I shook my head for her. Even if I hated to do that.

"No," Rosie said with a fake laugh. "Us in a stall would be crazy! And stupid."

My stomach soured at her words, but I picked up the gown from the floor, where it had ended when I'd pounced on her, and I helped her in in silence.

Only when she was dressed and zipped up did she meet my gaze again.

I could tell she was doing her best to hide how she felt about all of this, which wasn't good, but as much as I didn't like it myself, I had no choice but to mouth, *You go first. I'll wait.*

With a nod, she left the stall and joined my cousin. I heard their steps as they made their way out. Leaving me to my own thoughts while I waited to leave, long enough so I wouldn't get caught.

Get caught.

Never in my life had I let anybody sway my actions. Never allowed the world, or their opinions, to dictate how I lived. Who I befriended, dated, or fucked. I'd never cared enough. And I didn't care what Lina would think of Rosie and me.

I cared about Rosie.

About her trust, and about our friendship. I wanted to do right by her. I wanted her to have everything she deserved. Because she deserved *everything*, as much as that wasn't me.

Because you're leaving, I reminded myself.

Yeah. That, too.

CHAPTER NINETEEN

Rosie

A week after the Masquerade Ball party, two things had become clear.

The first was that as much as I thought it would, what had gone down between Lucas and me in that bathroom stall hadn't changed anything between us.

His smiles hadn't grown smaller or fewer in number. Our routine was still the same: he cooked for me every night and I watched him from my post at the kitchen island. After dinner, we binged on our show, and when we slipped in bed—and couch—he asked me how many words I'd written that day, and I asked him to tell me something about his day.

His answers usually included something funny or strange he had seen or experienced that day, and mine a decent word count.

Finally.

Because I was writing. Our experiment, our research, even if technically incomplete, was already working. For better or for worse, I was beginning to realize that Lucas might be the closest thing I'd ever have to a *muse*. And that was . . . exhilarating and terrifying.

We were friends. We lived together. We went on dates that were not real, that weren't meant to make a relationship move forward. We shared hot, intimate, hushed moments in bathroom stalls and went on like they hadn't been more than a dream.

Which brought me to the second thing I'd realized: I was playing a dangerous game. Because as much as this whole thing was helping me, the fact that Lucas's stay in New York—in my life—had an expiration date was starting to take more and more space in my mind. It was starting to make me desperate to grab every single thing I could take from him before he left. Not for Rosie, Date Night. But for Rosie, Every Other Night.

And I seemed willing to ignore the consequences. The price. Like ignoring I could still feel the imprint of his hands on my skin, or pretending I couldn't summon the words he'd whispered in my ear. We'd made a pact anyway. We'd said we wouldn't let the experiment change things between us, affect our friendship. He'd promised he wouldn't fall in love with me, for crying out loud. And that was probably why nothing had changed for him after the Masquerade Ball.

"You done with this, Rosie?" Sally—the barista at my favorite café in Manhattan—said, jolting me back to reality. She balanced a tray on her hip. "I'll take your mug away if you are."

"Yes, thank you." I grabbed my empty mug and plate for her. "The new cinnamon rolls are amazing, by the way. I'm thinking of taking a couple of them home."

Because Lucas would love them.

"Want another one for now? Looks like you're working." She pointed at the laptop sitting on the table. "You can use some extra fuel."

"No, thanks. I think I'm going to start wrapping up and head home soon."

With a nod, she placed everything on the tray and walked back to the counter.

As I finished saving my security backup, a man near the counter caught my attention. He wore a sleek black tux and was tapping his foot on the floor. He stood out like a sore thumb in the casual atmosphere of the coffee shop.

Just like it used to happen once upon a time, my head started imagining the possible scenarios that had brought him here. Maybe he was on his way to a gala, not exactly unusual in Manhattan. Or perhaps he was returning from one and was in sheer need of caffeine. Or who knew, maybe he had slipped unnoticed out of an event and what I'd thought was impatience was actually him fighting the urge to bolt before getting caught. He could be a . . . runaway groom.

Runaway groom leaves bride at the altar and falls in love at first sight with a barista. Or the pastry master. Or the patron that he spills coffee all over in his haste to escape.

I was smiling to myself, thinking that would be a romance book I'd love to read, when the man turned around and met my gaze.

His eyes widened with recognition.

Runaway Groom was Aiden Castillo, the contractor.

He waved a tentative hand and I returned the gesture with a nod. Then he collected his order and strode in my direction. And as he did, I couldn't help but notice that I'd overlooked how handsome Aiden Castillo was that day we'd met.

"You look great, Mr. Castillo," I blurted absently when he reached my table. His eyebrows arched and I shook my head. "Which is a weird way of saying, hi, how are you?"

Mr. Castillo laughed. "I'm doing good, and thank you, I appreciate the compliment." He lowered his voice as if he was letting me into a secret: "Although if I'm being completely honest . . . I hate the tux and after the day I've had, I'm dying to get it off."

As curious as I was, asking him to elaborate would be none of my business. So I went with, "Well, that's too bad." A loud giggle came from the table closest to the window, and a quick glance told me the source was a small group of teenagers. "Don't look," I told him. "But I think you might have a little fan club over there. And they'd be super disappointed if they heard you saying that."

Mr. Castillo's expression filled with humor. "Well, I wouldn't want to disappoint them, so I guess we can keep that between us."

He was a nice man, I thought.

And for some reason, a flashback of me bawling on Lucas's chest came to mind. "About the other day, during the visit at my apartment, I should probably apologize for how . . . very uncomfortable that visit must have been for you, so now that I see you here"—I shrugged a shoulder—"I want to, you know, say sorry."

"No need to apologize," he said with a wave of his hand. "There's no point in denying my brother-in-law is an asshole."

"Oh, so you're family with Mr. Allen?"

He nodded with a sigh. "For better or for worse." He seemed to think of something. "Which reminds me, I'm not sure if he's called you yet and gave you the news."

I frowned. *The news?*

"Okay," Mr. Castillo said. "So he hasn't, I see." He shook his head. "I have this policy of no work talk on a Sunday but I think I can make an exception." A pause. "Your apartment will be ready for you to move back in soon. On Friday, probably."

Friday.

That was . . . in five days. Less than a week.

He smiled, and in that moment, I thought of Lucas's grin. And how Mr. Castillo's didn't make me feel . . . anything.

"Oh," I breathed out, disappointment settling deep in my stomach. *Disappointment.*

Because that meant no more living with Lucas. And soon, our four experimental dates would run out. Because we were on date three out of four, if we counted Halloween as one. Which we probably should; where else would that night fit otherwise?

And after our research was over, if we didn't live together, I wouldn't be spending any more time with Lucas.

No more Lucas.

Because after that he'd leave New York, too.

Taking in a deep, shaky breath, I noticed Mr. Castillo frowning.

"That's good," I croaked when I recovered. "Really good. Very good. Thank you."

He tilted his head.

I shook mine, cursing myself for being so silly. I should be happy. This was good news.

"Sorry, I'm just . . ." Why was my throat feeling dry? "I'm tired and that's why my face is not showing it, but I'm really happy. Thanks for letting me know, Mr. Castillo."

That seemed to appease him somehow, because he waved his hand in front of him and said with a new smile, "Please, call me Aiden."

"Oh, sure." I tried to return it, willing my lips up. "You can call me Rosie, too."

"Perfect." He nodded his head slowly, as if coming up to a decision. "You know, I'm actually very happy I ran into you. I was wondering, now that we . . ."

The door opened behind Mr. Castillo, his voice fading into the background the moment I noticed the man entering the coffee shop.

My heart did a cartwheel in my chest, the sweetest brand of surprise filling my tummy, even if I had told Lucas that I'd be working here.

Lucas spotted me immediately. He was wearing his blue *I* ♥ *NYC* cap and his face was parting with that bright smile I wished was just for me. *Me*, Rosie. Not for Rosie, his roommate or friend.

I watched Lucas stride in my direction, his gaze fastened to mine, moving like a man on a mission, closing the distance almost as quickly as the beating of my heart.

He came to a stop beside Aiden, his focus on me, and said, "Hello, *preciosa*."

"Hi," I answered, the word coming out wobbly at that *preciosa*.

I'd looked it up. I knew what it meant, and it might be one of my favorite words now that he'd decided to use it on me every time he saw me.

Preciosa. Beautiful. Precious. Gorgeous.

Aiden cleared his throat, reminding me that he was still there. And judging by his expression, he was waiting for . . . something?

"So, what do you say, Rosie?" Aiden said, looking at me with a small frown. "I know this great place. It's not far from here, actually."

I blinked at Aiden. Crap. I had no idea what he might have asked me. I'd gotten distracted. Befuddled by Lucas's arrival. By that *preciosa*. By him.

Aiden's smile faltered, gradually falling. "I was saying that if you're done here, we could head out and grab a bite." He paused, and I watched his eyes bouncing up, probably following the motion of my brows shooting to my hairline with shock. *Was he . . . asking me out?* He scratched the back of his neck. "I said that if you really didn't mind the tux, or my fan club, I could take you. I was hoping you . . ." A strange laugh left him, and I was pretty sure he blushed. "But I think I might have read all of that wrong."

Okay, he *had been* asking me out.

My cheeks flamed.

And Lucas was standing right there, not saying a word. Just . . . watching. In silence. Probably feeling awkward and thinking of a joke he'd make later on.

"I . . ." I scrambled for an answer. "No, you got that right, Mr. Castillo. The tux is great. You look really handsome."

It was then that I somehow decided to look over at Lucas. And I couldn't miss the way he tensed up. In fact, it was hard to miss how he looked down at himself. A quick glance down, as if checking for something.

And because my own gaze followed the motion, it was only then that I spotted the bag hanging off Lucas's hand. I immediately recognized the takeaway logo on its side.

I looked back at Mr. Castillo, and as if he had been waiting for me to return my attention to him, he said, "Aiden is fine, remember?"

Out of the corner of my eye, I saw Lucas's fingers tightening around the handles of the bag.

My eyes returned to Lucas's face, his expression neutral, his smile stiff.

"Lucas," I said, hating the way his mouth pressed in something that wasn't *his* smile. "Do you remember Aiden, the contractor?"

Lucas gave him a nod. "Yes, I remember."

Aiden returned it. "Glad to see you again, Lucas. You're Rosie's . . ." He trailed off.

My heart seemed to stop, waiting, even though I had no reason to anticipate his answer.

It was after what seemed the longest five seconds of my life that Lucas said, "Rosie's friend."

I'd be lying if that didn't hurt the teeniest, tiniest bit. Because it did. As much as it was true.

"Okay, good." I clapped my hands softly, pushing down what I had no business feeling. "Everyone remembers everyone, that's good. Really good."

My eyes bounced from one man to the other, finally settling on Aiden, to whom I still owed an answer.

Rosie's friend.

Lucas and I were friends.

So I could tell Aiden yes. I could go on this date. It wouldn't be more than just that, dinner, but I could still go. Perhaps I should go. But every single cell in my body told me that there was food for two in that plastic bag Lucas held in his hand. That Lucas had already planned to have dinner with me, just like we did every day. And as much as it probably didn't mean anything for Lucas, not more than sharing a meal with his roommate, his friend, it did for me. So much that I realized now how badly I wanted Lucas to be the one asking me out. Taking me, Rosie, out on a date. A real one.

But Lucas didn't do real dates. Not anymore. Not now. He'd been clear about that.

"Thank you for the offer, Aiden." I gave him a polite smile. "But I think I'm going to head home."

I was busy gauging Aiden's reaction, because disappointing people gave me anxiety and because I liked Aiden and I feared I was making him feel awkward, when Lucas spoke.

"With me," he said, making my heart flap, flap, flap in my chest. "She's going home with me."

His tone hadn't been loud, or brash. He hadn't even injected any emotion in his words, which was so rare for him. And yet, that "with me" had been so powerful, so meaningful for me, that I knew it'd be imprinted in my memory for a long time.

Because he'd talked as if I were his.

"Yeah," I felt the need to explain. To Aiden? Myself? I didn't know. "We're living together at the moment, while my apartment is being fixed."

Understanding dawned in Aiden's expression. "Oh, right. That makes sense." He nodded his head. "Okay, so I guess Ed—Mr. Allen—will give you a call at some point this week to talk details about you moving back." He gave me one last smile. "Have a good night, Rosie." He turned to his left. "Lucas."

And with that, Aiden disappeared through the door of the café.

When I finally looked over at Lucas, I found his eyes on me. His expression was still the same. Off. "Moving back?"

"Oh," I said, busying myself as I gathered my stuff and threw it in my laptop bag. "Aiden told me that I might be able to move back to my place on Friday." Hearing how somber my voice had sounded, I faked an enthusiastic, "Yay!"

Lucas hesitated for the tiniest moment, but then a genuine, real smile—not whatever had been going on with his mouth until now—took over his face. "Ah, that's amazing, Ro." He placed his hands on my shoulders, then turned me around to face him before bringing me to his chest. And I . . . I melted right into him, because I was foolish and helpless where Lucas was concerned. "This is great news."

At least someone thought it was.

He released me and watched me as I stumbled backward. I fumbled with my jacket, trying to hide my dazed expression.

"We should celebrate," Lucas suggested. And I nodded with more fake enthusiasm. "Good that I have Chicken Karaage. For two. Probably for four, actually." He lifted the takeaway bag in the air, and my chest constricted because I had been right. He'd picked up dinner for me, too. Of course he had. "We can open some wine, too."

"Sounds amazing." I managed a wobbly smile.

Lucas reached for my packed laptop bag and hung it across his chest. "Let's go home, then." He took a tiny step backward, letting me through first. "After you, *preciosa*."

My step faltered at hearing that word again, but I kept moving forward.

Let's go home, then.

Home. With Lucas.

Not for much longer, though.

CHAPTER TWENTY

Lucas

*J*ealousy. That was new.

It was nothing like those quick and thoughtless gut reactions I'd experienced in the past. Oh no, this was more intense than fast, and certainly not thoughtless. It was the full thing. The full-on blood-boiling, gut-wrenching, want-to-growl thing.

I'd wanted to say something back at the café. I'd wanted to mark my territory and say *mine*, like a Neanderthal. An animal.

Just like I'd behaved at the Halloween party.

But I wasn't supposed to think about that.

I'd tried my best these past few days, and failed. I'd tried to pretend that those moments in that stall weren't all I thought of when Rosie bit her lip in thought, or when she came close and I got a whiff of her scent, or when our hands brushed reaching for the salt and caramel popcorn I made for her.

Some days, I found excuses to touch her. I'd tell her she had something in her hair. Or that I'd thought there had been something clinging to her clothes. Sometimes, I reached for her and didn't come up with an excuse in time so I just smiled at her like a total idiot, and hoped for the best.

And here I was, feeling jealous. Like I had any right to claim ownership over Rosie after a couple of experimental dates and whispering some dirty words in her ear.

How did I dare to call her mine after just that?

She deserved men in tuxedos that took her to fancy places in Manhattan. And I . . . didn't even own a tux. I didn't even have a button-down shirt or a blazer with me, for crying out loud.

It was laughable, really.

No wonder Lina had flipped at the idea of us becoming . . . whatever, everything, anything.

"Lucas?" Rosie's voice drew my attention back to her as we exited the subway station closest to our place. *Our place*, which wasn't even ours and we wouldn't be sharing for much longer.

I sighed. "Yeah, Ro?"

"I've been thinking," she said so slowly that it made me glance over at her. "Actually, I haven't been thinking this for long, but I was wondering, you know, now that I'm writing, and our experiment is working, if it makes sense anymore."

My fingers tightened around the bag I was carrying. "What do you mean?"

"Well, you've helped me so much already, you know? I think I might have everything under control. It has been all slowly coming to me, and I'm no longer lost, poking around in a fog. And we said we wouldn't allow this arrangement to put any awkwardness between us but I . . . " She blew air through her mouth. "I . . . I don't know, Lucas, it felt a little awkward at the coffee shop so I just—"

She stopped herself. She was looking everywhere but at me, and I didn't like that. Not one bit. Because I wanted her eyes on me, especially if she was talking about something important.

I came to a stop on the sidewalk and waited until she met my gaze. "Do you want to date him? Aiden?" I asked, keeping my voice as light as I possibly could. Because if that was the reason, I wanted to hear it. I needed to hear it. "You want to go on real dates?"

I wanted to take back the word *real*, because whatever had happened between us, on those two experimental dates or even at the

Masquerade Ball, hadn't been faked, forced, or *not real* in any way. But I'd used it, because if she wanted real dates with other men, who was I to stop her?

But Rosie didn't seem to mind my use of the word and I'd be lying if I said that that didn't sting. "Maybe I want the real thing. Not with Aiden, but maybe I want the real dates."

Of course, she did.

And that felt like a sucker punch to the gut.

Could I even give her that? No, I couldn't when I was leaving. I wanted to give her things I didn't have.

Something must have changed in my expression because her brows furrowed in confusion. "The three experimental dates we've gone on have been more than I could have asked for."

"Two dates." I carefully placed a hand at the small of her back and resumed walking. "We've only gone on two, Ro."

"I thought we were counting the masquerade as one."

I retracted my arm, readjusting the strap of her laptop bag on my shoulder just so I wouldn't do something stupid. Or reckless. "Why? I didn't plan anything. In fact, I didn't do a single thing."

Phase three. Infatuation. Intimacy. Seduction. I remembered those three points perfectly. I'd been thinking about them a lot.

"You did, Lucas," she said, returning her gaze to the sidewalk ahead of us. "In phase three, the physical connection takes the wheel. The infatuation becomes tangible, a breathing living thing between the two . . . parties. It's about breaking that barrier that holds you back and letting go. See if that person pulls you in enough to want to move things forward. Let them progress into physical intimacy."

"I see." I didn't just *see*; I felt it in my pulse. I felt it drum in my body.

Rosie chuckled and it was soft and self-conscious. "I don't think I'd ever been properly seduced," she told me, as if that wasn't supposed to make me want to howl at the moon like a lunatic. What the hell was wrong with me? She continued, "Like, sure, all men I've dated have said or done things to get in my panties. Successfully, I may add." And that didn't do anything to appease the beast, if my knuckles turning white around the bag were anything to go by. "But never, like, you know. What happened."

What happened.

Before I knew what I was doing, I had come to a stop again. "Rosie—"

"I don't want to make this weird," she said, stopping a step ahead of me. "Because I'm sure it was like a lapse in judgment or whatever." Her cheeks turned pink. "I mean, I literally had to force you to look at me. But it still counts. Research is research."

That was what she thought?

"Force me?" I spat out, stepping in her direction. "You think you had to *force me* to look at you? In the name of research?"

"You don't have to explain anything. And I shouldn't have phrased it like that, either."

My teeth ground. My disbelief turned to frustration, because how could she ever think that I—

"Rosie," I said, making sure I was coming as close as possible to her without touching her. Because if I did, I knew it'd be game over for me. "If we weren't friends," I told her, voice like gravel. "Good friends like we are, best friends"—I watched her eyelids flutter shut—"I would take you somewhere dark and rip your clothes off with my teeth without caring to have a good reason. Just so I could see you, have you to myself."

Rosie's lips parted, and when her tongue came out and wet her lips, it almost became physically impossible for me to hold back any longer. God, I wanted to touch her, lick her, kiss her everywhere.

I stepped away in a brisk motion. Then I moved forward again, and as if compelled, I grabbed her hand.

"Count the Halloween party as an experimental date if you like," I told her, leading her forward with me. "But we shook on four. We agreed four dates."

Her fingers tightened around mine.

"So, I already planned for the next one," I continued. "I was going to tell you to keep your schedule free on Thursday." I remembered Aiden Castillo's *great* news. "Or if you want to pack on Thursday, I can help you and we could postpone. I guess—"

"No," she finally said, and the way that word left her mouth made me look over at her. "Thursday night is okay. It's a date."

Nodding my head, I ripped my gaze off her and clamped down my mouth before I said something stupid, like how neither of us had called this fourth date experimental.

A few minutes later, we were climbing the stairs to the apartment, Rosie's hand still in mine, when she called. "Lucas?"

"Yeah?"

"I hope . . . I hope this makes you happy."

Puzzled by her words, I frowned. My mouth opened just as we entered the hallway and I spotted the door of the apartment, which was thrown wide open.

Shouting came from the inside and then, a blur of black fur was shooting in my direction.

"Pero qué cojones—"

I was toppled over, my ass landing on the cold floor, and a soft, energetic ball of warmth settled in my lap.

"¡Te dije que lo sujetaras!" came from the apartment.

I looked down, the familiarity of this, of the furry ball currently curling around me hitting me like a freight train. "Taco," I said, hearing the surge of emotion in my voice. *"Taco, chico. ¿Qué haces aquí?"*

My Belgian shepherd jumped out of my arms and circled around me before returning to my lap and placing a wet kiss on my cheek.

I tried to mumble something, but words had really been knocked out of me. All I could feel was happiness at seeing my pup, at having him here with me.

Placing a hard kiss on top of his fur, I released him and let out a strange laugh myself.

"I can't believe you're here." I patted his side. He whined. "I've missed you, too, *chico.*"

God, and I had. So much.

Slowly, I started making sense of my surroundings, and I wasn't surprised when the first thing my eyes found was Rosie. She was standing a couple of feet to my right, her eyes watery despite the bright smile adorning her beautiful face.

"Taco's here," I told her, as if she couldn't see that.

She nodded, that big smile widening.

Her eyes darted to my bad leg, as it stretched on the ground in front of me.

"I'm okay," I whispered before she asked. "I'm more than okay."

And she nodded again.

"*Hermanito*," a voice I hadn't been expecting called. "*Este perro es incontrolable.*"

Little brother, this dog is unmanageable.

"Charo?" I croaked. She was here, too, leaning against the frame of the door. Two new heads popped up behind her.

"Surprise!" Lina shouted, Aaron behind her. "Fine, we're not a surprise. Charo and Taco are the surprise. We're here just for fun and giggles. Also, to ask you for joint custody of Taco? Please? Maybe not tonight, but tomorrow?"

"But—" I started, then stopped myself. "How?"

Charo's flaming red hair swayed when she shrugged. "I was feeling in the mood for a little adventure, and you know Tía Tere? Well, her best friend's cousin is a flight attendant and—"

"Charo," Lina chimed. "*No te enrolles.*"

My sister sighed. "*Ay*, anyway. We flew in to see you. Especially Taco, who will stay with you. I'm only spending a couple nights with Lina and Aaron and then I will fly to Boston, where my friend Alicia moved last year after—"

Lina elbowed my sister, making her stop again.

Taco, who had calmed down by now, was curled between my legs, nudging my leg, and my palm fell on his head without much thought. I petted him between his ears. "How did you fly him in? How—"

"Well . . ." Charo cut me off with a wicked smile. "It's funny that you ask that."

I frowned and Lina said, "We made sure he was safe and comfortable."

Shaking my head, I was about to say thank you and tell them that this meant the world to me, when Charo said, "Rosie took care of everything." And my head swiveled in her direction. Her eyes were wide. "She was the one who did all the research we needed to fly Taco in the cabin. She even took care of most of the paperwork, paid for Taco's ticket. Actually, us coming to the States was her idea."

Rosie blushed when she murmured, "That was supposed to be a secret, remember, Charo?"

"*Ay mujer.*" Charo laughed. "You're family, there's no such thing as secrets when we're family."

You're family, she'd told Rosie.

And my chest swelled with that possibility.

"You did this, Ro?" I rasped. "For me?"

Rosie shrugged. "Lina mentioned Taco had emotional support training, and with Charo's—"

"It all worked out," my sister interrupted her. "No need to get into all the details."

I swallowed, my brain trying to put the pieces together.

I had noticed how Charo had stopped Rosie from saying more but I couldn't see past what Taco being here meant. Rosie had done this. For me. To make me happy.

I wanted to lay myself at her feet because no one had ever done something so thoughtful for me. Something this personal, something that had been designed to bring only me happiness.

I wanted to pull her into my arms and thank her, worship her, make sure she knew how grateful I was. Fuck. I wanted her. Now more than ever.

Taco barked, snapping me out of those dangerous, dangerous thoughts. Rosie took a tentative step toward Taco, her hand outstretched. "Can I?"

"Of course. He doesn't bite," I said. And when she sidled up beside us, I added so only she could hear, "Me, on the other side? I could eat you right up."

Rosie snorted, as if I'd been joking. I hadn't been. I'd start at her mouth.

Then, she said very quietly, "I want him to like me."

"Rosie," I told her, aware of the group assembled nearby. "Taco will—"

He pounced on Rosie, bringing her down to the ground.

"Love you," I finished, watching him plant kisses all over her face. Rosie laughed like it was the best thing to ever happen to her. "Taco will love you."

A pang of the emotion I'd been experiencing earlier tonight was back, and I couldn't believe it myself, I wouldn't have if I weren't feeling it in my gut.

But as I kept my eyes on Taco and Rosie, it was impossible to deny that I was jealous of my dog for being in her arms, free to plant kisses all over her face.

Ah, jealousy. My old friend.

CHAPTER TWENTY-ONE

Rosie

Something about Lucas was different.

It wasn't just the button-down shirt and two-piece suit.

And it wasn't the fact that he had styled his hair in a way that made me itch to slip my fingers through it to check if it was as soft and smooth as it looked.

It was something about the way he smiled, moved, or even breathed around me. The way he'd whispered in my ear how beautiful I looked tonight. Or the way he'd placed his hand at the small of my back when we'd entered Alexia's restaurant. That intensity I'd felt from him in the past was back, but this time . . . this time it felt like more. Greater, bigger, like a separate, inescapable force.

It felt like gravity.

I looked around us, taking in every detail about the restaurant, Zarato, and finding myself in awe of the place. I felt as if we were in a bubble, a dream where we weren't meant to be only friends, or roommates, where the purpose of tonight wasn't about helping my writing, and where Lucas's presence in my life didn't have an expiration date. A dream where we were real, permanent.

I sighed, falling back into reality and feeling the walls of that bubble thin.

But not burst, I told myself. *Not yet. Because I still have tonight.*

It was the first time I'd ever had dinner at a restaurant like this, so I wanted to make sure to enjoy the experience as much as the company of the amazing man sitting by my side.

The atmosphere was refined but relaxed, and we had been placed at the bar, made of sleek wrought iron in the shape of a horseshoe. The best spot, according to Alexia, who had received us when we'd arrived.

Lucas's hand grazed the skin between my bare shoulder blades, the touch sending a delicious shiver down my arms and validating my decision to wear a backless dress despite the drop in temperature and the dark heavy clouds hovering above New York today.

"You look happy," Lucas told me in the deep, stern voice he'd been using all night. "Did you like everything?"

"I am happy." I smiled at him, and when his eyes jumped down to my mouth his gaze darkened. My next words left me in a choppy, breathless way. "Everything was amazing. Thank you so much for bringing me here."

"I wouldn't want anyone else with me tonight, Rosie."

My heart jumped at his words, hungry for more. And even if it was the stupidest thing to say, I found myself needing to make light of the situation: "Not even Taco?"

"No," he said with a shake of his head, as if I'd said something serious. And then he leaned down his head, closing the distance between our faces until our noses almost brushed. "You're the only one I want here with me, sharing food with me, and sitting so close I'm having a hard time keeping my hands to myself."

And I—*Okay*.

I got this, I told myself. The pounding in my chest was under control. And the way it traveled to all kinds of interesting places in my body was one hundred percent imperceptible.

I just needed to say something. Anything. Keep the conversation flowing. "I think . . . I think Argentinian Japanese fusion cuisine is my new obsession."

Lucas chuckled and shifted a few inches away. "Alexia and Akane have done an amazing job with the tasting menu. I don't think I can pick a favorite from all the dishes they served."

We had learned that Zarato's Argentinian Japanese fusion specialties had only come to be after Alexia had fallen in love and married Akane, her sous chef. And that was what had elevated the restaurant's reputation and standing, Alexia had told us during the quick tour she'd given us of the restaurant and the kitchen. A tour that had had Lucas eyes flickering with a kind of interest I'd only seen him show while cooking, he'd been so absorbed that he didn't notice me studying him. Committing him to memory.

Lucas's fingers skimmed along one of the thin straps of my dress, sidetracking all my thoughts.

"What was your favorite?" he asked in a low voice. "The one thing you enjoyed the most."

I was tempted to tell him, *You, you are. You are the thing I enjoy the most.* "I loved everything."

"I know you have one," he said with a knowing smile. "And I think I can guess which one, but I want to hear it from you."

I did. *He knows me so well at this point.* "It was the mochi."

He hummed, and the pad of his thumb traced the length of my spine, stopping at the dip of my back. "I knew the moment you took that first bite. It was the *dulce de leche* filling, right?"

I nodded, feeling myself sigh at the Spanish words on his lips. I was never going to get over him speaking his mother tongue.

"What was that?" he asked, a new spark of interest in his gaze. "That thing you did."

Dammit, he could be so perceptive.

I swallowed. "It was nothing. I was thinking of the mochi."

"It wasn't nothing. You let out this little sigh," he said, and to my utter surprise he brought that thumb that had been caressing my back to my cheek. He grazed my now flaming skin. "Then there's this. This beautiful blush. What's causing this, Rosie?" He lowered his voice. "What's making you hot?"

His words echoed in my ears, reaching a spot between my

thighs. Seconds ticked by and I didn't answer. Frankly, I didn't think I could.

"Hey." Lucas tugged at a runaway curl that had come out of the loose braid I'd attempted tonight. And only when my lips parted did he tuck the lock behind my ear with a gentleness that made me short of breath again. "Don't be shy, Rosie. It's me."

And wasn't that the problem? Wasn't I so transparent, so affected, because it was him who was the one here with me?

After a heartbeat I finally admitted, "It was your hand. On my back. The words in Spanish, too. It was all . . . distracting. Especially the words."

That interest in his gaze sharpened. "What was so distracting about them, exactly?"

I went with the truth because what did I have to lose now? "The *dulce de leche*," I tried, sure that I was butchering the pronunciation. "I just thought it was . . . sexy when you said it."

Lucas blinked, one single slow blink, then his eyes filled with something else. Something wicked and a little dark. "You like it when I speak in Spanish to you."

Yes. Obviously. "I guess I do."

"I can say it again for you, would you like that?" he offered, and then, instead of waiting for my answer—*Yes please, sir, and can you record it, too, so I can play it for years to come?*—he leaned in. Close. Really, really freaking close. Until his mouth fell on the shell of my ear. *"Dulce de leche."*

If I could have evaporated into a cloud of steam, I would have.

That was how hot this man made me with nothing more than three words that weren't even supposed to be arousing. But I was, my God. I was so aroused.

"Was that good?" he asked, keeping his mouth right where it was, the touch of his lips on my skin sending wave after wave of shivers down my arms. "More?"

To my utter surprise, I nodded my head and said, "Please."

I heard him inhale deeply, slowly, then he said, *"Eres preciosa. Me recuerdas a una flor. A una rosa."*

My lips parted. My whole body churned now. "What does that mean?"

Lucas's voice was impossibly low when he answered, "You're stunning. You remind me of a flower. A beautiful rose." My breath caught. "You blush like one, too, Rosie. It's so fitting. So . . . goddamn gorgeous."

And I . . . I wasn't okay.

The way this felt wasn't normal. The way my heart raced and my body pulsed with need, longing, yearning for him, couldn't possibly be normal.

It couldn't be. And if it was, I didn't think I could take it. It was too much.

But Lucas had said that; he had called me beautiful. Said I was stunning. In two different languages, and I . . . knew he'd meant it. I knew it in my bones.

The way I feel has never been more real, I thought.

But I couldn't allow myself to acknowledge that out loud. Because tonight was supposed to be research, an experiment—our last experimental date—and now I knew I was at risk of having my heart broken. It could happen tomorrow, when I returned to my apartment, and I wouldn't see him every day. Or it could happen in a matter of weeks, when he went back to Spain.

I let out a breath, the sound rocky, unsteady. "Thank you."

Lucas's head reared back slowly. "Thank you?"

I averted my eyes, and as much as I didn't want to stop looking at him, I did. "Yeah. That was very deserving of a grand gesture kind of night."

Because that was what tonight was about. Phase four, the grand gesture.

Usually, in novels, it came after a black moment, after feelings are put to the test. But in this case—being this was nothing but an experiment—that hadn't made sense. So, we'd jumped ahead.

Lucas didn't answer, not for a while. He just looked at me, his lips curled into the smallest smile he'd ever given me.

Reaching for my glass of wine, I mused over what to say, finally settling for something that had crossed my mind, but I had never asked. "Can I ask you something, Lucas?"

"You know you can ask me anything."

"You never talk about Spain." I was trying my luck here. He didn't want to talk about his injury, or whatever had happened to him, I knew that much. But I couldn't stop thinking about him going back. "You've only talked about Abuela. Or Taco." I paused. "You know, the plan had been to fly your grandma here. With Taco. But she said she'd had enough of New York when she visited Lina a couple of years ago. She said everything's so big here it gives her *chicken skin*? Charo wasn't able to translate that."

"*Piel de gallina*. Goosebumps. That just means that it gives her goosebumps." Lucas let out a chuckle, but his heart wasn't in it. Then, he said, "What do you want to know, beautiful Rosie?"

Everything. "Do you miss home?"

"Yes and no."

I shifted to the edge of the stool, my knees moving into the space between his. "What do you miss about it?"

He seemed to deflate at the question, so I placed a hand on his knee. Encouraging him. He pressed his thigh against mine in response. "I miss . . . my life. How my life was before. Some days I wake up thinking I'm back in time, and my head starts pondering what beach I can drive to before the crowd gets in. Then I remember."

"You remember what?"

His gaze zeroed in on my fingers as they rested on his knee. "That I'm not there anymore. That I'm no longer myself."

"Lucas?" I said, and whatever he heard in my voice made him retrieve my hand from his knee and take it in his. "Why come here? Are you running from something? From whatever happened?"

He brought our hands to his mouth and placed his lips on my wrist. "I'm not running, *ángel*. Some days I'm not even moving."

Ángel. My heart pounded. "What do you need?" I asked, because whatever that was, I wanted to get it for him. "To feel like you're moving forward again."

His gaze searched my face. "I don't know, Rosie. And that's what scares me the most."

Something in my chest broke for him. The need to make it better growing by the minute. "I'll take your hand," I told him, tightening my grip around his fingers. "And keep you moving. Until you figure it out."

And I'll take that ángel, too. And keep it.

Keep it for when he left, and I had these memories instead of him.

He didn't speak, not right away. Then, he said, "I hope you're ready for your grand gesture."

CHAPTER TWENTY-TWO

Rosie

"*I* have no idea if I got this right," he said from behind me, his hands covering my eyes.

After leaving the restaurant, Lucas had ushered me into the elevator—the one inside the building where Zarato was located—and took us up to the top floor.

Before the doors opened, he told me to close my eyes and laid both hands over them, saying, "For good measure."

We walked very slowly now, Lucas guiding me forward. His legs tangled with mine, and I grasped both his wrists to keep myself from falling.

"Is this really necessary?"

"Yes," he confirmed, bringing me to a stop. "*Cosmo* said that the element of surprise was very important."

"*Cosmo*?" A bark of laughter left me. "As in *Cosmopolitan*, the magazine?"

"What's so funny?" he asked, and I could hear the smile in his voice.

"Nothing." I let my hands fall from his wrists. "Just that you sound like a guy from a chick flick from the noughties."

His hands shifted so only one palm was covering my eyes. Then when I felt his other one at my waist, tickling my side.

"Hey!" I squealed, breaking into a fit of giggles. "What was that for? That's a compliment. It doesn't get better than 2000s Matthew McConaughey." I waited for his laughter, but it didn't come. "It was all innocent teasing."

"Nothing innocent about it, Rosie. You know how much I like it," he said. And before I could utter a word, his arm wrapped around me, the tips of his fingers making contact with the bare skin of my back. "Careful with the step," he added before lifting me up in the air.

And just as swiftly, I was placed back on the floor. And I . . . was too stunned, distracted, to even say thanks.

Lucas chuckled darkly as he guided us forward again. "Just so you know, I used other sources that weren't magazines." We turned to the right, and then stopped again. "Hold on one sec. Keep your eyes closed. I'll be right back."

I heard his steps as he walked away.

"I watched a few movie endings," he said in the distance. "Classics, for the most part. Until I discovered that people put together grand gesture compilations on YouTube." His voice grew closer, and then, his hands were back on me. On my waist this time. "And I also had your book."

My heart pounded.

"The ending was a pretty good reference. Insightful."

My book's ending. That I'd written. Lucas had read it. He—

"You can open your eyes now."

As if on autopilot, my eyelids lifted.

And I . . . Oh God. I wished I never had. I wished I hadn't opened my eyes to something like this.

Because whatever I had been feeling a few seconds, minutes, hours ago had been nothing, nothing, compared to what was flooding my chest now. My body. I felt so light, so elated and moved, that I could take flight and float into the dark, stormy night.

"Lucas," I whispered.

His hands trailed up to my shoulders, his palms warm, so warm, against my skin and he said, "What do you think?"

We were on the rooftop of the building. Half of it was a greenhouse, flowers of all colors scattered around us, while the other half was open and exposed to the overcast November sky, that now seemed lit by strings of fairy lights that crisscrossed above us.

It was a beautiful place. Magical. Transcendent. It felt like a moment you know will become a memory before it's even passed.

Dad's words came back, *Remember to pick the boy that will plant a garden for you instead of just getting you the flowers, Bean.*

"I'm not sure if I did this right," Lucas said. "This is my first grand gesture."

Battling against the emotion clogging my voice, I shook my head.

"You did. It's perfect, Lucas. This is all so beautiful, I . . ." God, I needed to keep it together. I couldn't let him know how *much* I was feeling in that moment. "I wouldn't change a thing. Not one."

"You flatter me, *ángel*. But this is not all. This is not what I hoped I got right."

He dipped his head and brushed his lips over my cheek very softly, surprising me at how different this felt compared to every other time he'd done that. Breaking my heart, too, because I wanted so much more than a simple kiss on the cheek.

Lucas grasped my hand, pulling me forward with him. We stopped only when we reached a bench where he had laid a blanket, a Bluetooth speaker, a bottle of wine, and a pink box with a ribbon.

He pulled his phone from the pocket of his suit and tapped on the screen. Music filled the space around us. "You said you wished we'd met at Aaron and Lina's wedding," he said, his expression turning grim. He took one determined step toward me. "I thought that tonight, for this one last date, we could pretend we were doing that. Meeting for the first time."

The thrumming in my chest resumed. Louder. Bigger. Overcoming me with an emotion so powerful I found it hard to breathe.

Lucas smiled, and it was one of those rare bashful smiles. "What do you think? Is it . . . Is it grand enough?"

This selfless, considerate, good man, openly anxious over something like this. Over me liking his grand gesture. Me considering it grand enough.

I wanted to scream. At the world for being so unfair. At him, for going after my heart like this. For making it his in such a short amount of time.

Because he'd made it his, hadn't he? He'd made me his without even trying. Not really. Without my knowing when exactly it had happened.

God, I loved him. I had fallen in love with Lucas Martín.

And I knew it with a certainty that made my chest tight.

I had never stood a chance, not really.

I stood there, breathless, motionless, the realization rocking my body, as I watched Lucas's hands come to the front of his slacks and running his palms along the fabric covering his thighs.

He cleared his throat before speaking. "I know this is not even close to a garden with a view of the Bay of Biscay, so . . . I also have this."

He knelt and fumbled with something below the bench. A beam of light appeared, illuminating the wall behind us. Photos of Lina and Aaron's wedding flashed on the smooth surface. The venue, the ceremony, Aaron's and Lina's happy faces, Abuela, Lina's parents, little snippets of that day played across that wall.

And I . . . I just . . . couldn't do this.

With him. With the knowledge that his presence in my life had an expiration date.

A blanket was thrown over my shoulders, and it was only then that I noticed I was shivering. "Say something, Ro."

Ro.

He'd never called me that on a date. That was his name for *every other night.*

"I—" I breathed. There was nothing I could say to make him understand what this meant to me. How wonderful this was. How deeply I had fallen in love with him. "I can't believe you did this. That you thought of this. For me. You're just . . ."

Perfect.

Amazing.

The best man I could ever ask for.

Lucas angled his body so he was all I could see, and then, he brushed the back of his fingers against my cheek.

"Rosie." He said my name tenderly, so tenderly, that I wanted to beg him to take it back. "Had I been at the wedding," he continued, and my heart stopped beating all over again when he met my gaze, "had I spotted you across that hall, I would have thought *wow*." He paused, his face lighting up. "That girl takes my breath away, she's so beautiful. And she sure looks like she loves cake."

An airy chuckle escaped my lips, dazed by his words.

He reached for the box that sat on the bench and threw the lid open. Inside, a single slice of strawberry and cream cake sat on a little plate. And I recognized it immediately. It was the same kind that had been served at Lina and Aaron's wedding. But—*how?*

Lucas extracted the plate and held it in his hand, placing the box by his feet. Then he said, "I would have crossed the busy hall, cake in hand, and I would have approached you with a dashing smile."

God.

All those women that had had him at some point in the past and let him go had been so stupid. Crazy.

"And I . . ." I trailed off, my voice thick with emotion, needing a few more seconds to collect myself. "I would have looked at you up and down with a frown," I told him, doing exactly that. "And I would have thought, hmm, he's a total weirdo, but at least he brought something sweet." I took the plate from him and when he laughed, I added, "And he has a good laugh, and a handsome smile, so I guess . . . I guess I'll stay. Accept the cake."

His gaze warmed as it roamed over my face. "Because I *am* a weirdo, I would have asked if you were going to share. That'd be the least you could do, after I made it all the way to you with the cake, dodging drunk uncles and inquisitive aunties that wanted to know if I was going to stay single forever."

Not caring about not having a fork, or a napkin, I bit into it. It was sweeter, softer, far better than the one served at the wedding. And I knew without a doubt that he had baked it. Lucas had baked this cake.

My next words barely made it out. "And I . . . would have probably told you that maybe, you were single because you went around offering cake to women you knew nothing about." With shaky hands, I held the plate in front of his face. "But that maybe, just this one time, this girl who might or might not be available, and who might or might not like you, would share some."

Lucas leaned down, taking a bite from the other side and licking the cream off his lips. He savored it, exactly like I knew he would, keeping his eyes on mine as he did. He swallowed. "And after thanking you, I would have respectfully disagreed." I tilted my head, watching all lightness leave his expression. "Because I would have known then"—Lucas stepped forward, his chin dipping to look straight into my eyes—"that I'd been single only because no one had ever stolen my attention, scattered my thoughts so effortlessly. So completely. Not the way you did."

His words danced around us, waltzing straight into my heart.

The energy shifted as we stared into each other's eyes, a hundred thousand unsaid things hanging between us.

The air around turned thicker, heavier, and I thought I heard thunder in the distance, but I'd been sucked into a vacuum. I couldn't care about anything but him. Us.

Lucas snatched the half-eaten cake from me. Then he removed the blanket from my shoulders, took my hand in his, and placed his other one on the small of my back.

"And then," he told me in a voice I had never heard from him. One that I'd never ever forget. "I would have begged you to save me a dance. Or two. Or every dance until the night was over and our feet hurt. And after that, I would have *begged* you to please let me take you home with me. To my bed. Into my heart."

I felt myself expand, float away and up into the stormy sky. Adrift if not for Lucas's arms holding me back.

As if he had known, he pulled me closer, starting to move along to the music, and in silence, we danced. We spun and swayed, his arms around me and my cheek coming to rest on his chest. And I swore, in that moment nothing, not a single thing in the world, could have taken me away from him. Not a thunderclap, not the place bursting into flames, not even the apocalypse or King Kong climbing the side of the building we were in.

Not one single thing.

Because I was in Lucas's arms, and I knew how ephemeral this moment was. How soon I would lose this, him, his body around mine. I'd have nothing but a memory. An imprint that would fade.

That was probably why, when the sky was lit with a lightning bolt, I didn't find it in me to care. To let go of him.

And when the clouds above us shook with a peal of thunder, I remained in Lucas's arms.

Not even when the sky opened and water started pouring on us, did I move to leave his arms.

It was Lucas's chest that shook under my face with laughter and a curse. "For Christ's sake."

I shook my head, my arms tightening around his waist. "I don't care about the rain."

"You're getting drenched, Rosie. We should go."

"No," I told him, looking up so he could see my face. "I'm okay, right here. I don't want to go."

Another thunderclap roared, as if the sky was trying to prove a point.

Without giving it any thought, Lucas took off his jacket as best as he could with my arms around his waist and held it above my head. He met my gaze. "Rosie, please. You're going to get sick. You can't get sick, what about your book? Your deadline is in less than three weeks. You're on the clock. Let me take you home."

There he went, with my heart again. Putting me first. Making it even more impossible for me not to love him the way I did.

"What about you, though?" I shook my head, feeling my hair stick to my cheeks because the jacket above my head was now dripping water, too. "What if I want to take care of you, too?"

Lucas swallowed.

"What if you're important to me, Lucas?" I told him, because he was. He needed to hear it. I placed my palms on his chest and said very slowly, "What if I wanted to be the person you let take care of you, too?"

Lucas's expression changed, morphed. As if he couldn't compute my words.

Which was probably why I continued, "You're always watching over me, taking care of me. Helping me." I watched his eyes close, his head shake. "Giving me everything without asking for a single thing in return. And I . . . I want to give you things, too. I want to give you everything. I want you to want that from me, too." I felt my chest heaving, heart racing, daring me to ask the question I knew I shouldn't. "Do you want that from me, Lucas?"

Lucas stared at me as if my words had been nothing but a blow to his chest. As if I'd just hit him, punched him, and knocked him stunned. He remained silent as water fell in rivulets down his face and gathered at his jaw.

"You understand what I'm saying," I said, everything I had so carefully kept together slipping away. "Yes, you do, and that's why you're looking like that at me."

A muscle pulsed in his jaw.

No answer.

My hands fell to my sides in defeat. "Well, it's on me," I murmured. "We said that things wouldn't change between us, and I let them. I . . . I'm sorry I did that, Lucas."

I turned around and gathered our belongings on the bench, my face turned so he wouldn't see how big of a fool I felt. How much lay underneath my confession. In how many pieces he was breaking my heart.

"Rosie." His fingers wrapped around my wrist.

I shook my head. "It's okay."

He turned me around. Water dripped from his hair, falling down his face. "You're crying, Rosie." A sound escaped his lips, and he pulled at me again, wanting to bring me to him. "*Ángel, por favor.* Don't cry. Don't do that to me."

"I'm not crying," I lied. "It's just the rain. I'm okay."

His fingers cupped my jaw and he tilted my head upward until I met his gaze.

"You're lying. You're crying and it's breaking my heart," he said in a desperate voice. "Rosie, *preciosa*." He moved closer, as if he couldn't help himself. "Tell me what to do to stop this."

I tried to keep it in. Not to let it out, but that Rosie, that *preciosa*, did me in.

And everything just . . . escaped.

"Want me," I said, and God, how desperate it was to beg for something like this. "Want me like I want you. Because these glimpses of what we could be are killing me, Lucas. That's why I'm crying, because I'm frustrated, devastated, by the fact that I can't have you. That I want you and I can't have you."

Lucas was so still. He had remained unmovable under the rain, but it was only then, when my last words rang, that his whole body came alive. Like a match thrown into a fire, something roared alive inside of him.

He pulled me closer. "You think you can't have me?" His breath fell on my mouth. "Am I the one making those tears fall down your face?"

My heart surrendered then. "I'm crying because we're just friends, because none of this is real. Because maybe all I am to you is that. Your roommate. Ro. *Graham*."

His palms went to my cheeks, cupping my face, and I could feel them shaking, trembling. Another thunderclap cracked in the distance. "Rosie," he said. And the sound of my name rivaled the roaring in the sky. "Every single time I've called you Graham, I've done it to remind myself that I couldn't want you the way I do. Every time I've taken you on a date, I've had to tell myself that it was part of an agreement. And every time I've said I wanted to be your best friend, all I'd wanted was to take from you as much as you could possibly give me."

All the air in my lungs left my body.

"If you want anything from me, you only have to ask." Lucas's forehead came to rest against mine, his breath now leaving him shakily. "Don't you see that I'll break my back to provide anything you could possibly need? Have I not made myself obvious?"

"You can't mean that. You—"

"I mean it with everything I am."

Fighting my own fear, the certainty that this couldn't be really happening, because how could it be? I said, "If you do, if you really mean it, then I want you to kiss me, Lucas."

One second Lucas's hands were around my jaw, and the next they were slipping behind my head, inside the locks of wet hair.

His lips took mine like he was fighting for his last breath, like the rain falling around us signaled the end of the world. Lucas kissed me like this was our first and last kiss, as if this was the only chance he had to give me what I had asked of him. And that should have alerted me of something, but I didn't care. I couldn't care when his mouth was against mine, parting my lips and devouring mine. Devouring me.

His body stepped into mine, one of his hands leaving the nape of my neck and trailing down my spine until it curled around my back. A groan climbed his throat when I went willingly, without any kind of resistance because how could I resist when his fingers splayed over the small of my back, holding me firmly to him, his hips pressing into my belly, my breasts against his chest.

Desperate for more, I linked my arms around his neck and rose to my tiptoes, wishing the heavy and soaked layers of fabric between us hadn't been there. Wishing I could strip him naked, so I'd have as much from him as possible, as much as I'd be able to memorize.

His mouth left mine, his lips trailing down the side of my neck and soliciting a whimper from me. The sound fueled him, encouraging his hands to grab the back of my knees and hike me up his body.

As if it had been choreographed, my legs clamped around him, and he secured me against him again.

"Lucas," I breathed out, pulsing with a new surge of need, letting my fingers into his hair. "You—" His teeth nipped at the lobe of my ear. "You can't—"

"I'll be careful," he said, rearranging me around him, the new position making me know, feel, how big and hard he was. "There are things more important than that. You. You wanted a kiss." He met my gaze, a feral expression contorting his face. His mouth. Hunger flooding his eyes. "What else do you want from me?"

Everything. "Another kiss. A second one. And a third. And a fourth, and—"

His hand returned to my hair, fisting it in his fingers, pulling at it so I'd expose my neck. "Is that all you want?" he said against my pulse, nipping at my skin with his teeth.

No, I wanted to say, but then, he was cupping my head and bringing our mouths together. Then, his hips were punching up, right against the junction of my thighs and he was so hard, so hot against me that I—

"Lucas," I whimpered, my lids fluttering shut.

"I asked you a question," he rasped even when his breath seemed to catch, too. "I said I'd give you whatever you asked. And you wanted my mouth. A kiss. And now." He stopped himself, rearranging me around him, the friction feeling impossibly good and not at all enough at the same time. "Now I want to give you more. Now I don't want to stop at your mouth, Rosie."

I was the one who shifted next, sliding down along his pulsing length, bringing the same expressions of delicious pain to both our faces. I pulled at the hair at the nape of his neck when I expelled my next words, "Then, don't stop. Give me more than that. Give me what you promised me at the Masquerade Ball."

His throat worked, his eyes darkening with a realization, with a thought. "You had to be perfect, didn't you? You had to be capable of taming and pulling at everything that's inside of me?"

Yes. "Everything. I want it all."

Lucas's expression changed, and God, he looked ready to succumb, to give me exactly what I had just asked of him, and I wanted to let him. So, I took his mouth that time, encouraging him. He groaned deep in his throat and . . . a ringtone sounded.

I barely registered it as mine at first. Not until it rang again and infiltrated our bubble, making us come up for air.

Lucas's voice was barely a rasp, but he said, "That's your phone, *preciosa.*"

Still dazed, I fought against the remnants of the fog while the incoming call stopped and started again.

Lucas placed a kiss on the corner of my mouth, then another one on my forehead and placed me back on the floor. He walked us where we'd left our coats, back at the entrance to the roof. Fishing for my purse, he opened it and extracted my ringing phone.

I checked the screen—unknown—and answered the call.

"Rosie," I heard. "I'm ready to go home."

"Olly?" Every single cell in my body that had been burning scalding hot just seconds ago turned to ice. "Where are you?"

My brother didn't answer, not right away, but I could hear the noise in the background. Music. The nightclub.

"Text me the address," I told him. "Do you hear me, Olly? Text me where you are. I'm on my way."

There was a curt, "Thank you." And then, the line went dead.

CHAPTER TWENTY-THREE

Rosie

*L*ucas's hand squeezed mine again.

He'd been doing that the whole ride, and I knew what it meant. He didn't need to voice the words "I got you, I'm here," because that gentle but fierce squeeze of my hand as it lay cocooned in his was enough. No. It was more than enough, really. Him being here, not hesitating to hail a cab without asking for the full story or details, and taking the reins of a situation I was having a hard time keeping up with was more than enough.

It was everything.

The image of the busted lip Olly had sported the last time I'd seen him flashed in front of my eyes.

God, what the hell have you gotten yourself into, Olly?

Lucas's fingers squeezed mine again, and I thought he murmured something, something soothing, but all I was hearing in my head was *Please, let him be okay. Whatever this is, please, please, please, let him be okay.*

The taxi pulled up to the address Olly had texted, and I unclasped my fingers from Lucas's grasp so fast that he couldn't do anything to stop me from jumping out of the vehicle.

"Rosie, don't!" He cursed. But I kept on walking. I was on autopilot.

His steps sounded behind me, quick, fast, as if he'd been running after me, and I felt like a jerk, because I shouldn't have made Lucas run, not with his injury. But I—

He grabbed my hand and pulled at it, bringing me to a stop. He walked around me and faced me. "Don't do that to me ever again, please."

His hair was still wet. The clothes beneath both our coats were so damp, they weighed twice as much as they would have dry. He was probably feeling as cold as I did, and yet, I knew that wasn't the reason why he looked so miserable.

"I'm sorry," I told him, because I really was. "I shouldn't have done that."

I squeezed his hand and relief spread across his face.

With another sigh, I took note of our surroundings, the rumble of music in the distance indistinguishable. It had to be coming from the nightclub down the street, the one Olly had texted before. Pink Flamingo.

"Do you know this part of the city?" Lucas asked.

"Never been here." I shook my head. "But it's not exactly known for its good rep." I paused. "There's something I should probably tell you, Lucas." He remained in silence, laser focused on me, waiting. "My brother . . . he had a black eye. A few weeks ago. And I . . ."

And I hadn't done anything. Not a single thing. I'd let him walk away.

Lucas processed that information. Then, looked left and right. "Text him that we're here. If he doesn't answer, then we're going to find him and get him out."

I nodded my head, already inching toward the neon-lit entrance.

Lucas tugged at my hand. "You're going to stay behind me, okay? I'm not playing overprotective hero, Rosie, but if someone tries to get close to you, don't engage, yeah?" He patted his chest with his fist. "You stay with me."

My throat worked. "But what if—"

"*Ángel*," he said almost painfully. "I've traveled, stumbled upon people I shouldn't have and got into a few ugly messes myself. So please, please stay with me. Just trust me with—"

"Okay." I nodded my head. No hesitation. "I trust you. I'll stay with you. I won't engage." His features relaxed. "But only if you don't, either. I don't want you to get into trouble, not because of me."

Something shifted in his gaze and then, without giving me any kind of warning, he was brushing a kiss on the corner of my lips. "I trust you, too, *ángel*."

And just like that, we were moving again.

Lucas stopped a few steps away from the neon sign. A bouncer stood guard, the door covered by a maroon curtain.

I took one last look at my phone to see if Olly had answered my text. He hadn't. "Let's go," I told Lucas.

We stepped forward, Lucas slightly ahead of me, and the bouncer looked us up and down with a frown.

"No couples allowed. Performers through the back."

I stepped around Lucas, coming to his side so I could explain to the bouncer why we needed to go in. Both of us.

But the mountain of a man stopped me with a hand. "No couples allowed," he repeated, before returning to his position and parting the curtain. "The lady can go in." He pointed to Lucas. "You, out. Or through the back."

"No," Lucas refused. I took another step forward, and a warning left Lucas in a growl. "Rosie, please."

I was ready to let go of his hand, to tell him that it was okay, when the curtain opened. Then, I heard my name.

"Rosie," my brother, my *little* brother, said.

And he was . . . shirtless. Covered in what looked like . . . oil. And glitter.

I threw myself at him, wrapping my arms around his shoulders. "Are you okay? Please, tell me you're okay."

Olly's eyes darted around.

"I'm okay," he croaked. "But we should really go, now."

I released him, clasped my hands around his cheeks, and inspected his face. God, when had he turned into the man in front of me? "What the hell is going on, Olly?"

The bouncer spoke before Olly could respond. "Graham, you know the rules. No hanging out in the entrance. Performers through the goddamn back. You've got five seconds."

"Olly—"

My brother shook his head and ushered us away from the club. "Let's go, Rosie. I'll tell you everything but not here, okay?"

Lucas's hand grazed the small of my back. "I called an Uber the moment Olly got out that door. It'll be here in a few minutes," he said as he came up behind us and led us away from the entrance to the club.

He took his coat off and threw it in my arms. "Put it on your brother."

"Who's this?" Olly asked.

I looked at my brother just in time to see him take in Lucas's suit. Then, glancing at me and inspecting my attire. He came to a stop. "Oh God, you were on a date."

I picked up my pace, pulling him after me, the answer to that question too complicated for me to elaborate. "And now I'm here. I'm so glad you called, Olly."

Just as Lucas was nodding, I heard heavy steps behind us. I turned around—we all did—and took in the man that had just exited the club and was now looking our way.

"Jimmy," Olly muttered. "Fuck."

"Well, well," Jimmy drawled. "Olly, if you were going to invite your pretty sister to watch a show, you should have given me a heads-up." He looked me up and down with a sneer. "I would have cleaned up."

I recognized him as the man who had picked up my brother outside Penn Station weeks ago.

Both my brother and Lucas moved forward, partly in front of me.

But I managed to make eye contact with Jimmy. I knew a bully when I saw one.

"Not even a hello?" He clicked his tongue. "That's not very friendly, now, is it?"

Lucas, who I noticed now had been inching toward Jimmy, came to a stop a few feet in front of Olly and me.

I watched the muscles in his back straighten, his shoulders somehow expanding. "Don't talk to her," Lucas said in a hard voice I'd never heard from him. "Don't even look her way. You have something to say to her, or Olly, you go through me."

Jimmy snickered. "Well then, tell pretty boy next show is in fifteen. The crowd is already feral, so he better throw on some more oil and get in." *Next show*. It really dawned then, Olly, my brother, a performer. A stripper. "Or now that his girl is tucked away he's not taking the stage anymore?"

Tucked away. Oh, Olly. Whatever trouble he'd gotten into was over protecting a girl, of course, it was.

Jimmy's words were still echoing in the night when a vehicle came to a stop behind us.

I watched the man's eyes narrow.

Lucas didn't turn to look at us—at me—when he said, "Rosie, get your brother in the car."

Still shocked, I hesitated. Lucas stood there like a statue, serving as a wall between Jimmy and me and my brother.

"*Ángel*," Lucas's deep and commanding voice came again, breaking through my hesitance. "Car, now. *Please*."

Snapping into action, I linked arms with my brother and headed for the Uber. Once my brother was sitting inside, I turned back to check on Lucas. He remained in the same position, only now Jimmy was right in front of him, the two of them talking. Nothing more than gritted words between their teeth, not loud enough for me to make out a single thing.

I didn't like it. Not one bit. Every cell in my body demanded that I go to Lucas and drag him away.

"Stay in the car, Olly," I said, and gestured for the driver to wait.

I had dragged Lucas into this mess, and I'd be damned if something happened to him because of me. I had almost made it to Lucas, my arms ready and stretched in his direction, reaching for him, when Jimmy threw back his shoulders and shoved at Lucas's chest.

The man I loved so much for his kindness, his warmth, his selfless heart, stumbled back before straightening. And instead of retaliating, instead of returning the shove or throwing a punch, he took another step back.

"You're a lucky man," Lucas told him, ice in his voice. "I promised her I wouldn't engage."

The other man scoffed, the sound weak and his next words uncertain: "Oh yeah?"

Lucas stared down the other man for a long moment, and then, he turned, leaving him behind. He was keeping his promise to me; he wasn't engaging.

But then, so quickly the motion hardly registered, Jimmy charged forward, his boot making impact against Lucas's calf. His right calf.

Lucas went down, falling to his knees with hardly a sound. His head hung low between his shoulders, and his chest heaved.

My vision blurred, my ears rang, and everything turned red. As if I were no longer myself, I darted forward.

"You son of a bitch!" I cried.

"My bad," I heard Jimmy drawl. "See, promises don't mean much to me."

Ignoring all caution, my rage bubbled to the surface.

I looked around, desperate to do something, anything, to make him hurt, finding nothing but my purse hanging off my shoulder.

I gripped it by the handle and raised my arm, ready to fling the clutch at him if it was the best I could come up with, overlooking how harmless it would really be. How ridiculous.

Warm fingers wrapped around my wrist, and the only voice in the world that could have stopped me from doing something so stupid spoke, "Rosie, *no.*"

My lips parted, and I heard myself saying, "*Yes.*"

Those fingers spread, their touch anchoring me. Grounding me. "Don't engage. You promised me." I had, but that had been before Lucas had taken that ugly hit. "Put down the bag."

It wasn't the plea in his voice. It was the knowledge of him standing on his feet, the pain lacing his voice, that made me obey. I looked at him, and he even managed a smile. "He's not worth it."

He wasn't.

But for the first time in my life, I wanted to choose violence.

"Let's go home." Lucas's fingers pulled at my arm, extricating my purse from my death grip. He slipped it on his arm, even when I told him I could carry it myself. But Lucas didn't listen. He straightened and threw an arm around my shoulders, leaning some of his weight on me. He walked with me, and I could tell he was biting through the pain. When we reached the car, Lucas turned. "I have *nothing* to lose, Jimmy. Nothing. And you'd be wise to remember that, because next time I won't be walking away."

CHAPTER TWENTY-FOUR

Rosie

*N*obody said a word on the way back to the apartment.

Olly gazed out the window, his bare torso covered by Lucas's coat.

I sat between the two men, linking my arm with my brother. And Lucas, whose face had been void of any kind of emotion, held my hand tightly. As if I was the one in need of support.

Me, when it had been *him* on the ground. Me, when *he* was the one in pain. In pain because of me.

I felt so guilty, I could hardly breathe. That was probably why I slipped into management mode the moment we finally entered Lina's studio for what was supposed to be my final night. Because I couldn't allow myself to think too much, either.

I shoved my brother into the bathroom and forced him to take a shower. When he was out, I did the same with Lucas. I took the pair of sweats and hoodie Lucas offered and shoved them in Olly's hands, making sure he changed into the warm clothes. I prepared tea. I grabbed blankets from the closet and placed them on the armrest of the couch, ready to wrap the two men up in them if they so much as looked chilly. Then, I put ice in a cloth for Lucas, not even knowing if that would help. And after that, I went on a scavenger hunt for painkillers. Because this wasn't my place, and I didn't know where Lina might keep some.

"What are you looking for?" Lucas asked as I crouched on the kitchen floor, still in my dress.

"What are *you* doing, Lucas?" I answered. "Take the ice and go sit down, please."

"Not until you tell me what you're looking for."

"I'm searching for painkillers. For you." Moving a large pan to one side, I sighed. "I've looked everywhere, bathroom, drawers . . . I have no idea if Lina has any."

"Rosie," Lucas said, and his voice made me look up. He didn't seem happy, which I guessed wasn't surprising given the circumstances. "There are no painkillers in there. Only pots."

"You're right," I said, coming to a standing position and feeling the still damp fabric shifting against my legs. "There's a CVS down the street. It should be open."

"You're not going anywhere," he said simply. "You're staying right where you are. With me. And you're getting out of this dress and jumping into the shower, too."

"But—"

He came forward, getting close, really close. He tucked a lock of hair behind my ear. "This is not a one-way street, Rosie. You look after me, and I look after you. We take care of each other. We're a team."

"A team." I sighed, my eyelids falling closed.

His thumb swiped along my jaw so softly I could barely feel it. "Yes. So, get in the shower and change into dry clothes. I'll keep an eye on Olly."

Afraid of blurting out how good he was and how much I loved him, I just nodded.

On my way to the bathroom, I tried to calm my pulse, all the conflicting emotions threatening to burst out of me. Guilt and gratitude. Love and terrifying fear of getting my heart broken.

Once done with the shower, hair towel-dried, and clad in my

pajamas, I opened the bathroom door to Olly wrapped in a blanket on one corner of the couch and Lucas sitting on the floor with his back against the opposite side.

He was pressing the ice pack on his knee and when our gazes met, his eyes warmed. Then, as I stood there in my sleeping shorts, he looked down my bare legs and that warmth turned into heat.

A few hours ago, a look like that would have left me tingling, hoping for more, but now all of that . . . had soured. Because I had ruined tonight. And I hated it. I hated that I was responsible for him being in pain.

"Come here," Lucas said, patting the couch cushion behind his head. "I was asking Olly what we should watch."

I sighed. "It's so late, Lucas I . . ."

Before I could properly complain, though, Lucas's lips curled, giving me a distracting smile. "We all need to unwind, take our minds off tonight. I would cook something but—"

"No." I instinctively shot forward. Just so he wouldn't move from where he was. "No cooking or anything that imp es being on your feet for you. Stay put."

He smiled wider, and dammit, it was hard not t feel good seeing that smile.

"I think he's right, Rosie," my brother offered.

"You two ganging up on me?" With a sigh, I came to a stop in front of Lucas. "Why don't you take the couch? There's enough space for you to stretch your leg."

He shook his head. "The floor is fine."

I pinned him with a look.

And instead of fighting me over it, instead of trying to say something that would convince me or make me feel better, he placed the palm of his hand to the side of my thigh. And slowly, ever so slowly, he squeezed. The pads of his fingers were right against my bare skin, and everywhere that our skin touched heated up. Intense awareness spread out, traveling to all parts of my body.

Lucas let his hand rest there as he looked up at me, straight into my eyes. His jaw set into a line, his features serious. "Don't make me get on my feet and pick you up myself, *ángel*." And I knew he meant it. "Because I'll carry you to the couch if I have to."

God, this man. "Fine," I relented.

His hand fell off my skin at the same time as a grunt of agreement left his lips.

Choosing to ignore how that little sound affected me, I plopped myself down on the couch, watching as Lucas repositioned himself so his shoulders and head were between my legs.

He curled the arm that wasn't holding the ice around my shin. "Now the floor isn't just fine," he said quietly. "It's perfect."

I laughed, secretly cursing him for thinking he could go around saying stuff like that like it was nothing. Like it wasn't supposed to make me want to scramble off the couch and camp in his lap.

"Bean?" my brother called from the other side of the couch.

I looked over at him. "Yeah, Olly?"

"Why are we at Lina's place?"

"That's a bit of a long story. I'll be moving back to my apartment tomorrow."

Lucas nudged my knee with his head, and my hand unconsciously dragged along my thigh, stopping when my fingertips reached his hair. Slipping them in, I absently stroked a few chocolate-colored strands back.

"After I drop you off at Dad's," I added, watching with infinite pleasure how Lucas's head rolled to one side under my touch. "I'll take the train to Philly with you and then get back to the city."

"Okay," Olly accepted without a complaint. And that made me so relieved I barely handled not crying. "I already told your boyfriend while you were in the shower, but . . . I'm sorry I ruined your night," he continued, and the man sitting between my legs on the floor, the one whose head was leaning on my thigh and whose hand was latched on my ankle, didn't utter a word at the label my brother had used. Didn't even tense or flinch at all. Olly went on, "I owe you an explanation, Rosie. For being an idiot and dragging you into my mess tonight. Because if you had shown up alone, Jimmy—"

"But she didn't," Lucas cut my brother off. "And that's what matters."

"That's right. And I know you're sorry, Olly." There wasn't a doubt in my mind or heart about it. Olly was sorry, and this whole ordeal would weigh on him for a long time. "But I need to know what happened, whatever it was."

Olly nodded, falling so quiet that I thought he wouldn't say anything, but then he did. "There's this girl, Lexie. It all started with her really." He shook his head, and the gesture somehow reminded me of how much he'd changed. How much older he looked now. "It was a bet. I was trying to impress her and . . . it turned out to be fun. More fun than I thought. And the money was good. That movie isn't lying." He chuckled bitterly. "I made enough to come back the next night. But it was because of her that I went back every night after that. To keep an eye on her."

I swallowed, processing everything he was telling me, coming up with a hundred questions. But the one that seemed to matter the most was, "Is Lexie okay now?"

He nodded. "Yeah, we're . . . it doesn't matter. I got her out of trouble, Rosie. That was why I didn't want to do it anymore." His expression turned heavy. "Jimmy is the owner's right hand, and he wasn't happy about me quitting. I apparently attracted a good . . . audience. But I knew that if I involved you, he would let me walk away. He wouldn't want to attract too much attention or trouble. Calling you was selfish."

"Oh, sweetie." I sighed, my heart aching. "I'm your sister. Asking for my help isn't selfish."

"But I got your boyfriend hurt. You could have been, too."

Lucas reacted then, and what he said was, "Jimmy did, not you. And I'd never let anyone hurt Rosie, Olly. Just like I told you earlier."

"Thanks," Olly whispered.

Other than that, my brother didn't say anything else, and neither did the amazing, selfless man nestled between my legs. So, I continued playing with Lucas's hair for a long time, scratching his scalp gently. And even when his body slumped against my legs, and his chest rumbled against my skin, I still kept going. Because as much as touching Lucas usually left every cell in my body tingling, I was beginning to understand that touching someone you loved was about much more than just that. It wasn't always about the sparks and the fireworks. Not exclusively. It could also be about the peace it brought you. The comfort. And for all the romances I'd read and the one, almost two, I'd written, I hadn't known that. I would have *never* imagined that touching a man could light me up inside and quiet every worry and every noise in the world.

We stayed like that for a long while, none of us paying any attention to what was playing on the TV. Only when Olly's breath deepened and snores sounded from his side of the couch did I lean forward to whisper in Lucas's ear.

"Let's go to bed."

I moved around him, standing up and offering him both hands. With a tired expression that told me he'd been about to follow my brother's example, he took them, letting me pull him up.

And just like it happened every time I came within hugging distance of this man, I ended up wrapped in his arms for a long, heavenly moment.

His head dipped. "You did so well tonight, Rosie. So well."

It felt like I hadn't done a single thing *right* tonight. Or lately.

I shook my head and turned around, making my way to the bed.

"Rosie?" Lucas's hushed voice reached me from where he was, still at the foot of the sofa. "I think that if you help me"—his features hardened as he seemed to think about something—"maybe we can get your brother into the bed."

"Come here," I whispered back, throwing open the covers of the bed. But he hesitated, not moving. Turning that tender spot in my chest even softer. "Leave Olly. You sleep here tonight. With me."

His jaw tensed.

"Lucas Martín," I said, hearing the edge in my voice, even if hushed, "if you don't get in this bed, with me, right this second, you're going to break my heart. And I don't think I will be able to take it. Not tonight."

I wasn't even joking.

Because only a few hours ago, I'd been in his arms, and he'd been kissing me. And as much as we hadn't talked about it, something had . . . opened between us. Something *more.*

All of that must have been written all over my face because Lucas's hesitation melted away.

Choosing not to ask him for the hundredth time if he was in pain, I joined him in bed and threw the covers over us. I rolled on my side with a long and deep sigh, and faced him while he remained on his back, his head turned toward me.

"Are you comfortable?"

"As much as I'll ever be, *ángel.*"

I swallowed, searching his face for the meaning behind that. Was he hurting? Did he regret coming with me tonight? Did he regret kissing me?

"I'm sorry you got hurt, Lucas. I hate that you did, but . . ." I trailed off, hating myself a little bit for what I was going to say. "Does it make me a horrible person to say that despite everything, I'm glad you were there? With me?"

He shook his head. "You have nothing to be sorry for, okay?" He looked at me as if he was waiting for something. "I would have never let you go in there alone, Rosie. Never."

I shifted, moving a little closer to him.

Lucas reached out a hand, the pads of his fingers brushing the corner of my lips lightly. Too quickly. "I can't believe you were ready to hit him with your purse. For me."

He wasn't smiling. Or laughing. And I didn't want to, either, because I had been dead serious about that. "And I can't believe you stopped me from doing that."

"You're always beautiful," he shocked me by saying, and my heart sped up. "But seeing you like that? Ready to claw your way forward to protect me?" He paused, his eyes filling with something that would have been awe if not for the heavy and sultry quality that coated them. "You were breathtaking. Like an avenging angel. I had to stop myself from kissing you there and then."

My lips parted, and my face flushed. Not from embarrassment, but from the wave of need that in that moment washed over my whole body. Because Lucas was not only saying he'd wanted to kiss me, but he was also looking at me like he'd die if he didn't.

"We shouldn't," he breathed out. "It's late, and we should get some sleep."

Reluctantly, I nodded.

Lucas added, "My leg will be better tomorrow, I promise."

I didn't believe him. But I loved him for still trying. "You told me I could ask you anything, always, so I want to know about something." He nodded. "Why do you have nightmares?"

Lucas tried to roll on his side and winced in pain.

"The accident," he admitted, falling quiet for a full minute. "It's ironic because I'm drowning in those nightmares. And that was not how it happened. It's as if my head has come up with new different ways to haunt me in my sleep." A long and shaky breath left his lips. "I haven't been able to bring myself to talk about it, not since it happened."

I scooted closer to him. "Why?"

"There hasn't been anyone I've . . . wanted to tell, until now. Someone who wouldn't want to fix me. Because there's nothing left to fix, Rosie."

Fix him? Didn't he see that he was perfect? There was nothing about Lucas that needed fixing. "You can't fix something that's not broken, Lucas."

He reached an arm around my waist, bringing me closer to him. "I was prepping for a competition in Hossegor, weeks before Lina's wedding," he said, voice like gravel. And just like that, I knew that he was going to open up. He was finally going to talk about it. With me. And I felt the luckiest woman in the world to have him trust me first.

"Hossegor?"

"In France," he paused. "It's not a particularly dangerous beach but . . . there's this one spot with one of my favorite breaks. Rosie"—he sighed, and it was somehow hopeful, happy—"it's such a beautiful place. The conditions have to be right, but the wave can hold shape up to three meters, which is almost ten feet, I think. Big, wonderful waves. That's why I'd always try to visit at least once a year. Even if some days it's just close-outs you can't ride."

He was talking with a kind of passion I recognized. It was the same one I heard in my voice when I talked about writing. About my dream. Or the one I'd seen glimpses of in him when he talked about cooking.

"The problem with that spot, though," he continued, his tone no longer the same, "is the shore break. If you're riding a wave that breaks directly onshore, it can propel your body out and onto the sand. With that speed and force, it's like hitting concrete. You can break your neck. Damage your spinal cord. Or your extremities if you fall in a certain way." His voice broke, his eyes fluttering closed. "And I knew all of that. I knew the risks. It's a gnarly place, reserved for pros for a reason. And yet . . ."

And yet it somehow happened.

My palm landed on his chest, and I could feel his heart pounding under my fingers.

"And yet," he repeated, still not finishing the statement, his breath going in and out of his lungs in a broken rhythm, "my knee was shattered. I needed surgery. Everything was . . ." A ghostly expression that broke my heart in a million pieces came over him. I wanted to scream at the injustice of the accident, at all the things he'd lost, and I wanted to somehow return them all to him. "I'll never be able to get that back. My right leg just . . . I can't, Rosie. I'm too old to do it all over again, to recover and climb back to top form. Physical therapy would get me back to fine—not great, not prime shape, just *fine.*"

I cupped his jaw, grazing my thumb over his cheek.

"One hit. That was all it took. One bad hit and I . . ." he trailed off, looking disoriented for a few seconds. "I went under, Rosie. Sunk straight to the bottom."

"You didn't," I told him, slipping my fingers in his hair, clasping the back of his neck. "You're here. Breathing. Whole. Alive."

Lucas's features pinched.

"You lost so much that day, and yet, you're here," I repeated, allowing myself to say what he needed to hear. "You're not the same, and you don't need to be. Because you're here, with me. Opening your eyes every morning and smiling at the world in a way only you know how to do. You lost something, but you didn't lose everything, Lucas. You didn't lose yourself; you just . . . changed."

He tilted his head, resting his cheek against my wrist.

And after a heartbeat, both his arms were around me, and he was saying, "*Ven aquí*."

I didn't recognize the Spanish words, but it didn't matter because I knew what they meant. Come here. Closer.

So I went to him. Because where Lucas was concerned, I'd never hesitate. And so, I curled against his chest, resting my head over his heart.

"You're right. I'm right here, *ángel*," he whispered before brushing his lips on the top of my head. "And I can't believe I found you."

He was wrong. He hadn't found me.

I had.

CHAPTER TWENTY-FIVE

Lucas

A cramp gripping the whole length of my leg woke me.

I knew the consequences of not going through the advised physical therapy sessions. I hadn't nurtured my rebuilt joints and atrophied muscles back to health, and this was their way to protest. Seize control. I had only my own stubbornness to blame.

Up until last night, I hadn't really cared. There hadn't been a reason to. But then, that bastard had kicked me, coming at me from the back, and I'd been on my knees. Gasping for fucking air and incapable of moving, terrified that he'd go after Rosie next, and I wouldn't have been able to stop him. It had been that fear that had somehow brought me up. Only to find her wielding her purse, like a warrior princess.

My thigh spasmed again, and I winced. Realizing I was on my side and all the weight of my body fell on my bad leg, I tried to roll onto my back. But something stopped me. *Peaches*.

I peeked down, finding the source of that intoxicating, delicious scent.

Rosie. Her body was cocooned by mine.

We spooned, the back of her head resting against my throat, her back flush against my chest, our thighs pressed together, and her ass nestled in my lap.

Nestled against my morning wood.

Dios. Never had a hard-on felt so good, and never had it been so . . . inconvenient. Inconvenient for . . . reasons I couldn't recall.

Reasons my dick didn't care for when Rosie's body was so warm and soft against mine. Reasons that seemed unimportant the more time passed with my arms around her waist, or the higher my palm hiked up her stomach, or the deeper my nose dug into her hair.

Rosie shifted, her ass wiggling in my lap, and my hard-on stood to attention, any remaining trace of sleep dissipating and bringing me fully awake.

A breath left my mouth forcefully, and I had to still myself from doing something crazy, something bad. Something like positioning her body so she would rub against me just right. Just—

Rosie's hips moved again, sliding along my length and turning my dick to steel.

"Ah, joder," I breathed out.

Without being able to help myself, I splayed my fingers on her stomach, letting the tops of my fingertips reach her ribs. I needed to stop this, to stop myself, but I couldn't. Didn't really want to. Everything in me wanted her closer, fused against me, and that overpowered any good intentions I might have had at some point in the past. That was probably why I couldn't stop my arms from curling around her, why I couldn't stop myself from pulling her back, right up against me.

Her breath caught.

"Is this okay, *ángel*?" I whispered in her ear, feeling like a selfish bastard even when I asked.

A small part of me expected her to complain, hoped that she would turn and ask what the hell I was doing, what kind of liberties I was taking, but a contented sigh left her lips.

"I thought I'd been dreaming," she said low, so low, her hands coming to grip my forearms and snuggling against me. She *fucking* snuggled into my hard-on, like there was nowhere else she'd rather be. "But it's real. You're here."

My mouth teased the shell of her ear. "You're not dreaming; you're awake." And because I was in fact a selfish bastard and I had happily learned what it did to her, I made sure to murmur in Spanish, *"Buenos días, preciosa."*

A puff of air left her, and her backside shifted again, rubbing herself against my cock. She moved up and down, knowing exactly what she was doing to me.

My lips parted, a groan wanting to escape, my hips dying to move against her, my teeth ready to nibble her ear while I whispered all the things I wanted to do to her.

"Hmm, it still feels like a dream," she said in a breathy voice that sent more blood straight to my dick, making it pulse with need.

I hummed in response, allowing that hand on her stomach to search for the edge of her top. I slipped my fingers underneath, the contact of our skin heating my blood, obscuring everything but my need for her.

"You feel like a dream, too," I told her, burrowing my nose in her hair, inhaling slowly. "Smell like one, too."

A shiver rocked Rosie's body, and her fingers wrapped around my wrist, urging me to touch her, as if I needed any encouragement.

Letting more of my weight fall on her, I trailed my hand up, up, up, passing her stomach, her ribs, reaching the underswell of her breasts. A groan slipped from my mouth when I was reminded she wasn't wearing a bra.

Rosie pressed her ass to my cock again, spurring me on. And once more, I didn't stop myself. I couldn't when she felt so good against me, under my touch.

The back of my fingers grazed the warm skin, making her shiver. And Lord, it took me less than a second to have my hand cupping the fullness of her breast.

Something close to a "Yes" left her lips and my fingers shifted, the pad of my thumb flicking over her nipple.

I wanted to hear that *yes* again, but louder. Clearer. Leaving her mouth in a cry of pleasure, followed by my name. I wanted to fuck all of that right out of her. But there was something I was forgetting. Something that—

Fuck.

"Rosie," I rasped out. "Your brother's sleeping on the couch, less than fifteen feet away."

Her head shook, her back arching further, luring me right back into the haze, pushing me closer and closer to a point of no return.

"He sleeps like the dead," she slurred.

My index finger joined my thumb, closing around her nipple, and I wanted to roar in frustration at knowing that I couldn't tease her as hard or as long as I wanted. That I'd need to stop myself soon.

Rosie whimpered very softly, her ass now moving up and down in my lap, teasing my cock with swaying motions.

Taking my hand off her breast with what took all my goddamn willpower, I stilled her roughly against me.

I counted down to three.

"Rosie," I warned her, bringing my mouth to her ear. Grazing my teeth over the sensitive skin, even when I shouldn't have. "You need to stop that."

But she didn't. She moved again, making my cock swell and pulse with a blinding wave of need. "But it feels so good," she mumbled, sounding out of breath. "Doesn't it feel good for you, too?"

It did.

"*Preciosa*," I growled in her ear. "It feels fucking amazing." And I shouldn't have, I really shouldn't have, but I thrusted against her. Just once. "So good I'll come in my sweats if you keep this on."

"That's not a bad thing," she answered quickly, need coating her hushed words. "I like that."

She tried to move again, but I managed to stop that, turning her and pinning her with the full weight of my body. And I *felt* the shift, the moment it registered in her how much she loved being pinned under me. A moan rumbled in her chest.

I cursed myself.

"You love this, beautiful Rosie?" I heard myself whispering, locking her between me and the mattress. She nodded, her breathing turning labored, hectic. "You love giving me control, having me all over you?" Another nod. And without being able to stop myself, I thrusted against her ass again. One last stroke. The last one. "It'd feel so good if I made you come like this, Rosie."

Rosie whimpered, loudly this time, making the blood traveling straight to my dick swirl with desperation. I covered her mouth.

And that—

Fuck. That didn't help, because her body was now melting like fucking butter left out in the sun.

"Rosie," I said, voice low, so low I didn't recognize it. "I'm not going to make you come with your brother within earshot. Sorry, *preciosa.* I'm sorry."

And I was, God knew I was.

Rosie nodded her head in understanding, and when her eyes opened, I let go of her mouth.

I brushed my lips over her temple. "When I make you come, I'll want to hear those moans." I trailed my mouth down until I reached her jaw, and I nibbled at the soft line. I left soft kisses all along that beautiful line. "If I make you come, I need to hear you calling my name."

And then, I did one of the hardest things I'd ever had to do: I ripped myself off her.

Slowly, I rolled onto my back, my leg thanking me for the shift, and my dick . . . tenting the comforter.

Rosie turned on her side to face me, eyes roaming up and down my body. She licked her lips, and I heard myself letting out a harsh breath.

"*Ángel,*" I breathed out. "Keep looking and licking your lips like that but please, please don't reach out and touch me because I—" I'd lose it. I'd one hundred percent lose it. I wouldn't fucking care who was in the room. I'd make her scream my name.

"I'll be good," she answered.

And why did that make me want to . . . do bad things to her?

My dick twitched.

Keep it together, I told myself. *Think unsexy things. Like trash cans. Or . . . that time Taco had diarrhea.*

"Lucas?"

I glanced back at her, finding her lips curled into a smile, and it hit me like a ton of bricks how beautiful she was in the mornings. In this light. In my bed. "Yeah?"

She tucked her hands beneath her cheek. "I really wish this apartment had a few more walls."

I huffed a laugh. "Yeah. I'm not a big fan of these fancy Brooklyn studio apartments, either, Ro."

She chuckled softly.

"I am a fan of the views, though," I added, looking straight into her eyes. "Big fan of them."

That blush that made her so uniquely her reappeared. "You're so full of compliments today, Mr. McConaughey."

"I live to make you swoon."

My mind returned to last night when we'd kissed. Something had snapped in two the moment her mouth met mine. I wasn't oblivious; it had been simmering between us for a long time but it had solidified on that rooftop.

We needed to talk about that. I had promised her honesty, and I didn't want Rosie to think that it hadn't meant anything to me, or that I was ignoring it. But I wanted to do this right—where Rosie was concerned, I needed to do right by her—and now it wasn't the best moment to talk about it.

"I need to pick up Taco from Lina and Aaron's."

She nodded. "I should probably wake Olly and head to Dad's," she said, confirming that there were much more urgent things to deal with. "Long day ahead."

"Do you want me to come with you?" I asked.

"I'd love to introduce you to my dad, but maybe under better circumstances." She seemed to think of something. "How about we call Lina and ask if she can drop Taco off? You should stay in today, rest."

I nodded, swallowing hard. "You're probably right."

"I'm always right. So . . . will you ask Lina to come?"

I rolled my eyes.

She laughed, and it was a magical sound. "Don't make me fight you over this, Lucas Martín. I will win."

It was my turn to smile. "Don't threaten me with a good time, Rosalyn Graham."

Her mouth opened but before she could say anything, a different voice spoke up in the room.

"Rosie?" Olly called from the couch, stifling whatever had been between us. "You up?"

CHAPTER TWENTY-SIX

Lucas

$\mathcal{B}$eing alone in the apartment left me with more time to myself than I knew what to do with.

Rosie had gone with Olly soon after he woke up, and as restless as I felt for staying behind, I understood why she had told me it wasn't a good idea to tag along.

This was time that Rosie, her brother, and dad needed for themselves. As a family. And very much necessary time I could use to cool myself off after what I'd been so close to doing to Rosie earlier in the morning.

Besides, I had been counting on Lina dropping Taco off soon after Rosie departed. Of course, Lina, being the dog-hogger she was, had rescheduled. And now the plan was that Lina would bring Taco here later today when she picked us up to move Rosie's stuff back to her apartment. Because Rosie was leaving today. She was going back to her place.

And I was coming with her. Unfortunately, not in the way I wanted. I was only going to help, even though I wasn't going to be of much help. But I . . . needed to see her back to her apartment. Make sure everything was mended and sorted. See for myself that she'd be safe. Okay.

Liar, a voice in my head claimed. *What you want is an excuse to spend more time with her. An excuse to haul her back here, with you, if something in her apartment is marginally out of order.*

Yes. *Yes.* Because after kissing her and having her sleeping beside me, it was hard to ignore this part of me, this beating, pulsing, emotion inside of me, that wanted Rosie. Wanted her *badly.*

And now . . . now I was hard again. Just like I'd been the whole day, but worse, because now my head was busy with thoughts of her moving back to her place, of not seeing her anymore.

With a shaky sigh, I checked my watch and noticed I at least had some time before Rosie was back from Philly and Lina came over with Taco.

A shower. Cold. I needed to cool off before either of them showed up.

Slipping inside the bathroom in a rush, I undressed myself. I took a good look in the mirror, pointed a finger at my reflection. "*Contrólate, Lucas,*" I told my reflection, as if it would help. "You're being a horny idiot, and this cannot stand."

But the need in my expression didn't get any duller and my dick didn't get any less hard.

With a shake of my head, I turned on the shower—as cold as it'd go—and jumped under the stream of water, closing my eyes the moment it hit my shoulders.

I shouldn't be feeling this way for a woman I had met just a few weeks ago. A woman I had promised she'd be safe with me. A woman who had become one of my closest friends. *My closest friend.*

How had this happened?

Rosie affected me in ways no other woman ever had. I wanted to do things for her, everything and anything if she let me. I wanted to make sure that she was okay. More than okay. Not good, but *happy.* That she accomplished whatever she dreamed of. That she was cared for, cherished.

And *God*, I wanted to fuck her. Venerate her body. Give her pleasure. With my hands. My mouth. My cock if I'd ever be so lucky. I wanted to treat her like she deserved to be treated, like a gift.

There was no way around it. All of that was there, bubbling under my skin. Demanding to be appeased.

My hands fell to my hips, and I . . . God. It had been a long time since I relieved all this pressure.

Our living arrangement had lots of perks, but it also had one big disadvantage: the lack of rooms. Of walls. Privacy. We'd proved as much this morning.

The image of Rosie, shifting in my lap, flashed behind my eyes, setting my skin on fire, making my hand slip low, encouraged by the water falling down the sleek planes of my body. Incapable of stopping myself, I finally gave in to the overpowering need I'd been trying to keep at bay for hours and curled my fingers around my cock.

A groan slipped out of my mouth.

Jesus, I was so fucking hard. I was shocked I hadn't burst when I'd had her body tucked against my lap. Pinned underneath me.

With a labored breath, I stroked myself, base to tip. And my legs almost buckled beneath me.

Bracing my other hand on the cool and slippery tiles of the shower, I continued fisting my hard length. Slow, rough strokes that had me shut my eyes in pain and relief. Torture and pleasure.

My mind summoned images from that morning when it had been Rosie's ass stroking me. I pictured myself flipping her on her belly, readying myself to make her scream the way I'd promised her. My fist moved up and down my length, keeping the rhythm as I imagined her taste, the feel of her soft body underneath mine, the pink of her skin, the curl of her lips when I finally gave her the orgasm we both craved.

Me vuelve loco.

She drove me crazy. Just the thought of her did, and I'd tell her myself. I'd gladly watch her squirm out of her skin with lust when I hummed those words in Spanish the way she loved so much. I—

"Lucas?"

Her voice broke through the haze, coiling around me like smoke.

"Rosie?" I replied, longing and surprise coating her name.

Without stopping my hand, because I couldn't, I just couldn't stop, I turned around. Rosie stood in the open bathroom doorway, in her coat, her keys dangling off her hand. Her cheeks were a deep shade of pink I wanted to taste with my tongue, and she was transfixed. Her eyes on my fist as it closed around my cock.

"Rosie, *mi ángel*," I rasped out, turning my body. Letting her see all of me because I was at her mercy. I wasn't even ashamed when I told her, "This is what you do to me."

Her throat bobbed and I saw her whole body reacting to the sight. At me naked, stroking myself under the water stream. The green in her eyes liquefied. Her blush spread. Her mouth turned into a beautiful *O* I was already fantasizing about. Over my skin, around my hardness, on my mouth.

My cock got harder.

"I can't stop," I said, my voice gravel, desperate, forcing my hand to slow down.

Rosie's gaze met mine. "Don't stop." Those glassy eyes confirming that she wasn't appalled by my lack of control. Not at all. She was excited, flattered. In need. "I heard a cry, and I thought you were hurt."

I let my forehead drop to the glass door of the shower, a bitter laugh escaping my lips. "I am in pain, *ángel*." I pushed away, straightening my back, looking at her straight in her eyes, giving her a show if that was what she wanted. "So much I had to fuck myself."

She shifted, her gaze returning to my fist. My cock. And I stroked myself harder. Bringing myself closer and closer to the edge. Her eyes moved lower, and I saw the shock, the concern, in her eyes when she noticed the scar on my knee.

"Eyes up, Rosie," I commanded. I was ready to detonate like a goddamn bomb and I wanted her with me.

She obeyed. And soon, her hand absentmindedly going to her chest, her palm moving down to rest between her breasts.

"You like what you see, Rosie?" I asked her, enraptured by the look of bliss on her face. "You like seeing me like this? Being responsible for it?"

She nodded her head. "So much."

Fuck.

"Rosie," I gritted between my teeth. "*Rosie.* The things I want to tell you. To *do* to you."

She swallowed, and we were suspended in time for a long moment. Then, slowly, very slowly, she let the keys drop to the floor. She opened her coat, revealing the plaid button-down shirt I'd watched her put on that morning. Very delicately, like we weren't in a rush, and she didn't know that I was about to come out of my skin with pure lust, she let her coat fall to the floor.

"We're past playing coy. Tell me everything," she said, meeting my gaze with something that did mad, crazy things to me. "I want to hear it. I want you to watch me like I'm watching you."

A groan rumbled in my chest, climbing up my throat and leaving me in a burst. "You want me to tell you how to tease your beautiful body the way I would? Want to give me a show and make me crazy like only you can?"

She nodded, her eyes tipping down to my fist, and back up to my face.

I felt myself baring my teeth, the beast unbound, severing and slipping out of the leash.

"Unbutton that shirt," I instructed, and she did, tugging hard at the neckline of her shirt. So hard that the two top buttons snapped and dropped to the floor, revealing a cotton bra. I let out a grunt of desperation at the sight. "Bring that hand back to your breast."

She did, and my pulse sprinted, my cock throbbing in my fist.

Rosie whimpered, palming her breast while she never stopped watching me.

"You're in pain, too, Rosie." I exhaled through my nose, my eyes raking her body and drinking in the needy motions, wanting out of this shower. "You're hurting and we can't have that."

She nodded and I swallowed, wishing it was my hand around her breast. My fingers on her. My tongue on that rosy peak I needed to see.

My voice dropped when I spoke next. "Bring down the bra." And turned into nothing more than a rasp when I continued, "Let me look at you, *preciosa.*"

The sight of her breast, with her standing there, panting with her shirt half open, could have brought me to my knees, but instead it broke something else. My restraint to stay away. To keep myself at bay.

Gritting my teeth, I opened the shower door with one hand as I teased my shaft with the other. Her gaze dropped again, and she let out a whimper. "Do this to your nipple, Rosie. With your palm, then your fingers."

Rosie did as instructed, and she moaned again, her eyes fluttering closed for an instant only to open back up and zero in on me with a hunger that I knew mirrored the one etched in my face.

"This isn't enough," I grunted.

I stepped forward, ready to get out of this shower and fuck her against the floor like a goddamn animal, forgetting all the reasons why I shouldn't. But Rosie moved at the same time, desperate need pouring out of her as she slipped out of her shoes and stalked in my direction, joining me under the stream of water, drenching her clothes. Her palm fell on my chest and red exploded behind my eyes.

In one swift motion, I had her back against the slippery tiles. In the next, I watched her unzip her jeans, revealing the white lace of her panties.

A growl left my lips and I instinctively thrusted into my hand. "You want to watch, Rosie. Then you can watch me up close," I panted, my fist moving roughly over my pulsing length. "You want me to guide you, then slip those fingers inside of you, please. *Please.* Slip them before I do."

She brought her hand inside her panties, obeying. And, oh, the moan that left her mouth brought me so close that I could feel myself dripping with pre-cum.

"Tease your clit, tease it like I would," I urged her, barely recognizing my own voice, her hand and my hand moving urgently. "*Ah, preciosa,* just like that."

The sound of our breathing overpowered the water falling on top of us, and I couldn't stop myself from coming closer, I couldn't stop my hand from rising to her neck, closing around her throat very gently.

"Is this okay?" I asked her, watching her face very closely. "Tell me if it isn't."

She gave a curt nod, as if incapable of more. "Yes. Oh my God, yes."

Both our motions turned quicker, more desperate, our hips thrusting as if we were fucking each other and not our own hands.

"Lucas?" Her breath hitched. "I'm going to come, oh God. I— *Lucas.*"

I pressed my thighs against hers, tightened the pressure of my fingers around her throat only slightly, held myself back until she came. "Come, Rosie," I growled, letting go of my cock and moving my hand over hers. "Just like I have been fantasizing since Halloween. Ride our fingers and come for me."

She exploded with a loud moan, just like I wanted, and before my eyes, her eyelids fluttered and her whole body trembled. And when her hand became limp with the wave of pleasure rocking her, I took over, riding her out of the orgasm.

My forehead fell on hers, and I waited for her to open her eyes once again to resume my own strokes. She licked her parted lips as I thrusted into my hand, roughly, as roughly as I ever did, my spine tightening, everything coiling in down, bringing me to my limit. "This is what you do to me, Rosie."

Her hands fell on my shoulders, moved to my pecs, her nails grazed my skin down my stomach.

I hissed a breath, fisting myself desperately, nothing but need left. "Can I come on you, Rosie, *ángel*, please?"

"*Yes,*" she breathed out. "Yes."

Rosie lifted her shirt, forcing the rest of the buttons open, and I stroked my cock one more time before bursting. With a hoarse groan, I came on her smooth skin, squeezing until the last drop with my fist. Wishing I was inside of her. Wishing this would have lasted for hours, for days.

"Rosie," I breathed out, bracing myself on the wall behind her head, feeling my dick still pulsing with release, watching the water wash my spent from her stomach. *"Estoy a tus pies. A tus pies, preciosa."*

We stood under the stream, foreheads together and heaving chests for a long time, until eventually I turned the water off and picked her up in my arms without another word. My leg complained, and Rosie noticed, demanding to be put down, but I refused. I didn't have much time left with her, and that made me reckless. That was probably why instead of letting go of her, instead of putting distance between us and talk about what had just happened, I placed her on the ground and stripped her of her wet clothes. I kissed her lips again. I helped her putting fresh clothes on. And then, I let her do the same to me.

Because time was working against me, now. Everything was. And perhaps, it had always been.

CHAPTER TWENTY-SEVEN

Rosie

"*I* barely brushed the curb. You're making it look like I drove over a . . . squirrel or something."

I chuckled.

"A squirrel? Really?" Lucas asked.

Lina shot him a look.

"It could happen." Then, she lowered her voice to a whisper, eyeing Taco. "I didn't want to use a p-u-p as an example, okay?"

Taco whimpered at my side, and the man I'd spent an outrageous amount of time checking out on our drive to my place muttered under his breath, "Whatever. I'm not covering for you with Aaron. I like him and I'm sure there's some bro-code I'd be breaking."

"Oh," I added. "I'm not covering for you, either, sorry."

Lina rolled her eyes. "Aaron knew what he was doing when he let me borrow his car. He's the one who told me I shouldn't be scared of New York traffic, *smart-asses*."

Lucas grazed his hand over the small of my back, bringing a powerful rush of awareness to my skin even at that brief of a touch.

"Sure," he said, going for the bag that was hanging off my shoulder. "It's New York's traffic who should be terrified," he said, looking at me. "Of her."

Letting out a laugh, I shook my head. These two were ridiculous, and there was no way I was surrendering the bag to him.

Lucas narrowed his eyes.

"Funny," Lina said from the trunk of Aaron's car. "Someone's eaten a little clown today."

Lucas ignored Lina's comment and went for the suitcase resting at my feet.

I did, too, because I only had an idea what she might have meant. Plus, I was too busy pinning Lucas with another hard look. I lowered my voice. "You shouldn't be taking anything heavy."

He seemed ready to fight me, but he said, "You're right."

"Told you, I'm always right," I murmured, my lips twitching. Then, I took the handle from him. "Gimme."

"Nope," he shot back, and picked the bag anyways. "You're right, but that doesn't mean I'm going to let you carry all this weight up the stairs." He shrugged, and it was my turn to narrow my eyes, giving him my meanest face. "That look is not deterring me, Rosie." He came close and added only so I could hear it, "It's only making me hard."

My lips parted, and I . . .

I hadn't expected him to say that, but I liked that he had. A lot. *Too much.*

I wanted his hands on me again, just like earlier today, but this time I wanted more. This time, I wanted all of him.

Lucas's eyes hooded. "*Preciosa*, don't look at me like that. You're only making it worse."

Lina cleared her throat loudly, and when I glanced at her, her eyes had turned to thin slits. "What are you two whispering about?"

"I was telling Rosie that I was glad we were alive," Lucas was quick to answer, his face telling me a completely different story. Then, he turned to face his cousin, "Don't you agree we're lucky, *Ms. Fast and the Furious*?"

"Ha," Lina shot back. "Hilarious."

With a sigh, I turned to my best friend. "Here." I placed my key in her palm. "You go first. We'll get the rest."

Shockingly, Lina didn't question me, just called for Taco and headed for the staircase.

I grabbed the lightest bag I could find—one with a pillow—and placed it on Lucas's shoulder. Then I retrieved the suitcase he thought he was taking upstairs. "There." I patted his chest. "Up you go, Martín number two."

He grabbed my wrist, a wild, all-powerful sensation flooding my body under his touch. I looked up at him, the heaviness and lust dissipating slightly when his lips pursed into the cutest pout.

I snickered. "Don't be a grouch," I told him, trying to keep the tone light. "You can't win all the time. Now up."

He scoffed. "I'm a ray of sunshine." Lucas's gaze tipped down to the fingers that were around my arm. He moved my hand so it lay against his chest, right over his heart. "I just . . . want to help."

He didn't want to; he needed to. And I understood that.

So, I splayed my fingers over his sweater, making sure he felt my touch through the layers of clothing that separated my hand from his skin. And only when he seemed as distracted as I was by that, I told him, "Your being here with me. That's all I need from you."

I was looking straight at him, so it was impossible to miss the way his face changed when my words registered.

He probably wanted to talk about what had happened today, or last night, because we hadn't and we really, really should have. But once again, this wasn't the time, so I cleared my throat and said, "Let's go. Lina is probably wondering what's taking us so long."

With a nod, he headed up.

A little over two hours later, we had all my stuff up and the big mess the contractors had left behind was cleaned up.

"I am dead," Lina grunted from her post at the end of my couch. "This was worth at least three months of exercise."

I chuckled and Lucas scoffed with disbelief. "I think the several ten-minute breaks you took to snack on Pringles cancel out the workout, *prima*."

"What a total party pooper." She threw her hands in the air. "You're in such a mood today, Lucas. I didn't even know you could *do* grumpy." Lina wasn't lying: Lucas hadn't been his usual self these last few hours. He'd been sighing and grunting and barely smiling at all. "Maybe you should take a nap when you get home, *sí*? You're acting like a baby that needs some sleep."

"I slept fine last night," he said, his gaze falling on me from across the living room. "In fact, sleep is the last thing in my mind now."

My pulse rose, because I could see what was flickering in those two brown eyes that were on me. I could feel it on my skin.

Lina cleared her throat.

I ripped my gaze off Lucas, clapped my hands. "All right. Thanks so much for helping out, guys," I said, standing up. Taco nudged my leg with his head. I crouched and planted a big kiss on him. "And thank you, too, for being the handsomest of them all."

Lucas grunted, and Taco went immediately to him. He seemed to relax slightly.

My gaze slid to the loveseat where Lina was sitting, and it hit me then that there was no reason for them to hang around. There was no reason for Lucas to stay. He'd return to Lina's studio. And soon, he'd return to Spain, too.

Panic swirled inside of me, making my next breath a little harder.

I blurted out the first thing that crossed my mind. "You guys want to eat something? The fridge is empty but I can order pizza." I turned to my best friend, because if I looked at Lucas, I might do something very stupid. Like jump in his lap and beg him not to leave. "It's the least I can do."

Lina sighed, clasping her hands together under her chin. "I promised Aaron I'd pick him up from InTech after I was done here." She stood up. "And I'll take any chance I have to get him out of there early. Because one day, I'll have to rip his ass off that office chair before he fuses to his laptop."

I nodded, debating whether I should tell Lucas that if he wanted to stay, he should. That I really wanted him to.

But then, Lina spoke again. "So we should really get going. I'll drop Lucas off before heading into Manhattan. It's on my way."

"Of course," I said, because what else could I say?

I didn't even know if Lucas wanted to stay, and he wasn't saying anything.

Grabbing my phone from the coffee table, I checked the time. "Okay, sure. Then, you should really go if—"

"I'm hungry," Lucas offered casually. "And those pizzas sound like a good idea."

My head swiveled in his direction so quickly I almost got dizzy. He met my gaze with determination.

Lina spoke. "You can call Alessandro's on our way back." She picked up her coat and purse. "He'll have your order ready by the time I drop you off."

Lucas's eyes didn't leave mine when he said, "Maybe I'm hungry now."

My heart rate sped up, the poor, hopeful organ climbing up my throat.

I heard Lina's exhale.

"You are not going to eat in Aaron's car. He'll murder your ass, and as grumpy as you are today, you really are my favorite cousin."

I watched Lucas breathe very slowly through his nose, almost as if he was gathering strength. And for the first time ever, I was shocked to see him snap.

"Are you always this oblivious, Lina?"

I had to stifle a gasp. *"Lucas."*

"See what I mean?" My best friend narrowed her eyes at her cousin again. "You're in such a mood, today."

Lucas's eyes fluttered closed, and he said, "Sorry. I'm sorry. I— *Soy un gilipollas.*"

"Yep, you are. But apology accepted." Lina came to a stand before him. "And just so you know, I'm not blind. I've seen you limping your way around this apartment, and I've seen Rosie checking on you every five minutes, too." That made my eyes widen. "I also feel this crazy sexual energy thing around you two. So, unless you want to have a conversation right now about all of those things, I'm driving you home. And if you stop being a jerk, I might not grill you with questions about why Aaron gets all quiet when I bring you up. And trust me, I really want to, because this is the first time my husband is somehow keeping a secret from me, and while it's adorable that he's covering for you in some bro-way, it still makes me sad that I'm being left out."

Lucas stood up and pulled Lina into a hug. "*Soy un idiota,*" he told her. "I'm sorry. You're right. I might need that nap."

My chest tightened at Lina's words. I'd been such an awful friend keeping this from her.

"You guys should go," I said softly, trying to keep my thoughts from clogging my voice. "I might pass on the pizzas and hit the bed anyway. I'm dead on my feet."

The two Martíns broke the embrace, and next thing I knew I was in my best friend's arms. "I'm not mad," she said just for me. "You'll tell me everything, I know that. And I'll be there when you're ready, okay?"

A strangled sound left my throat. "Okay."

God, she really was the best.

When she released me, Lucas was there, as if he'd been waiting in line to get his hug. And I . . . Ugh. I couldn't wait to throw myself in his arms. In his warmth, his scent, his strength. He wrapped his arms around me and I felt him drop a silent kiss on the side of my head, close to my ear. Then, he whispered, "*Buenas noches, preciosa.*"

Taco nuzzled at my feet, a whimper leaving him.

But I didn't say a word to any of them. And it was probably for the best. Because I would have probably said something stupid. Something like "Stay."

Stay for good.

So I limited myself to watching Lucas, Lina, and Taco leave, and a few minutes later, I was alone. Again. Just how I'd been before Lucas had slipped into my life and somehow made himself . . . irreplaceable.

"All right," I said to my empty apartment. "I'm on my own. And that's good. It's okay."

Only it wasn't. Not really.

Because I already missed him, and that was crazy. It was . . . ridiculous. Outrageously so. But there was this beating, breathing thing inside of me, demanding to be let out.

And just like that, it was as if a lightbulb had lit up in my head. One that was wired to the organ in the middle of my chest. I grabbed my laptop bag, pulling out my computer and plopping back down on the couch. I opened my manuscript and did the only thing I had known how to do once upon a time. I wrote about every single thing I didn't know how to . . . handle. How to process. Every fear in my head, every powerful emotion raging in my heart, every terrifying question, and every suffocating certainty. Every hope. And I just wrote. I released them into my story, so I was able to untangle them the best way I knew. On paper.

Hours later, I was lying in bed. Wide awake.

I'd somehow managed to work until past midnight, and I'd thought that the exhaustion from the day and the productive writing session would knock me out. But nope.

I stared at the dark ceiling of my bedroom. Stealing glances at my phone. Wishing it would light up with a message or a call. Wishing I was brave enough to grab it and reach out myself.

But the screen remained pitch black. The device silent.

I wasn't daring to do anything about it, and I was driving myself crazy.

Squeezing my eyes closed, I let out a groan.

There were so many unwritten rules about how women should behave with men they were interested in. Men they'd kissed and wanted to kiss again and again and again. But this was Lucas. This was me. It didn't feel like those rules should apply to us.

I had seen him naked, beautifully imposing as he stood under the stream of water, with his hand on his dick. Hurting for me. Vulnerable. Powerful.

And before that, I had kissed him in the rain, not caring about anything but his lips, as they moved around mine.

I had danced with him to *our* soundtrack, spinning in his arms while I bathed in his laughter.

I had comforted him when he'd had nightmares, wishing I could take the fear away.

I had let him hold my hand in his when I needed someone to comfort me. And I'd let something that had started like an experiment turn into something real.

The rules didn't apply.

I was a grown-ass woman. I didn't need a reason to send a message to him. To my friend. To one of my best friends. To the man I couldn't stop thinking about.

I started for the phone. "Fuck it—"

And in that exact moment, the screen lit up.

Heart in my throat, I scrambled for it, managing to tangle my legs in the comforter and flinging myself to the ground. "Ouch! Dammit."

From my position sprawled on the carpet, I stretched an arm and grabbed the device from the nightstand, not bothering to return to the bed. It was a text.

Lucas: I might have separation anxiety.

My lips stretched into the biggest, most ridiculous grin ever, and my fingers rushed to type an answer.

Rosie: I thought only pets got that.

Lucas: You're up.

Lucas: Did I wake you?

Rosie: Nope. I was wide awake. I've been working for hours.

Lucas: That makes me happy. How many words?

Rosie: Lots 😊

Lucas: That's my girl.

Lucas: You must be exhausted, though. I should let you go to sleep.

The thrumming in my rib cage rose to my temples as I came up with an excuse to keep him with me.

Rosie: Don't worry. My brain is still on so I can't sleep.

Rosie: You could . . . keep me company? Maybe?

Rosie: Until I fall asleep.

Lucas: 😇 Oh yeah? You'd like that?

Rosie: Yep.

Lucas: Well, you're lucky I'm an excellent entertainer and great company.

Lucas: Most of the time.

Rosie: I know.

Rosie: All of the time. Even when you're a grouch.

A picture appeared on my screen. It was a selfie, and he was frowning. Pouting.

Lucas: a grouch like this?

Lucas: I still think I look handsome. Sexy, even.

He did. He always did.
Another message came in.

Lucas: would you entertain me, too?

Lucas: send me a pic.

Lucas: for the sake of my separation anxiety.

Lucas: I'm scared I'll forget your face.

Rosie: are you . . . flirting with me, Lucas Martín?

Lucas: is it working?

With a nervous snicker, I snapped a selfie and sent it.

Lucas: is that . . . the floor? Why are you laying at the foot of the bed?

Oops. My Lucas-hazed brain hadn't thought of that.
Another photo of him popped up on my screen. It was taken from a longer distance, as if he'd stretched his arm to snap the shot so I could see that he was lying in bed. On top of the covers. Shirtless. His glorious, glorious chest on display, his tattoo peeking out of a corner of the screen.

Lucas: This is how beds are meant to be used, Ro. You lay on top of them.

Rosie: thank you for the lesson, professor.

Lucas: What can I say? I'm well versed in the many uses of beds.

Rosie: Oh?

Oh?

Really, Rosie? Oh?

I could have done much, much better. Much sexier. But my brain was . . . scattered.

Lucas: don't sound so surprised.

I waited, thinking of how to answer. But he beat me.

Lucas: have you forgotten this morning? Because I haven't.

Lucas: it's all I've thought about.

Lucas: well, not all. I've thought about that shower too. About you coming so sweetly.

I stared at that word on my screen, a heated sensation pooling low and gathering between my legs. I just didn't know what to say to that.

My brain scrambled for a good answer, for something, anything, I could say. This was good, it was just sexting. And I was a romance writer, I'd written sex scenes. I could be sexy. I could be daring. I could sext.

But nothing came to mind. Nothing. Only flashes of that morning, of us in bed, under the covers. Of that shower and Lucas naked, coming on my stomach. Which had been the hottest, most erotic sexual experience of my life and I—

I might have spent a long time thinking because Lucas texted again.

Lucas: Rosie?

Rosie: Still here.

Lucas: Sorry. I'm an idiot. I wasn't trying to have phone sex or text sex with you, I promise.

Rosie: You weren't?

Lucas: No.

Well, that was disappointing. I would have been all in for any of those two options; I just needed . . . a little more time.

Lucas: I was texting you because I miss you like crazy. The apartment is too quiet. Too empty. Even with Taco here. Nothing feels right. I want you back.

My chest swelled to the point of hurting.
I want you back.
That was exactly how I felt in my own home. That was how much he'd ruined me. Could it be possible that we were feeling the exact same way?

Rosie: I miss you, too

And then, because I clearly had no self-preservation instinct when it came to this man, I sent him the words I wanted him to hear. The truth that I wanted him to see, that I wanted to scream at him until my voice grew raw.

Rosie: I want you back too, Lucas. I wish you were here with me. In my bed.

Lucas: . . .

Lucas: I wish you hadn't told me that.

Rosie: Why?

The three points danced on the screen of my phone for a few seconds, and then disappeared.

Remaining very, very still, I waited for a minute.

Then, two. Three, five, ten, fifteen.

Thirty minutes.

Lucas didn't answer.

Maybe he'd . . . fallen asleep.

Or maybe he'd gotten hungry and decided to grab a snack. Knowing him, that involved something more sophisticated than opening a bag of cereal and a carton of milk even at one in the morning.

Or maybe . . .

"Jesus Christ," I said into the empty room. "Listen to yourself, Rosie."

I cursed, realizing that not only was I being ridiculous, but I was also on my feet, pacing in front of my bed, and about to give myself a headache.

The intercom downstairs blared through the apartment, startling me and making me drop the phone on the floor. The screen lit up at my feet.

Lucas: It's me.

I left the phone there, not caring about anything but the door.

Because . . . he was here.

I ran to the entrance and when I buzzed him in and threw my door open, my panting had nothing to do with my sprint.

The handsomest face I'd ever seen in my life appeared in the hallway after a few seconds. And the man that had somehow become my favorite person in New York City—in the country, the whole world—made his way to me.

"This is why," he said, smiling his Lucas smile. The one that was bright and happy and had the power to set a flock of birds free in my stomach. To make my skin tingle and every nerve flutter. "So,

I wouldn't run here, uninvited, and show up past midnight at your door. That's why I wished you hadn't told me you missed me."

My heart sung.

"You said you missed me," he repeated, as if he was still processing my words.

And without meaning to, without knowing how, I threw myself at him. I would have climbed him up like a tree, had I not known that his leg was not up to the task. But I still tangled myself around him as best as I could. Breathed him in, welcomed his scent, the toned muscles under the layers of clothes he wore against the chilly weather of New York. Welcoming *him*.

"And it's the best thing I've ever said," I told him, the words spilling out of me and falling on his chest. Close to his heart, where I wanted to burrow myself. Then, I said something that perhaps I shouldn't have, but I wasn't able to stop myself anymore. "I'll say it again if it makes you stay. I'll say it a hundred million times."

His arms tightened around me, the long breath he let out warming the skin of my neck.

And because he'd cracked me open and everything was coming out now, I continued, "I've missed you since you stepped out of this apartment, hours ago. And I had missed you for a long time before then, Lucas."

Lucas's chest rumbled with a deep growl that rattled me with anticipation, need, with whatever this thing growing between us was.

Then, his arms were around my waist, and he was walking us inside, the door closing behind us. The next second, I was pushed against it.

Lucas braced his arms on each side of my head, caging me against the wooden surface.

"Again," he commanded, meeting my gaze. "Nobody has ever missed me that much or needed me like this. Say it again."

My mouth dried at the look on his face. At the way his eyes darkened, and his jaw turned into a sharp line. "I've missed you, Lucas. So much. Please, stay with me. Stay tonight."

Stay tonight and every single night after that.

His right hand came to cup my face, the pad of his index finger trailing across my cheek, to my bottom lip, swiping along the line of my mouth. "If I stay . . ." He closed his eyes, exhaling shakily. "I've seen you come apart before my eyes, Rosie. And I barely had the chance to touch you. If I stay, that's going to change. If I stay, we're going to fuck."

I shivered at the thought of how much I wanted him to follow through with that warning. "Good."

"I need you to hear something," he said, his gaze hardening. "I am leaving in a week, and I was serious when I said that I can't— My life is in shambles, Rosie. I have nothing to offer. But I . . . I'm selfish when it comes to you. I'll give you my mouth if you ask me. My touch, my body. It's not much, certainly less than what you deserve, but if you want that, if you want me—"

I kissed him.

Stopping his words.

I didn't need them. Didn't need anything but him right now.

And I would have told him so if he hadn't returned the kiss with an urgency that rivaled mine.

So I kissed him. I kissed him like I had wanted to do for so long, finally letting go of everything that had held me back until this moment. Because he was leaving soon, and perhaps, this was all I would ever have from him, so I was going to take it.

I pulled him closer with a kind of desperation that I had never known, wanting him against me as he ravished my mouth. Lucas's arm came around my waist, bringing my hips into his and leaving my shoulders to press against the door. A whimper left me at the contact, and Lucas took the chance to part my lips and brush my tongue with his.

My head was spinning with every sensation flooding my body, leaving me unbalanced. I pulled at his coat, wanting that extra barrier gone, but he wouldn't budge.

A complaint rose to my lips as he dragged his mouth down my

neck very slowly, nipping at my skin and turning the sound into a loud moan.

Lucas's lips went up to my ear. He said against the sensitive skin, "That sound."

"Which one?" I struggled to ask.

His teeth grazed the lobe, tugged at it.

My reaction was immediate. A new whimper climbed up my throat.

"That one," he whispered. "I'd do crazy things for that sound, Rosie."

"What things?" I breathed out. But all I wanted to say was, *Please. All things. Now.*

Lucas's hips pushed against mine in response, punching the air out of my lungs at the need surging through my body. *Hard.* He was so hard and big. "Things like fucking you against this door, right now."

I wanted to scream at him to go ahead.

But before any words came out, his mouth was retracing the path back to mine, leaving behind a trail of tingles that spread down my arms. His lips stopped over mine. Not making contact.

Not kissing me.

Why wasn't he kissing me?

His nose dragged along mine. "I was so close to fucking you this afternoon," he confessed, his voice dropping. "Taking you on the floor of that bathroom."

I whimpered, pulling at his clothes again, but he wouldn't move.

All he did was take my bottom lip between his teeth and say, "Do you want to hear what other crazy things I'm close to doing now?"

"Yes."

"I want to bring down these little pajama shorts you've been driving me crazy with," he told me low, so low, against my mouth. "Panties off, too." His lips flicked along my jaw. "Just so I can get deep, deep inside of you until the only thing you feel is me."

My eyelids fluttered shut at his words.

"Do it," I pleaded, hearing the outrageous need in my voice. "All of that. Please."

"No." He scraped his teeth along the shell of my ear again, making my toes curl. "Not now." His words felt like torture, taking away the possibility, the idea of having this right now. Of having him as soon and as fast as I could. "Do you know what I'll do instead?"

My eyes opened just in time to see his lips part in a slow grin. This was a new type of smile. It wasn't the happy and bright curl of his mouth; it was dark. Sultry. A warning and a promise. One that I wanted him to keep.

"Tonight," he said, and I knew before his next words that there was no turning back, that after tonight I would never be the same, because I was getting him, all of him. "Tonight, I'm taking you to bed. Fucking you deep and slow. And I won't settle for that beautiful whimper. Tonight, I'm making you scream my name, Rosie."

If I thought he had come undone at any point before, I couldn't have been any more wrong.

Because the moment those words left his lips, Lucas unraveled.

He lifted me up again, and before I could complain, before I could really think, he was guiding my legs around his hips as he stalked to my bedroom.

My heart toppled. My need stirred. And next thing I knew I was being dropped on top of my comforter.

His head tilted very slowly, and his eyes trailed up and down my body, and God, never in my life had I been looked at like that. Like he was ready to eat me alive.

Lips parted, I watched him finally rid himself of his coat. Then, he reached for the hem of his hoodie and pulled it off in one smooth motion.

He hadn't been wearing anything underneath.

A sound of need climbed up my throat because I might have already seen him naked, I might have already seen the indents of his hips and every lean muscle flexed, but not like this. Not even in the shower earlier today. Not with that dark glim to his eyes, or that knowing bend to his lips.

"No shirt?" I heard myself ask.

His chuckle was smooth, secretive. "I was in a rush when I left the apartment. I still don't know how I managed to leave Aaron a message so he'd get Taco. He must hate me right now, but I can't seem to care."

My throat dried up, his expression turning serious when he stepped closer to the bed.

He stopped right beside the edge, then said, "Come here."

Without losing a single second, I got on my knees and crawled until I was right in front of him.

Lucas looked at me, something breaking, softening. The back of his fingers brushed my cheek and he said, "All this pink covering your skin. *Eres preciosa.*" He inched closer, his face tilting down so he could meet my eyes. "I'm dying to see how low it spreads."

Sitting on my knees, I stretched my arms up. Giving him every green light ever.

Lucas didn't hesitate to take my offer, and he pulled my shirt over my head.

A broken breath left his lips as his eyes roamed up and down my body. Taking in my bare breasts.

"Me robas el sentido," he murmured. "You take away my breath."

I reached for him, placed my palms on his chest very gently, and then dragged them down, memorizing the map of warm and taut skin under the tips of my fingers. Committing it all to memory. And when my hands reached the band of his jeans, I leaned down, grazing my lips over the center of his chest. Then, I pressed them above his heart. Next, I went over his ribs, close to the ink that painted his skin and without thinking about it, I placed an open-mouth kiss on the crest of the wave, letting my tongue trace the beautiful design.

Lucas's stomach flexed, strained, and I felt him shudder under my tongue.

I looked up at him, the confession slipping out. "I've wanted to do this ever since I saw it for the first time."

A groan left his lips, and next thing I knew, he was pulling me up and taking my mouth in his.

When he broke the kiss, he rasped, "You've been fantasizing about this? With me?"

A nod. "Every day. Every night before sleep. Every time I've closed my eyes."

He exhaled roughly. "What else have you imagined doing to me?"

I dragged my hands along the band of his jeans, then let my thumbs draw the indents in his hips, finally returning my fingers to the button and hearing his hiss. "Today, when I caught you in the shower," I said, making a work of it and feeling the intense heat coming off him, "I wished it was my hand. Or my mouth."

Lucas's hips thrusted upward in what I knew had been a reflex.

I peered up at him and added, "I wished you'd been coming inside me."

His hands came to the sides of my face, his fingers tangling in my hair as I brought the zipper down.

I wrapped my hand around him through the stretched fabric of his black boxers and Lucas hissed out a breath.

"You liked seeing me stroke myself," he said, moving against my hand. "But you wished it had been you."

I nodded my head.

His fingers tugged at my hair a little tighter. "Take me out and show me how."

I brought his boxers down, licking my lips at the sight of him springing free. Without thinking about it, I closed my hand around his length, stroking him up and down very slowly, wanting to give him pleasure. To make him feel good. Better than good.

Lucas's chest grumbled with a growl, his back arching back. "One more," he demanded. "Harder than that, *preciosa*. Don't be shy."

I obeyed, giving him one firm stroke and seeing him swell in my hand.

Another groan left him, this one loud and short, and that was my last warning before Lucas's hands left my hair and went to my shoulders, returning me to the middle of the bed.

"No more playing," he said, his arms landing on the sides of my head, and placing a hard kiss on my lips.

Then, his mouth was traveling down my body, and his teeth were pulling at my sleeping shorts. In a brisk motion, I was in nothing but my undies, and Lucas's head was right above the juncture of my thighs. His mouth followed the seam of the underwear, his teeth scraping over the fabric, and my back arched at the contact. My head spinning out into space.

"Lucas," I breathed out, almost coming right then and there.

His tongue grazed my clit over the flimsy fabric covering me. Then, he moved the panties aside, revealing all my wetness and dipping into my flesh.

"Oh God." I moaned. And when he continued, I could only repeat my words. *"Oh God."*

I felt his hum fall on my skin. "Not God," he said, before retracing my opening with his tongue. "Lucas."

I whimpered, and his hands brought my knees apart, his palms falling down the inside of my thighs and making sure I kept them open as his tongue descended again.

"Say it."

Letting out a groan, I lifted my hips.

"I told you I want to hear my name, loud and clear," he repeated, thrusting in again, and again, and again. "Say it."

One of his hands moved, his thumb starting to rub circles around my clit, and sending my body straight into a frenzy. "Lucas," I gasped brokenly.

Lucas's tongue did something then, something I'd never experienced before and just like that, my arms were flying back, holding on to the first thing they found, a pillow. My hips thrusted into his mouth, urging him to go faster, deeper, and when he did, my mouth parted, the cry ready to fall off my lips and just like Lucas promised, I screamed his name.

The spasms of my orgasm subsided, my body lax, and he straightened on his knees. He grasped his cock, still looking at me. "I could come right now, just tasting you on my tongue and watching you like this."

Before I could process how those words seemed to bring me back alive, he was climbing off the bed and ridding himself of his boxers and jeans.

When he settled between my legs again, he let his cock rest against me, and the contact, him naked, against me, here with me, knocked the breath out of me.

"Put it in," I said so breathlessly that I barely recognized the words. "I'm on the pill. Last time I got tested I was okay, and I haven't been with anyone in a long time. You said you hadn't, either."

Lucas shuddered, focused on my face as he led his swollen tip to my entrance and dragged it along my slit. "I'm clean, too. I've never fucked without a condom, Rosie."

He seemed lost in thought, then he looked at me with something new in his eyes, in his face. Something that I loved and something that terrified me.

That was why I said, "I know what I'm doing. I know what I'm getting. I want everything I have in front of me." His jaw set, and I made sure to meet his gaze when I spoke. "I want you inside of me, Lucas. I'll have whatever you have to give me."

Lucas grunted at my words and without breaking eye contact, he slid inside of me. One hard and firm thrust.

My eyes shut, pleasure shooting up and down my body, gripping my spine.

"No," he said in that commanding voice. "Look at me, Rosie."

And because I was at his mercy, my eyes fluttered open. I looked into his eyes just as he grabbed my thighs and thrusted again, getting even deeper. "How does this feel? How do I feel inside of you?"

"Good," I answered, moving against him. "So good."

"Good's not enough." He drove into me again, and I saw tiny stars behind my eyes. "This is not a *good* fuck."

I didn't answer, I couldn't when his pace did nothing but increase. So I reached for him, bringing him down, fusing our mouths.

His chest rumbled and his thrusts grew deeper, pushing me up the bed. So much that he had to grip my waist.

He moved to his knees, making my back arch with the change in position, but I wanted him even deeper. Faster. Harder. I just wanted . . . him. His weight. His body. All. Over. Me.

Next thing I knew, those two hands that had been around my waist, pulling me to him, flipped me onto my belly. My cheek rested on top of the covers, my hands fisting them as he slipped back inside me from behind.

"I read you like you were my favorite book, Rosie. Like I've memorized you." He lifted my hips, so we were both on our knees. "Is this deep enough? Am I more than just good now?"

Oh my Lord, he was.

"I'm going to erase from your memory every loser that had you and didn't deserve you." One of his hands came around the base of my throat, not exerting delicious gentle pressure like this afternoon, but holding me in place, and the other one returned to my breast, all the while his hips keeping his pace. Pushing me closer and closer to the edge. Making me whimper with abandon. "That's it. Now, a little louder."

I obeyed.

"*Vamos, preciosa,*" he rasped in my ear, as he moved in and out of me from behind. "Come apart. Come, Rosie. Come all over me and take me straight to heaven."

He let a hand drop to my clit, rubbing circles with his fingers as he kept thrusting, fucking me just like I'd begged him. "Lucas, I—" I never got to finish that, because Lucas drove briskly into me one more time, and I felt the pulse of his cock inside of me, felt the grunt leave his lips, and I went off with him. Screaming his name one more time. One last time.

His arms snaked around my middle, keeping me flush to him, as he spent himself inside of me and I continued coming all over him.

After a blissful moment, he brushed a kiss on my jaw. Then,

without slipping out of me, he guided both our bodies to the bed until we were lying on our sides.

I grabbed on to his arms, because I really, really didn't want to let go.

A hum left my throat, and his chuckle was easy, happy.

Sighing deeply with contentment I eventually turned in his arms until I was facing him. I studied him, his smile, the creases in the corners of his eyes, the lips I already wanted to kiss again.

"You okay?"

"Never been better." His mouth grazed mine with a softness that would have brought me to my knees if I hadn't been lying down. "But it should be me the one asking that question."

"Why?"

"Because I want to." He placed a kiss on my nose. "Because you deserve to be asked."

He really was the best man.

"But—"

He stopped me with another kiss, this one on my lips. "Next time, I'll let you fuck me. You'll ride me while I watch you move over me," he said so simply, so matter-of-factly that it made me want to roll him on his back and make him keep his word.

But instead, I asked, "Next time?"

"If you'll have me." His lips fell. "I don't think I can stay away, Rosie. Not now that I've tasted you. Not now that I've had you. Not when I have only a week to feel you here, against me."

There were many questions I could have asked right at that moment.

What happens after you leave?

What are we doing?

Do you also feel this powerful, beating force right in the middle of your chest?

But a big part of me didn't want to hear his answer to any of those questions. I wanted to live in this moment, right here, right now. I wanted to have this one *next time* he was talking about and all the times after that. For as long as I had him. Even if that was only a week. I didn't want Lucas to have to define what we were or weren't on top of having to do that with himself after he'd lost so much.

So I said the only thing I could. "Then, don't. Don't stay away."

CHAPTER TWENTY-EIGHT

Rosie

There were a few things that could stir me awake with only a whiff. Number one was the smell of smoke, embedded in my brain since that time Mr. Brown decided to microwave a wig at three in the morning. No, I never asked for the whole story. I simply took the experience as a life lesson and rolled with it.

Number two, however, was a far more pleasant way to be welcomed into the day—or night. It was pancakes.

And that was the scent filling my apartment.

My stomach grumbled in delicious anticipation.

Anticipation that soon morphed into a different kind of hunger when I patted the bed and immediately remembered who had been filling that space beside me. Holding me all night. Placing slow kisses on the back of my neck. Wrapping himself around me like he never wanted to let go.

Lucas.

A wave of need surged through me, settling deep in my belly, and pushing me out of the bed like a woman on a mission. I snagged the first piece of clothing I found lying around—Lucas's hoodie—and slipped it on.

Never in my life had the distance between my bedroom and the kitchen seemed so long.

When I finally reached the threshold of the kitchen, music was filling the space. It was a song I'd never heard before, that Lucas had never played before, but had a bright and upbeat rhythm.

My gaze zeroed in on the man at the stove, pink spatula in hand and apron tied around his trim waist. He was in his boxers, shifting his weight from side to side, in perfect sync with the music, doing a little ass wiggle every couple of beats.

And . . . Lord. My poor, puffy heart tripped and then swelled at the sight of him, knowing with absolute certainty that I was so gone for this man, it wasn't even funny.

I must have let out a sound of some kind because Lucas turned. His beautiful grin caught me completely off guard, and I thought I mumbled something stupid like, "Hi."

His eyes met mine with the same big emotion he had looked at me with last night, when he'd told me he wouldn't stay away, and said, *"Buenos días, Bella Durmiente."*

Lucas's gaze swept up and down my body. Very slowly. And his smile changed. It didn't fall, not exactly, but it turned serious, focused, as it thoroughly inspected my legs.

"I grabbed the first thing I found," I said a little too breathlessly, waving at his hoodie. "Is that ok—"

"Yes," he rushed out. His voice deep and low. "Please keep it, wear it all the time." He inhaled slowly, as if he had needed the extra oxygen. "You know what? How about you keep all my hoodies? T-shirts, pants, too. Keep everything, I don't mind. I rather see them on you than on me."

My lips twitched. "But what will you wear then?"

He nodded his head, still distracted. "We'll figure that out later."

The laughter I had been holding in escaped my lips and I sounded like a teenager in sweet, sticky love. "Okay, deal," I told him, delighted to hold that kind of power over him. "But only if you keep dancing."

I moved to one of the chairs that sat around my kitchen table, taking it out and plopping myself onto it. I braced my elbows on the table and my chin on my fists, waiting.

"I'm ready to watch now."

The smirk that curled his mouth was delicious. "You saw that?"

I nodded.

"You liked it?"

I pretended to think. "It's a . . . nine out of ten from me."

He placed the spatula on the counter and took one step in my direction. "And this?" he asked repeating his last ass wiggle. "What's the verdict on this?" His hips swayed left to right, matching the new song's rhythm.

I made a show out of inspecting his movements. "Oh, that gets you to a nine point five. But probably only because you've bribed the jury by giving me *all* your clothes."

He let out a deep belly laugh. "You calling me out, Ro?" He stepped in my direction. "Making fun of me because I got a little distracted seeing you prancing around in my clothes, looking ready to eat?"

"It was cute," I told him, my heartbeat's speed increasing as he moved closer. "So cute."

Lucas stopped in front of me. He leaned down a little. His arm reached out, his hand grabbing the edge of the chair, right below the side of my ass. And then, he pulled the chair—with me on it—in his direction. Bringing me right under him.

He braced a hand on the back of the chair, behind my head.

"You scatter my thoughts, Rosie," he said, his mouth a few inches above mine as I looked up at him. "There'll never be a moment when you don't distract me from whatever I'm thinking or doing." He trailed his nose along mine, his lips barely brushing mine. "You have that power over me."

I exhaled shakily, wanting him to close the distance, to take me in this chair.

He brushed a kiss on the corner of my lips. "I want you so badly already. Again," he whispered. And it was impossible not to notice his arm flexing beside my head, holding himself back from doing what I desperately wanted him to do. "One look, Rosie. That's all it takes. That's all it took."

I kissed him in response. Because that was the best kind of answer I could ever give him. He groaned deep in his throat, his hand moving to the back of my neck, tilting my head further, angling me so he could part my lips.

Linking my arms behind his head, he somehow pulled me up, bringing us both to a standing position. His other arm wrapped around my waist, letting me feel how hard he was, how much I affected him, how much he wanted me, just like he'd said. So I grabbed on to him even tighter, whimpering. Cursing the thick hoodie hanging off my shoulders. Letting him feel how much I needed him, too.

Lucas broke the kiss, meeting my gaze with a million things dancing in his eyes. "As good as you feel," he said nonchalantly, like that wasn't supposed to make me all the more soft and hot. "I'm not letting our breakfast burn. I haven't gotten over the loss of those pizzas yet."

My shoulders fell, and I let my arms fall back to my sides as I nodded and readied myself to return to the chair, because if we weren't going to kiss—or do *other* sexy things—then I'd settle for a cooking show. But Lucas didn't let go of my waist, and instead, he turned me around and guided us to the stove.

He assembled behind me, and I felt his breath on my temple. "That didn't mean I'm giving you up," he murmured in my ear as he placed the spatula in my hand. "First, breakfast. Then, we'll go pick up Taco."

We. Us, together.

"Lucas?" I asked through a ridiculously big grin. "Will you and Taco stay here? With me?"

"Only if you'll have us."

"Yes," I rushed out, and he placed a kiss on my hair. Heart singing, I glanced down at the dark brown pancake that sizzled on the pan. "Do you think we can save this one?"

He reached for the bowl of batter, stretching an arm and putting his biceps right on my face. *Yummy.* "Let's discard that one and start over."

"Okay, chef."

"Ah," he said, throwing the almost-charred pancake away. "I love when you talk dirty to me, Rosie."

A glass of water appeared next to my laptop.

Well, it didn't exactly pop out of thin air. I *noticed* it had been placed there at some point.

By Lucas.

Since Friday, we hadn't left my apartment, at least not for more than a few hours to pick up Taco and Lucas's things once we both accepted that he wasn't sleeping anywhere else but in my bed. Although, saying that we were sleeping was a bit of a stretch. Not that I was complaining, I'd probably be hanging off him right now if I didn't have to work. Because I was still on a deadline that was a little less than three weeks away, and as good as my progress had been since Lucas and my experiment began, I still had work to do. Words to write.

"You can't sleep on it now, Ro. You're so close," Lucas had insisted when I so much as suggested that I could dedicate more time to being with him.

But Lucas was right. I was so very close that I could already feel the band at the finish line breaking against my chest as I crossed it.

So even though Lucas's time in New York, in my apartment, was coming to an end, I worked mornings and afternoons while he lounged somewhere in my apartment, reading one of the many romance books I owned, and made sure I always had snacks and stayed hydrated. We had lunch and dinner together; we walked Taco in the evenings together and snuggled on the sofa every night. And we had sex. More than just good sex. Mind-blowing sex. The best sex of my life.

The fact that he was leaving was a constant in the back of my mind, like a low buzz that I couldn't ignore but could learn to live with. Because I couldn't let that sour my time with him. I wouldn't. So, for once in my life, I decided not to plan. Enjoy the moment.

Enjoy him. If this was supposed to last a week, a week was all I'd take. I'd deal with the aftermath when I had to.

"Rosie?" A low voice fell close to my ear, returning me to the present.

Delicious awareness washed down over me at the realization that Lucas was right behind me.

"Yeah?" I answered, relishing in the way his scent wrapped around me.

He braced both hands on my desk, caging me in. God, I loved when he did this. "You spaced out, Ro."

"And how can you possibly know that?"

His nose dragged along my cheek, making my skin tingle. "You were staring at the glass of water." He let out a low laugh. "For a very long time."

"I was thinking."

He leaned over me a little more, resting his chin on my shoulder. "Were you thinking about me? About us?"

I blushed, my heart racing at how close to the truth he was. "Maybe."

"Was I naked?" he asked next.

I bit my lip. "Possibly."

"Were you naked?"

"Definitely."

He hummed. "Ah, those are my favorite kind of thoughts."

I turned around very quickly, placing a kiss on his lips, and returning my attention to the laptop. To my manuscript.

Lucas must have been dazzled for a moment because he didn't say a single word. He just . . . seemed to need a moment to catch his breath.

I smiled to myself.

"So, Rosie," he finally said, "when are you going to let me read it? I've been craving more ever since I finished book one."

I didn't even try to conceal how happy that made me. "It's not ready yet."

It took him a moment to answer. "How about just a taste? A . . . snippet. A teaser. It's Tuesday, you owe it to your fans, and I'm your biggest one. Hashtag Team Rosie. Hashtag Teaser Tuesday. Hashtag Friday Kiss."

My head swiveled very slowly. "Where did you learn that?"

His grin was big and proud, unashamedly beautiful, just like him. "I have my ways. You should know how good of a researcher I am by now."

"You're actually right," I told him. Then, I turned around and smiled to myself because, whoa, had Lucas looked into the *bookish-phere*? For me? "I'm sorry I underestimated you, Matthew McConaughey. But no teasers for you."

No way in hell.

I was extremely proud of this first draft, but I didn't know how I felt about Lucas reading it when there was so much . . . inspiration drawn from him. From us.

"Not even a peek into a spicy scene? I could help by bringing some more inspiration in there."

Delicious warmth filled my belly, but I shook my head.

"Okay." He sighed, but I knew it was more for the theatrics. "How many words away, then?"

My lips curled up, unstoppable. "Not many."

His arms wrapped around my middle from behind, his face burrowing in my neck. "That's my girl," he said, my heart losing it just like the first time he'd ever uttered those words. "I'm so proud of you, Ro. So, so proud." And for some reason, hearing that from him, that he was proud of me, felt like I'd accomplished something big.

Something amazing.

Something extraordinary.

That was how much he meant to me. "All thanks to you," I breathed out, overwhelmed by my own thoughts. "To your help. Our experiment."

"It was all you, *preciosa*. I didn't write a word. You did."

Tonight was Lucas's last night in New York. In the States. In my apartment, my bed, my time zone. And with every passing second that pushed us closer to tomorrow morning, my mood plummeted to the ground.

Together with my heart.

During the week we'd spent together in my apartment we never discussed what would come next after he and Taco jumped on that flight and returned to Spain. For good. It had been as if none of us had wanted to burst the blissful bubble we had slipped in. And that was probably a mistake.

Not probably, it definitely was one.

But what was I supposed to say? How would I broach the topic? Hey, Lucas, I have fallen in love with you. And I know your life is in shambles, and I know you are struggling to come to terms with what you've lost and who you are right now, but what are we?

That would be so selfish.

Even thinking of burdening Lucas with that conversation made me sick to my stomach. All I wanted was to protect him, to make it all better for him, to see him find his way and thrive in his new life, and I knew this—a long-distance relationship with someone he'd met a handful of weeks ago—wasn't a way to make any of that easier.

Or was it?

I didn't know at this point. And it made me so unbelievably sad.

So yeah, my mood. Plummeting.

And Lucas noticed. Of course, he did.

That was why he had been trying to make me smile all evening. He hadn't even held back in front of Aaron and Lina when we'd met them for his goodbye dinner. He'd held my hand, touched my back, whispered in my ear, and just . . . acted like the man I wanted him to be for me. Like he was mine.

Standing in the bathroom, in front of the mirror as I brushed my teeth, I checked my phone.

I had a trail of messages from Lina. Understandably so. She knew there was something between us, and I owed her an explanation. But that could wait until tomorrow, I hoped. She could deal with the fallout of my broken heart, too, if she wasn't too mad at me. Two birds with a stone.

Locking the device, I placed it screen down on the vanity and continued staring into empty space until I was done and ready for bed.

I walked back to the bedroom and found Lucas zipping up his backpack. Taco at his feet. The sight made me want to scream. It made me angry at myself, at time for going by so fast, at fate for crossing our paths only to take him away from me.

What would he say if I took that stupid backpack, ran to the window, and flung it out?

What would he say if I asked him to stay? He couldn't stay more than three months without a visa. But I could hide him and Taco.

What would he say if I told him that I didn't care about whatever he thought he could or couldn't give me? I'd take it. I'd move to Spain myself. I'd—

"Hey." Lucas's voice made me jump.

There was something in his face that looked a lot like . . . pain. Concern.

He walked up where I was, and his arms came instinctively around my waist.

"What are you thinking?" he asked me.

"Honestly?"

He nodded.

"I was considering how pissed off you'd be if I threw your backpack out the window."

He let out a laugh, and not even that lifted my mood. "Do you want an honest answer, too?"

"Always."

"I wouldn't be all that mad about it." His hands came to cup my face. He tilted my face up and looked right into my eyes. "I don't think I could ever be angry at you, Rosie. Not really."

I frowned and said through my pout, "Why?"

"Because everything you do is for a reason." His thumb traveled along my lower lip, erasing that pout out of my face. "So, if you threw all my things out, I'd know it wasn't irrational. I'd grab my coat with a smile and go salvage whatever was left."

A kind of pressure I knew very well rushed from my chest to my face, building up behind my eyelids. "Seems pretty irrational to me."

"Maybe," he admitted. "But it wouldn't matter because I'd know what it meant. Why you did it. And that's a good enough reason to smile."

I exhaled, the burst of air leaving my mouth forcefully. "Well, I'm happy you're happy."

Lucas's chuckle was low, and it made me scoff.

"Do you find this entertaining?" Taking a step back I tried to cross my arms over my chest but then Lucas leaned down, brushing his mouth over my lips and killing my intention of going anywhere that wasn't straight back into his arms.

His kiss was slow and soft, and it made me want to cry.

When we came up for air, I struggled to make my vocal cords function. "Lucas?"

"Yeah?" he answered, the brown in his eyes simmering with a gravity that hadn't been there before.

"I don't think I can say goodbye to you." Because it wasn't just about saying goodbye. It was about seeing him slip out of my life without being able to do anything about it. It was about how unfair it was that timing hadn't been on our side. It was about how much I wanted him not to go. "I . . . don't think I can go with you to the airport and watch you leave. I—" I closed my eyes. Shook my head. "I can't, Lucas. I just—"

I felt his mouth on my forehead, his lips pressing on my skin for a long moment.

"It's okay, Ro," he told me in a whisper. "You don't have to come. I understand."

I didn't want him to understand, though.

I wanted him to fight me. To make me say the words I hadn't yet uttered out loud because he needed them. To tell me that he wouldn't leave, or that we wouldn't become nothing but a memory. To tell me that as much as he hadn't figured out his new life, he wanted me in it. Needed me.

But I couldn't make him say those things. And I'd understand if he didn't.

It broke my heart, but I wouldn't make him put my heart before himself. "Okay," I breathed out. And when I opened my eyes, I wasn't ready to see what was staring back at me.

There was an emotion flooding Lucas's face, his eyes, the way his features were arranged right this moment. As if he was in far more pain than I was. As if he couldn't bear the thought of leaving. As if he loved me.

Without a word, he clasped my hand and pulled me toward the bed.

And without a word, I went.

He guided me onto my back and braced his hands on each side of my head.

His gaze met mine, and I swore he was looking at me with this emotion I didn't want to acknowledge out loud. That powerful, all-consuming emotion that mirrored mine.

"What do you need?" he said, placing a kiss on the corner of my mouth. "I'll give it to you, Rosie."

The answer was so simple, so obvious, that I didn't even understand why he asked.

I grabbed on to him almost desperately, and told him, "You."

Because it was only him I needed.

CHAPTER TWENTY-NINE

Lucas

I rested my elbows on my knees and let my head fall between my shoulders. Closing my eyes, I told myself for the hundredth time that I'd done the right thing.

The only thing I could have done.

Rosie wasn't the only one struggling with the idea of saying goodbye. I was, too. I . . . didn't think I could have gone through it if I hadn't left the way I did.

I snuck out while she was still asleep.

I was a coward.

But it was about survival.

I couldn't give her what she deserved. I was . . . a man with no plan. No life. No purpose. *Sin oficio ni beneficio*, like Abuela would say.

And if I had stayed one more minute in that bed with her all soft and warm and wonderful against me, I would have never left her side. I would have only delayed what was to come: her finding someone else that could give her all the things she wanted and deserved. Everything we'd had, *and* stability. Someone that had goddamn plan, a future. Someone who had his shit together.

I didn't want Rosie to settle for me. And I wouldn't let myself use her, use us, to ignore reality.

Eyeing the counter again, I finally saw my destination displayed on the screen above it indicating that it was open for check-in.

"Fucking finally," I muttered under my breath, even when I knew that this was on me for showing up at the airport hours early.

Instead of enjoying that time with Rosie.

With a sigh that wasn't of relief, I stood up, grabbed my back-pack from the floor, and called for Taco, *"Vamos, chico."* Then I headed to the queue before it got too long.

Checking my phone as I stood there, I fired a text to my sister, who had arrived in Spain from Boston yesterday. With the time difference, I knew it had to be around lunchtime in Spain.

Lucas: At the airport. Will you pick us up?

Lucas: Can we stay at your place tonight?

Charo: first, I babysit your dog. Now, the two of you?

I rolled my eyes; she was just being difficult by default. I knew my big sister.

Charo: Abuela is staying here too, she planted herself here today. So we'll go pick you up. I'll bring sandwiches to the airport; I know flying gets you hungry. Jamón or chorizo?

Lucas: Jamón.

Charo: How about please and thank you?

Lucas: Please. Thanks.

Lucas: And why is Abuela with you?

Charo: Rude. I hope you got her a gift. Mamá, too.

Lucas: oh.

Ah mierda. I hadn't thought of getting anything for anyone. Not even the Empire State Building key ring Mamá had asked for.

Charo: oh? That's all you got?

Lucas: what do you mean?

Charo: first you say please and thank you without being snarky about it. Then, you don't even try to sell me something like "I'm bringing myself, I'm the gift." Or like being your usual . . . charm-man.

Lucas: I'm sorry.

Charo: . . . Now you're apologizing?

Charo: are you okay?

That was a loaded question. How I was, was something I didn't have the energy to dissect myself, much less via text with Charo. I started typing an answer.

Lucas: I'm okay. Just tired, we'll talk when I get there okay? I will land at—

"Lucas!"
My head lifted off my screen, my eyebrows knitting because that couldn't be the voice I thought it was. Her voice. She couldn't—
"Lucas! Wait!"
I turned around.

My eyes scanned the crowd behind me, jumping from head to head, from face to face, until settling on one. Just one. The one face I could never miss. Not even in a packed airport terminal.

And then, everything slowed down.

As if I was starring in a dream, Rosie parted the sea of busy people. Her hair was a beautiful mess of curls, her eyes burning green, her cheeks flushed, and those full lips I'd memorized parted. She was wearing the short-sleeved shirt she had been sleeping in—my shirt—the front tucked into her jeans and . . . God, why didn't she have a goddamn coat on? It was November and freezing outside.

"Lucas!" Rosie repeated. She closed the distance while I stood there like a statue. Like a total dumbass, watching her run toward me, and hearing Taco bark excitedly. "Oh my God, you're still here. Thank God."

The last three steps she took felt like a haze. Like she wasn't real, and this couldn't be happening. I'd have to be imagining it.

"Rosie?"

But instead of answering, she threw herself at me, landing on my chest, and it was as if the ground beneath my feet had finally settled. Everything around me disappeared.

I wrapped myself around her, breathed her in, rejoiced in having her in my arms, being able to do all those things I'd regretted not doing one last time.

She looked up, meeting my gaze with those eyes I'd never forget.

Unable to stop myself, I leaned down and kissed her. Simply content to get one more kiss from her lips.

When I came up for air, I moved us out of the line, not giving a damn if I lost my spot. I looked into her face. "Rosie, what are you doing here?"

She shivered in answer and I took off my coat and placed it around her shoulders. Her head shook but she didn't complain. Good. I wanted her warm. Safe.

"I . . ." she trailed off, taking one step back. "I couldn't do it, Lucas."

I didn't like the space between us, but I had the feeling she needed it.

"I thought you didn't want to do goodbyes," I told her. "That's why I left."

Liar, it was you who couldn't bear the thought of saying goodbye to her.

"And you're right." Her throat bobbed. "I can't. I can't say goodbye to you, Lucas. That's why I'm here."

I frowned, feeling there was more. Something else.

She pulled out her phone from the back of her jeans. Unlocked it and looked for something. "Here," she said showing the screen to me.

It was a photo. A selfie of me and Taco on a beach. An old one. From way before the accident and before we'd ever met. I—

"Here," she repeated. "I've been keeping this on my phone ever since you posted it on your Instagram." The pace of her breathing increased, the air leaving her mouth in big gulps. "I . . . sort of followed you, Lucas, without actually following you. I checked for new posts every day, went to bed thinking of them, of you, of your face, of Taco, too."

My own chest mimicked hers, oxygen suddenly struggling to enter and exit my lungs.

"For months," she added. "Then, you didn't come to Lina and Aaron's wedding, and I was heartbroken over missing the chance to meet you in person. Devastated. But I told myself I was being stupid, that it was just a silly online crush." She shook her head. "But I was fooling myself. I . . . never stopped thinking of you, Lucas."

My mouth opened and closed, but nothing came out. I just . . . What was there to say? I was trying to process everything she was telling me. How fucking good it made me feel. How my chest and head were growing a couple sizes too big.

"Do you think I'm a weirdo? A stalker?" Rosie whispered. "Because if you think that of me now, you have to tell me before I—"

"No," I finally rushed to say. "No. God, no." I clasped her cheeks, my thumbs caressing them. "I'm flattered, Rosie. I'm . . . I'd never think you're weird. I love that you liked what you saw. I love that you wanted me." I kissed her forehead. "If anything, I'm flattered, *preciosa*."

"Okay," she murmured. "That's good. That's really good."

"I wasn't lying, Rosie." I tilted her head back with my hands, making sure she was looking at me. "Everything I said on that rooftop about us, if we'd met at the wedding, was true. Do you understand?"

Her gaze filled with something. Something that made me short of breath. Something that resembled the way she had looked at me that night, seconds before asking me to kiss her.

"Lucas," she said, staring into my eyes. "I'm glad you say that. Because I . . ." Her eyelids fluttered closed very briefly, then opened again. "This is my grand gesture."

My heart thrummed recklessly in my rib cage.

"I've told myself a hundred times that I shouldn't do this, but I can't not do it," she said, looking at me with a million different things dancing in her beautiful eyes. "Stay with me, Lucas. Be with me. I want you. I've wanted you for a long time. I know that you can't stay in the country without a visa, that you squeezed that time to the last second. So, I'll come with you. I'll get myself a ticket right now, I—" She shook her head. "I haven't packed or have anything with me right now but that doesn't matter. I'll buy what I need in Spain. You are all I need, Lucas. I want *you*. I want to go on dates that are not experimental. I want to kiss you under the rain a hundred times more. I want to dance with you in the kitchen every morning. I want to bring you a box of Cronuts when I want to say thank you. And not because we're friends."

My heart had halted in my chest.

My lungs stopped functioning and no air got in or out.

My hands fell to my sides.

And I . . . I didn't know how I was still standing.

Then, Rosie went for the final blow. "But because we're more. Because we're everything. And we can do that here, or in Spain."

I blinked, everything inside of me breaking.

Shattering with a big loud bang.

Rosie must have felt it, too, because her face fell. She took a step back.

"Rosie," I somehow rasped, the word barely coming out. I reached for her face, but she shook her head. Because she knew; I didn't need to tell her. She could read me. "You can't leave your life behind and follow me. I—"

She took another step back, merely a few inches this time, but it was enough for my blood to drain from my face.

I needed to hold her. I . . . just couldn't bear seeing her hurt and knowing I was the one responsible.

"Rosie, *preciosa*," I reached for her again. But she shook her head. Something lodged in my chest, cutting the air. "Rosie . . . I . . ."

I couldn't make the words form, climb to my mouth, and leave my lips. Everything in me stuttered, watching this beautiful woman be shredded to pieces. By me.

By what I couldn't bring myself to say out loud. To give her.

"It's okay," she whispered. But it wasn't. "It's okay. That was very selfish of me, reckless. I put you in a hard spot." Her throat bobbed. "I knew the last thing you needed right now was this. You said so yourself, that you were not in the market for a relationship, right? That you didn't date. I just thought . . . I thought maybe that had . . . changed. Because of me."

"Rosie," I said, her name again, and for the first time, it felt wrong rolling off my tongue, like I had no right to utter those five letters together anymore. Like I'd lost that the moment I'd hesitated. "I . . ." *Want to. There's nothing I want more than you*, I wanted to tell her. "I can't."

I can't make you do this. I can't let you uproot your life for me. Not when nothing is waiting in Spain for me.

But the words wouldn't come out, paralyzing anxiety, fear, flooding me.

One single tear slipped down her cheek and it killed something inside of me. It smothered a light, bringing only darkness.

I managed to step forward, opened my mouth to beg her not to cry, but she stopped me with a hand. "I knew what I was doing. I was happy to have this one week with you, even if it was the last. So I don't regret you, Lucas Martín. I don't regret doing what I just did, either." Her arm dropped, coming around her middle. "I just really wish you wanted me as much as I want you."

But I do.

I want you with every cell in my body. Every nerve ending. Every bone. Every ounce of who I am.

"Have a safe flight, Lucas," she whispered.

Then, she turned around, and even when Taco whimpered and nudged my leg maniacally, I still didn't move. I remained rooted in place, gasping for air, and watching her walk away with my jacket hanging off her shoulders.

CHAPTER THIRTY

Rosie

I stared at the wall of my dad's guest bedroom.

With a sigh, I braced myself for a new wave of tears, but it didn't come.

I must have emptied my tank by now—which, all things considered, was only natural when one cried for hours. To my credit, I'd held it all in on my way out of the airport. I hadn't shed one tear on my way back to the city or in the train to Philly, either. Not even when I realized that I still had Lucas's bomber jacket wrapped around me, his scent surrounding me.

Only when I climbed the steps to Dad's door did my eyes start burning, readying me for what was to come. And just as Dad opened it I finally broke down.

He pulled me to him like the hundreds of times he'd done when I was a kid and I just wept. I let it all out.

I still had no idea why I'd gone to him, all the way to Philadelphia; I'd never done this as an adult before. Not once. Every time I'd been dumped, or my relationship had gone sideways I'd always called Lina, downed a pint of ice cream, felt bad for myself for a couple of days, and moved on.

But this didn't feel like any of those times. It felt like someone had pulled me apart. Disassembled me and left all the parts scattered around. Too dispersed for me to attempt to piece anything back together.

And after staring at this wall for the longest time, I had realized that none of what I'd experienced up to this day had been heartbreak.

This was heartbreak.

So I guessed that was why I'd come here. To the place that would provide the type of comfort I hadn't needed in years. *My dad's.*

By the time I'd run out of tears, I'd opened a different kind of gate. The one that had been keeping in all the things I hadn't told Dad and Olly. So I told them about writing that first book, about the way I'd felt when that door had somehow opened for me and I'd felt happy, blessed, complete in a way I hadn't before. I told them about quitting my job and hiding it from them, about lying, because I'd been terrified, paralyzed by the pressure I'd put on myself. The stakes. The possibility of them not understanding how important this dream was for me. And they had listened. Just like a small part of me, the one that hadn't been ridden with fear and insecurities, knew they would.

"Bean," Dad said when I'd finished. "Why would you ever think you had to keep this from me?"

I hiccupped and told him, "I was terrified you'd be disappointed in me. Scared for me, when I was plenty scared for the both of us. I . . . didn't want to hear that the one leap of faith I'd ever taken was a mistake. I didn't think you'd understand. I thought that perhaps you'd judge me. I don't know."

"Of course, I'm scared," Dad had answered. "I'm terrified for you. I will always be, Bean. But that's part of loving someone. You want them to thrive, to succeed, to accomplish any dream they reach for, but you also want to protect them. To soften any blow that might come. But I'd never be disappointed in you." He had paused and then added, "And I'll always make an effort to understand, Bean."

I hugged him tightly. "Even if you've never read a romance book?"

"There's a first time for everything. And who cares what an old man like me thinks? Who cares what anyone thinks?" He'd sighed. "You shouldn't have kept this from me."

And I really, really shouldn't have.

I shouldn't have kept from Lucas how I really felt about him, either. That I loved him. Even if that wouldn't have changed a single thing.

Life was too short, too brittle, to keep secrets and live in half-truths. Even when we thought that we were protecting those we loved. Or protecting ourselves. Our hearts. Because the reality was that without honesty, without truth, we never lived fully.

And I was starting to understand just how much.

"And now about this boy . . ." Dad had said after that, reminding me of a time when everything was far simpler, because I'd just been Bean and Dad had been able to fix everything with a plate of waffles for dinner.

But I wasn't a kid anymore, and Lucas wasn't a boy whose name I'd scribbled in my diary.

Lucas was the man I'd fallen in love with. The man I'd chased through an airport in an attempt to become my own romance heroine. Only, in this story, the hero had taken flight and left me on land with a broken heart.

A knock startled me, making my gaze sway to the door.

"Rosie, *cariño*," Lina said, looking at me in that way only your best friend would. Like they were ready to kill whoever hurt you but also smack you up the head if you pulled off something stupid. "Your dad called me. And wow, Joe wasn't lying. You look like shit."

I didn't know if it was the look on her face, or the fact that I had been needing my best friend and I had kept her away because of my own stupidity, but I burst into tears again.

Lina rushed to the bed, and before I knew what was happening, her arms were around me.

She waited while I let it all out, again, just like I had done with

Dad, only this was different. Because this was Lina, and there was no one in the world who understood me better than she did.

After a while, we lay on our sides, her body stretched beside mine, and I told her everything. Like I should have done when I realized I was falling in love with her cousin. When I finished, Lina remained quiet, understanding across her face.

"I'm so sorry, Lina," I murmured, my voice scratchy and rough from all the talking and crying. "I didn't mean to keep this from you. Not for this long but it all happened so . . . fast."

She reached out for my hand and clasped it in hers. "I get it, you know?" she admitted with a shrug. "I might have been a little . . . hard on the idea of the two of you together. And that wasn't fair to you or Lucas."

"I guess it doesn't matter anymore."

"It does, Rosie. You're my best friend and I love you." She grabbed my hand. "So of course it matters. Also . . . it's really hard to be mad at you when you're crying. It would be like kicking a cute but very sad puppy."

That only managed to remind me of Taco, of Lucas.

I sighed. "I'm the furthest thing from cute right now, and we both know that."

Her head tilted. "Yeah, you're right. You've always been an ugly crier. But I still love you."

That didn't pull a laugh out of me, but I felt a little . . . lighter. Only because, if anything, I still had my best friend. That'd never change. Not even after I had kept something like this from her.

Lina hummed. "Can I ask you something?"

I nodded.

"Why did you think it would work?" she said, her expression turning serious. "Why did you think that this . . . dating experiment would lead to anything other than this?"

That was a very good question, I guessed. "I was desperate, Lina. Quitting InTech to write had somehow . . . increased the pressure I put on myself, so much that I felt sucked under a current. Dragged down by something I couldn't control. The higher the stakes, the more blocked I became. So, when Lucas offered"—my breath hitched at the memory of his smile—"I wanted to say yes. Because it was him, but also because I wanted it to work. Maybe somehow I knew that he'd manage to make it work."

And I guessed a part of me always knew that as long as it was him . . . I'd be inspired. I'd fall in love.

"So even after my own firsthand experience with faking love and dates and such," she said, "you still thought playing charades with someone you *might* like wouldn't confuse your feelings."

"They're not confused, Lina."

Her brows wrinkled.

And before she asked, I said it, because what was the point in keeping anything else from her?

"I love him, Lina. I'm in love with Lucas. There's nothing uncertain or confusing about how I feel."

Lina didn't speak for a few seconds, something in her eyes changing, dawning with more understanding.

"Did it help?" she asked. "Did Lucas make a difference in your book?"

"Yes," I told her and, God, I guessed my tank had been far from empty because I wanted to cry again. "So much. He's . . ." I shook my head.

She squeezed my hand. "Tell me."

"He's magic, Lina. He's selfless and kind. He's sweet and commanding. He managed to make me feel lighter, to make it all better. He has the most beautiful smile. And you probably don't want to hear it, but the sex with him was something I'd never experienced before, something . . ." The pressure in my chest increased, making everything feel tight. "Lucas is the best man I'd ever known and I . . . really, really wanted him to want me as much as I wanted him. I thought for a second that maybe he would and now—"

Now my eyes burned again and if I finished that statement I'd need to gasp for air.

Lina started blinking, her eyes getting watery in return.

"Don't you dare cry, too," I told her with a broken laugh.

"Jesus, Rosie. I had no idea." She shook her head. "But I guess . . . I guess it makes sense in a way."

I frowned. "What does?"

"You know I suspected you guys were probably hooking up from the moment I saw you together." My mouth opened, but she stopped me with a hand. "Maybe that was why I was a little hard on the idea. Even when Aaron told me a hundred times that you probably weren't *just* having sex." She shrugged. "I didn't believe him until he finally told me what Lucas had done for you on that rooftop. Did you know Aaron helped him with the photos and the cake? Without me knowing? It was in that moment that I knew. And after that, it was really hard not to notice how Lucas was . . . different."

"Different?" I breathed out.

"It was the way he moved around you, the way he watched you." My face must have filled with raw pain because Lina paled.

"Sorry, that's really not helping," she said quickly. "Okay, so is book two done? Ready?"

It was, for the most part. That was how much Lucas had changed everything. "Yes."

"Will you let me read it?"

"I'll send it to you tonight, when I get home."

"I'm so proud of you, Rosie." She scooted closer, placing a kiss on my cheek. When she returned to her position, she looked at me for a moment, amusement entering her expression. "I can't believe you ran after him at the airport like a total romance hero."

I groaned, not because I regretted it—I'd do it again—but because I knew that years from today, Lina was never going to let me forget this.

"Not my brightest idea."

We smiled at each other, but just as quickly, our lips fell.

"Did he at least give you a good reason?" my best friend asked.

The question seemed to spin in my head, and even after thinking for a long time I didn't seem to find an answer. So I told her the best next thing I could find, "Before we went on that first date, he promised me he would never fall in love in with me." I shifted so I could rest my head on her shoulder. "So maybe . . . maybe I shouldn't have forgotten that."

Lina didn't say anything, and I didn't, either.

We just lay on the bed, in silence, until Dad walked in and asked, "Waffles? Olly is setting the table."

CHAPTER THIRTY-ONE

Lucas

$\mathcal{M}$y phone rang again, displaying the name of the person I had been avoiding for the last three weeks. And just like it had done every day for the last twenty-one days, it stopped and a text lit up my screen.

Lina: *gallina.*

Chickenshit.

I agreed.

Not that it would make me pick up.

One, because my cousin was right: I was a coward. The biggest one she'd ever met, like she'd texted me yesterday. So why bother denying it?

And two, because I wasn't excited to discuss the way Lina wanted to make a necklace with my balls. I didn't want to hear that she'd murder me, make sure I suffered, and keep Taco for herself. I didn't want to hear her say that I never deserved Rosie.

Because I knew she thought all of that and I also knew she was right.

I hadn't deserved Rosie, and I'd have helped Lina with the kicking had I been in the mood to get my ass up from Abuela's couch. Although at this rate, Abuela would ship me off any day now. Probably even give Lina a hand and smack me up the head.

"Como un alma en pena," Abuela had said yesterday, *"pululando por la vida."*

Like a soul in sorrow, roaming around.

She wasn't wrong.

Dragging both hands through my hair, I tried to push all that out of my head. But then, my phone lit with another notification, and just like every time it did, I immediately picked it up from the table. Just in case in was her.

Lina: Call me, it's important. Something happened.

Desperately, my fingers flew over the screen of the device, and in less than two seconds I was doing what I hadn't brought myself to do in weeks.

"What's wrong?" I barked into the phone when Lina picked up. "What happened? Is Rosie okay?"

There was only silence.

"Lina, don't play with me." I didn't even recognize my own voice. "Tell me what happened."

A cackle came through the line. "I knew that was the only thing that would make you call me back." A huff. "I should have done that days ago, but I guess I was trying to be nice."

I grunted, slowly realizing I'd been played.

But my heart was still all over the place, and I was unable to calm myself down, to kill the idea that something might have happened to Rosie or ignore the fact that, with an ocean between us, there wouldn't be a single thing I could have done. "Rosie's okay?"

Lina snorted. "I'm not answering that."

"Lina, te lo juro—" I hated my harsh tone. "Is she okay, or not?"

Lina's exhale was long, loaded with what felt like sympathy. Laced with anger, too. "Just . . . calm down, will you? Nothing happened."

Only when I heard the confirmation, did I breathe a little easier. Only slightly.

Then, she added, "At least nothing other than *you* happened."

Swallowing, I tried really hard to keep myself from barking something I wouldn't be able to take back. I was well aware of how much I'd hurt Rosie. Nothing I could say would change that. I hated myself enough for it. I'd never forget the look on her face or forgive myself for putting it there. For inflicting on her a single second of pain.

Probably feeling the swing in my mood, Taco came to my side and rested his head on my knee. I patted him behind his ears, obtaining a quick woof of appreciation.

"Is that Taco?" Lina asked, her tone changing, lighting up. "Can you give him a kiss from—"

"No."

"Ugh. I don't like you too much right now, Lucas."

I shared the feeling. "What do you want, Lina? Besides almost giving me a heart attack and telling me something I already knew."

"Well, at least you know you suck. That's a good start. I thought you might be in denial, but at least it doesn't sound like you are. Good, because—"

"Lina," I growled. "I don't have energy for whatever this is. That was why I didn't call you back."

Another long sigh came through the line. "I was hoping you wouldn't, but you sound as miserable as she does. If not more."

Something inside of me stirred, and I didn't deserve to ask, or to know, but the words left my lips before I could stop them. "She's . . ." I could barely finish, "miserable?"

"Well . . ." Lina trailed off, making me shift in my chair. "That's a loaded question, *primo*. How are *you* doing?"

Miserable would be putting it lightly. The two things that had kept me going were Taco, who barely left my side, and Abuela, whose patience was obviously running thin. "I'm fine."

"Oh yeah? You're *fine*." My cousin dropped her voice, mimicking mine. "Well, Rosie's fine, too. And by the way, she hasn't told me whatever is wrong with you. That's who my best friend is, loyal to a fault."

The memory of her beautiful face, looking at me with hope as she asked me to be with her, to come with me, flashed behind my eyes. And I . . . God, I wanted to break something. I struggled for air, too. I didn't deserve her loyalty.

Taco nuzzled my leg, demanding my attention, so I resumed the scratching.

"*Lo sé, chico,*" I murmured. Then I told Lina, "Okay, if that's all then . . ."

"Wow," Lina spat. "Just wow. You really are a bigger idiot than I thought you were."

"I don't have time for this—"

"No," she cut me off. And the change in her voice was clear as day. I was going to listen to whatever she had called me to say. And if I hung up, she'd find a way. "You know you deserve to hear you're being an idiot. That's why you haven't had the balls to pick up or return my calls. Because you don't want to hear the truth. Because if you did hear the truth, you might open your eyes and see things differently and you might end up having to really dig into that hard head of yours."

My jaw clamped shut.

Relentless, she continued, "I told you, Lucas. I warned you. I said, *If you hurt her, I'll murder you.* Rosie's my best friend. She's my family here in New York. She was all I had before Aaron." A pause, and I could tell, she was trying to rein it in. "And I wasn't joking. I *should* want to murder you. But I said all of that when I assumed you two were just secretly fucking each other's brains out. For fun."

"It wasn't like that." I grunted. "It *never* was."

"I know," she admitted. "I know that now. That's the only reason why I might not try to kill you. Because now I know the whole story."

I was almost scared to ask. "The whole story?"

"Yes, Lucas. The *experiment* you two had going on," she said, and her tone shifted, like she could no longer hide her emotions. "Rosie told me about it. Told me everything. Every single thing you did for her. All the dates. The record store? Alessandro's? The *rooftop*?"

My eyelids fell shut at the memories. "I . . . I didn't mean for this to happen, Lina. I didn't want to hurt her. I'd never . . ." My voice cracked. "She's . . . so much more than . . . She's *Rosie*." My breathing turned labored, the tears I'd fought so hard to keep at bay rushing to my eyes, so the best I could manage was to repeat my words. "I didn't mean for this to happen."

My cousin remained silent for a long moment. So long that I thought that was all, that this was it, that she'd had her say and now I was left alone.

But then she sighed, and the sound was so sad that I almost severed the call myself. "Lucas . . ." She trailed off, and I could picture her shaking her head. "You couldn't predict that you two would do all of this and she would fall head over heels in love with you?"

My world halted.

Just like when I'd spotted her in that terminal as she ran toward me. Or when I'd kissed her and I hadn't even felt the water pouring down on us—hadn't even cared. Or when she'd told me that she missed me when I ran to her apartment at one in the morning.

Only this time was different, because the gravity, the meaning, of what I was hearing was . . . too much.

She would fall head over heels in love with you?

My limbs felt numb.

My chest too tight.

I was no longer sure if I was sitting, standing, or lying on the floor. I couldn't even tell if the phone had slipped off my hand until Lina's voice somehow made it through the haze.

"You're telling me," Lina said, "that you took her to Zarato, managed to somehow convince the owner to let you use their greenhouse, hung lights, and installed a projector just so you could re-create the night she'd wished she'd met you, and you didn't think this could happen?"

Lina's words were barely registering in my head, merely getting in and out, my mind still processing—stuck on—what she'd said earlier.

"You're telling me that you even went through the trouble of baking her my wedding cake—and yes, Aaron told me he helped you with that, and trust me, he's paid for keeping that little secret—that you could dance with her, and kiss her under the freaking rain like a modern-day Mr. Darcy, and you still thought none of that would make her love you?"

Lina gave me an opening to say something, but I was too slow.

"Are you telling me that she chased you down in an airport—"

"Lina," I finally managed to speak. *Pleaded.*

She just waited for me to continue.

I hardly got my breathing on track before saying something, and that was probably why the words left me in a hard gulp of air. "She loves me? She said that? Rosie said that she's in love with me?"

Seconds stretched into an eternity. "Lucas, are you joking right now?"

"Answer me."

"Jesus Christ," she muttered. "Yes, Lucas. Of course, Rosie loves you. She's in love with you." *She's in love with you. She's in love with me.* "Why else would she chase you down at a freaking airport and offer to follow you anywhere? That was her grand gesture, and trust me, as big into romance as she is, she's never done something like that. Not for anyone. Not ever. Rosie thinks everything through; she plans. And she blew up her rules for you."

And I didn't even say a word when she did. I broke her heart instead. "I can't give her anything, Lina. Not a single thing."

Because life wasn't as easy as saying yes and being with her. Life wasn't as simple as following your heart and hoping for the best.

What kind of a man would she have beside her every day? One that didn't live up to her expectations. One that couldn't give her anything. One without a future or a plan.

"She doesn't want anything from you. She just wants you. Loves *you.* Don't you understand?" Lina said after a beat.

I did and I didn't.

Just *me* wasn't enough. Perhaps that would be enough for now, but not in the long run. "Just me is not enough."

"Oh, Lucas." Lina sighed. "You really don't see, do you?"

I didn't have an answer for that because Lina didn't even know the whole story. Unless Rosie had told her, which I doubted. She'd never do that, I fully trusted her. I—

"Rosie . . ." She trailed off, as if hesitating whether she should say. "She'll kill me if she finds out I told you but . . . she wrote you a goddamn book."

The ground under my feet shook again.

"She *what*?"

"Her book. I'd read her first one, obviously. And it was good. She's—"

"I know," I rasped. I'd read it, too. I had it memorized by now.

"But this one? This one story you somehow inspired with your little experiment?" A pause, and I felt the thrumming of my heart in my temples, banging in my ears. "Jesus, that freaking book punched the air straight out of my chest. I don't remember ever smiling that big, crying that bad, or clutching my chest that hard. And I . . ."

Lina trailed off again, leaving that unfinished.

"And what?" I breathed out.

"I could see you in those pages, Lucas. It was you. I have no idea how she did it, how she turned something great into something breathtakingly beautiful, but she did. And it's like a goddamn love letter. To you."

CHAPTER THIRTY-TWO

Rosie

*O*nce upon a time I loved Christmas.

As a kid, I'd lived for this time of the year. It had nothing to do with the gifts or the never-ending supply of sweets. It had always been about the magic. The love.

It was suspended in the air, like pixie dust, sprinkled on top of everything and everyone, making the world look a little brighter. A lot better.

I thought I'd grow out of it at some point in my life, probably in middle school. It was only natural to stop being as excited for things like putting up the tree or getting your old Santa jammies out of the closet. I thought that I'd become a little more irritated by the snow blanketing the city or the harrowing quest to find gifts for everyone. But that never really happened.

My love for Christmas never faded.

Until this year.

For the first time in my life, the season had knocked on my door and I couldn't have cared less.

I didn't put up a tree. I left those red and green pajamas in the drawer. I finally saw the snow for what it was—a muddy and gray mess. And I hadn't bought gifts for anyone.

I had even been tempted to pack my things and leave for somewhere far, far away. Somewhere where they didn't celebrate Christmas.

Yes. Against all odds, I'd turned into the Grinch. My chest, once filled with fuzzy feelings, was nothing more than an open pit now. And the worst part? It wasn't even bitterness. It wasn't anger or frustration; it was hopelessness. The joke was on me, I guessed, because I couldn't even become the grouchy, irritable Grinch. Instead, I had to be a sad, heartsick version of it.

Just like I'd figured out that day I showed up at my dad's from the airport, for the first time in my life I had had my heart broken. Truly broken. And that took time to . . . deal with, to learn how to live with the notion of missing a future I'd barely had any time to imagine. To learn how to live missing him.

Because I missed Lucas.

I missed being in love with the idea of love, too.

Because now, I was an engineer turned romance writer who barely survived the most magical and romantic time of the year.

The irony wasn't lost on me.

And yet, I somehow managed to go through Christmas without a breakdown, only leaving the apartment twice—on Thanksgiving and Christmas Day—just to pretend that I was doing fine, that I was kind of okay. And eventually, my inner Grinch and I watched everyone take their trees down and sighed in relief thinking, *Well, fucking finally*.

And without really knowing how, I miscalculated and ended up faced with everything I had tried so hard to avoid.

New Year's Eve.

New Year's *freaking* Eve.

So here I was, in the middle of the fanciest party my best friend had managed to find, clad in a cocktail dress and a pair of high heels she had picked out for me. Holding a flute glass that she had placed in my hand. And trying and failing to smile at all these people drunk with hope and new resolutions.

"More champagne, Rosie?"

"Sure," I absentmindedly answered, nodding my head. "I might as well drown it."

Lina snickered. "Drown what?"

Sad Grinch Rosie. "Nothing." She refilled my glass, and I noticed the bottle in her hand. "Where did you get that bottle from?"

"Contacts." She smiled, pouring golden liquid until it reached the brim. "Now drink up."

I narrowed my eyes. "What about your glass?"

"Oh." She waved a hand, and I noticed that she didn't have a glass in front of her. Had she been even drinking tonight? Heck if I knew. "The champagne is just for you, bestie. So you loosen up a little."

My eyes turned to thin slits.

Lina rolled hers. "Don't look at me like that, I'm not trying to get you drunk." A pause, then she muttered under her breath, "Trust me."

Before I could even attempt to parse that last part, Aaron reappeared. He placed himself behind his wife, just like he always did, snaking an arm around her in that organic and natural way that would have made two-months-ago-Rosie swoon. Sad Grinch Rosie sighed and averted her eyes.

Without any kind of warning a memory flashed: Lucas, standing behind me, just like Aaron did with Lina. But we hadn't been at a fancy party; we'd been in my kitchen, cooking breakfast, and Lucas had been laughing, the sound rumbling out of his chest and making me smile.

Ugh.

Would I ever stop missing him?

What was I even doing here?

Pulling out my phone, I checked the time. Fifteen minutes until midnight. And I was giving myself sixteen before I left. I'd give the woo-hoo to the new year and then scatter. That was all I promised Lina and myself.

I glanced at my best friend, finding her looking at me with a big, scary smile.

"Hmm . . ." I said, frowning. "What are you grinning about?"

She didn't answer, and slid my glass closer to my hand.

The people around us started shifting, the atmosphere growing restless as they looked for that person they'd be kissing at the end of the countdown.

I grabbed the glass and tipped it back, emptying it in one gulp.

"It's okay, bestie," Lina said patting my free hand. "It'll all be over soon."

Yes, because I'd be going home to hide under my comforter. "Right."

For some reason, I glanced at Aaron, and I found him smiling, too. I did a double take, taking them in for a moment. "Are you two . . . *okay*?"

Their twin smiles widened, making me wonder if they were high. Because Aaron had never ever grinned like this, like a . . . maniac, except for the day they got married, and because Lina kept saying weird stuff, looking at me funny. And it was all freaking me out.

Unless . . . unless they were just high on life and love and whatever this stupid night represented.

"I'm happy you're . . . happy." I checked my phone again. Ten minutes to go. "Can I get more champagne?"

"How's Olly doing, by the way?" Lina asked through her psycho grin as she refilled my glass. Again.

I knew what she was doing—entertaining me, distracting me, because she had been going at it the whole evening—but I humored her. At least Olly was a topic that brought me some solace. "He's good. Happy to be home."

"Joe finally wrapped his head around what happened?"

"Took some time, but yes. Mostly, because no matter what happened, it doesn't change the fact that Olly's back."

Lina nodded her head, her gaze warming. "He's one big piece of bread, your dad."

Aaron snickered. "That doesn't translate literally, baby. You mean Joe is a teddy bear."

My best friend rolled her eyes. "Yes, and Rosie got it anyway. You guys understand what I mean just fine."

That made the corners of my mouth tip up because contrary to what she believed, I actually had no idea what she had meant. All I knew was that it had been something good because Lina adored my dad.

"And look"—Lina pointed a finger at my face—"I even got a teeny-tiny smile out of her. It's the first one in weeks!"

That teeny-tiny smile fell off my face. "Anyway." I shrugged. "I got Olly an interview with the contractor that took care of my apartment."

I had been talking to Aiden on the phone after Mr. Allen had passed on his contact, when he'd told me he needed more manpower and was considering taking apprentices. So I'd asked him if he might be open to hiring someone without experience. He'd said yes, and when I brought it up with Olly, he not only seemed interested, but excited about the idea.

"That's amazing, Rosie," Lina said with a little clap. "Let's hope for the best. And if he needs any tips, we can send Aaron to prep him for the interview. If Olly survives that, he'll get any job he wants. You know how scary Aaron can be and—"

"Funny." Aaron cut her off with a quick kiss on her temple, leaving my best friend a little dazzled. Then, he turned to me. "But if you think it will help, send him to me."

"Thanks, Aaron," I told him honestly. I knew Aaron had plenty experience conducting interviews, and while InTech and Aiden's business were completely different beasts, any help would be welcome. "I think it's a good idea, but I'll let Olly decide how he wants to prepare for it."

Without any kind of warning, the lights dimmed, and a single beam illuminated a screen that had been installed high on one of the walls.

Cheers erupted around us, signaling the moment everyone had been waiting for.

Everyone except for me, of course.

Lina clapped her hands under her chin, her grin growing impossibly wider, and I made myself smile at her with something that wasn't sadness. I didn't think I was very successful at it, but her expression didn't fall, so I guessed it didn't completely suck. Then, she grabbed my hand and dragged us away from the table and into the agitated throng of people.

"Do we really have to?" I asked.

She patted my hand. "Yes."

Two golden numbers flashed bright on the big screen, a one and a zero; and I could taste on my tongue the anticipation of everyone around me.

Okay, just a few more seconds to go and I'll be free.

My best friend situated herself between her husband and me, people moving past us, around us, probably between us if we had let them, wanting to get closer to the screen, or looking for those they wanted by their side when those numbers started making their way back to zero.

Lina turned her head and met my gaze. There was something in her gaze, something I couldn't decipher. She looked at me like she never had before, like . . . like she'd walk through fire for me. Like she was holding herself from hugging me. Her eyes watered, and exactly a second before the countdown started and chaos ensued, she said, "Make a wish, Rosie. It might come true."

A little taken aback by her words, I unconsciously closed my eyes and listened to the chanted numbers as we strolled straight into the new year, unable to shake Lina's words.

Ten!

Make a wish.

Nine!

It might come true.

Eight!

I wanted nothing. Nothing . . . except for one thing.

Seven!

One person.

Six!

The one person in the world I wished with all my heart were here. With me.

Five!

The man I was helplessly in love with.

Four!

The man I wished I could kiss tonight. And every single night after this.

Three!

And while my eyes were still closed, I felt someone grab my hand. The grip was warm, strong. Familiar.

Two!

My heart tumbled in my rib cage, coming alive after being dormant for weeks.

I was gently tugged forward, brought against a chest.

The scent of clean soap and sea salt hit me, making everything inside my body tighten and shake. Vibrate with possibility.

One!

Air stuck in my throat as I felt a breath against my lips.

A kiss was brushed against my jaw.

And then, when I thought it couldn't be, that my mind was playing games because this was too much, four words were whispered in my ear. "Open your eyes, *preciosa*."

Happy New Year!

My eyes blinked open, and I . . . *Lord*.

A sob climbed up my throat. I didn't know why, or how, because I thought I'd cried all the tears I had, but it did. I cried because standing in front of me was my wish. My one and only wish.

Lucas.

And there was so much I didn't understand, so much to figure out, but I was a fool in love who had missed him with all my being, so I couldn't do anything but stumble into him. I questioned my sight, my sanity, the banging in my chest, as I felt tears trailing down my cheeks. Happy tears, sad tears, all kinds of tears. Because he was here. Somehow, he was standing in front of me, in a dark suit, his hair disheveled, and his eyes the warmest I'd ever seen.

He'd come back? How? Why?

Lucas's hands clasped my face, that grin of his parting his handsome face. "Don't cry, Rosie." He pressed his forehead to mine, his hold on my face growing desperate, pleading. "No more tears, no more."

Aware only of him, I didn't know where the tiny sparks of color falling around us came from; I just knew Lucas was here, with me. And he was holding on to me like I had wished he had that day at the airport.

I felt the words against the skin of my temple when he said, "Happy New Year, *ángel*. I've missed you so much."

My lips parted, and my hands went to his wrists, my fingers closing around them, feeling his pulse under his warm skin.

"Lucas," I whispered. "You're here. Why are you here?"

His forehead came against mine, and his body stepped even closer to mine, causing a shiver to trail down my spine at the feel of him. "I'm here because I love you. Because I thought I had to walk away, Rosie. Because I didn't feel worthy of you. Of us. And because I'm ready to grovel as much as I need to to get you back."

A sound I didn't understand climbed up my throat.

His hold of my face tightened. "Walking away from you like that was the hardest thing I'd ever had to do. But now, I understand. Now I know that I couldn't claim you without wanting to become a better man for myself. Without wanting to get there on my own." His nose trailed along mine, his lips coming so very close to mine, hovering with the promise of a kiss I desperately needed. "But I'm not going anywhere now. If you'll take me back. If you'll have me." The pads of his fingers tangled in my hair as he tilted my head back so he could look at me. "Will you? Do you still want me?"

The question left me so breathless that I couldn't utter a word.

"I have so much to tell you, Rosie. So much to explain, but—" He stopped himself, coming even closer, his hold turning more urgent, his voice dropping with the need I felt surging through me, too. "I need you. I need you to take me back so I can show you."

"*Lucas*," I finally said, "would you just . . . stop talking and kiss me? Please."

I didn't need to look at him, to see him, to know that he was smiling when he took my mouth. Because when his lips finally met mine, I felt it. Deep in my bones. I felt his beautiful smile, his kindness, his selflessness, his honesty, his love. I felt all the things that made him *him* and that I adored so much. Everything that had made me fall so helplessly in love with him.

He parted my lips, deepening the kiss, telling me with it how much he'd missed me, how sorry he was, how much he needed me and wanted me. And I took all of it. I took it for myself, keeping it in the safe place where I'd stored everything else he'd given me and I'd thought I'd lost. Only now, it didn't hurt anymore. Now it only filled me with happiness. It made me float.

When we came up for air, his gaze met mine, looking at me like he had something precious in front of him. Something invaluable. Something he wasn't planning on ever letting go.

"You've killed Sad Grinch Rosie," I croaked in a broken voice.

Lucas laughed. "I've missed you so much, Rosie." His throat bobbed. "This mouth." The pad of his thumb grazed my bottom lip. "These eyes." It moved to my brow. "This beautiful face." He leaned down, brushing his lips along my cheek. "But most of all, I've missed this." Lucas's palm pressed against my chest, where my heart was thrumming out of control, wanting out, wanting to leave me and go to him. "And I have no right over it anymore, but God, I want it for myself. I want it so badly." He paused, like it was impossibly hard for him to continue. "I hope I can have it."

My hands trailed up his arms, reaching his face. I brushed his hair back. "You do," I told him, looking up at him, letting him see just how much. "You always did and you always will."

I hadn't realized he had been holding his breath until his chest moved, and air left his nose shakily. "Good," he said, leaning his face on my touch. "That's good. Otherwise what's coming next would have been a little awkward."

My mouth parted, but before I could utter a word, the song over the speakers registered.

Slowly, I became aware of my surroundings. New Year's Eve. The party. Lina and Aaron. Confetti dusted over every surface. The opening line of the track that had marked the start of something before I could know what it would lead to.

I glanced up at Lucas again, finding that pair of brown eyes filled with the same emotion flooding my chest.

"Our song," I barely managed to say, something clogging my throat. "Rosie and Lucas's Soundtrack."

Lucas shrugged, the corner of his lips tipping up, and then he lowered his head, grazing my ear with his mouth. "I told you to make it count." A shiver crawled down my arms, my whole body coming alive at that simple touch. "Will you dance with me, Rosalyn Graham?"

"Yes," I told him. Then, I repeated it for good measure. "Yes, yes."

His arms rearranged around me, one of his hands traveling all the way to the nape of my neck and slipping in my hair. "I know this is not a song to slow-dance to, but I don't think I can stay away from you a second longer."

Lucas tilted my head back, and he kissed me again. Intently. Honestly. Wordlessly granting me a little piece of himself I hadn't had access to before. My arms linked behind his neck and I couldn't do anything but pull him to me and give him access to whatever I had left.

His mouth left mine, his lips soft along my jaw. "I wish we weren't in the middle of a party," he admitted low and only for me. "That I had you all to myself right now. But that needs to wait, anyway. There's so much I need you to hear first."

Sobering up, I nodded, letting him sway us softly. "Then tell me. Tell me everything, Lucas."

"I left you without an explanation, back there at the airport," he said, swallowing hard. "And for that, I'm sorry. I'm sorry I hurt you, and I'm sorry I somehow let you believe that what I was feeling for you wasn't strong enough, powerful enough for me to be with you. I let you believe that you weren't enough for me, and I'll never forgive myself for it."

My palms grabbed the back of his neck, my fingers slipping in his soft hair. "Lucas, you don't have to apologize for that." And he shouldn't. He really shouldn't. "I blindsided you in an attempt at making you understand what I felt for you. It was too much, too soon."

"It wasn't. That's why I need you to hear this, Rosie. Because you—" His features pinched. "Because you were everything. You *are*. Don't you see?"

"Then . . ." I trailed off, terrified of asking. Because I'd played with the question so often that I no longer knew what to expect. "Why did you leave like that?"

"I was convinced that I was doing the right thing." A muscle in his jaw jumped. "I never doubted that you wanted me, but I didn't think you always would. I thought you were settling, Rosie. And if I didn't believe I was the man for you, why would you?"

His words broke my heart all over again, because how could this kind, thoughtful, and selfless man ever think that of himself?

"I left Spain a shell of myself, and I'd been that way for a while before that. The rug had been pulled from under my feet, Rosie, and I was left without the single thing I knew how to do, without the person I knew how to be. I couldn't offer you just that, Rosie." He shook his head. "You deserve someone who challenges you, who shares the weight on your shoulders, someone who lays the world at your feet. And I . . . could barely manage to walk without cracking under my own weight. So how was I supposed to do any of that for you?"

I rose to my tiptoes, and kissed the corner of his mouth, telling him I was listening, I understood.

"But then," Lucas continued, and his voice cracked with barely contained emotion. "Then, I read your book. The one you wrote while we lived together, were together. The one born from our dates."

My lips parted, my heart raced in my chest. "Lina sent it to me, told me to read it. And I . . . *God*. Everything I didn't believe of myself, everything I couldn't possibly think you saw in me, was there. I saw myself through your eyes. You *loved* me. And knowing someone like you could love me when I wasn't whole only made me want to do more. Be more. It made me want to become a better man for myself. A worthy one, for me and you. To prove you right. It made me want to earn that love you were willing to give me, Rosie. And that's what I'm doing. Or trying to do."

There was something else in his gaze, something fierce, passionate, something I had only gotten small glimpses of in the time I'd known him.

"I wasted so much time pitying myself, thinking of what I had lost, that I didn't see what I still had. What I could have." His palm moved to cup my face. "I'm back to physical therapy; I've only done a few sessions, but I'm committed. I'm also talking to someone about my panic attacks, learning to process what happened. I finally told everyone about the accident, apologized for being an idiot, and I . . . thought about you, Rosie. Every day, every night. Until what you said that night with Alexia and Adele, in Lina's studio, came back to me. It was an itch, a buzz in the back of my head. And . . . it suddenly made sense. I think it always had."

"What did?"

"Culinary school. I was just too blind to see it. Too stubborn and hopeless. I still believe I'm too old for it, and I know I might fail, but I'm determined to try. Because it's what I want, the thing, beside you, that makes me dream of a future again."

Tears rushed to my ears, happiness swelling my chest.

He continued, "I got in touch with Alexia and she's going to help me with everything. I will apply to school, Rosie. Here in New York."

I jumped into his arms, bringing my face to his neck, and he laughed. He let out a deep and honest laugh.

"It will take some time to get everything ready: the paperwork for the visa, the school application, everything," he said in my ear. "So, I really hope you're open to do long distance with me, *ángel*. I'm praying that you will because—"

"Yes, Lucas. *Yes*." I moved so I could plant a kiss on his lips. "I'll visit you in Spain as often as I can, write from there. And the rest of the time, we'll do long distance. Even if I'll miss you every day. For as long as we have to."

He laughed again, and it was a glorious sound. "We're talking long months of phone sex, *ángel.*"

I grinned. "Can't think of a better way to use our phones."

Lucas's eyes filled with a kind of wonder that left me breathless, the kind that had the power to change a life. He placed his hands on my shoulders and turned me around. I felt him lean down and then he said, "Good, because remember I said this could get awkward if you didn't want me back?"

He pointed at the screen where the countdown had been.

I blinked, a new rush of happy tears making it hard for me to see what was displayed. And right there, right in front of me, it read,

Rosalyn Graham,
Will you be my best friend?
My roommate.
My Dancing Queen.
My ~~experiment~~ life partner.
My heart.
Will you be mine, just like I'm completely, hopelessly yours?

Then, the words "I love you, Rosie," from the lips of the man I loved were whispered in my ear. "I love you like I'd never loved anything before. And I'll love you for the rest of my life if you let me." And before I could even process what I was doing, I was turning in his arms and I was looking into his brown eyes, giving him the easiest *yes* I'd ever have to give anyone.

EPILOGUE

A little more than a year later . . .

Lucas

"You sure you have everything?" she asked me again. "That all your things are in the boxes Charo will ship and your essentials are in your backpack?"

"*Preciosa,*" I told her, the grin in my face growing impossibly big, "you're all I need with me."

"You wouldn't care if you forgot your socks?" Her voice was strawberry sweet. "Or your underwear? That is a very annoying thing to replace."

"Couldn't care less." And I wasn't lying. "Less layers for you to peel off me."

She let out a soft sigh. I knew the sound very well. I'd grown very familiar with those light exhales of breath, with what they signaled. I'd learned in the many, many occasions we'd had to resort to our phones in the time we'd been apart.

We'd tried to see each other as much and as often as we could, but it was still not enough. It would never be. I still counted the time I didn't have her by my side.

Ten weeks, five days, and fourteen hours since her last visit.

And this time, not only had I been without her, but without

Taco, too, as Rosie had taken him with her when she'd returned to New York.

"I know, *ángel*." I lowered my voice so the cabdriver wouldn't hear me say the next words. Not because I cared if he did, but because they were only for her. "I'm also dying to touch you. To have my hands on you. To feel you under me."

Another sigh came, but this one was different. It was the one that told me she missed far more than my touch. And I was right there with her. I missed every single thing about her.

"Oh, well," Rosie finally said. "At least, I hope you didn't forget your toothbrush because sharing one is a big step."

She clicked her tongue, and her teasing me instead of saying what we were both thinking—how hard long distance was and how much we hated it—made me want to jump out of the cab, into traffic, and run to her. Sprint.

Something that after the physical therapy plan I'd religiously followed I was able to do without a limp or major consequences. On the occasion.

"*Preciosa*, there's no step we're not ready for."

And there wasn't. I would have already married her if we had been living in the same time zone. Walking away from her that one time over a year ago was something I was having trouble forgetting or coming to terms with. I'd almost lost Rosie, the love of my goddamn life, in my attempt to protect her, to protect myself too, as I'd been able to finally understand after my due sessions with a therapist. But just like Dr. Vera said, it's not about forgetting, but about forgiving yourself and putting in the work to be better. And I tried every day to do that. I'd also learned to live with who I was today without resenting what I'd lost. And I sure as hell knew what I wanted in my future.

I had always wanted Rosie. But now I was ready to take everything and anything she'd give me. I was counting the seconds to start a life with her, in New York, while I attended culinary school to build a new future for myself. While she thrived in her career as a romance writer. While we built a future together.

"You're in the cab, then?" Rosie asked, jolting me back to the conversation. "On your way to the airport?"

"I'm in the cab, yes." Only I wasn't on my way to the airport; I was on my way to her. I'd landed in New York an hour ago, as much as Rosie thought I hadn't boarded my flight yet.

"Ugh, I already feel like the last ten weeks have been the longest of my life. And now, I must wait another full night. It's not fair."

I watched Rosie's building come into view. "I'm almost there, Rosie."

"I know." She sighed. "But I want you here now."

The cab pulled up. "What will you do when you see me, *ángel*?"

A deep, sultry laugh left her. "What will I not do?"

I pulled out my wallet and paid the driver. "Describe it for me."

"I'll jump in your arms," she said, no hesitation.

I hung my trusted and beat backpack on a shoulder and made my way to her building. I pushed at the entrance door and found it open. I made a note of getting someone to fix it and went in.

She continued, "I'll cover you in kisses. Your mouth, your neck, your eyelids, your ears, everything I can reach."

"Everything?" I asked as I climbed the steps to her floor.

"Every single spot I can get my lips on," she confirmed, and I hummed. "Then, only when I'm done and satisfied with my job, I will very kindly climb off you, tug at the hem of your shirt, and peel it right off you so I can start working on getting you—"

I knocked on the door.

I heard Taco's excited bark.

And through the line, I heard Rosie suck in a breath.

I asked her, "At getting me what?"

"Naked," she mumbled. She exhaled shakily. Emotion was clogging her voice when she added, "Lucas?"

"Rosie?"

"Your flight," she answered, and I could hear everything in those two words: the surprise, the relief, the love, the joy. "You told me it was today. That you would get here tomorrow."

"I did," I confirmed. "And I didn't lie. My flight was tomorrow. But I couldn't wait, Rosie. So, I got myself an earlier one."

"You did?"

"I did, *preciosa*." I heard her soft steps. Quick. As desperate as I was for her. "I couldn't wait a single second more to see you, Rosie. To kiss you, to wake up every morning beside you for the rest of my days. To cook for you and remind you to drink water when you're too lost in your writing. To hear my name off your lips every time I'm inside you. I couldn't wait a second more to start our new life together, Rosie. I've waited enough. I've waited a lifetime without me knowing. So why don't you open this door and let me show you?"

ACKNOWLEDGMENTS

Holy smokes. So that really happened, huh?

To say the past twelve months have been a wild ride would be a complete understatement. And believe me, I don't say that lightly. If you're new here, and this is the first time you've heard of me, you probably have no idea what I'm talking about, and that's okay-I'll just THANK you for trusting me with your book moonies and hope you loved Rosie and Lucas as much as I do. But if you do know what I'm referring to . . . that means you were there about a year ago. It means that you picked up my debut, *The Spanish Love Deception*, read it, and felt passionate enough to talk about it. To do your magic. And yes, you probably screamed to everyone and their mother (me included) about our grumpy homemade-granola-bar lover: Aaron Blackford. So it means that thanks to YOU, and your love and your passion, I am here, typing these acknowledgements while I sit in my full-time writer's office, instead of on some corporate laptop, sneaking hours in-between a job that didn't make me happy and a life that was missing something. This. So thank you. To every single one of you that made this possible, THANK YOU.

Ella, hi. I know you're going to roll your eyes, but you started this. You've been here since that sucky first manuscript of *The Spanish Love Deception*, and even when it sucked (I can't stress that enough how sucky it was) you still encouraged me. Because that's who you are. That's why I love you and value our friendship so much. That's why you will never get rid of me and why you're stuck in my acknowledgements—FOREVER.

Jessica, you've held my hand, pushed me forward, guided me through the craziness, told me when to chill and take a breath, and reminded me when I should be proud of myself. Honestly, I think I'd be rocking in some corner without you. Thank you. Andrea, Jenn and everyone at Dijkstra, thank you for your infinite patience (and sorry for continuously cramping your inbox).

Kaitlin, I *just* read your note on the print proofs I *just* received in the mail, so overall, I'm a little emotional. I won't repeat the words you dared write about me but I will say that having your trust and faith in my words and work is something I value more than I can say. And something I'm still coming to terms with, not gonna lie. Megan, Katelyn, Morgan, and the incredible Atria team, you guys have been working on the clock for months now and I couldn't be more grateful and thankful to have you in my corner. Thanks to you I have accomplished things I never even dreamed of.

Molly and the marvellous team at Simon and Schuster UK, thank you for always being amazing and for the incredible job you are doing. The day I finally get to experience seeing my books on Waterstones, I'll probably faint.

Mr. B, you once told me "you're not *just* lucky. For luck to find you, you have to work hard and put yourself out there first" when I was having One Of Those Days, and somehow, that managed to be the most reassuring thing I've ever been told. I love you. Even when you don't get me flowers on release day. Or a cover-themed cake? Or, like, a puppy? Honestly, I don't ask for much.

To you, the reader, hi again. Thank you again. Rosie and Lucas's story was a little more emotional and a lot more personal, and I really, really hope you loved it. I also hope that if, like Rosie or Lucas, you feel lost, or stuck, you don't ever, ever stop pushing forward. I mean, come on, like Joey would say, you can't give up. Is that what a dinosaur would do?

ABOUT THE AUTHOR

ELENA ARMAS is a Spanish writer, a self-confessed hopeless romantic, and proud book hoarder. After years of devouring HEAs and talking—okay, fine, yelling—nonstop about them, she has finally taken the leap and decided to create some of her own.

She hopes these stories make your heart skip a beat or two, your palms a little sweaty, and your cheeks flush in that rosy pink that makes other people want to peek at the page you are reading.

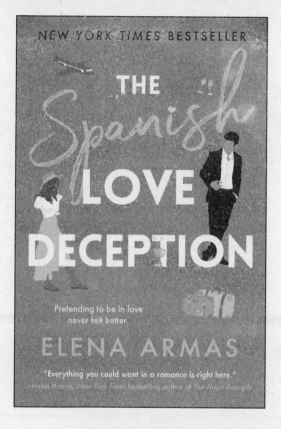